THE CURSED DRAGON
BOOK ONE OF THE AGE OF ACAMA SERIES

BY:

RACHAL M. ROBERTS

www.TotalPublishingAndMedia.com

ISBN 978-1-63302-016-0

Total Publishing And Media
www.TotalPublishingAndMedia.com

For Jason, my wizard

Acknowledgments

Thanks and appreciation to all the folk kind enough to let me interview them, Jenniffer Martin, Todd Ray, Jeremy Roberts, Josie Sickler, Mallie Whorton, and countless others. It is a work of fiction but a lot of research was conducted to make this book, thank you to Dr. Anna Cruse for the geochemisty, Dr. Martin Heimann for the extreme cold temperatures and carbon dioxide, and Dr. D. E. Wadsworth, Jr for the mummy eyes. Additional works were studied from the research of Simon Martin and Ramon Carrasco about the Maya, as well as Xu Xing and his fabulous work with digging up feathered dinosaurs. Jim C., without you, one of my favorite characters, Tamtoc, wouldn't exist, many thanks to you. And lastly I drew a lot from my history, love and blessings to my parents Calvin and Sylvia for raising me right, Dianna, Rianna, Veronica, as well as Jayne and Marshea for convincing me to take that job which began this path.

These artists' songs fueled my passion and perseverance to finish this work. Countless hours I listened and sang to this playlist as I wrote or drove my car. Each one of them in some way exemplifies the emotions in the book and I encourage you to enjoy them as you proceed.

Believer, Dimensions: Movement I: The Lie, Movement II: The Truth, Movement III: The Key
Brainchild, Metamorphosis: Deviate (Sawed-Off Shotgun Edit)
Celldweller, Soundtrack for the Voices In My Head, Vol. 02 (Chapter 1) – EP: The Wings of Icarus (feat. James Dooley)
The Cranberries, No Need to Argue: Zombie
Dragonforce, Inhuman Rampage: **entire album**
Dream Theater, Awake: Space Dye Vest
Enigma, The Cross of Changes: Return to Innocence
Enigma, MCMXC a.D.: Sadeness (Part I)
Enya, Shepherd Moons: Book Of Days
Evanescence, Fallen: **entire album**
Living Sacrifice, Metamorphosis: Black Veil, Desolate
Nightwish, Oceanborn: Gethsemane, Swanheart, Walking In The Air
Nightwish, Once (Bonus Track): Dark Chest Of Wonders, The Siren, Dead Gardens, Ghost Love Score, Kuolema Tekee Taiteilijan, Higher Than Hope
Nightwish, Over the Hills and Far Away: Over the Hills and Far Away
Nightwish, Wishmaster: Sleepwalker, The Kinslayer, Crownless, Fantasmic
Rhapsody, The Dark Secret – EP: **entire album**
Rhapsody of Fire, From Chaos to Eternity: **entire album**
Rhapsody of Fire, Triumph or Agony: **entire album**
Therion, Crowning of Atlantis: Mark of Cain, Thor
Therion, Deggial: Emerald Crown
Therion, Lemuria: Lemuria, An Arrow From The Sun, Abraxas
Therion, Secret Of The Runes: Muspelheim, Secret Of The Runes
Therion, Sirius B: The Blood of Kingu, Dark Venus Persephone, Kali Yuga Part 2, Voyage of Gurdjieff (The Fourth Way)
Therion, Theli: To Mega Therion, In The Desert of Set, Grand Finale / Postludium
Therion, Vovin: Black Sun
Within Temptation, The Silent Force: Angels

Table of Contents

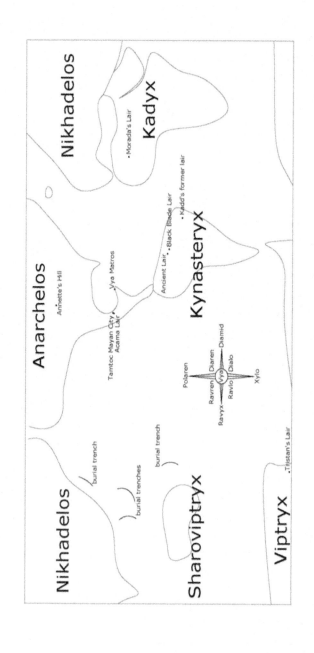

Prologue

Deep in the Amazon rain forest of Brazil between Manaus and Boa Vista, amidst tall trees and countless animals there was a certain tepui that loomed over the vast green world below and sleeping on the sunny ledge of that tepui was a purple dragon, an Acama.

A sound pricked her ears which caused her purple eyes to open and squint at the bright day. Hearing the sound again, she rolled over and scanned the forest below but couldn't see through the canopy of trees. The hunt was on, the dragoness bounded into the air to catch its scent. The tips of her massive purple wings brushed the trees as they pumped silently. The delightful smell of human was in the air.

She flew high and cast *"MORPH TO HUMAN"*. In a gravity-defying aerial, thousands of feet above the forest canopy, she shrank from her 70 foot frame, her black horns softened into dark tresses, her purple scales lightened into pale skin and wings folded to sink into her back. With her naked human frame, the enchantress dived down to pick up the fragrant trail. Landing without making a sound, she cast *"DRAPE CREAM RUNES"* and *"EVOKE GREEN PACK"* and began a steady gait, clothed and armed. The fire opals on her cream robe lit the forest floor around her feet and cleared a path, burning and vaporizing branches and thorns.

Far ahead, her amethyst eyes spotted her target's leg. The Acama calmly reached into a green bag and retrieved its contents. In her open palm were grains of green sand; bringing them to her lips, she whispered the spell *"CONSTRUCT"*. The green sand blew of its own accord, fusing together and pulling the remaining grains in the bag to it. The tiny green tornado became a short bow, made of olivine crystal and intricately laden with small gemstones of tiny enchanting runes. When her fingers came to the string, an arrow magically appeared with a malicious-looking tip – ready for use. Just as she started to aim, her prey ducked behind a bush.

The shot was gone, but the Acama kept the bow readied while she advanced at a snail's pace. She found the human again and prepared to shoot, but her target darted to a nearby tree. The hunt was proving to be a great one. She cast "*ERODE*"; the crystalline bow blew away and the Green Pack was full once more.

She made a wide arc through the trees but the human wasn't where it should have been. Curiosity piqued, she continued on to see the back side of the tree. She noticed the weathered split at the base. With wild joy she knew the human had to be cowered inside the tree, the Acama once again cast "*CONSTRUCT*". Her fingers deftly touched the arrow materialized at her finger tips and she waited. Her prey was in there, she knew it. She could almost taste the salty flavorful blood; she salivated with the thought of its heart gushing with fear. Her eyes now nailed to the dark heart of the tree with anticipation. Finally a shadow moved and that was all she needed. She aimed to light up the target with the bow's inherent spell starlight, she pulled the arrow back. All she had to do was release it.

Chapter 1

A death match was in progress between four house cats, it ranged all over. The only spectator at the event was Kalara who was sitting on the couch. Her favorite was Seven (named for his seven toes on each paw) and he was winning with his vicious claws. She could almost predict the battles of the games they played. Even her roommate Jenniffer, who owned and had rescued each of them, had to admit that Kalara had an uncanny connection with them.

Kalara heard her roommate rustling around after having just gotten out of bed so she stood up to take her empty bowl back to the kitchen. It was a typical Saturday morning with Jenniffer sleeping in until noon. Kalara had been up for seven hours and had eaten three times. Even in her down-hearted state she could eat. She was always hungry it seemed but Kalara was constantly depressed at her lost past. Ever since she was found nearly a year ago, Kalara's life was one of disappointment. Even though Jenniffer was nice to her and tried to hide how she truly felt, it was obvious that Kalara was a nuisance in her roommate's life. Her memory and state of mind wasn't improving as Annette the Medicine Woman had said it would. She'd fixed the confusion but all that remained was a hard wall.

In the beginning Annette had been helpful. She discovered Kalara in the Brazilian jungle and offered to take her to her home in the forested country of northeast Oklahoma until her memory returned. Those first few weeks Annette studied Kalara's every word and had kept a close eye on her – using medicinal herbs and sweat lodge to extract Kalara's memories from the Nether Realms, but with no success. Yet for all the time they spent together, Annette seemed to be aloof, never allowing Kalara to get to know her better. In words, Annette cared enough to help her; in actions, Annette maintained the distance of a doctor who was exhausting every possible effort to cure a highly contagious and dying patient. Annette was cold and analytical. Having tried every idea twice over, she seemed to have given up. Kalara knew Annette had found a roommate for her to get her out of her house, Annette's phone calls had even become scarce. Kalara was practically a prisoner with no hope of ever leaving Jenniffer's apartment in Tulsa.

No one had come looking for her. No TV broadcast searching for a woman of Kalara's description – Caucasian female with long dark hair and purple eyes. The only people who even knew she lived were doing their best to avoid her and at the same time keeping her "safe" in the apartment.

Kalara sat on the balcony taking in the crisp feeling of the day. Even in the stuffy and crowded city the death throws of summer were gone in the wind and fall had made her entrance with shades of old green and dried-up brown. The sun felt different to Kalara. She wondered if she had always been like that, attuned to nature and reading the signs in the air.

Jenniffer finally joined her. She opened the door and took the remaining seat on their small sun deck, eating her cookie dough and cola breakfast. Their fenced deck faced a car dealership and couldn't hold more than two people. It was their little claim on the outside world. Also competing for space was the thirsty petunia in the corner, it wasn't doing well in the shade and would most likely give up trying to add color to Kalara's life in the next few days. Jenniffer poured the rest of her cola on the poor plant. "You know, cola is good for the roots, the fizz cleans them," she snidely commented, knowing that Kalara had no clue.

"Aren't they supposed to be dirty? They live in dirt."

"No, the fizz bubbles away the slime from the fertilizer."

Kalara looked at her ugly plant. "Let's go buy a new plant, it would be great to get out."

Jenniffer mulled the idea over, "Oh, I don't know about that, are you sure you can handle it?"

"Of course I can, I'm perfectly fine. Besides, remember? - Annette gave me this ring to protect me." Kalara held up her right hand to show off her only jewelry. It was a dark colored ring woven from a braid of her own hair and Annette's. When Annette finally presented it to her, she said it had taken a while to make it, and it had been steeped in a special brew to ward off harmful spirits.

Jenniffer politely smiled because she knew Annette's true intention of the gift. "OK. But first we have got to clean the kitchen. Do you not remember me asking you to do that yesterday before I left for work?"

"You did?"

"Yeah I did. Right after you said you could help out around the place."

"Oh, sorry about that."

"So, what did you do yesterday?"

"Not much, I fell asleep after lunch. I dreamed I was hunting."

Jenniffer's ears perked up, the dream would need to be reported to Annette. She wondered if anything in it was different this time. "Well? Tell me about it."

"OK. I was hunting in a forest with a magic bow. My mouth was watering with the anticipation of tasting hot blood and then all the sudden I was in a fog, hearing that voice again."

"You mean the Acama voice?"

"Yea. Hearing it woke me up. But I tell you, I could almost taste the blood, I wanted it."

Jenniffer made a face, "That's gross. – hot blood? You are so weird." She rolled her eyes. "We should tell Annette about it even though it is nothing new. She might be able to help you sleep better. For right now just don't worry. It was only a dream and dreams aren't real. You aren't some great hunter and there is no such thing as a magic bow. You need to remember that magic isn't real, you *know* it isn't. How many times have I told you this? Say it with me – 'magic isn't real'."

Kalara obeyed and said it, although she resented it every time Jenniffer asked her to say it. It was enough, she got it she understood. From watching people on TV and on the streets outside there was no such thing as magic. If there was magic she would not have the problems she has. Some time ago she had dismissed the notion of magic and was really getting tired of reciting the mantra with Jenniffer.

With the dishes finally clean the pair was out looking at plants. After the garden store Jenniffer was ready to take Kalara back home. She was at her wits end and trying to figure out a way to tell Annette to shove it. If only Annette would find someone else to babysit the dazed Kalara. Not even the meager amount of money or the new cell phone plan Annette had given her was enough to make her keep watching her. Kalara suggested they shop separately at the mall for a while then meet up to eat at the food court. Jenniffer didn't argue the point like she normally would. At the moment she was so annoyed a break sounded good. She could agree to let Kalara be alone, then hang so far back Kalara wouldn't notice her keeping an eye on her. That way, Jenniffer could say that she was indeed doing her job when Annette asked during their weekly phone call.

They entered the mall and Kalara made off on her own. "Be careful and try not to forget we are meeting at the hot dog stand in one hour OK?" Jenniffer yelled to her.

"No problem. See ya."

Jenniffer hung back so their gap would widen. She knew there was no way Kalara would remember when and where to meet, the stupid woman could hardly remember how to get home.

Kalara wasn't shopping, she was searching. Of the many people at the mall, at least one person might possibly know her, recognize her. But on this day no one spoke to her and everyone she made eye contact with gave her an odd look and circled wide around her.

There were so many faces to watch, Kalara made it a point to check each one even though they all seemed to look the same. Aside from hair color, it was very hard to tell people apart. Even though Kalara visually blended in with her average height and slender body, she felt at odds with people, always different than everyone else. She was out of touch with everyone and everything. It all seemed so foreign.

Kalara had just passed the lower level bookstore when she noticed a man in his 30s keeping pace with her and looking in her direction. Clean shaved, expensive jeans and blue shirt, without want. He was taller than most men, broad, and handsome with loose dark hair that fell to his mid-back; the image of a perfect man. He wasn't menacing or threatening in any way but the fact he seemed to be studying Kalara's every detail was disquieting. She changed paths and he adjusted accordingly. The guy was definitely following her. He must know who she was so why didn't he just come up and talk to her?

She turned towards him and started to greet him when suddenly she was mute and couldn't move a muscle, rigid and vulnerable, she stood there. The she heard him say *"CALM"* as he approached her with an air of confidence. Her breath slowed down and her heart relaxed. Standing frozen, she was interested in what he knew about her and only mildly concerned he was controlling her, but she didn't mind it.

The tall, blue-eyed man came close enough to whisper in her ear "I placed a hold on you because you are acting really odd Kalara. I'm not going to hurt you. I just want to know what you are doing here."

Seeing no recognition in her eyes, the man thought carefully about his next words. He started again "My name is Ravanan of Kynasteryx Diamid and I have been looking for you for some time now. You need not fear me, the calming spell should help you relax. Kalara, I don't know why you are here, but I *will* find out. Do this one thing for me, give me this one moment. Just jump in the air and I promise you will stay there, hovering. Your magical blood is eagerly waiting to carry out your commands. I will even jump with you. This is all I ask and I will release you to do it. If you come back down, I will walk away and you will never see me again."

Kalara was skeptical but intrigued. Magical blood? Magic wasn't real. Yet, how was he able to stop her movements? Why wasn't anyone noticing them or caring that she was frozen? He knew her and that made her mood lift considerably despite the calming spell. She would jump to get him to stay and talk more. She had to find out what he knew about her. Feeling his release she jumped and hovered about six inches off the ground. Luckily he did the same thing so she didn't feel completely odd. People around them didn't seem to notice or care, too busy and wrapped up in their lives of purchasing. Was she staying there, or was he causing her to hover off the ground?

He grinned and said "Follow me". Barely forming the thought to consider it, Kalara's body started flying as fast as if she were running. Before she realized it they were six shops away from where they had started. The shoppers didn't seem to notice them soaring above their heads as if a spell of invisibility was emanating from them. Ravanan flew towards the atrium and found a bench to sit down. Kalara followed and sat down beside him.

Kalara's mind was racing, she had to ask, "How were we flying? That's not possible!"

Searching her eyes, Ravanan replied "Of course it is, it's very natural for us. You seem to have forgotten. You don't know who I am do you?"

Kalara looked away and focused on a frazzled young mother forcing four kids into the glass elevator. She replied "No, I don't know you. Nor do I understand how we were flying or that you were able to hold me still back there. You know my name and said that you have been looking for me. I would very much like to hear what you know of my past and how you know me. I was found alone and confused with no idea of who I was other than my name."

Ravanan sat back to consider the words he had just heard. What Kalara told him greatly influenced his next course of action. The thought of leaving crossed his mind. He would now have to account for her memory loss and adjust accordingly if he wanted to keep her with him. Perhaps it would be easiest to kill her before she was discovered. Walking away and leaving her as he had found her was not an option. Yet escorting her back, ruined, with no mind, was not what he had expected. She was tainted by them, the humans, believing she was one of them. She was of no use and dead weight to him.

Finally coming to a decision, Ravanan devised a new strategy "I will tell you what I know about you. You are a dragoness currently trapped in your own morph spell. Your name is Kalara of Kynasteryx Ravyx. Your memory loss would explain why you didn't defend against my spells, but regardless of that, you are still a dragon whether you use magic or not."

Kalara was at a loss as to what to say and ended up reciting the mantra "That can't be, magic isn't real. Dragons aren't real."

Ravanan was prepared for the closed-minded response. "Just because humans can't access magic doesn't make it myth. Here are some facts you used to know about it before you accepted ignorant human beliefs as truth. First, humans don't know about us, their minds don't want to know either. The terror they would feel, knowing they aren't the most powerful creatures on the earth would destroy all they have done and ruin their societies. After the initial shock wore off, the vile, inventive creatures would undoubtedly find a way to hunt us down and kill us all. So we use magic for a mind-blanketing effect that radiates from our blood to blind their senses, as opposed to sending out wild fear and panic, which we are also very good at doing. We have eluded humans by using magic; it is the one thing that sets us apart from other large predators easily run into extinction by humans."

Kalara was trying to find anything that might falsify Ravanan. She countered with "So why do you and I look like humans then?"

Ravanan could see she was listening and had his answer prepared. "There are so many humans around us we often use transformation magic to mimic them and blend in. We can attain nearly 100% of the human form minus the mind and blood which holds consciousness and magic by casting a morphing spell that has been meticulously crafted to keep the benefits of both species, while denying the negative aspects of body density, frail tissue, and the smaller food portion that would normally hamper using magic.

"Somehow, while you were in human form, your dragon qualities must have been made invisible to you, unreachable without help. This would prevent you from casting the reversal spell to change back to your base form. I can't cast the reversal for you. You alone are the only one who can reverse it since spells of transforming are largely nonverbal visualizations executed by the caster's blood. No other dragon would know your body or your particular human form exactly like you do. You have to be able to feel the shape you want to attain – you need to know what it is you want to do. You need to identify with the shape before you can take it as your own.

"Once in human form we have to eat more often to keep the spell going, but in smaller amounts obviously. Your blood has been continuously keeping the human form all this time and it has been needing extra energy to do so. You have been led to believe you are human and you have been trying to blend in with them since you were discovered, thus eating every bit of food you can." Ravanan knew this was where he needed to end the conversation with Kalara. He smiled, "You must be hungry even now. Do you want to go eat?" Kalara couldn't deny she was famished, human or not. "You are right, I am hungry."

She began to walk, but Ravanan gently reached out and held her back. He said "Let's fly again to help you reaffirm your magic". He saw she was unsure so he jumped up as they had before. Kalara copied him and again they were flying, slower this time.

Going to eat was a way Jenniffer could meet him as well. Gliding through the air liberated Kalara from her woes. She smiled at the thought of leaving her problems behind her. Even her purse seem to be weighing her down. Flying was really fun, Kalara smiled. She wanted to believe every word he said after all of the frustrated time spent desperately wanting to know who she was. She had just about given up hope of ever knowing. No one could lament with her because there was no bond there, no connection. Tthis was something tangible to hang on to; a shining beacon to lead her to herself. The fantastic feeling of soaring above the crowd and not having to fight her way through the mall ended all too soon as the smell of fried foods filled her nares. Landing she looked around for Jenniffer but didn't see her. It was no matter though, she would eat with Ravanan and then wait for her to show up.

She turned in a friendly fashion and asked Ravanan "What are you going to eat? I'm going over to get a hot dog." Ravanan replied "I'm not eating, but you go ahead. I'll follow you."

After finding a table and starting to eat, Kalara wanted to keep things light and asked "Aren't you hungry? You've been using magic too." He smiled and answered "I didn't come here to eat."

Ravanan seemed genuinely pleased and relieved to have found her. Sitting at the small table, he was close enough that Kalara could have reached out and taken his hand. He was handsome and disarming. Kalara got the feeling he would fiercely defend her against the entire crowd in the room if need be. He would see to her health and help her discover who she was.

Kalara picked over the few fries that were left. She was eager to learn about who she was and yet on edge that Ravanan could do impossible things. She wanted to ask him about herself but her thoughts were taken up with trying to figure out how he was making them fly. Annette and Jenniffer had drilled it into her that magic was not real. It was not real. Jenn's cynical attitude had rubbed off on her.

8

Ravanan was watching the lunch crowd, studying every face like a hunter looking for prey that might be away from the others, alone and defenseless. He was actually scanning the room for any possible threat. Kalara made sure his attention was elsewhere and caught a few glimpses of him. Well-defined muscles rippled under his tan skin as he drummed his fingers on the table. The slight movements of his tendons mesmerized Kalara who had never noticed before just how sexy a man's wrist could be. She tried to imagine how solid and hard it must feel. By looking at the way his clothes fit, his whole body was that way. She longed to run her hands all over him to find out for sure. Her observations were at the front of her mind and were quickly evolving into a need to softly stroke his wrist with her fingertips. She toyed with an idea of how to accidentally brush up against his arm. It would be a small move, nothing noticeable. There was nothing wrong with that. The urge was becoming a monster she had to tame.

Kalara wondered if he could tell what she was thinking and if he was experiencing the same desire she was. It couldn't be, he wasn't even looking in her direction. She purposely held her hands together in her lap, as if to hold them back from grabbing Ravanan's wrist in her palms. Her fingers found the woven ring Annette had made and she tried to focus on feeling the ring's smooth plaits instead of Ravanan's smooth skin; it was no use. No matter where she looked he was in her vision – his perfect skin and well-built form getting in the way.

It was at that moment Kalara noticed how warm she felt. It was the type of heat generated from warm blood pulsing through a body. It was in the air moving towards her instead of coming from within. The hairs on her skin indicated the subtle warmth was coming from Ravanan. It was enticing and fanned the flames of desire within her. Kalara's skin tuned into it slowly at first but increasing rapidly until the full effect was felt. The warmth of his skin was constant and undeniable, but not uncomfortably warm. She wished he was closer to her. After some serious self-control Kalara was finally able to chain the beastly urge.

Even though no sound had passed her lips and she had made no outward motion, Ravanan turned to squarely face Kalara and lock his azure-blue eyes on hers. His stare was like a spotlight on her. Had she done something to turn his head? Could he read her thoughts? Had she said or done something unaware? After a few embarrassingly long seconds Ravanan asked "Are you ready to go then?"

Kalara sighed with relief that her thoughts hadn't been exposed. Answering back, she said "Go where? Let's stay here, I want you to meet my roommate and then we can talk about my past."

Ravanan had no intention of lingering among the humans. Even though he felt no other dragon blood in the vicinity, it was time to leave. "No. We should go." And he stood up to walk away.

"But what of my past? Won't you help me?" She said in an attempt to stall him - it failed. Kalara stood up and pleaded "Please stay. I need you." At those words, Ravanan ceased his movements. He held her eyes once more then said "Come with me then. I will find a way to recover your loss."

Ravanan walked away. Kalara hurried to catch up before she lost him, so intent on staying with him she forgot her purse hanging on the back of the chair.

She felt much better after the meal; not just better, but invigorated. She was going to finally find her past. Life seemed more vivid to her now. Her senses were sharper somehow, making her more conscious of the world around her. The noise of the lunch crowd was louder, and she could separate out many individual sounds, much more than before. Aside from the sounds, the place reeked with a myriad of odors ranging from sticky spills inside trash cans to long forgotten chunks of food that had rolled under tables. Ready to get away from the putrid smell of human filth she followed Ravanan as he turned the corner from the food court.

Kalara was a few paces behind his quick steps when she saw him stop walking, oddly glance around, then turn back towards her. Ravanan looked very concerned and was about to take her hand when he vanished. Not just invisible, but no longer near her – somehow she knew he was gone.

Kalara stepped to where he had been and felt nothing but air. She looked around for clues and found none. There was no indication that there had ever been a dragon in the shape of a human with her. But he had been there. He had turned around, tried to get to her, and he looked worried. What had happened to him? Would it happen to her as well?

Alone she made her way through the pedestrian traffic to a bench. Kalara felt a quiet rage coalesce in her blood as she sat down. Why couldn't she have vanished with him? She didn't want to be left behind. How would she ever find him again? He hadn't told her anything about himself. Kalara clung to the image of his face and tried to burn the image into her memory, she must never forget him. She couldn't even remember his last name.

She meant something to somebody, she must keep telling herself that. How could she ever return to the hollow world she had known just a short while ago? She couldn't, not now. Not now that she was so close to figuring out who she had been. To go back to that apartment would be like death.

She didn't belong with these people. The gulf between her and the humans around her was greater than ever before. It was like looking at an exhibit in a zoo, separated from the creatures within the cages. The long blank faces she saw seemed to be outward manifestations of pointless errands to fill up a Saturday; and there were so many of them. After a while they really did begin to resemble a herd that was milling about, waiting for death to find them. She couldn't be a part of the crowd any longer. She was done trying to fit in with them, they disgusted her. The rage inside Kalara was now constructing an almost tangible wall about her, separating her from the masses of humans on the outside.

All she wanted to do now was get away from them. The fastest way she knew to exit the mall was to fly. She hadn't imagined it. Ravanan had been real and he had helped her to realize she could fly. She mustn't forget that. Humans couldn't fly, but she could. She could fly out of there right now. In a mighty declaration Kalara's will to be a dragon won out. Standing up, she told herself "I am not a boring human any longer, I am a dragon!" Then she jumped............and fell back to earth. 'It can't be!' Her mind screamed at her body. 'Fly! damn it!' Kalara commanded her body as she jumped again. Her feet touched the ground. She had been so sure. Tears welled up in her eyes.

Doubt took root in her mind. Had she imagined it? For nearly a year she had been desperately searching, trying to find anyone who might know her, She was driven to find herself. Was her thirst for her past so great she had created Ravanan in her mind? The tears broke free and moistened her face.

Ravanan was real – wasn't he? Ravanan was going to give her memory to her. He had seen her, he had froze her, he talked to her. Kalara ran her fingers through her dark hair, pulling it back off her face as she sat down again. She had been flying hadn't she? She had seen the tops of people's heads, it had seemed so real but maybe it was all in her head. She wasn't so sure now. She needed to hear someone tell her that he was real, that dragons existed and she was one, there had to be an eyewitness who saw her flying. She looked around but only saw shoppers who knew magic wasn't real.

Had Ravanan ever really been there? Was her mind playing tricks? The hot tears on her face might as well have been blood drawn by her jagged fingernails as she clawed at the walls of sanity. She was desperate to find herself and the mysterious Ravanan.

Kalara's ears replayed Jenniffer's scoffing laugh over and over in her mind. Did she really think she could fly? How foolish of her! Magic wasn't real, she knew better. Jenn's laughter echoed in her head. She was losing it. The small cord of belief began to fray. She wasn't a dragon. She was a fool to believe otherwise. Dragons weren't real. She couldn't escape being human, an unwanted human. She was crazy to think otherwise.

Kalara could feel her grasp of reality unraveling. With every minute the memories of Ravanan the dragon faded a little more. She sat there crying, the rift of frustration in her mind was leaking Ravanan's very existence. Her mind created him; there, in the mall, created a friend to give her what she wanted. He wasn't real. No one had seen him but her. He was nothing more than a figment of her imagination.

Was she so desperate after the months of no memories she had to resort to fantasy? To think she was flying, it wasn't possible. She wasn't a dragon and had made the whole thing up. She was creating stories that seemed like they were real, so real she believed them to be factual. This was it then, this was to be the end of a pitiful life. After months of amnesia her final story would be dying while trapped within herself living a fantasy life that only she could see. It hadn't been enough that her memories were lost, but no, fate would take her sanity as well, leaving behind a babbling idiot who was having a wonderful time inside her own head.

Her wet eyes were closed, when a warmth came over her that coaxed her eyes open. Before she could turn to look, Kalara heard Ravanan's voice cast *"HOLD"*. She tried to turn her head towards the source, but again, Kalara couldn't move. She felt Ravanan's warm hand grab hers and they were flying in a heartbeat. They reached the doors, Ravanan used such force opening them the handicapped gear broke and the heavy glass doors swung open freely. Once outside, he launched them into the sky. She couldn't have broken his grasp even if she had wanted to. Kalara could feel his hard muscles flexing to maintain their hold on her, making the necessary small adjustments as needed – it felt good. Their altitude increased high above the parking lot where Jenniffer's 1973 red corvette convertible was parked, now a tiny speck among the many cars.

Within seconds they reached a rocky outcrop over-looking the city. Although she felt the release to move again Ravanan held her hand tightly and walked a few yards towards the cliff.

He spoke finally, "I'm going to get you out of here. Hold on...." He scanned the weathered sandstone to find the unremarkable center of a single large rock. In a firm voice he cast *"ANCHOR"*. Blood-red iron began to weep from the rock to form finely etched markings on the surface – it was a sketch of a hill top with four scraggly trees. The spell had taken all the available iron from the rock matrix and used it for ink to write on its surface. Runes of an ancient spell circled the two foot sketch.

Ravanan watched the deep red lines thicken. He explained "I'm taking you away from here as fast as I can before anything else happens. I need to make sense of what is going on." When the anchor stabilized, he stepped onto it, pulling Kalara with him. As soon as their feet touched the anchor their bodies wisped away in red smoke forming balls of lightning that catapulted into the air. As they left, the sketch seeped back into the sandstone bluff leaving no trace.

Chapter 2

Annette sat on her front porch watching the morning fog that was rising from a distant pond. The still water of the pond was one of her favorite things about the country... and to see its golden mirror reflecting the morning sun was perfection. She puffed on her pipe, the wisps of smoke were poor imitations of the low fog that filled the valley. She loved pipe smoke, its sweet aroma worked its own special magic on the sick and those who needed her services.

The rest of the world, impatient and worried, was starting their day in the distant cities and towns – Annette made sure to live as far away as she could from any one community or train track. Nothing disturbed her world more than man-made noises and odors. She would take the smell of a skunk any day rather than the odor of human filth, and the security lights, every home had one blocking the natural starlight she loved to view. She always marveled at people's fear of the dark. The dark was part of life, just about half of it the way she figured it.

Annette was a tribal medicine woman despite being only 42 years old. Sure there were others who claimed the title and they were much older, wiser and deserving great respect, but she was the best. Her medicine seemed to always work, especially when men were making the request. No one could deny her strong connection with the ancestors either, not even the tribal elders. Somehow she always knew things about people's deceased grandparents that no one could possibly know. Just little things they remembered from their childhood, like grandpa's favorite fishing hole, or the way granny would cut up her peaches. The only explanation of her knowledge and abilities was that Annette communicated with their deceased kin; it was surprising and comforting to those who came to her for help.

And they did come, nearly the whole tribe thought of Annette as the one person they could not live without. Annette knew the heartbeat of the tribe, where it had come from and where it was going. The full bloods believed she could walk through time, forward and back, they considered her a living ancestor, a time-walking spirit.

Pipe smoke curled.

The air spoke of harvest time, each day the wind stole more of the trees' fall foliage and within a week the trees would be fully whipped about, changed into dark skeletons of their former green selves. The season represented Annette well for she was wise, experienced, and producing perfection in everything she touched. She was the epitome of late summer-sweetened fruit, those final tomatoes that had bloomed late but still grew to beautiful plump red berries. The passing of time gave Annette perfection, an edge in the world around her.

She was waiting for Todd to arrive. He was her understudy and helper, but by the time he showed up everyday Annette had most of the chores done. This morning she even had time to go hunt for mushrooms. Annette watched the smoke wickedly rise into the quiet air and dance in a lacy pattern before vanishing.

Todd wasn't just a strong back, he was her stepson, she had no children of her own and had never married – though most could argue she received more love than any married woman did. Todd and his sister Jenniffer had been placed in Annette's care when their mother mysteriously died some 15 years previously. Taking a puff from her pipe and then braiding her long dark hair, Annette reflected on her stepchildren. Todd was her favorite, he was turning out to be a great learner, always listening, never questioning her. His rich heritage obvious in his dark skin and bone features, he looked as though he could be Annette's biological son. There was no doubt he was a full blood.

Jenniffer was Todd's younger sister, his opposite, and Annette's expression turned foul at the thought of her. Jenniffer had a serious dislike of all medicine – or magic as Jenniffer called it – and always pulled away from Annette's teachings. She wanted to move away to the city and study architecture of all things. Such a disappointment, Annette should have seen years ago when in puberty Jenniffer's fair complexion needed sunscreen of all things! Annette didn't doubt they were brother and sister, for she was there at each of their births, but their differences were quite notable, causing question of their paternity. One day Jenniffer would regret turning her back on her blood and her tribe.

Todd finally pulled into the driveway. Annette took the basket of mushrooms with their rich, earthy smell into the house and returned to greet Todd in the yard. "How did it go last night?" she asked.

"We did pretty good. I ran out of those pearl beads you made. We got $148. total." he said as he hoisted the remainder of their wares out of his truck. As he did his long black braid swung against his back.

Annette always sent Todd to the pow-wows, he needed the exposure if he was ever going to be her replacement and she didn't like being out late. "How did it go with Melissa, did she forgive you?"

Todd showed her a big smile that softened his stern and chiseled face, "No, in fact she broke up with me. But we did have one great last time together after the pow-wow was over." he paused at the memory, "Good riddance I say, she was too jealous anyways."

"You should have tried what I told you, women like that."

"I did, kinda. But she didn't go for it." He shrugged and passed it off as he retrieved his chainsaw from the bed of his pickup. "Not all women are open like you. But hey, Bill got great news last night, his drum group was asked to be the main drum at the next pow-wow..." Todd was lost in thought for a moment, "Can you believe he asked about Jenniffer again?"

Annette shook her head, "I don't know what he sees in her, she won't even go to pow-wows and we all know how she feels about cockfighting. He'd have to get rid of all his chickens!"

Todd added "He's too good for her. He probably just thinks it would be cool to date my sister, it would make us closer, like brothers."

Later when they were sawing up a black oak tree that had fallen across a foot path, Todd got into a mess of stretch-berry vines. His legs were snagged and cut up by the vicious little thorns. After the tree was cleaned up and firewood stacked Annette took him inside to clean up the bloodied cuts. Todd watched calmly as Annette began chanting a healing song and took out her jar of salve.

He loved watching her work, so much so that sometimes he purposely got hurt just to see her heal his wounds, it was amazing. He couldn't explain how her medicine healed, it had to be supernatural rather than physical because he was the one who made the salve with Annette's guidance and the ingredients were simple, ground up cat bone, fresh aloe vera gel, dried grass seeds (any variety), the sap of an oak tree, milk of milk weed, and a little whiskey. He didn't see how any of those things could really heal on their own. The salve didn't keep very long and he knew the recipe by heart because he had to make it every month. Even as he watched and listened to her droning voice, the deep scratches and snags of skin healed over before his eyes as Annette massaged the salve into them. Her touch was relaxing, he could easily lay back and take a nap, Annette had ways about her that were simply mesmerizing and impossible to put into words.

In his eyes, Annette was a superwoman and he was attracted to her connection with the spirit world. He was twelve years old when Annette began to care for him and Jenniffer, she was only 14 years older than him. He adored Annette and her ministrations and was attracted to the Native American medicine woman to the point he would get aroused in a certain setting. She was the reason he hadn't married yet, no other woman could ever match her. He was over eighteen and what did it matter if he liked her, Annette wasn't his blood relative. He would just wait and see what the Great Spirit called him to do.

The two of them had sat down to eat when Annette paused and her dark gray eyes got a worried, knowing look.

"What is it?" Todd asked.

"Something has happened to Kalara, I feel it in my chest. I think she has finally begun to follow her vision quest. Todd, help me outside, I've got to get to the prayer stone." The pain in her chest was from anxiety, a sudden realization she had missed something important, it wasn't crippling, just distracting; she needed to know what was going on.

Annette's house was more of a cabin, an ancient cabin. No one could remember exactly when it was built; it seemed to have always been there, nestled in the trees. It had undergone several remodels yet none could take out the mold inside the walls. She owned the entire hill and aside from a small shaded lawn, the hill was covered with old-growth black oak forest. In the summer, everything was a rich green color and serenaded by June bugs and cicadas. In the winter, Annette's hill was brown and dormant with the occasional reverberating crash of tree tops being snapped off from ice storms. At the top of the hill were a few rocky but moss-covered, vine-laced, snake-infested bluffs only to be seen by birds flying directly over them. These stone bluffs were where Annette had sent many a young native to find their vision quest and spirit guide. On certain mornings, foggy patches could be seen rising from the oak forest, a gray mist escaping from the numerous small cave openings found on different parts of the hill. All in all, it was a beautiful hill, part of the foothills of the Ozark mountain range.

Her small lawn was, for the most part, clean, aside from the brush piles that needed burning, the tool shed / green house combo, the rusty 55-gallon drum where she burned her trash, five ricks of firewood, three overgrown and rocky flower beds, the well house, the storm cellar, the small vegetable garden that was strategically placed in the only sunny (but rocky) spot, the compost pile, the butchering table, the rabbit hutches, the chicken coop, and the bigger discarded items that had been waiting for years to be hauled off and would most likely have to wait a few more.

The focal point of her outdoor living space was the natural stone altar in her front yard that was not placed there by man; it was part of the hillside that time had weathered and exposed. Todd had helped her position smaller rocks around it for seating.

In the backyard was her sweat lodge, it was the size of a small shed. The well-thought-out earthen structure allowed for greater concentrations of steam to build up; it was her pride and joy. Her design of the lodge was masterful, near the back wall of it was the sacred fire that was never allowed to burn out, always alive, connecting her and the tribe to the spirits.

The only way to drive into Annette's homestead fortress was a long gravel road that winded around the hill, its entrance from the road marked by boulders that originally had been on top of the hill.

The stone altar in the front yard greeted them as Todd helped Annette kneel down in front of it. He lit the incense sconces that stood at each side of the stone altar and added oil to the flames as Annette instructed. As the flames grew tall he left the sacred circle to stand watch and beat a small ceremonial drum.

Annette dropped some sage into the flames and dealt fifty peacock feathers in five rows of ten onto the flat prayer stone, she preferred using organic tools rather than cold, lifeless rocks and crystals because things of life always gave better results. The severed "eyes" were roughly the same size as a deck of cards, each one reflected in Annette's eyes a thousand rainbows.

The bleached shell of a baby box turtle laid against her chest dangling from a simple leather cord necklace. Annette's spirit guide, a gray snake, was painted on the shell. She grasped the dangling turtle shell and began to rattle it in rhythm to the drum and chanted a summoning song to awaken the ancestors. When the song ended she raised both hands high, taking in the heady smell of burning sage. With a strong and earnest voice she prayed "Great Spirit, be honored this day, please draw near unto me." She shook the turtle rattle upside down in her hand to dispense a few tiny pearls and gallstones she had harvested personally. She then blessed the prayer stone with the sacred elements by reverently casting them onto it.

Smoke billowed unnaturally from the two flames. The medicine woman sat motionless as the smoke filled the air around her, sinking low down to the ground instead of floating up. The Great Spirit thickened the smoke to where Todd had to squint to see her inside the haze. He could see the peacock eyes were no longer fifty feathers but a single watery pool with a rainbow sheen on it, much like how gasoline appears on a mud puddle after a rain shower. He heard Annette commune with the Great Spirit. "Ancestors, Great Spirit, see the woman Kalara. Something has just happened with her. Show her to me."

Todd took a few steps forward, not enough to insult, and looked into the oily iridescent pool where he saw Kalara walking in a shopping mall. He looked quickly at Annette who was watching the pool intently, she seemed pissed off and slightly surprised at what she saw.

Where was his sister Jenniffer? She wasn't in the pool, she should be right there watching Kalara. Then he saw a man in a blue shirt turn around and walk to Kalara but he disappeared before he could get to her. Todd didn't recognize the man and wondered who he could be.

Then the smokey air filled with unseen splinters of ash and Todd had to step away or else be gagged by the abrasive cloud. He wasn't scared, he knew the Great Spirit when it descended. The ancestors favored Annette, the ash cloud of the Great Spirit never made her cough or gag. It was now so dense he couldn't see into it at all. He could hear the familiar shattered voice speaking but he couldn't make out the words. The voice always sounded strange to him, if glass shards could talk, they would sound like that voice. Todd wondered if Annette heard it the same way he did, he knew it wasn't her talking, no human could make those sounds. It had to be the Great Spirit, because the voice was other-worldly and fragmented.

Todd was so enamored with Annette and the great power she had tapped into, her house was the only place he ever wanted to be. He wanted to learn everything and be just like her, he wanted to be in that cloud with her, communing with the Great Spirit of Mother Earth.

Soon the smoke around Annette faded and she made her way out of the sacred stone circle. As she approached Todd, he asked "What did the spirits tell you?"

Annette didn't waste time answering him, instead she was moving fast devising a plan, she commanded him "Fetch me a couple of river rocks about yeah-big" - she gestured with her hands - "and that bobcat skull in the round flower bed, then build up an oak fire where I was sitting in front of the prayer stone."

With orders given, Annette made her way to the house and the back room where she kept a special chest that held Kalara's dress; it was the robe Kalara was wearing when Annette had found her. The exquisite cream-colored robe was embossed with runes and adorned with fire opals that had a light all their own, they were unnaturally beautiful. She carefully unfolded the white robe to retrieve an ermine pelt she had nestled into the bodice to absorb Kalara's residual self. She pulled out the small white fur and went out the door.

Todd was adding more oak twigs to the smoldering pile when she arrived. Annette waited for the fire to catch and carefully held the ermine pelt in her hands, straightening the strands of Kalara's dark hair that she had sewn to the head of it. The weather conditions were not cooperating with the meager coals, she finally added some oil to the fire and commenced with chanting a curse.

Chanting all the while, she punctured the torso of the pelt on the sharp saber teeth of the bleached bobcat skull as Todd held it firm. The holes left behind were jagged when she pulled the skin away. The rhythmic chant of her dark curse continued as Annette took the river rock and broke the back legs of the small bones which had been left in the ermine skin. Lastly, she placed the back feet of the pelt into the flames and watched as the fur singed and skin burned away. The lingering putrid smell of burning hair made Todd want to vomit, but he dared not. She finished the cursing chant with ugly, guttural tones.

Annette cast Kalara's Pelt aside and stood up to dust herself off. She collected the peacock eyes off the altar and slipped them back into her medicine bag while Todd quieted the fire. He glanced over at the little white ermine pelt, not wanting to get near it, he asked "What about Kalara's Pelt?"

"Put it on the honey locust tree out past your deer stand, you know the one. Stick it on the thorns. Be sure it won't come off."

Using a stick to carry the mangled fur, Todd headed off for the woods knowing exactly where to go. The honey locust tree was something to be avoided. Its old bark was densely covered in woody thorns, each one nearly a foot long. The thorns were tough and could poke right through a rubber-soled boot. There were thorns on top of thorns, the whole tree trunk was a horrible nightmare, protected from any animal who might think to climb it. Todd recalled the time he had to clean one in his childhood, it took him and Jenniffer three days using pliers, buckets, and ladders to get it free enough for a chainsaw to cut it up. Each thorn had to be carefully disposed of, you sure didn't want to drop one because they blended in perfectly with the forest floor making walking around the tree very hazardous.

The awful tree stood gravely before him, a sentinel of the woods. Todd carefully pushed the small pelt onto the pristine thorns, it stuck nicely with a satisfying friction. He spoke under his breath with a quiet reverence, "Take care of Kalara's Pelt, cause it pain." Suspended and crucified in the air, Kalara's dark hair waving in the breeze, the little white ermine fur was now firmly held and decorating a very evil and black tree.

After Todd left, Annette's cell phone rang while she was putting away their interrupted meal, Jenniffer was on the other end her worried voice was loud in the quiet kitchen. Annette had been awaiting Jenniffer's call. She didn't comfort her step-daughter but upon hearing of Kalara's disappearance ordered her to come straight to her house. It would be more than an hour before Jenniffer got there so Annette settled down with some rum and her pipe.

How could Kalara be gone? What was she even doing outside of the apartment? The trapping enchantments she had placed over the apartment only worked if Kalara was in it, the foolish girl knew better than to take Kalara out of there. What would prompt Kalara to run away now, after all this time? Maybe it would have been better to at least let Kalara know that she was Jenniffer's step-mom, maybe then she would have felt safer in Tulsa. How was it that the magic of Kalara's Pelt failed to stop her? She should be in tremendous pain, unable to move, and that phone call should have been Kalara asking for medicine to stop the pain. Annette puffed on her pipe, causing tendrils of smoke to search for a way out of the house. She had to try the feathers again to look for Kalara. The late afternoon had brought a thunderhead which Annette would use to her advantage.

The storm front was quick to move on and left plenty of rain puddles. Annette went to the low spot on her back porch and placed the feathered eyes on the calm pooled water. Soon the puddle acquired the familiar dazzling colors but it only showed grass and no Kalara. If the pool couldn't target Kalara's ring, then no spell could. Where could she be?

Annette was mad at herself. She never should have sent Kalara away to stay with Jenniffer, if only she hadn't feared what would happen if she'd kept Kalara close by.... and now Kalara was lost to her. Jenniffer would soon regret losing her.

The night sky had settled in by the time Jenniffer showed up and Annette was more than ready for her. "You lost her? Tell me everything – leave nothing out."

Jenniffer was smart enough to do as she was told. No good ever came from lying to the woman, her paraplegic ex-boyfriend was testament to that. She sat down on the chair by the front window and recounted the day, "... I had my eye on her, honestly, she was just walking along and I was tagging her from behind, giving her some space. I thought that would be better than having her resentment keep building up – you do realize she hadn't left the apartment in two months? She was acting like her normal self, we had only parted ways for maybe five or ten minutes when she simply vanished. I saw it happen. I was watching her when she disappeared right before my eyes. I ran to where she had been and there was nothing there. I asked the other people who had been right there and no one saw anything. I searched the mall twice over. I found her purse hanging from a chair back in the food court. It was undisturbed with everything still in it. Here, I brought it for you."

Annette rummaged through the purse, finally dumping it out on the coffee table. "Her ring isn't here. Did you see her ring anywhere?"

"No, Annette, I looked for it and it wasn't anywhere near that purse or in it. Do you think I'm that stupid? I know what you instructed of me and I did it. How can I help it if she vanished? She would have vanished with you too!"

Annette said nothing and allowed the uncomfortable silence to build. She knew that in the absence of speech the guilty would spill out their secret thoughts. 'Let them stew in their misery' was Annette's motto. It would do no good to yell, screaming is for the young and foolish, a quiet reply is all that is needed to make a point. She lit her pipe once more, enjoyed several slow puffs and ruminated over a fitting punishment.

Jenniffer worriedly looked about for something to take her mind off of the moment. She hated it when Annette did this and refused to say another word. Anything more would only imply guilt. Her eyes found the large dream catcher that Annette had made a few years back, all the windows in the house were protected by them. This one spanned the whole window with a three foot diameter. The familiar dust it had collected while guarding the window had been cleaned off of the sinew webbing, but something else was different about it too. The adorning beads looked odd, more like raisins than clay. It looked like Annette had recently restrung the dream catcher.

Finally, Annette set her pipe down and spoke just loud enough for her venom to be heard "You are foolish and stupid. Stupid! I told you to keep her inside that apartment with your damned cats. You can't even follow simple instructions. After all I've done for you..... you lose her?" She took a moment to regain her composure "Tell me, had anything odd happened lately?"

Jenniffer remembered Kalara's dream, "Yes, I meant to tell you the next time you called, this morning Kalara had another dream, this time she was hunting and she heard the voice again. I told her again that magic isn't real. She wasn't upset from it and quickly forgot about the dream. Jenniffer dreaded the consequences of not mentioning that sooner.

Annette shivered secretly at hearing about Kalara hunting even though it had been a mere dream. She pushed that aside and leaned forward to pick up a small house spider that had come up from under the coffee table, and she watched it move to the top of her finger.

"Jenniffer, you should have called me about that rather than wait for me to call you. You say she disappeared before your very eyes..." The spider posed itself, ready to strike. "...Since you can't use your eyes and body properly, I will."

With that, Annette flicked her wrist and flung the spider onto Jenniffer, it landed on her shirt. The moment the spider touched its target, Annette's spell began to unfold. The webbing of the giant dream catcher un-knotted itself and reached down to bind Jenniffer's arms and legs. The "raisins" weren't dried fruit after all, they were dried hearts of some small animal that began to beat in unison with Annette who had begun to sing a cursing chant. Jenniffer's pulse joined the rhythm as the sinew tightened around her neck and mouth.

She didn't try to avoid the trap, she knew it was useless to fight the medicine woman's magic; but her eyes told the truth, she was scared.

Annette rose up and came around the table to Jenniffer, grabbing a magnifying glass as she did. The beat of the chant continued even as she paused the horrible song to say "How far have you fallen from being the skilled daughter I always wanted? Let me just have a look into those stupid eyes and see if there is anything in you worth saving." She peered into Jenniffer's eyes and then backed away.

"You are pretty much useless to me, however I shouldn't waste your perfectly good body on the compost pile." Annette slammed the magnifying glass onto the coffee table, shattering the lens, and picked up the curse where she had left off.

Annette walked out of the room leaving Jenniffer firmly bound to her chair. Jenniffer couldn't move, the spider was long gone and still the beating hearts kept time for her. There was no escape, she never should have agreed to help the witch, no matter what she offered. The sinew finally stopped its advance. She had been gagged with a throbbing heart in the back of her throat, her saliva was moistening it, making it gooey.

When Annette came back to the living room, she was carrying a cutting board with a nine-inch slicing knife on it. She sat down across from Jenniffer who could only watch and hear her step-mom sing her curse - hoping it wasn't a death sentence.

Annette sharpened the slicer and peered down the length of the blade to make sure all remaining nicks were gone. She took a yellow cooking onion from her pocket, the stoutest, strongest variety on the market. Holding her face over it, she sliced and ate the onion to make her tears flow. She looked at her disappointing excuse for a daughter and laughed a sharp, cutting laugh. Her chant continued in perfect time with the beating hearts - the evil song filled the air.

Annette picked up the lens shards, reserving the longest two she could find. She rolled the shards down her own face, cutting her cheeks, unflinching, a mixture of blood and tears coated them. Then she took from her pocket two peacock eyes, the iridescent feathers reflected the dim lighting of the room, and soaked them on her face as she had the shards, singing all the while.

Jenniffer could feel the beat of the music on her throat and taste the hot onion from the air which was an improvement over the rotten, gummy hearts. She shut her eyes, refusing to watch anymore. But eyesight wasn't needed for what happened next, she felt the wet, soft feathers cover her eyelids. She shook her head vehemently and leaned far back from Annette, but the strong sinew fought back, growing longer and tighter, immobilizing her head and curling like grape vines holding the peacock feathers in place. Jenniffer then heard the final notes of the curse as she felt the sharp prick of two bloody shards piercing her eyes.

Chapter 3

The magical journey from the anchor was startling. It was as though a giant fish hook had snagged Kalara and was yanking her to shore. She tried to see where they were going, but her eyeballs had been atomized along with every other body part making normal vision impossible. Only her consciousness remained intact; electricity held it together with thousands of spider-webbed arcs of lightning as her matter formed a cloud around her. Somehow she knew they were traveling fast, the wind was biting at her raw flayed-open mind; trying to break the connecting bolts. The intensity of the trip didn't let up until they came to be standing on a table top hill with four wind-whipped trees that loomed over a wide desert plain, the landscape was identical to the sketch in the anchor.

Kalara was light-headed and held onto Ravanan for support. It took her a second to reconnect to herself. Her eyeballs worked – she could see again. She shook her head trying to sync with her newly reformed body then did her best to stand on her own.

Ravanan looked over at her, "You'll be fine. Stay here. I won't be long." He walked some distance away from her and as he did his clothes disappeared. Then he knelt down with his fingertips barely touching the earth. All at once his fingernails grew and changed to black talons, his tan skin became brilliant blue scales and his dark hair whipped up furiously to become black horns. The bumps of his spine extended into black spikes and folded wings rose out of his back while his neck and tail bones lengthened so that his frame grew eleven times larger. His muscles tensed, his wings unfurled and he took off to fly a perimeter. The transformation took mere heartbeats to complete.

Completely stunned at the magnificent dragon she had just seen, Kalara sat down and tried to focus on the most basic functions of life; checking that her whole body was there. She was dumbfounded. The man had been telling the truth and he was big.

'...nine ten.' she counted to herself, happy that all her toes were present.

Kalara didn't recognize the terrain. She didn't know what to think. There was shock at seeing a mythical being, elation that he had come back for her, worry that she didn't know where she was, fear that she might actually be laying in a coma on the floor of the mall and there was the bizarre feeling of being separated into billions of pieces, and the attraction at seeing a very well-toned man bare his body before her. It was all too much for her to take in.

Ravanan made three full passes around her, the third engulfed Kalara in a wide dome of faint, glittering blue fog that covered the entire hill they had landed on. It was beautiful and all around her, touching her, blocking her from the outside world. Kalara rose up and took a few steps to explore the feeling. The blue fog was neither moist nor dry, but in perfect balance with the weather. She could move through it with no hindrance. She reached out to collect a sparkle that was slowly hovering near her face, it evaded her grasp just as a dust particle would in a sunlight beam.

Kalara peered into the millions of sparkles, mesmerized by them. As she did the blue fog in the distance seemed to be coalescing into a thicker cloud. She refocused her eyes, trying to see better into the glittery cloud. Suddenly she realized it wasn't a cloud, but the shape of a massive blue dragon coming towards her. It was as though he had appeared from out of nowhere because she hadn't heard him land.

She watched him approach. From inside her mind Kalara heard the dragon's full title, Ravanan of Kynasteryx Diamid the Malefic Azure, as it heralded before him.

She stood transfixed as he drew closer still, close enough to eat her.

Ravanan did not come to stand before Kalara. Instead he circled her, keeping his blue eyes trained on her tiny human form. Amidst the quaking of his footfalls he cast "*ARMOR*". The look of his blue scales changed, they became blurry, as a thin layer of super dense air coated him with magical protection. His tenseness was palpable.

Something was up. Kalara broke the uncomfortable silence that hung in the air. "Ravanan, what is it? What happened back there at the mall?"

"*What happened*?" Ravanan flung her question back at her. "You tell me what happened." He kept walking slowly around her. "I don't suppose you want to tell me who dismissed me do you?"

"What?" Kalara burst out. "How should I know who it was? I was worried it would happen to me too!"

"Really." He said with a deep, flat tone. "Come now Kalara. Some dragon must have known where you were..... saw us together..... and then cast a dismissal spell on me." Ravanan's voice was thick with suspicion. "Now I wonder, who? I know it wasn't you, at least not directly." he sneered at her. "Tell me who it was."

Kalara was silent and wide-eyed, fear washed over her.

With a defensive ire he continued "I sensed your surprise when I came back. You didn't think I would did you? What trap did you have planned for me? Who is helping you? And why?"

"I don't.....," Kalara shook her head, "You are helping me... you were...or so I thought." She was confused and growing more afraid. She had no idea where he had brought her to, and she was alone against him.

"Enough! You can stop the game Kalara."

The blue glittery mist grew brighter, the hairs on her arms raised up. Kalara looked away, a tear escaped from her eye. The longer she looked at the beautiful glitter, the more it seemed to be changing into something more than just glitter, perhaps tiny electrical sparks – but how was that possible?

Then Ravanan stopped his pacing to face her dead on. "What were you doing there? And don't tell me you have no memory. What an absurd story! What are you planning? Why did you leave the territory?"

The barrage pierced Kalara's mind and unseen pressure points compelled her to speak. Kalara could not believe he was doing this. She didn't know what to say. Her eyes welled up with tears. "I'm not planning anything! I promise!"

The pressure increased and so did the pitch of her voice. The mist was definitely brighter and becoming charged. She spoke quicker. "I don't know who you are. I don't even know who I am. Dragons aren't supposed to be real. I'm not even sure I'm really here. I don't remember anything of my past. Nothing. I swear it!"

The air around them started popping with sparks. Ravanan roared "WHO DISMISSED ME???!"

Kalara's hands flew to cover her ringing ears. She screamed back "I DON'T KNOW! Why are you doing this to me? I have nothing you want and I've told you all I know."

She had offered everything she knew. She couldn't give anymore, the next step was death. Not only did it feel as though she was drowning in deep water, but it looked like it also, everywhere around her was the electrically charged blue mist and the giant blue dragon blended perfectly with it.

He was turning up the pressure and Kalara's body was about to collapse under it. She didn't want this and didn't know how much longer she would last. Maybe she really wasn't there. Maybe it was all in her head and she was laying in the mall. The crushing pressure felt real enough though. The commanding power from Ravanan was impressive and even in her current predicament Kalara was in awe of him.

The pressure continued to increase slowly, at an imperceptible rate, like the slow turning of a screw as Ravanan analyzed her answer. Then he dug deeper with icy cold prying tendrils to force out information from every crevice of her brain. "Who is watching you Kalara? What color are his eyes? Why are you helping him?

"WHAT IS HIS NAME?" Ravanan's voice rolled across the plains. Or maybe his voice was in her head, Kalara was getting dizzy, she couldn't tell the source anymore, just the pounding, ringing, dizzying pressure from her inquisitor.

A shiver ran down her spine, she closed her eyes and screamed out. "I don't know! I didn't know I was being followed. All I had been thinking of is that you must know my past and could help me sort out my memories. I'm so sorry! When you disappeared back there, I didn't know what to do." she wailed. "I wished you would come back and had no way of finding where you had gone."

Revisiting her despair caused Kalara to shudder with gasping sobs against the pressure. Her world was going black – at any time now she would pass out. She waited for it, for anything, something would have to give and it would most likely be her life.

Even with her eyes closed, she knew the angry dragon was still there. What had she gotten herself into? What did Ravanan want with her? Finally she felt a release and dropped limply to the earth.

When Kalara opened her eyes again the blue dragon was where she remembered him, standing right in front of her. His massive head was above her some ten feet in the air. He spoke with disgust. "The human body is so small, bite size really."

Kalara wiped the old tears from her face, not saying a word. She didn't want any of this. He went on "Of all the forms you could have taken, all the places you could have went, why a human up in Anarchelos Vya?"

"I told you – I *don't know*." she answered angrily, not looking at him.

"It does appear that your mind is missing. You really don't know anything about yourself."

He went on "You think what you know is actuality and truth, but what I see is a game, nothing more than a temporary situation that you have placed yourself in and you had another dragon help you do it."

Seeing that Kalara did not deny it, Ravanan spoke further. "My banishment could only have been caused by a very serious and high level spell. It seems as though you were bait for me, or that some other dragon doesn't want me near you. Which is it I wonder."

Again Kalara said nothing, she was rubbing her chest where it hurt the most.

Ravanan watched her. He could see that her once strong mind was now hindered with fragility and fear, even though it was inconceivable to him that a powerful dragoness would allow herself to be victimized for any reason.

He was getting nowhere with her. Ravanan rose up to walk away.

That got Kalara to talk. She said "So what now? How do I get back home?"

"You're not going back there."

"I'm not staying here." The tone of her voice was obvious; she deserved to be taken home.

"Finally, a truth from you. You are coming with me so I can get your memories back. We'll leave after the sun rises." Ravanan started to leave.

"Wait, don't walk away. The night is early, let's talk – and without the use of pain."

Ravanan the Malefic Azure contemplated her demand. After some thought, he responded "You are ordering me? I don't think so my little Kalara. You should be grateful you are even being rescued. I need to eat, I'll be back. Gather some wood and then I'll hear your words."

As she searched for wood Kalara rubbed her arms to bring back the feeling that the ocean pressure had taken from her. She was thankful she wasn't his foe and tried to massage away the lingering pain. She was still angry at him for torturing her like he did but she needed him for answers. She had to get over it and go on.

As she threw dead wood onto the pile she'd made, she muttered to herself, "I don't see why he won't just tell me right now who I am. 'hear my words'!" she huffed, "I have nothing to say. I want to hear his words!"

"It's not that simple." Again, Ravanan startled her from the darkness made darker by his blue mist. How could he have heard her say that? She had practically whispered it to herself.

Ravanan went on "The moment you told me you didn't know who you were, was when I knew that you were not safe. I know you need answers, you need a lot of them. But before anything else, we must get away from the dragon who did this to you. You don't realize the powerful magic that has been over you all this time, silent, watching, and waiting from far away. You don't understand how vulnerable you have been."

He tossed a blackened dead cow onto the rock near Kalara.

Ravanan rose up high and cast *"MORPH TO HUMAN"*. The large dragon practically vanished because the spell happened so fast and in his place stood a man whose dark hair was still falling down over his shoulders. His naked human body didn't bother him, but like all dragons, Ravanan cared deeply about blending in when morphed to the human form so he then cast *"DRAPE SAPPHIRE"*. Ravanan the Azure

Wizard walked up to Kalara wearing his favorite apparel. His blue velvet robes were embellished with sapphires and light blue topaz gems that set off his blue eyes. The heaviness of the velvet accentuated his broad shoulders giving him an even more impressive build.

For the first time since they traveled through the anchor Ravanan looked Kalara over as if to make sure she was still herself and alright. "Did anything happen to you after I vanished from the mall? Did you see or hear anything?"

"No, nothing. What happened to you? Where did you go?"

"I was banished as I told you." Ravanan knelt down and cast *"EVOKE BOLT"*. A dirk appeared in his outstretched hand that had a jagged crystal blue blade with edges shaped like a lightning bolt and he savagely cut the cow's throat with it.

Ravanan waited for the blood to collect on the rock and said "Until your memories come back you will have to work on learning your magic again the hard way. It's in you, but you have no understanding of it and it is lost to you. Just watch everything I do.

"The way we craft spells is to just do it. It is physically and mentally exhausting at first, using our blood to work the magic and causing us to eat great amounts of food. But with each repetition the chosen spell slowly becomes easier. It takes a long time to refine a spell to perfection. But finally if a spell is cast enough times it hardly uses any magic at all. This does not give us unlimited power, it just rewards the work we put in towards a particular spell. Such as the dismissal spell that was cast on me. Whoever that dragon is he probably tired himself out completely just vanishing me. That was powerful magic to watch a dragon through a seer pool and then displace it from its point of origin. It was a rare spell, not needed for normal living."

The small pool of bovine blood was overflowing now. Ravanan cast *"ANCHOR"* and he watched it form on the rock where they had landed. Seeing where the anchor was located, he dipped his finger in the blood and quickly drew a two foot circle next to it. The first anchor faded after a few heartbeats as Ravanan worked on the second anchor.

He wrote out a spell using the same runes Kalara had seen on the other anchor around the edge of his circle and he explained "What I'm writing is the command to break apart our molecular bonds and to send our atomized flesh to the place I'll draw in the center."

Kalara was distracted by the flies that had started buzzing around the dead cow and disgustingly asked "Why did you need cow's blood for this? Have you ever heard of a magic marker? Humans make them to write on things....."

Ravanan smiled to hide his shock at her total memory loss, 'How could she not know this?' he thought to himself. He tried the best he could to put on a teacher's face for her, amazed he would even go the trouble, and answered. "I'm drawing an anchor, it needs iron-filled ink to call forth the iron in the rock. I will go back and kill the dragon responsible for banishing me and taking your memories, this anchor will make it faster to get there." Now he was deftly sketching the cliff they had flown to in Tulsa.

Kalara watched him draw with the cow blood and asked "What is this blue mist?"

He paused to look at the mist "It's a barrier that protects against outside magic and prevents those outside of it from seeing us. In here we are hidden from the world."

After he finished his sketch he cast "*IMPRINT*" which caused the blood ink to soak totally into the rock.

By then Ravanan was ready to eat. He was exhausted from casting the protective blue mist spell. The wizard breathed a quick jet of fire on the wood and sat back to wait on a rare steak.

Kalara watched the flames grow tall. "Who am I?" she asked.

He replied "I know who you were, but telling you about yourself won't help you. I could tell you about any dragoness and say it was you and you wouldn't know the difference. What you really want to know is your memories; once you get those back you can decide if you still want to be who you were. Until then, you must be who you are right now."

"Alright, can you help me get my memories back? Do you have a spell for that?"

"Yes, I do, but you might lose your recent knowledge in the process and the possible clues about who did this to you. I need those clues intact, your memories can wait."

Kalara was disappointed. "Wait? But I don't want to wait! How did this happen to me? Can you at least tell me that?"

Ravanan's voice remained low and paced, as if time had no hold on him "I wasn't with you when you lost your memories therefore I don't know how it happened."

"So that's it then, you don't care that I've been like this for months. What's a little longer gonna matter? All you are wanting to do is take me far away from all I know. Why? Why you? Who are you to me? And where are you taking me? Why not help me get the one thing I need, the very thing I crave more than anything else?"

His answer was tinted with a scoff, "You don't know your needs. I was chosen to escort you back to your true home, Kynasteryx. You are a dragon and you'll not be left to the fate of a common animal, lost in a herd of humans."

"And if I refuse to go with you?"

Without pause Ravanan gave her a choice "You'll go or you'll die."

Kalara came undone. "WHAT?!"

With cold reason he answered her "You are dangerous. Your ignorance is too great a risk for discovery of our kind. Either return with me or prepare yourself for total destruction; which, I assure you, would happen should you choose to fight me. Even in the extreme chance you could kill me, you'd still die.

"You see, I've modified the common burial spell. Normally the burial spell activates when the body dies. But my spell will bind you to my carcass; and your last breath will be taken from your lungs as our bodies sink to the deepest ocean trench where the earth will erase all traces of our blood and bones.

"But try not to think about it like that. I really don't mean you any harm, far from it actually; and I think you honestly want to come with me, or at least you did back in the mall."

Kalara couldn't dismiss what he had just revealed. She had been captured. She couldn't fight him. But did she want to escape? No. The only thing she was living for now was answers. If finding her identity meant being his prisoner, then she would endure that. Really, was it any different than Jenniffer keeping her locked away in that miserable apartment? She would get her answers eventually. She just needed to hang on.

Ravanan seemed to know what she was thinking "Kalara, you don't have to suffer. You can relax. Yes, I could tear you limb from limb, but there would be no sport or reason in that. If you suffer at all it will be fully self-inflicted I assure you, it will not be from me. If you truly want help then work with me. Tell me about your recent memories, like what you were doing in that city."

Kalara was still tense despite his nice words. "There is nothing to tell, I have been lost for months. I know nothing to tell you. My existence has been uneventful and boring."

She just wanted answers and now she was being taken even further away from Annette and her only alternative was death by his hand. Relaxing on demand was not going to happen. She didn't want to talk with a man ready to kill her. If he truly knew who she was why not just tell her, it wouldn't take very long. Once she had her past, then she would know who did this to her and could go after them.

Ravanan sighed "I can see you're not going to tell me. You know I could force you to, but I won't." He got up and walked away to make his own bed on the other end of the blue mist.

With him gone, Kalara thought back on her day. So dragons and their magic was real, just as real as the bumpy and flat rock she was laying on. How could people not know there were dragons big as houses living among them? Ravanan was huge. Kalara wondered what her base dragon form looked like and if she was really as large as he was. Knowing she was a dragon didn't make her feel any different really. She still didn't know who she was.

How would she get him to tell her about her past? Ravanan was so set on getting her away rather than helping her find her memories. Why? With each anchor she was moving further from Annette. How long was she willing to follow him without getting her answers? Or was she even being willing at all? He so easily held her still, calmed her heart crushed her with pressure. Could he be controlling her mind too? How would she know it if he was?

He was handsome though. As she tried to find comfort on the hard ground, she allowed herself to run free with the image of his disrobing. How could she be attracted to a dragon that threatened and hurt her? Yes, his human form was so tantalizing, but he wasn't human. Why was she so strongly attracted to someone she had just met? What if he was causing her to desire him? If he was manipulating and commanding her, how then could she trust that he would tell her the truth when she asked him to? No, he was nice, mostly, he couldn't possibly want to harm her. He did come back for her and said he would help her.

Nonstop images of his cloths vanishing from his lean body ran through her mind. He was hot. She didn't know if her former dragon self enjoyed the human male form or not, but her current self did. Had living among humans changed her? Changed who she had been and her personality? Was it for better or worse? Deep in thought, she drifted to sleep.

Kalara's eyes began to flutter from her dreams. Jumbled images flashed before her, they were mostly clips from the past day. She saw and smelled the grease cesspool behind the mall as she flew over it with Ravanan the giant blue dragon. Then Jenniffer was poisoning her plant with cola and Seven the house cat came and clawed up Jenniffer's arm to punish her for it. The dreams all converged with Kalara following a naked Ravanan through the woods, after some time she became lost. The woods filled with smoke and ash and she could feel tiny shards of glass cutting her throat as she breathed in the toxic air. She covered her mouth, but it was difficult to do because she had black talons for fingernails that were way too long. From the ash cloud Kalara heard a distant voice that sounded like shattering glass "Stay lost Acama, don't ever come this way again."

In her dream she was coughing up blood as the splintered voice faded away. All the coughing and spitting made her wake up spitting nothing but air.

Kalara tried to recapture her sleep. She didn't care for the dreams of ash and hated waking up that way. She liked the dreams where she was hunting. If she could just get back to sleep then maybe she would dream a hunting dream.

In her dreams though she was always a human. Try as she might, Kalara couldn't grasp feeling like a large dragon. She wasn't what Ravanan said she was. There was no way she could be a dragon; surely she couldn't have forgotten something as basic as that.

Sleep wouldn't come back. Her mind was frustratingly awake for the day, it was busy thinking as the sun was thinking about rising.

"I must still be laying on the floor at the mall." she mumbled. The floor was not comfortable. She wondered what Jenniffer was doing. How did Jenniffer react to her disappearance? Kalara wondered if she even called Annette about it; probably not.

Suddenly she was fully awake. "Annette!" she said and sat up, worried, wanting to talk with the Medicine Woman to sort out her dream. "What?" Kalara looked around her, she was on a cold rock that brought her back to cold reality. The stars were still fighting the dawn, trying to give light to the world, they glistened abnormally beautiful from beyond the blue mist.

She had slept on a rock all night in the middle of a wide plain. She needed to call Annette. She wasn't laying on the floor of the mall, drooling and babbling about a fictitious life. She hadn't imagined the whole thing! She really was in the middle of nowhere.

Kalara searched for her cellphone in her purse only to realize she had left it behind. "Shit!" she paused and absentmindedly played with the ring on her finger. There was nothing else to do except go forward with Ravanan the dragon, assuming he was still there somewhere, and try to get him to stay in his charming human form rather than the menacing dragon one.

This life did seem easier to handle, just move along as his prisoner. Months of complexity – learning how to get along with Annette and Jenniffer, learning how to do the things that no one else had problems with, things that had been stolen by her amnesia – now they were no longer needed. It was incredible to think that in the short span of an afternoon none of it mattered anymore. She was relieved that for the first time she wouldn't have to worry about conforming to a society that she had no recollection of. She could relax, just be what she was, a living being of questionable origin and expected to do nothing. Annette and Jenniffer didn't matter anymore, she wasn't going to waste another second trying to fit in with them or any human. She had moved on and wasn't looking back to that small apartment. No matter what, she was finally truly free from that place.

Her past would find her, it had to, Ravanan seemed so sure and so *knowing*......... perhaps today was the day she was going to get her memory back. Kalara's excitement grew.

She watched the sun appear and finally spotted Ravanan as he walked towards their small campfire site to relight it.

Watching the fire grow, she asked, "Do you always cook your food?"

He chuckled as he turned the meat over, "No, not always, I like it both ways, hot with blood or flavored by flame. I assumed you are used to flavor and went with that. We'll head out in a moment, no sense in staying here."

"So you're taking me to Brazil? How long will that take?"

"Not long, Brazil is another eight anchors away. The longest part will be making the return anchors at each one."

"You know I was found in Brazil."

Ravanan seemed indifferent, "Your home was in Brazil so it would make sense."

"Do you think that dragon followed us?"

"Are we in a duel right now with another dragon? No, we're not." he answered himself. "That dragon watched our electrical clouds leave and then lost us as we went out of range. He would have been too tired to try and follow. But it's still a good idea to keep going and burn our tracks."

After Kalara's quick meal he erased all signs of their presence and gestured for her to get ready. Then he cast *"ANCHOR"* on the cap rock.

Kalara mentally prepared herself to be turned into a cloud as the dark red anchor started to form, this time with two destinations.

Ravanan was careful to synchronize the dissolving of the protective blue dome with the forming of the anchor. Kalara felt a low sonic boom when he released the mist to expand into nothing.

Following the sound wave, when the anchor was at its zenith, they were in mid-step and Kalara doubled over, screaming in agony from stomach pain. She was being attacked and couldn't tell from where.

Popping sounds could be heard coming from her legs as they broke then she went down.

Holding her stomach, Kalara knew something was really wrong. She pressed her palm closer to herself and discovered that her belly skin had large jagged holes in it. Her skin had curled away from massive cuts. It felt strange without the sense of touch on her belly because the injury didn't hurt and guts don't have sensitive nerve endings. Her fingers felt her own hot, wet guts like she was butchering someone else's stomach. With the skin gone, her hand fell in and her organs slid past before she could stop them. Her hand was covered in blood as she tried to hold the intestines in place, but they kept slipping through.

Kalara was curled up on the ground in so much pain, the soles of her feet were now bubbling and searing as if on fire. She looked at where she had been standing and saw melted pieces of her feet stuck to the rock.

Ravanan scooped Kalara up with awesome speed, stepped onto the older of the two anchors, then their bodies vanished into turbulent clouds of lightning. Her last thought before changing into a cloud was that magic had to be real because her pain sure was.

Chapter 4

Todd woke in a sweat, his dreams were of his spirit guide, a bull. It was mating with all the cows in a field except that the bull's member was a gray snake. There were so many cows that needed him, the bull was incapable of satisfying them all. Getting tired he ate other bulls to keep up his strength, the task was never-ending. Todd couldn't get back to sleep after that and decided to drive over to Annette's to get her opinion of the nightmare. He'd just wait on the couch for her to wake up.

As he was pulling up, Jared Brownfield was leaving. Todd found Annette in the kitchen eating a nibble of fruit before bed, her housecoat was pulled up to cover her nightgown and he could see a bruise on her neck that wasn't there yesterday "What's up with Mr. Brownfield?"

"His wife had to go pick up their daughter from county jail. That girl is nothing but trouble for him. The sheriff said that next time, the girl will get two months minimum. He was pretty upset and sent his wife to go get her because he knew he would make a scene if he went."

"So what did you do about it?"

"Well, Jared wants her to behave, you know he's wanting her to enroll in junior college. We consulted his ancestors and with their blessing I placed a hex on her group of friends. I don't think they will be wanting to spend another night with her because she is a lying, thieving maggot. She didn't need them anyway, they were holding her back. With them gone, she will fall into school because it will be the only way to ditch mom and dad. Remember Todd, it is a whole lot easier to make someone look bad rather than make 'em a saint." She lit her pipe.

"Is that how he paid?" Todd indicated with his eyes to the hickey.

Annette puffed on her pipe, smiled and looked at the smoke in the air "He brought some ground deer meat and his litter of kittens that were ready to leave their momma. Enough of that. Why are you here Todd?"

Todd told her about the dream.

Like the night Annette was quiet, he shared her pipe and waited, just comforted to be in her kitchen. Annette looked exhausted, from the stress of losing Kalara to endlessly serving the tribe with her special medicine, it had been a long day.

Annette got up and fixed him a stiff White Russian that she warmed in the microwave. She handed it to him "Go to sleep Todd, I'm tired, we'll consult your ancestors in the morning." She went on to bed, Todd found his old bed and he fell fast asleep. The mere fact that Annette was never in a hurry made him feel better.

The following morning Todd closed the door to the sweat lodge and prepared the ceremony as fire keeper. As the steam built up they shared the Ancestors Pipe, he let his mind go and hovered near the ceiling. Annette chanted and then meditated, listening to all that Todd's ancestors had to say. The ancestors knew of his vision quest and they knew the path that his spirit guide had set before him. Annette began to speak to Todd. She told him of a great task that would soon fall on him. He needed to be ready, it would be an enjoyable task for him, but tiring – he needed strength and endurance. Although the ancestors were silent on exactly what the task was, they did say that he would know what to do when the task presented itself. As he was now, he couldn't handle the great quest that the bull was asking of him. She opened her glassy eyes and took her stepson's hands in hers, then Annette told him what the ancestors needed him to do to prepare himself.

After the ceremony, Annette and Todd went out to the chicken coop. The chickens' long wing feathers were already growing back from the last clipping, soon they'd have to be clipped again to keep them from flying away. But for now, the chickens were easy to handle. Annette took the meanest of her three roosters, placed him under a five-gallon bucket with his head sticking out, she sat on it to kill him fast and clean. After the thumping stopped Annette plucked the bird and saved the meat for a stew. All the innards would go to the compost, but she took the rooster's gonads and handed them to Todd.

He knew what the ancestors had instructed, he asked her "Can I have a drink with them?"

"We don't question the ancestors." Annette chuckled. "It's your vision quest, your dream. I know if it were me I'd strictly obey to get the purest blessing. I wouldn't water down the gift for fear that it would make it less powerful. And I would hurry, the ancestors did say fresh with no rot."

It was a hard thing to do, with each passing minute, the bloody pieces were drying and flies were hovering – Todd kept shooing them away. He'd take a breath, get ready...and then exhale with a small chuckle and huff of doubt.

Annette could see the hardship on his face, she said "On the count of three. Ready?"

Todd held them in his palm, they were slightly cold to the touch but warm inside still and the fringes of the blood puddle were drying in the creases of his fingers. He locked eyes with his step-mom.

"One, two..... three."

He poured them into his mouth, not chewing, just letting them slide down his throat as the spirits said fighting the gag reflex. He swallowed and grimaced in disgust. It was over, he did it.

Suddenly an unexpected, quick, sharp pain cut across the back of his tongue, he grabbed at his neck, it felt like there was a knife in there cutting his throat from the inside out. The pain made him want to scream out but he didn't want to disappoint Annette who seemed oblivious to what was happening to him. If he screamed out now he would surely be sick and he must keep them down, no matter what. He didn't know what was happening to him but it hurt like hell. His body wanted to gag so bad he was sweating and breathing heavy. He was panting strongly and started to bend over but Annette went to him and held him tight, trying to keep him from gagging.

As quickly as the pain came on, it went away. Annette seemed to sense it also, perhaps she felt his tensed shoulders relax a little, she patted his back softly, "Hold it down Todd. Hold it down. Don't throw up, not yet. Wait, it'll heal." He could hardly breathe, his stomach was twisting and his eyes were tearing up. A warm feeling came over his tongue and throat, it was the warmth of healing. He couldn't hold it any longer, he was trying, but they were coming back up, he started to heave. He had failed her and the spirits because he wasn't strong enough to keep them down. His muscles lurched, it was coming up, the bloody balls of meat rose to the back of his tongue and he emptied his stomach. His eyes caught the contents on the ground. Amidst his partially digested breakfast, the balls were slightly bigger and they looked different than before. "That is not what I swallowed! What are those?" he gasped.

Annette grimaced as she took a stick and poked at them. "Your tonsils. You didn't need them anyway, toss 'em in the bucket." She smiled, happy with the transplant.

"But there was nothing wrong with them!" Todd protested.

"Wouldn't you rather please your ancestors and the Great Spirit? You'll do better with those than with useless tonsils."

"I thought I was supposed to eat them!"

"Now that would be a waste. Consider them a gift from Mother Earth you did good. Now let's go rinse your mouth and get you some steak to eat. You'll need to keep your protein up so you can make plenty of muscle, you need to be healthy and strong – like the bull."

Todd was insulted "I didn't think I needed help down there."

"Don't be so touchy, there was nothing wrong with you, but now you'll be even better. The tonsils are plumbed directly to the blood so you'll feel the new boost of hormones from their replacements almost immediately. Let me look....." Todd opened his mouth wide and Annette peered in. "They look like they belong there, no one will notice anything different."

Todd made a sour face, afraid that everyone was going to know that he had done the most disgusting thing ever.

"Oh, come on already, was it that bad?" Annette guffawed. "Besides, until we find Kalara and discover who that man was, I'm going to need a guardian while I sleep and I'll be turning in early from now on. Don't you want to be big and strong as possible to protect you mother?"

From her words Todd knew his step-mom was done talking about it, to her it was no big deal and she went inside to go make some lunch.

Annette pushed her plate away and lit her pipe. "I've got to go find Kalara, you'll take my place while I'm gone won't you?" she said between puffs.

"Why? Why do you have to? She was nothing but trouble and we owe her nothing."

"I wasn't done with her."

"You could have fooled me" Todd remarked "- you hardly even thought about her after Jenniffer took her to Tulsa."

"You don't know how often I thought about her." Annette scolded him with a gravelly voice. "Kalara was special, it wasn't just her eyes, she was powerful and I want to know why."

"OK," Todd had heard her say that about Kalara before. "I'm sorry" he muttered.

Annette wasn't finished with her thought, as if even now she was mulling things over in her head, trying to work it out. "I've never understood why my medicine could not recover her memories. You know how powerful I am – the whole tribe does. Yet Kalara eludes me. It doesn't make any sense."

Todd waited quietly while Annette did more thinking.

She pointed at him with her pipe to stress her point, "There are answers in her head, secrets. That is why I've got to find her. I want them. We just need to figure out how to clear her mind and get them out of her. Now she is gone thanks to that twit of a sister you have."

Todd shook his head "I guess I don't understand why you were never very forceful with Kalara. You could have been, I've seen you do it and you had plenty of chances."

Annette absolutely did not want to discuss that matter with Todd and she had to move him away from it. "Perhaps I will when I get her back. Which reminds me, do you have everything you need while I'm away? How much healing salve is left?"

"I made some more last week."

"And you remember the chant I sing to use it?"

"Yes Mom, I learned well."

"Well then," she stood up and began clearing the dishes "Do you remember how to properly thank the spirits and anoint the prayer stone?"

"Yes."

She paused to smile at him, "Of course you do. Look at you, how far you've come. I think you are ready to lead the prayers of our people." Turning back to the dishes she added, "Now you go and prepare the prayer stone, I'll need the blessings of our ancestors if I'm to find Kalara."

Annette opened the ceremony with her turtle shell rattle, making a hypnotic beat. Then she added her voice to sing a short chant. The song ended but the rattling continued on until it too finally died away into a time of meditation.

Todd may have been near her standing guard outside the circle but Annette was alone with her thoughts. She raised her face to the sky and beckoned, "Ancestors, Great Spirit, be honored this day."

The air grew thick with heavy smoke signaling the spirits had come. Annette loved that smell. She touched her forehead to the ground and communed with them "I am going on a great journey to find Kalara. I ask your blessings to protect me on the way. Guide me to her."

The loving voice of Mother Earth filled her ears and mind "You have been given all the power of the Earth. Your thoughts are amplified to higher planes, your will has been given action, and yet you seek the power of a woman that doesn't exist anymore?"

"But I know it's still there inside her, I have felt her threatening me many times with her power."

"Feeling threatened can be a warning, a fear to be heeded rather than ignored."

"I will find the source of her power no matter how much it frightens me and take it for myself."

"Then do what you will, knowing that your actions *may* bring you suffering. But also be warned, do not bring that woman back to this place or you *will certainly* suffer a great deal."

"Thank you for your warnings Great Spirit. But how can I find her now when I can no longer see her?"

"She will be where you found her before, you know this already."

"But I only know the area, not the exact location."

"Then look up to the cliffs, there is a black sword that cuts across the rock, begin at that point with this." On the prayer stone appeared a small greenish-black crystal – a gift from the Spirit.

Annette picked up the boring-looking crystal, trying to see what made it important.

"After dipping it in the waterfall near there, touch it only with gloves. Pull the fern away and place the crystal in the hole only after the wall is covered with the mist of dawn and your eyes closed, working only with feeling. This key is but a beginning to a most arduous journey through rock." The voice and smoke faded away.

Annette tucked the little shard in her bra and concluded the ceremony. She called over to Todd and handed him her turtle rattle necklace, keeping hold of his hand as she did.

Todd (who had heard only the glassy-sharp voice the whole time but not any clear words) thought this was a little strange but did not pull his hand away.

"Todd," Annette said softly, "take this rattle, make it yours and always keep it full."

Their gazes were locked, Todd could feel a warmth from her skin flowing into him, moving up his arm and into his heart.

His step-mom continued, "I'm not allowed to bring Kalara back here and I don't know when I will return. But some day I will and I will have her power when I do. Until then take care of the tribe, use the power I'm giving you, Mother Earth will guide you as she has me. Always listen to the Great Spirit first, before the tribal elders, they don't realize the power that Mother Earth has given to us. You are an extension of the Earth itself. With time you'll understand and learn how to push your will into the world, making it work for you. That is all there is to it, make a decision for good or bad, and there it will be for all to see."

When their hands finally parted Todd looked down to see that Annette had added burrs to the rattle that had pierced his skin and hers. They'd shared blood.

Annette went to bed early, the sun was barely touching the trees. Todd noticed she seemed eager to retire. After he cleaned the dishes from their evening meal, he unpacked his overnight bag and settled down to some TV and a beer or two.

It was a dark night, Todd got up on a commercial break to stretch his legs and water the lawn. In the corner of his eye, he saw movement going towards the backyard, he followed it but lost it by the time he got there. He decided to check the shadows for the varmint.

Todd neared the sweat lodge, it seemed to be in use which he knew it shouldn't be, his alertness turned to anger. Who would dare trespass onto Annette's land and go into such a sacred place? He wished he would have brought the flashlight with him. He prepared to open the door, maybe Annette was in there, he wondered how she could have made it outside without him seeing her. Not knowing who he'd find, Todd swung open the door, sweltering steam overtook him. "Annette?" he called out.

There was no answer. He could hardly see anything because of the dark night and the lodge didn't have lights, but he could tell there was smoke. He didn't see any flames though and there was no sound, it didn't look like the lodge was on fire. He stepped inside and felt with his hands but no one was there. Someone had definitely been there to create the steam but they must have just left.

Todd turned around to chase down the trespassers but had to stop for a second to cough from ash and soot. He knew the Great Spirit was upon him. He was amazed and in total disbelief. He was inside a manifestation cloud of Mother Earth! He leaned with his hands against the door frame and struggled to find fresh air, he was coughing and needed to get out, even though he didn't want to leave the spirit cloud. He wasn't strong like Annette, he couldn't handle the ash of Mother Earth in his throat. Tasting the ash reminded him how he was always the last in the circle to share the pipe, it never failed that when it got to him there was more ash than tobacco. Then he heard the Great Spirit speak with the sound of glass breaking, he was unable to figure out what it said because it was so highly distorted and it came from all around him and from no where at the same time, but somehow he understood Mother Earth wanted him held there, forcing him to breathe the noxious air.

As his stomach muscles flexed from the violent coughing, he felt something big appear out of the smoke around his waist, it was hard against him and it was alive. Todd couldn't see what it was through the dark cloud, nor could he drop his hands to feel it, but before long there was no mistaking, it felt to him like the body of a giant python. He panicked, it wasn't coiled but was just one large, scaly loop around him. He tried to release his hands from the doorway but they were stuck and he was held there, arms extended. He was afraid.

Despite being unable to move he remarkably found it easier to breathe as time passed. The ash cloud still enveloped him, but it no longer affected him, it was like Mother Earth was helping him handle it.

The shattered glass spoke and this time he heard it in two ways, the familiar broken shards and also a very well-defined soft voice inside his head, "Todd" it soothed like a cactus, "Why are you scared?"

"I'm not scared" he stammered. "I'm not really, I'm just not used to this.... but it's OK" he said quickly as to not offend, "I can breathe, I'm alright." He wanted to experience Mother Earth in her fullness.

There was silence as the Great Spirit listened.

"Are... are you really a snake?"

There was a sound that would have sounded like a laughing woman had the voice not been filled with broken glass and then it said *"REDUCE MORPH"*. The great python around his waist wreathed about, he felt the large girth of the snake shrink to become a slender, long body the size of a woman's arm, it crawled over his torso, Todd held his breath.

The splintery voice asked "Is this form less troubling to you?"

"Ye...yes." Todd managed to say.

The snake wrapped around him, clinging to him, exploring his frame. It gently traveled up his arms and down the length of his legs, paused wherever it felt warmth on its way, it roped tightly around his neck, feeling his pulse, it slithered through his hair, it's movements were tender, slow, methodical, the working of the snake's many muscles soothed and massaged his skin. It was almost like the snake was moving in the pattern of words, magical words of calming. Todd began to relax, it wasn't so bad, but Annette had never mentioned snakes. The way the snake moved across his sweaty, wet skin made him feel like he was resting in a heated stream, any tension he felt washed away with every movement the snake made.

Then he remembered Annette's spirit guide was a gray snake, at that thought he became slightly nervous, with a confused and slow but shaky voice he asked "Annette, is that you? Are you here? Who is behind me? Mother Earth, please, allow me to turn around, I'll stay here, I promise. I just need to see who is here."

He heard nothing but the normal faint crackle of the small fire used for the steam. Annette was there, he knew it. Who else could make the fire and steam so perfect? And who else had such a strong bond with the spirit world?

He tried to look behind him into the gray cloud, even though his head didn't move he strained his eyes to their corners, it was hard to see, there was nothing but thick smoke. Was she still back there or had she left? "Annette?" he wished his voice wasn't trembling but he couldn't help it, he knew there was a presence in the steamy lodge that was greater than both of them.

Despite the cool night air in front of him, sweat was running off his face, trickling down his neck. His hands were still glued to the door frame so he was unable to wipe the beads of sweat away. With his arms and legs spread open, he was facing the outside, Todd noticed the steam coming from behind was great despite the door being wide open; he knew it wasn't natural, even his best fires were never that good. The snake slid along his shoulders, sticking its forked tongue out to taste his salty skin, it licked and tickled his skin, the hairs on the back of his neck rose in shock, the snake moved with purpose, it was *enjoying* him. Still, the voice said nothing and then the snake found its way inside his shirt, its slick thick scales felt soft to him. Then he heard the voice of glass say *"TWIN MORPH"*. Now there were two snakes running around inside his shirt and still he could not move or twist out of his position.

Todd had disturbing thoughts. How was he being held there? Was Annette controlling the snakes or had she somehow turned into one of them? Why wouldn't she talk? Was she in a trance? Did she know what she was doing? Did she even know who she was touching? He knew the ash cloud was from the Great Spirit, but why were there snakes? Annette must be there. He wished he could turn around and not be spread-eagled, vulnerable, facing the wrong way, even though he couldn't see anything through the darkness at least he'd feel more like he was meant to be inside the manifestation with Annette. What if he had erred by entering the lodge? Did she want him to be there?"

"Annette can you hear me?"

The tingly sound of glass shards crescendo into Mother Earth's voice "What does it matter if you are alone or not? Is my ash not soothing to you?" her voice sounded hurt and the snakes writhed and squeezed Todd with an uncomfortable pressure, hinting at hidden reserves of power.

After a moment the snakes eased up and resumed their courses along his torso.

"No one can see you and have you ever been able to see me? You're safe inside my cloud of ash." her voice took on a hint of a sinister smile as she continued, "Anyone else who enters will be sanded with hot wind and shredded by millions of splintery shards of razor-sharp glass. It is by my power alone that you are unscathed."

The voice quieted then "I would think you would want to be alone inside my cloud. I've waited for you Todd, waited until you, the bull, were ready for me. I set you apart and chose you from the moment you were born... and now you are ready."

The snakes dipped low to fully explore the hottest part of his flesh, the surprising sensation aroused him - it caught him off guard. He couldn't tell exactly what they were doing, but it felt good and caused his breath to stop in his throat. He thought it odd that Annette would be like this with him, she had never given any indication of desire. It seemed so carnal in the presence of the Great Spirit. Even though he didn't understand it all, he was thoroughly enjoying the ash-filled cloud. It all felt *so right* to him, Mother Earth must be blessing his union with Annette, it was meant to be. He wondered who was talking to him, was it Annette or the Earth itself, wanting to be with her creation? Was Annette so connected with the Great Spirit that they spoke and acted as one being?" He didn't know, couldn't know the difference without seeing, but he wanted to stay right where he was for the rest of the night, soaked with sweat. The thought of being with the woman he'd loved for years brought him to full arousal, if only he was able to move....

The sinuous snakes slithered up his body while their nimble tails continued down below, he couldn't stop them, he didn't want to. He felt intoxicated with desire. The snakes latched onto his neck, there was no venom, just wet mouths and fangs, sucking his salty skin, kissing it, bruising it, their mouths working in rhythm with their tails, titillating him with the perfect amount of lust-bringing pain; it felt good, but it hurt also, and it was getting to the point where Todd would have ripped them from his neck if he could. Then the twisting snakes let go and bit his shirt instead. He heard the splintered voice laugh in pleasure, how did Annette make her voice sound like that? The snakes became violent and together they ripped his damp shirt away from his body, freeing him and exposing his wet skin to the steamy night air, the sensation made him dizzy.

Then he felt the twin snakes wrap around his bare, sweaty chest, their tails knotted together behind his back and their mouths clinched his nipples. Mother Earth said something at that point so splintery and jagged Todd couldn't understand. The hard scales changed to soft, smooth human skin. In a matter of seconds, a naked woman was standing behind him with her arms wrapped around him, and her hands running over his wet chest and hard nipples. She felt great up against him her breasts were full - he wanted to turn around so badly.

With the same other-worldly voice she giggled and said "Shall we test what I gave you?"

Todd felt the release to move and he spun around. Even as close as the woman was to him, all he could make out in the dark smoke was her long, black hair flowing down around her tan skin and her dark eyes. "Annette" he whispered. The Native American woman was hauntingly beautiful. Without another thought, he took her down and gave her everything he'd been given, all of it, every ounce of power, semen and might, he was sure that even though it had only been a day the rooster's gonads had already enhanced his own body. The whole experience was indescribable for him and he made sure it translated to her as well. He gave her so much of himself that he fell into a deep sleep only moments later.

He woke later in the night, there were headlights headed up the driveway, he looked beside him for Annette, but there was no trace of her, he did find a few shreds of his shirt and he had a wallop of a headache. A smile fell across his face. That had been some wild sex, he still felt exhausted from it. He wondered who could be driving up at that time of night in a yellow piece-of-junk sedan.....

Chapter 5

Kalara's electrical cloud was a welcomed change to the mangled body she was in just a heartbeat ago. But even in the form of ball lightning she was sickened by remembering the smell of her burning feet and of touching her own living entrails. As the anchor vaulted her away Kalara's consciousness received the final pain messages from her neurons, she was pain free. She wanted to stay that way forever and began to panic at the thought of taking form again. The spell was hurtling her to the next anchor and she could do nothing to stop the inevitable landing. She tried to veer off but with no eyeballs she couldn't tell if she did. Maybe she could alter her course and remain as lightning for eternity, causing pain to others and not feeling any herself.

The journey ended all too soon and she was solid again on a rocky outcrop overlooking a small pond. Pain hit her body again causing her to contort. Seeing her splintered leg bones jutting out of her jeans brought on new levels of anguish and she let out a scream. The forcefulness of her scream pushed even more guts out of her belly. Her hysterical eyes found Ravanan's, he was just as horrified as she was. The last thing she heard was him casting a sleeping spell on her.

Later, she awakened and glanced around. She was in an immense cavern, it was bright enough to see the air was glittering with hints of blue from protective mist. Intense pain distracted Kalara from seeing much else about her location. Her focus was on the gaping holes in her belly and guts that were dirty and drying out. She clinched her fists and grabbed at the soft furs beneath her trying to escape the pain.

Ravanan had morphed back into his massive dragon base form. He turned his great head towards her and cast "*CALM*".

Kalara could feel her heart instantly slow down, her hands relaxed and released their grip. While she disliked being controlled, she was glad to be at peace with the pain. He was obviously trying to help her, not maliciously control her. Why be upset about the spell? Everything was fine. Why be bothered by the pain? It was logical that her body would be hurting; tensing up wouldn't stop her guts from spilling out or snap her bones back in place. And so it was that Kalara casually accepted the tormenting pain. The pain was over her whole body yet her face was a picture of health and rest.

With an easy voice she notified him "I hurt really bad".

"Those wounds are deep. The best thing to do is to just sleep and let your body heal."

She was glad they had stopped to rest. Being in such a peaceful state allowed Kalara to notice Ravanan was terse and edgy, even though she hadn't known him very long she could tell the dragon was bothered by something.

"Where are we?" Kalara asked quietly.

"We're in Black Blade Lair, my lair. It has a protective mist so you can recover without further harm. I have suspicions about these wounds. Did you notice it happened to you after the dome faded away?"

"I did."

"That dragon must have magically hexed you with a continuous malediction. When my barrier was lifted the curse went directly to you, it was *waiting* for the barrier to lift so it could attack. If we dissolve this current barrier, the magic will cause new wounds. As it is, you are already hurt and must recover. I believe you will heal and I have a few spells to speed the process."

"How did you get me here?"

"I kept you asleep through all the anchors. And I'm sure you'll want me to keep you asleep as much as possible still."

"But don't you have some pain reliever – or magic to fix me?"

"It's called sleep. Be glad you have pain, it's telling you to fix yourself or die." Ravanan grumbled. "You speak like one of them. Humans think everything is solved with drugs. You have managed to live for 2200 years without drugs, I'm amazed at how thoroughly you've adopted their way of life."

He was on edge, Kalara was sure of it. However she didn't feel up to finding out why; it would probably lead to a fight and she didn't want to argue, "I'll sleep then. At least I won't be awake to feel the pain."

The next few days went by without incident, Kalara was hardly ever awake. Time meant nothing, keeping count of days was the furthest thing from her sleepy thoughts. One thing that changed after she stopped losing blood was what she was sleeping on – what had once been furs was now a bed.

Ravanan came and went. He didn't press her for any information, just let her be alone. Seeing her strength return one morning he asked her "Have any memories come back to you yet?"

Kalara could tell from the intonations in Ravanan's voice that he was just as anxious to get answers as she was, maybe more so. She answered quickly, afraid he might interrogate her again, "No. No they haven't, but I'm used to it. Thank you for taking care of me."

After not moving for so long Kalara felt stiff. She stretched to work out her muscles. Seeing that Ravanan wasn't going to proceed with more questions she asked "Who would have done this to me? And for what reason? I know it wasn't you."

"It had to be the same dragon that banished me and took your mind, I'm sure of it." Ravanan's quick answer revealed that this was all he had been thinking about since it had happened. He lifted up his head a little to shift focus "But don't worry, you'll live to fight again. Your skin is healed, the inside will take a little longer still you are doing fine."

Kalara winced as she propped herself up and wondered if she would ever be able to stand after her leg bones had poked out of her legs. She looked down to check out the wounds and holes in her jeans and saw a black robe instead. It was a thin ornamental robe that should not be worn in cold weather or by modest people. It was the kind of robe that warranted exclamatory remarks. She looked over at the dragon and demanded "What is this I'm wearing? Where are my clothes?"

Ravanan was smug. "You needed something to wear. That robe was all I could find with a healing enchantment on it. You'll want to keep it on until you're fully whole again."

"What was wrong with the clothes I had on? You didn't need to get this for me."

"Your clothes were ruined, I burned them." Ravanan reasoned, then swiveled his long neck and turned his giant head away from her to go back to sleep.

Kalara patted herself down and felt her broken body. Her leg bones were set back into place and the skin was healed over the exit points. Kalara examined the soles of her feet, new soft pink skin appeared ready to walk on. She recalled the pieces of melted tissue that hung from her feet and shuddered, she decided to wait a while longer before trying them out afraid she might step on a sharp stone. Her stomach felt smooth again, it too was healed with fresh perfect skin where just days ago there was none.

Eyes closed and feigning sleep, Ravanan was quiet, his shiny scales flexing with each breath as he listened to Kalara move around. He wasn't in a hurry, practically ageless having lived for over two millennia, he would get what he wanted – one step at a time. He could wait before pressing her for clues if he had to, but he did want them soon.

In the quiet cave Kalara wondered what the dragon intended by dressing her in that robe and what thoughts were going through his head. It wasn't just any old robe she was wearing, it caused certain thoughts to happen. Its design was formal, with a slight Spanish flair, and fitted at the waist. She looked down at her cleavage and how the robe decorated it. Her thoughts progressed, reminiscing about how good his human form looked and the warmth she had felt in the mall.

It had been an unusual feeling of heat, it was memorable. It came from him and she enjoyed it. Was he secretly doing something to her? It was uncanny how he had turned to look at her after she started feeling the warm sensation but what did his look mean? Maybe he was pushing the warmth towards her, influencing her, after all he could do powerful things.

Kalara had to find out about that warmth and what Ravanan's intentions were. She couldn't do magic, all she could do was talk – and anything she said would reveal her desire for him or confirm that he was successfully causing her to desire him; either way he would win, but so would she. The one tool she could use was what all females were born knowing: discern what is said, twist and repeat it back, then pick out the truth from the battle that followed. She readied herself for battle.

Dressed as she was, Kalara felt odd talking to a large dragon about such a sensitive subject and decided to try to balance things out visually. That way at least she got to enjoy looking at her opponent. She called out, "Ravanan, are you still awake?"

He turned his head towards her. Kalara stood up, her full height barely reaching his chin. He was so close to her. She pulled her shoulders back and lifted her face, not wanting to appear afraid, and said "I want to ask you something but can we discuss it as one 'human' to another 'human'? Can you transform into your human persona for me?"

Not necessarily bothered, but neither did he look happy, Ravanan answered her, "Kalara, you are not human, you should get used to seeing dragons, you are one. But perhaps starting on your end and working backwards is better than immersing you into a foreign world and hoping for an epiphany. I'll do this for you. *MORPH TO HUMAN.*"

His morph and draping spells worked quickly and Kalara was disappointed that she didn't get to see much of anything before he was wearing his sapphire robe.

Kalara barely had time to start feeling his warmth before the wizard approached her. Not detecting any temperature change from him, she simply said "Thank you."

"It's no matter, other than a small amount of magic. What do you want to ask?"

She looked down shyly at the bedding she was laying on "When we were at the mall and I was eating, I felt something. It was you, I felt a warmth coming from you. What was that? Why did I feel it?"

"That warmth is my aura. It can be detected from two striking distances away when it's fully charged."

"Do I have one?"

"All dragons have auras. I feel yours, it's full right now. It was how I was able to find you, along with using seer pools. Auras are an extension of the magic in our blood and announce our presence to others. Our magic recharges with food, the magic energy builds and causes an aura around us. They can be warm or cool depending on where the dragon hatched and they never change. Auras defend us when threatened, the color of a dragon determines how; azures like myself are electrical, and as an amethyst dragon, you are defended by frost despite your warm aura. It would be foolish of any creature to come in too close to an irate dragon."

Kalara remembered his interrogation, he was very close to her then and could have killed her with a thought. She pushed that unpleasant moment from her mind. "Well it was strange how it just kind of turned on with me. So why can't I feel your aura now?"

"It would seem your magic awareness is slowly returning to you. Rather than abruptly recalling it and the full capability of magic being available to you, it seems to be a function of belief. You've been brainwashed by human ideas and they permeate your thoughts. You need to trust your blood again and then control it. Me finding you and you learning you're a dragon must have awakened your magic, it's a start at least."

"So I started to feel your warm aura but now I can't?" Kalara charged on towards her goal of discovering the truth "You turned to look at me as soon as I started feeling it. How can I know for sure if I'm in control of myself or......" She hesitated to reveal her thoughts and took an extra second to add the right inflection to her voice. ".....if you are commanding me to do and feel things, manipulating me?" She quickly asked.

Ravanan was incredulous, "Is that what you think? That I'm influencing you?"

"I don't know! I just need to have some time alone, away from you, to put some distance between us so I can think." Kalara was flustered by his heated reaction.

"Why? Why would you do that when I'm trying to help you?"

"Look, I know you can calm me with a word, freeze me, who knows what else you can do? How can I ever trust you when you captured me!?!" Kalara yelled.

Each waited to see what the other one would say or do, taking time to consider their next course of action. Staring and thinking they rounded on each other, keeping their distance like fighters in a boxing ring. Kalara couldn't help but to once again become aware of his tall build and broad shoulders. Despite her efforts of confrontation she was drawn to him still, and didn't want to upset him. She became angry with herself, why couldn't she stop thinking such desirous thoughts? Ravanan had to be in her head, making her feel this way. Lust was winning over her anger and accusations. Kalara recalled the warmth of his body back at the mall, she wished he would come closer so she could feel it again. Even as she leered at Ravanan, she wanted him to take her hand in his. If she could just bring him closer...

Kalara stopped herself. Did she really want him or was she just unconsciously obeying his charming command? How could she know for sure? Was he summoning her or was it the other way around and she was wanting him? Just then, Ravanan took a step towards her.

Did she make him do that? She didn't think so. He must have stepped closer to gain more control over her. It scared Kalara. She didn't want to be helpless and be made to obey him.

She needed to get away from him. Kalara backed away on her newly healed feet and took off for the other side of the lair. The floor was smooth from centuries of sleeping but there were still rocks and mounds that she had to avoid, they slowed her escape. Even the smallest of step ups and downs were difficult for her stiff muscles. The black robe swished about her legs and did nothing to stop the cool cavern air from touching her skin and lace-covered breasts which in turn caused the sexual feelings within her to perk up. The way she was feeling about Ravanan was crazy and all too soon for having just met him, he wasn't even human. Something was going on. There had to be more to it than simply escorting her back to Brazil.

Kalara was winded and had to stop short of the wall, she rested on a large rock.

Just as a body guard always stands within arm's reach, Ravanan came to be at her side.

She couldn't take it anymore, her anger was rising in her throat. "Please leave me be! Get away from me! I don't even know you!" She glared at him. The fear in her eyes was dangerous and she was dizzy from trying to sort out her thoughts. She couldn't focus on any one thought for very long which only added to her aggravation. Deep down she knew she was hopelessly lost and that Ravanan was her only chance at finding herself, but how could she ever learn the truth with him manipulating her for his own dark purposes? She viciously lashed out, "You're only confusing me further! If you want to help then make me organize my thoughts – you've got magic, cast something! You obviously want to!"

"No, I don't." Ravanan's voice was level "But I'll listen while you set them in order." Seeing the rage in her eyes, her outburst was exactly what Ravanan worried would happen. He needed her and her memories intact, and he was afraid she might totally lose her sanity. Ravanan added "Kalara, I'm not controlling you. Once you're back to normal you'll understand."

"Normal? But what is normal for someone like me?" She screamed at him. "I've been living and believing I'm human, that magic wasn't real and my dreams were simply metaphors. But then you showed up with a far out explanation for my condition. A dragon. I was a powerful, magic using dragon, but not always. I don't remember being a dragon. It's not in me, and I can't explain you being one. I feel like a human with a human life back in Oklahoma, my human roommate probably called the cops for a missing human report. But they will never find my human body. I should call her to let her know I'm OK. But my phone and purse are back at that mall." she started to cry "Everything in it, my stuff, my cash, it's all gone. Everything that I had attained to start a new life, everything that defined me is worthless, and I'm back to being a lost soul.

"The whole city, everything I know, is nothing but dragon food. I bet you'd eat Jenniffer if you had the chance. Am I supposed to eat them too?"

Ravanan interrupted her "You're getting ahead of yourself, slow down. You never have to eat a human if you don't want to. Have you seen me eat a human?"

But Kalara drove on "I want a pizza damn it! I'm hungry and I'm tired of cooked unseasoned meat! Teach me how to summon a pizza with no cell phone. Go ahead, teach me how to control a dangerous thing like magic! Better yet, show me the manual that will explain everything for me. Take flying for instance, how was I flying? And what is it with the whole mind control thing? I just got the feeling that I was commanding you to come to me, or were you making me think I was? Somehow I was sensing your warmth and I know humans can't do that. But how am I making it all happen?

"How do I handle a sense of magic, a sense beyond the known five, assuming there really is one? Talking about senses, why am I so strongly attracted to you? That is not me, I keep my feelings in check, especially around guys I've just met. I practice self-control, I'm not some easy whore who is available on a first date. But this isn't a date, it's a rescue mission by an incredible hot guy – no, I take that back – dragon who could kill me with a breath. How can I fight against that? How would I even know if you were controlling me? I'm defenseless against you and I am messed up. I need my dragon memories back while keeping my human memories to save any clues I was too blind to notice while believing I was a human. I need confidence in abilities in which I just discovered in order to regain those same abilities back that I once had every confidence in!"

She was overwhelmed, her tears were a steady flow. Her newly healed legs were throbbing from the short jaunt and she knew there was no way she could ever get away from him.

Ravanan was already mentally working out ways to counteract her muddled mind. The confusion and memory loss had pushed her so far from herself that killing her would be easier than fixing her. But her death wouldn't help him; so rather than kill her where she stood, he would at least address her immediate problem to stabilize her long enough so they could eventually fix the rest. Attempting to help Kalara was the same as trying to hold a frantic tiger without hurting it.

"If you can trust me, you'll have the answers you seek." he answered back. "I can show you how it feels to be totally without magic, how bare it feels, and then when the spell ends you'll feel your magic rush back to you. Then maybe you'll recognize the subtle change you've made since I found you and you'll know if you're being controlled."

"Is that possible?" Kalara sniffed and asked through bleary eyes.

"Yes it is but only for a short moment. It's a terrible thing to do to another dragon; to strip their magic away – even though it's only for a few heartbeats. It's even worse to experience it first hand, but it may be just the thing you need."

She wiped her eyes, "I've got nothing to lose and nothing to fight you with. Do anything you want to me." Feeling dejected and tired, Kalara let herself slide down to the floor.

"Don't say that." Ravanan warned with a stern voice, "Don't give me that power."

"Why not? I can't stop you, I'm tiny next to you."

"Enough." He was repulsed by her attitude. "You were and will again be as powerful as I. Even though you have no memory of magic, you have to admit it is real."

His words snapped Kalara back to attention, "I know that I can't explain all the things you are able to do. I know that I was seriously injured from an unknown attacker. If that is magic, then yes it exists."

"It does exist. If you don't trust me then at least trust magic, it is neither good nor evil, and you'll find it to be your best asset."

"How is magic even real? Why aren't humans magical?"

Ravanan found a rock near her and sat down. "Our magical blood comes from the comet that destroyed the dinosaurs; we call the place where it landed Vya Matros because it is the center of where magic started. The impact would have killed us all if our lairs had not been underground, only a few of us remained, mostly those diamid dragons on the other side of the world far from the blast zone. In the long, dark aftermath that covered the whole planet our blood mutated and began to obey the instructions of the mind. We continued to exist, slowly, and we eradicated anything else with magic. Over the eons we studied and perfected it. We are the guardians of magic and thrive because of it. Humans came along only a few lifetimes ago – long after the infectious clouds had faded away."

Even though she'd seen a lot over the past few days, Kalara was still having a hard time settling into the idea of magic and dragons. She pointedly asked "Then how come dragon skeletons have never been found?

"Look, I really want to believe you, but humans are a great people – I've lived among them. It's all I know. They have done many things, they own the world. They've gone to the moon, they have radar. Their scientists have mastered the atom, they know how the continents fit together, and mapped DNA, but nowhere do intelligent humans think dragons or magic exist. How can they not know?"

Ravanan retorted "How can you not know? How can you have no recollection of the past 2,200 years that you have lived? You ought to know what I'm telling you is true. Yes, the herd is clever, inquisitive, and has made superb discoveries that dragonkind has learned from, but they are a wasteful species and have a remarkable knack for ignoring the problems they don't feel like dealing with. Dragons may lack curiosity and creativity, but humans more than make up for it in their blatant disregard. It's really quite easy to avoid humans.

"If you weren't so addled and gone you'd remember the deep ocean trenches are our grave yards, far from curious human eyes. We value our solitude from humans more than being careless enough to leave a dead dragon lying around. We even went so far as to erase our bones from the rock layers that record life to keep our secret.

"Not only do we carefully hide our dead, but we are also careful to not hunt too much. We purposely keep our population in check to maintain a healthy and growing herd. The more humans that disappear the more they would question it and find us. Then they'd never stop. They would hunt and search until we were all dead. Humans are forever searching; the search itself gives them a sense of purpose."

Kalara tried to understand "So dragons are always near humans then; hunting them and tending them like sheep? Why wasn't I eaten when I was among them?"

"We don't eat our own kind. Other dragons would have sensed your blood just as I did and assumed you were hunting or playing with your food."

Kalara had a look of disgust on her face but Ravanan didn't care and went on. "Humans are entertaining and they're everywhere now. Acama was right, their population did explode and we have had to adapt. Take Merlin the Topaz Wizard for instance, he really embraces humans and lives with them. He actually vacated his lair, gave it up completely, put all his treasure in a human bank except for a couple of pieces, and went to serve a human king until the king died of old age. As the court Wizard he advised the king on which fair maiden to sacrifice and then turned around to be the dragon that ate the girl. To hear him talk you would think he invented human sacrifice."

Kalara stopped him "Did you say Acama?"

"I did. Why? Do you remember something?!" Ravanan's voice raised with excitement, hope filled his eyes.

"I've heard that name in my dreams before but that isn't my name. Who is it?"

Ravanan answered "Acama was a dragon who died years ago. Death among dragons is rare, old age is our only real threat and we use magic against that. So his untimely death merits remembering, it wasn't for nothing."

"And.... is that all?"

"No. You see, before humans we were the biggest and best predator on earth. And even after they showed up we were still better. We noticed how they were self-aware, they had music and spirituality, different than all the other animals we ate. That was their business and we still hunted them – it made no difference to us.

"There weren't enough humans to worry about them seeing us and the few humans that did see us, and lived to tell about it, made up fantastic tales of monsters, wizards, and dragon slayers which all worked to our benefit.

"But who could have predicted the tremendous impact they would have on dragonkind? We blossomed because of them and we took their discoveries as our own. Dragonkind jumped forward. We took on their form and discovered the benefits of it, we've studied alongside humans, have even added their alchemical findings to our own. This is a new age for us.

"Then Acama the Malefic Jade Dragon hatched right in the center of the human Olmec empire in Anarchelos Xylo. They were his food source as a hatchling and on after he grew up. Word spread of the Olmec's numbers and a diamid dragon showed up to hunt. Acama fought hard, defending his herd, but when he got the upper hand the wounded diamid flew off and hid, only to be found by the Olmec and finished off.

When Acama saw how they mutilated the body he turned on the Olmec; eating every single human that had come in contact with that feathered dragon's blood. He became merciless in his feeding. The Olmec kings pleaded with Acama, offering cups of blood and bodies through ritual, and it worked for centuries until the younger generations forgot about the massacre and wondered why they had to offer anything. They rose up mightily, only to meet a terrible end by Acama. The few remaining Olmec scattered across the land.

"After that Acama didn't seem to mind if other dragons hunted in his territory. He invited us so that we all could feast at leisure, you were there too, just like me. In the Mayan lands he loved to pit city against city, having us all join in, we'd each take our own. It was like a giant game – and they would have been great warriors had they not been fighting dragons in disguise. The warring cities were devastated by dragons and a 200 year drought didn't help either. So we all left and went back to our own lairs and herds."

"But Acama stayed. It was a lean time and he never forgot how all that surplus of food had helped him study new spells and he wanted that energy again.

"Eventually he found that energy in the Aztecs, becoming their first Tlatoani and secretly eating their sacrifices, trying to be more careful about keeping the herd's numbers strong. The Aztecs called him Acamapichtli and hailed him as a mighty leader. And in his royal palace he sat alone, raising them for food.

"He watched them grow. He saw what they were capable of. They were intelligent, curious, and joining together into societies that were far greater than any one human or dragon could ever be on his own. There was power in having a society. He began to really think.

"Acama followed the thread of existence, looking ahead, and imagined a horrible road before us. He could see dragons wiped out by scores of humans, our blood used by them for their devious pursuits; it would be our annihilation. Humans were multiplying and they were so inquisitive. He also saw how the Olmec and Maya fell before him and how dragons could easily hunt humans into extinction. He believed humans and dragons had reached a critical moment, an impasse that had to be addressed.

"Now it's possible that other dragons in the world saw it also since we were thriving because of the human cities that were springing up everywhere. Take Atlantis for example, the older dragons at Acama's Calling spoke of their debacle there and the tragedy they had caused. But Acama was the one who did something about it. To make his plan work, every dragon in the world needed to know his concerns and ideas. But we are, by nature, solitary with no need of government and he knew the only way to get all dragons together was with a magical summoning. This had never been done before and hasn't been done since.

"Acama did something odd then. He used paper and ink to record his fears and proposals. It was odd because even though dragons can easily decipher human languages, we don't use books; we have our minds to preserve information for our young to inherit. He sealed the writing in a box that could only be retrieved and read by the final dragon to arrive. Then he chained the box around his neck and traveled to Vya Matros. Once there, he cast some type of high level spell to summon all dragons to him. Eventually all the dragons of the Earth arrived and found the box on his dried up carcass that was resting inside a bubble on the shallow ocean floor.

"The spell had taken every drop of his blood, vaporized it – he must have known it would kill him. Until then we didn't even know verbal spells used blood, for all the many verbal spells we cast only drops are lost. That was by far the highest level spell I'd ever seen cast, Acama must have ate thousands of Aztecs just to craft and practice an extreme spell like that. It was an ultimate spell, there can be none higher than the one that kills you.

"We took his body to shore, cleared the beach of the few humans there, then read his notes and agreed with his predictions that humans would rapidly multiply and find a way to defeat us. He wrote that we have an unending food supply in humans, that they also supply information to us, but that they are also dangerous. Because of his notes, Dragon Law was made, and it is very small and simple.

"It's two-fold, first is don't fight over food or hunt too much to avoid discovery and second is to completely hide from humans. Hiding is the main component of the law and the law would only work if every dragon in the world agreed to it. Because of the law we now hide our dead, place our eggs in solid rock, hide ourselves and lairs, and erased our story from the rock record. And for those eggs that were not at the summoning, each one was kept with its dragoness until it hatched so it could know the Dragon Law that resulted from Acama's Calling."

The story of Acama's Calling intrigued Kalara although she had no recollection of it; it was just like everything else, it meant nothing to her. Just like hearing about someone else's life that you don't even know, their story doesn't matter because it doesn't affect you. But there was something about that name, Acama. In the recesses of her mind, it was there, Acama was very important – it just wasn't the dragon Ravanan was talking about. Her mind knew that name well enough to dream about it and that one fact was monumental to Kalara. It was the first time she remembered something even if it was only in a dream, and she would cherish it like a life preserver, as something tangible she could hang onto.

Kalara crinkled her forehead in thought, trying hard to gather up the memory. "In the dream I'm always lost in a cloud of ash and smoke. Then I hear a hurting voice warning me to stay lost but it calls me Acama. It doesn't make any sense and doesn't go with what you just said."

Ravanan paused for a long moment to look into her violet eyes. He then said "There is more that I didn't say. The name Acama has another meaning and maybe you are ready to know since you dreamed about it. At Acama's Calling we were all appalled by his bizarre death. Every dragon there understood the importance of global communication but no one wanted to kill themselves to make it happen. In order to be unified against humans, dragonkind needed to stay connected – not with a government but with a forum. And since the idea was to keep the majority of us from having to be summoned again, the responsibility fell to the minority.

"You are one of only four amethyst dragons in the world. Each of you were given and accepted the title of Acama before leaving Vya Matros that day. The amethysts don't rule over any dragon, but you do answer to us all until death. It is your duty to be available to the dragons who live near you; to hear them and then relay their words to the other amethyst dragons who will tell the rest of dragonkind. You serve Kynasteryx and Anarchelos. Kadd of Kynasteryx Diamid left his lair and took a new one in Nikhadelos. The glass dragoness known as Morada of Kadyx Polaren covers Kadyx and Nikhadelos Ravyx and lastly Tristan the Malefic Amethyst, who is the only purple dragon with a cool aura, covers his frozen home land of Viptryx and also took on Sharoviptryx."

Ravanan had outlined the continents of the world using electrical sparks hung like tiny fireworks in the air, pointing to the lands as he named them.

"The amethysts bind all dragons together and the four of you crafted a spell to do just that, giving you the power to summon the dragons you serve and the other Acamas as well. There are some who question what you did and wonder how it works, but only you four know."

Kalara's heart filled with self-worth to discover that she had a title and a job.... that she was needed, maybe not by humans, but by dragons. Even though she had no familiarity with the role and still didn't feel like she was a dragon, she wanted it.

"Now see?" she smiled at him, "Was it so hard to tell me something about myself? It helps me. I don't understand why you are so intent on keeping my past a secret from me."

Ravanan looked ruggedly at her "Kalara, I want you to get better and this is a start, but it doesn't change things. Even if you were told everything about yourself, it wouldn't matter. Some things you must discover on your own. You have no understanding of your previous life and you haven't begun to truly embrace the role of Acama. How would you even fulfill the title right now?"

He sighed and ran his fingers through his hair. "Look Kalara, it is important you don't try anything that may arouse the other Acamas. According to Dragon Law they will kill you for your condition. We can fix this and find your memories before mistakes are made."

Kalara stood up, so did Ravanan. She knew he was right she just didn't want to admit it. It was one thing to recall a lone fact but quite another to be the dragon he spoke of. Even though she knew now she was an Acama, a purple dragon, she couldn't do what was required of her. She couldn't even leave his protective blue mist without taking damage.

"Alright. I'll let it go for now. But I'm not giving up." She said with determination. "Hearing the title Acama in my dreams is something from my past – I know this now. Just because I'm lost with no memories doesn't mean I'm not an Acama – I've got the violet eyes to prove it. Even if I have to start from the beginning again, I'll get it all back. You did say I've been unknowingly using magic all along to stay in human form, and my awareness of magic is returning to me. I can already feel your aura when I'm close to you, see?"

Kalara walked up to him hoping to feel his aura but there was no change in the air. She stepped even closer and took his hand in hers which felt like any other normal hand with no special heat. Tears filled her eyes as she released Ravanan's hand and backed away. "But I know I felt it.... back at the mall, I felt a warmth coming from you."

Ravanan noticed her shoulders slump with disappointment and reached out to comfort her, but stopped himself short. Instead he simply suggested, "Perhaps you can only detect it when you're relaxed."

Kalara didn't want to hear that, not from him. She hadn't known him long enough to speak of such personal things. Avoiding the topic she went on, "OK, fine. There is something else. I know I stayed in the air when I jumped in the mall, I was able to fly." She tried jumping up again.... and then came back down. Her failure burned into frustration and anger. "But I did do it! You saw me. You even somehow knew I would be able to. You were the one who told me to do it, you promised me I'd stay there."

"I knew you wouldn't, so I held you there." Ravanan hated to tell her the hard truth. "I had been watching you for a while before you even noticed me. I knew you weren't hunting humans, you were studying them, searching. I also knew you didn't or couldn't sense me which was strange. I watched you more until I was sure you weren't accessing your magic, only then did I reveal myself to you. I had to tell your body to fly. Then right about the time you began to sense my aura was when I knew you had a chance at recovery, when your magical awareness began anew."

Kalara came undone at hearing Ravanan's confession. It was never her doing the flying but him! "So you HAVE been making me do and feel things. I knew it! You've been controlling me this whole time!"

If Ravanan was without empathy her ashes would be blowing away. He shouted at her "Will you stop it with the accusations?!"

Ravanan's aura flashed bright with millions of tiny blue static sparks for only a heartbeat. "You haven't begun to experience the manipulation of a dragon! If manipulation were a mountain, you'd be so far away from it you'd wonder if the gray haze on the horizon was a summit or a cloud!

"I controlled you only when I needed you to do something I knew you couldn't do. But I'm not compelling you to think things. The thoughts in your head are yours. What you are suggesting is I'm the one who can't control my magic, that it runs rampant and I'm maliciously unleashing my intentions on you." he paused for a breath, "Kalara, I want to help you – not hurt you. Can't you see that? I've looked for you for months. I left Black Blade Lair unattended for you! And when I finally found you and saw your plight, I chose to help. I don't even recognize you anymore. Why would I bother manipulating you when I know your memory will return shortly and nullify any mind control? Influencing you would be pointless. I've not been controlling you. Your mind is free and you are free to leave my lair, just don't expect to live beyond this room.....You are right, you don't know me," he said coldly.

Kalara quickly changed her attitude. "No, no I want your help and I don't want to die. There is no one else to ask, please. My memories are the only thing I want, they are all I have in this world, I need to find them. I'm sorry, I was wrong about you. This is all my fault, I can't even have a normal conversation without messing it up. I can't do anything right. I can't even use magic, it may be real but it's not in me."

Ravanan didn't listen to her words, instead he breathed in her honest sadness "Kalara, listen to me. Don't go down this path. You have been using magic, you just haven't noticed or been sure about it. Magic is inherent and involuntary in dragons; it has been inside you all along and it is there now. It was your mind that vacated your body, not your magic. Allow me to show you the gradual difference you've developed. See instantly how the absence of all magic feels."

"Do you really think I'll feel anything?" She was skeptical.

"I do."

"Alright then, let's try it."

The wizard wasted no time "I'm going to begin by casting a spell called Anti Blood on you. This spell prevents the aura from leaving a dragon's veins and blocks the dragon from casting new spells. Your aura will not be able to help you, you won't have one. I'll then cast Magic Immunity on you so you can be sure I'm not affecting you in any way. The third and final spell of Anti Blood will be on myself as an extra assurance to you. Other than the barrier mist surrounding us, no magic – or myself – will be able to mess with your mind; and there is absolutely no way I'll drop the mist so don't ask it of me.

"These spells are high level and therefore short lived thankfully. After several heartbeats the magical build-up of the blood will burst through the spell and break it. It is also important the spells are cast in the correct order, if you are immune to magic then I can't cast Anti Blood on you. If I cast Anti Blood on myself first, I'll be unable to cast it on you. Be prepared, it will feel odd to you when I cast Anti Blood."

Seeing that she was still willing, he approached Kalara and cast *"ANTI BLOOD"* on her followed quickly by *"MAGIC IMMUNITY."* Then Ravanan hesitated, reluctant to become defenseless, even for a few heartbeats. He would rather cut his own arm off. But he was confident in his spell casting and told himself, 'it's only for a little while and she can't even remember how to use magic', he steeled himself to the task of isolating himself from magic by casting *"APPLY ANTI BLOOD."* Though not required, he took the extra care to use the word 'apply' on the front of the spell, going over and above what was needed to make doubly sure he had targeted himself then he walked away, tired and weakened from the high level spells.

Kalara's heart skipped a beat. Pain associated with lack of air grabbed hold of her. She gasped and her hand instinctively went to her chest that was quickly rising with shallow breaths. The pain felt like a bad hiccup caught on the up-swing. Around her, the lair was too quiet and the air was stagnant, her senses were numb and turning gray with death. She was out of sync with the world and her fingertips started to chill, she was one step behind time. She reminded herself Ravanan said it would feel weird; so by a mighty effort of willpower she forced herself to look beyond her distorted perception and the cold void her heart had become and test herself. Kalara jumped to fly but returned to the ground – she wasn't surprised. She tried hard to feel Ravanan's aura. She tried to pull him close but again nothing happened. Maybe she was too far away. She walked to within an arm's reach of Ravanan and tried to summon him but he did not take a step. The chilly subterranean air was around her, no warmth could be felt, even though Ravanan was right there watching her quietly, tensed and silent. He was closer to her now than he was at the mall when she had felt his aura, but now she felt nothing – absolutely nothing, magic was not in her.

She reached up, gently closed Ravanan's eyes, and then shut her own. All the frustration and tears she had shed over the past months seemed to settle on her shoulders making one great weight. She felt nothing but heaviness. She wanted to feel his muscular shoulders, wished he would hold her and take away her hurt. Surely he would reach out and save her. She couldn't use magic and she never would. Nothing had changed in her except for the sluggish and empty feelings she had. She continued to stand there with her eyes closed, in physical pain, and alone. She was amiss in the hollowness of the cold void and saddened by the absence she felt. She wished it would all be over – one way or another. All was hopeless.

Lost in her utter sadness, Kalara didn't know exactly how many heartbeats it would take, maybe too many and she would die of loneliness. But then a warmth overtook her ribcage that flowed like rum down her throat; it was invigorating.

At once, with lightning speed Ravanan took her up in his strong arms, holding her. Surprised and relieved, Kalara relaxed into his chest, reveling in the vividness of life. She was alive again, her warm magical blood was part of her, making her whole - she was a dragon. Then she smiled grandly at the thought she had just used magic. She felt her unspoken command that time, felt the magical message get sent out the instant it happened, just like turning on a light switch. She understood it now, feeling her magical blood carrying out her mind's orders. It was the same as telling your legs to walk; it just happens when you think about it. It's not complicated. This whole time she had been concentrating too hard when she didn't need to be. She was making mountains out of molehills! Kalara was jubilant at her discovery and wanted to try it again. Temptation filled her mind and she wondered what his kiss would feel like. The message sent, he obediently and without question heightened their embrace and covered her lips with his.

The kiss continued since Kalara kept thinking about it. She wanted it to be passionate and the blue wizard obeyed. The kiss was everything she'd hoped it would be, somehow he knew exactly how to please her.

There was just one thing bothering Kalara, if her control over him was complete he was only a puppet and it was eerily unsatisfying to her. She had to let him go; it wasn't right and she didn't want it. Just when she was about to release him from his servitude of endlessly kissing her Kalara felt another subtle warmth come over her but this time it was not hers and she felt it recklessly unleash into Black Blade Lair, rough and untamed, it was so intense it was palpable and it was all around her.

Ravanan's aura had returned to him and the blue wizard was no longer under her control. But the normally reserved wizard had let his guard down with the spell and the virile male beneath the sapphire robes intensified the kiss rather than ending it; turning the wizard's pleasing caress into a titillating clutch Kalara had to match with a passion all her own. Raw desire overtook them as they kissed; forming heat waves that shimmered in the air. She couldn't keep her hands off him, he felt as good as he looked, from the back of his neck to his arms, then waist and further down, he was hard everywhere. Inside Ravanan's powerful embrace, Kalara let him take more and more of her as he savagely pressed her body into his. She felt weak at the knees and faint.

He started to bring her legs up around him and push her robe up but then he paused; it was so abrupt Kalara lost her balance and leaned on him for support in a most unintentionally provocative way.

Unable to resist the opportunity, Ravanan seized hold of her once more and stole an extremely close kiss. The desire within him was unruly and lashing about like a monster, biting her ears and neck, wanting more of her, rubbing the back of her legs, his hands running higher, feeling her every curve and the hotness between her thighs. His honed muscles fiercely held her tight, there could be no escape even if she'd tried to get away; he was rigid and built with all the physical power of the massive dragon base form condensed into his small human shell. He could have easily crushed her body had he wanted to, but what he wanted was to press her body onto him so hard that they would fuse into one flesh.

It had almost gone too far for him to stop, he wanted Kalara so bad. Then, with his last thread of resolve he gave her a final deep kiss and grudgingly stood her back on her feet.

The Azure Wizard reined himself in. Ravanan tore his mouth from hers and began urgently kissing her hair instead, forcing himself to concentrate on its softness as he ruggedly kept her close. He had to stop the heated romance but it was proving difficult for him to do so when her warm flesh was so close and poorly covered by her robe. He was breathing heavily with desire, fighting it and trying to cool down.

Kalara reluctantly accepted his retreat and when they finally released each other, they were unable to look each other in the eyes for an uncomfortably long while.

Finally, Ravanan broke the silence. The blue wizard had fully returned, no longer the primal, loose man who had been kissing her. "You may be mad I walked away during that spell, but you were wondering if I was controlling you; so I put some distance between us."

Kalara was thankful he kept it cold. "You were right, I did want to be alone, I just had no idea the grief and pain I'd feel because of it. But from that loneliness I found my magic. I can recognize it now! I felt it the instant you took me....."

Embarrassment killing her joy, Kalara rerouted her thoughts. "I hope you're not mad at me for what I just did to you. It just kind of happened. I was lonely and then when the spell lifted, my blood jumped at the chance to serve me. I should have stopped it then. It was wrong to continue forcing......"

She stopped at that point, her mind caught what she'd just said and leaped to a realization. He'd had no access to magic to defend against her commands and she had *forced* him, she wanted him and forced him to kiss her. Without his magic he couldn't have been influencing her to desire him, it was from her. Her true desire was him and she hated herself for admitting it to his face and was embarrassed for demonstrating it just now.

Secondly she realized all along she has been defenseless because of her amnesia and unsure about magic. He could have had her anytime he wanted, forcing her just as she had forced him. She wouldn't have had a choice but to follow his dark wishes. But he hadn't forced her to lie with him. He was noble, and every feeling she'd had was coming from herself. Then Kalara noticed Ravanan was politely waiting for her to finish her sentence.

".....forcing you, forgive me." She really didn't want to look at him after that.

He smiled and shrugged it off, as if to imply her desirous feelings hadn't been noticed. "The magical blood that flows in our veins is raw, untamed power. We aren't slaves to it but you may have been feeling that way since you have forgotten about it."

Kalara had to change the uncomfortable topic of control and desire "Then why do you cast verbal spells if we have such powerful blood?"

Ravanan seemingly didn't mind moving on and answered "Verbal spells are even more powerful and have greater range than our auras. We can craft a spell for any purpose while the aura only carries out our dominant feelings; it is more primal than scholarly and....."

He caught her eye, signaling he hadn't moved on after all. He was reluctant to continue but knew he must ".....auras can be a detriment if not controlled because every being around you will know your thoughts. Being near you has caused my blood to work harder to resist your newly awakened magic and siren call. I knew I'd be powerless against you when I cast those spells – and I'm not mad about it – but it was the only way I could think of to bring you to this point. There was no way around deadening my magic, but it's over now and I'm glad to have it back."

Kalara was incredibly embarrassed after hearing that. "You mean to tell me this whole time you knew what I was thinking?!"

"Yes."

"Why did you let it go on? Why not say something?" Kalara frantically tried to hide her embarrassment with a shocked smile and gathered the black robe tightly around her to cover any exposed parts. He must have known she had been staring at him and wanting to touch him. He had known her lusty thoughts all along – every time he morphed. He knew how she felt exposed in that robe. He had to have also known about her manipulative plot to discover the truth, and he let her do it.

She shook her head and rubbed her forehead, "You're toying with me."

"I was observing you and your intentions." he explained "Only your feelings are sent out, nothing specific – like names, but it only takes one thought to give me sufficient warning. And why not listen to free thoughts? How could I not?"

"But they were my private thoughts! If I had wanted you to know them I would have told you." Kalara was reeling.

Ever the composed wizard Ravanan kept his voice even and with light-hearted reason "You did tell me – or have you already forgotten? Your thoughts are chaotic. I've felt no danger from you and I have no desire to act on your thoughts."

Kalara's embarrassment changed to a defensive resolve. "Now that I can command my blood, I'll block them from you."

"I hope you can." Ravanan was ready to place bets on the outcome. "Until then, I'll keep listening for any threat towards me." His sly smile became frosted with the icy edge she'd noticed earlier. "I don't trust you, Kalara of Kynasteryx Ravyx. Something is amiss and I will figure it out."

"If you don't trust me then why did you continue to kiss me once your magic came back and it could defend you again? Why not resist and pull away?" Kalara knew she had him that time. "Admit it, you feel the same as I do."

Ravanan wished she wouldn't have brought that kiss up and paused to find a good answer "I thought I would take a payment for helping you find your magic."

"By kissing me? You don't even like me! You've threatened to kill me. I would think biting my arm off would be a better payment."

"Are you offering it?" He smirked and began walking away.

"Fine! Leave! It's obvious how you really feel." Kalara haughtily remarked.

Ravanan turned on a point "Since I know you can't read my hidden thoughts I'll tell you what they are. That kiss was a moment of weakness, nothing more. I won't let it happen again."

Kalara was annoyed, somehow he was getting out of her trap. But also annoyed he wouldn't be kissing her again. "It didn't feel like a weak moment to me! There was something between us before wasn't there? There is something you're not saying."

His reply was honey-sweet, "What can I say? Your morph spell is really good. Your natural beauty as a dragon translates perfectly to the human form. I admit that I have always admired you – you are enchanting. I just couldn't help myself; especially when you were the one who started it."

Then Ravanan vanished before her eyes. Shortly after that, Kalara heard a splash in the distance and the battlefield in Black Blade Lair got a little cooler.

Chapter 6

Jenniffer woke with a start and discovered she was in her own bed. She looked around wildly for Annette, remembering what the witch had done to her. Why wasn't she blind, or in pain at least? She felt her eyes with her fingertips, they felt normal. She couldn't remember anything after the glass shards were shoved into her eyes. How did she get home? How long had it been? How long does it take to heal holes in eyelids?

She was grateful to be alive, that night could have gone so badly – she could be dead. But she was still breathing. She was never going near that bitch again. Who could she report her to? No one would listen to her. The police were no good and the elders wouldn't believe her if she tried to tell them, not to mention all the other medicine men were scared of Annette – and for good reason. The young men of the tribe would defend Annette, even her own brother would fight for their wicked step-mother.

She was going to be alright, she could see and she was free. Good riddance to the whole deal. She was glad Kalara was gone and glad to be done with serving Annette. She would forget about Todd also, he was trying to be just like Annette, he was her faithful lapdog and would tell her anything, she would have to stay away from both of them. She would get her own phone, mail Annette's phone back to tribal headquarters, get a new email address, get a post office box, switch apartments and maybe even find a new job. She would change her name if she had to. She was done with them, the map might as well end at the east edge of Tulsa.

Jenniffer stumbled out of bed and tripped on one of the cats, it howled and ran off. She went to the nearest mirror and gasped at what she saw. Her brown eyes were now an iridescent blueish-green like a peacock feather.

Why would Annette change her eye color? Everything else seemed fine, her vision was still good, and she had all her digits. She stripped and closely looked over her whole body for any new scars or tattoos, nothing was different other than her eyes, her hair wasn't cut – not even a few strands, all her fake nails were still on, and her toenails didn't look clipped. Jenniffer even looked at her eyelashes and eyebrows for anything missing or odd. Annette didn't take anything fresh from her that she could tell and Jenniffer knew that old body clippings didn't work as well. Maybe Annette only wanted to punish her with pain and couldn't bring herself to kill her stepchild – Annette was a healer after all, not a killer.

Maybe after she passed out from the pain Annette had driven her home. It didn't matter though, Annette had gone too far this time and she was done with all of it. No amount of motherly love could ever make Jenniffer forget about the dream catcher attack or the taste of aged sage-covered hearts. She wondered what animal the hearts had come from as she furiously brushed her teeth and tongue and gargled mouthwash three different times. She showered and scrubbed her skin raw, wanting to forget all about the horrors of last night.

The next thing she did before breakfast was to haul out anything and everything that Annette might have touched, given to her, or made for her. She cut up the credit cards, even threw out her high school memories album Annette had made, and her purse (just in case Annette touched it the night before) – putting all the contents in a plastic bag until she could replace them. She took another shower before going out to trade her car off for one Annette had nothing to do with, she hated to get rid of the corvette, it was her dream car and worth a lot as a trade in but no car was worth her life. Jenniffer erased every trace of Annette and her brother Todd from her life. She wanted to forget her entire life.

Jenniffer had done all she was able to since it was a weekend. She spent Sunday afternoon making a list of what else she needed to do to hide from her step-mom, then settled down with a cheeseburger in front of the TV. The cats, Seven, Sasha, Ming, and Ludwig, took over the remainder of her dinner then cuddled up with her on the couch. The shadows in the room grew long, tempting her with sleep and the youngest kitty, Ludwig, was purring in her lap, enjoying the petting Jenniffer was giving. The sun lowered and its orange reflection from the giant windows of the car dealership bounced warmly into Jenniffer's apartment.

As the orange windows faded to black Seven hissed at her and ran off. She felt an odd sensation come over her, as if she wasn't alone. The other cats were looking at her but not willing to leave their comfortable positions. Her hand kept petting Ludwig even though she tried to stop. She wanted to get up and make sure the door was locked but she couldn't make her body respond. There were no out-of-the-ordinary sounds, but a presence was with her. She wanted to ask 'Who is there?' but she couldn't make her mouth move, it didn't work anymore. She felt paralyzed but yet she kept petting the cat. Her body had a mind of its own, she couldn't even turn her head to look at the front door. Nobody could have come in, she would have heard them. Her heart sped up. What was happening to her? It had to have something to do with Annette, she was sure of it. Terror seized hold of her.

Her head bent down to watch as her left hand press Ludwig down into her lap at his shoulders so he couldn't get away or swing his claws. Then her right hand firmly grabbed Ludwig's head, causing her elbow to jut out high and away from her body. Jenniffer tried desperately to release him but she wasn't able to. He was such a trusting cat. Jenniffer's face belied the shock and horror of the moment when she began to twist her right hand. With a firm hold on his skull, her elbow came down, cranking smoothly until she felt maximum resistance. The final snap and popping of the neck bones made a terrible sound as her elbow locked down hard against her waist. Ludwig's life was over. Jenniffer was horrified at what she'd done but she couldn't cry about it. How was Annette able to keep her from crying when her very heart wanted to? She had never put much stock into Annette's mystic shit but maybe she should have.

Jenniffer was in a mental cage, unable to control her body. She carried the limp body into the kitchen to butcher it on a cutting board and there was nothing she could do to stop it.

Cat blood was all over her hands and the sink. Sasha and Ming sat nearby on the counter top, watching and hoping she would throw a scrap their way – but she did not. Her hands deftly worked, just like she had seen Annette do a hundred times with rabbits, armadillos, and chickens. She reserved the heart and stomach, putting them in a cereal bowl, chilling them in the fridge, everything else went to the trash can. Jenniffer was in utter disbelief of what Annette was doing. Did Todd know about this? How could he go along with it if he did?

Jenniffer looked over at her kitchen clock and then went and took a shower. She was so thankful the other cats were spared, she wondered what Annette was thinking. She wanted to cry. How could Annette be so cruel to her? The body possession continued throughout her shower, as Jenniffer piled on the make-up, she heard her own voice speak up for the first time that night "Oh, Jenniffer, this is so much fun. I should have done this a long time ago, your body is so young and beautiful, its fun to dress it up. We can wear a lot of different colors with your new eyes."

Jenniffer grabbed her car keys and headed towards the parking lot. Annette stopped her body then and looked around for her car. It wasn't there, the red corvette that Annette had bought for her wasn't there. Annette used her voice to ask "Jenniffer, what have you done? Where is your car?"

Jenniffer was hopeful, she was glad that Annette didn't know what she'd done during the day, she wanted to laugh.

But her joy was short-lived. Her head looked down and examined her keys, her fingers wrapped around the car keys, they were quite obvious because she'd left the dealership keyring on them. "Why would you trade your car? You are so stupid, that car was a collector's dream and it was reliable, you'll have problems with this new one, mark my words." It was easy for Annette to locate the new car, a yellow sedan, by its dealership tag and soon Jenniffer's body was hanging out at the red light district of Tulsa.

It wasn't long before she was picked up. Annette didn't say much and let the guy have his way with Jenniffer's body. The man was really smitten with Jenniffer's eyes, Annette told him they were contacts. He was an older man of normal height and light features, his ego more than made up for any short comings he might have had. Annette made him very happy with Jenniffer's body.

Something odd happened when he climaxed, Jenniffer didn't know exactly what it was, but it felt like a piece of his ego departed his body along with the normal fluid and she didn't know where it went. He seemed aware something was gone because he was anxious to leave, yet he was subdued and a whole lot tamer, if not a little skittish. Physically speaking he was fine and would have many more nights of romance in his life, they would just be passionless until his testosterone levels built back up from zero.

Jenniffer handled five men total and two of those were on the same ticket. The same weird toll was dished out to each of them as they finished, leaving them lesser men. She was literally beside herself, her body was sore and exhausted, she was mentally grieved and dismayed at what she'd been forced to do and no amount of money made it right in her opinion.

She also figured if she was going to suffer torture of that magnitude she would gladly take money for it. There would have been more money from the work but Annette insisted the men pay with their house cat for a hefty discount if they owned one.

After stopping for fresh sage at the 24-hour grocery store, Jenniffer had three more cats with her when her body arrived at her apartment. Sasha and Ming were laying on the couch but Seven was still hiding somewhere.

She took Ludwig's stomach from the fridge and tossed it onto the kitchen floor. The five cats ran for it and the unlucky one who reached it first got to enjoy his last meal before donating his heart and stomach to Annette's cause. Annette did this over and over again killing the one who ate the stomach, until all five cats were butchered with hearts reserved and a single stomach that actually held five other stomachs nested inside each other. There was just one more stomach to harvest....

Jenniffer's spirit cried even though her body couldn't, as Annette walked through the apartment sweetly calling for Seven. "Here kitty-kitty-kitty-kitty-kitty-kitty. Seven, come on out. Where are you?" Of course Jenniffer knew where the cats always hid, but Annette didn't, she hoped Annette couldn't find him.

Annette searched every room before kneeling down low to peer under the bed. She lifted the bed skirt and Seven lashed out, all claws and teeth, he growled feline profanities and hissed, his lightning fast right paw swept across Jenniffer's face. Seven's second strike caught her lip and his hooks-for-claws held onto her lip making a jagged tear. Any non-possessed human would have got the message and backed off, but not Jenniffer. Annette forced her to try to grab him. Despite the hurting pain of his stinging attack Jenniffer was proud of him. Her hand reached in and Seven clasped onto it, all fourteen of his back claws started tearing up her forearm.

By the time she dragged Seven out from under the bed, her arm was shredded. Annette made Jenniffer press all her weight, which wasn't much because she was so tall and thin, onto Seven's back, pushing him to the carpet. She wanted to scream 'FIGHT!' but her voice was soft and slow "Good kitty, shhhhhhh. Calm down Seven, calm down."

Her right hand was petting his head and scratching him under his chin. Seven wasn't calming down, his low growl was straight from hell. He lurched to bite her hand. Jenniffer wished she could show him it really wasn't her being mean to him. She didn't want his last thoughts to be that she had turned on him. She had cared for Seven since he was born, but that didn't matter to him. He could tell something was wrong with her.

He almost escaped but Jenniffer was able to hang onto his foot. She wanted to cry as she fiercely grabbed his fur. Seven swung around with twenty-one claws, it was ugly and so was the pain in Jenniffer's body. Annette was pissed now and she yanked the cat, flinging him into the back of the bathroom, Jenniffer heard him hit the porcelain. She saw him dazed and try to stand, he shook his head, then Annette shut the bathroom door.

Her burning cat scratches felt as though infection was trying to kill her, she wondered if Annette could feel the pain also. The ugly trip her body was on was wearing tremendously on Jenniffer's mind. She wanted it to stop and knew that it wouldn't. She was tired, powerless against the mad woman, and she was paying a hefty fine for losing Kalara, being forced to commit atrocities that surely damned her to hell.

She hated them both, Kalara and Annette. Ever since Annette had found Kalara things had changed. Annette had definitely become meaner, her mind was always working and she hated being bothered, she was consumed with studying Kalara. It seemed to Jenniffer that Annette was envious of Kalara, wanting something from her that Kalara wasn't able to give. Annette then sent the dazed Kalara off to live with her but never said why and Jenniffer was too afraid to ask her step-mom, not that she would get an answer if she did ask. Jenniffer wanted it all to be over. But as tired as Jenniffer's body felt to her Annette still had work for it to do.

She fetched the full cat stomach and pushed it under the door. After some time Seven ate it, she knew he would, that cat would eat anything – he might not keep whatever it was down, but he was greedy and gluttonous. Then Annette found the oven cleaner, Jenniffer's hands worked the nozzle under the door and emptied the can into the small bathroom. After waiting for the fumes to drug the cat, she went in and snapped his neck like the rest of her cuddly pets.

In the middle of the night, Annette, still possessing Jenniffer, loaded the car with the trash bags holding all the dead cats and a grocery bag of her newly harvested wicked ingredients then drove off into the night.

Only able to watch from inside her own eyes, Jenniffer knew where they were headed. When she arrived Jenniffer noticed Todd's pickup at Annette's house.

Annette made Jenniffer's body take the trash and sit it around the side of the house then she headed back to the car just as Todd was coming from the backyard with his rifle aimed at her head. Her brother was only wearing boxers, his shredded shirt was dangling from his non-trigger hand. Jenniffer wondered what his part in all this was.

"Jenniffer! What are you doing here this late?" he set his gun down against the house.

Annette answered in Jenniffer's voice "I could ask you the same thing."

"The thing is, little sister, I belong here. I do what Annette says – unlike you. How could you lose Kalara? Are you that stupid?"

"Todd, I'm not gonna fight with you. What are you doing wandering around outside? Why aren't you asleep? It's late." Jenniffer's voice sounded to her like Annette was surprised to see Todd awake.

"Your headlights woke me up."

"Oh." Her voice sounded as though Annette didn't believe him.

Jenniffer saw Todd shivering in the cool night air as if he'd been outside for a while. She knew her brother well enough to know when he was not being fully honest.

Whatever Annette may have thought about him, she went on despite her doubt "I brought some stuff for Annette that she asked for, she said it had to be fresh so I brought it over just as soon as it was ready. See? I can obey too." Jenniffer handed the closed paper bag to him. "Can you put this bag in the fridge for me? I also set a couple of bags of trash by the house, I didn't want to throw them away at my apartment building because of all the blood."

"Blood? What did you do? And what happened to your face and arms?!"

"Seven attacked me after I fell asleep, just like Annette said he would. I guess I should have believed her when she said that a seven-toed cat was a bad omen – maybe she really does know what she is talking about after all."

"Yeah, she's pretty smart if you'd just listen to her."

"I see you still think she hung the moon."

"Shut up Jenniffer, you don't understand."

Jenniffer's voice said "Oh I understand alright, I bet you'd just love it if she wasn't our step-mom and maybe ten years younger. I'm surprised you weren't in there right now jerking it on the couch." Jenniffer was shocked that Annette would say that and for once she wanted to give her step-mom a high-five because she knew it was true.

Todd threatened his little sister with the look that only a big brother can give. "I said shut up, you're just jealous because she loves me more."

"Hardly."

"Just admit it, the only love you can get is from your damned cats."

"Well, they're gone now, they're hearts are in that bag along with Seven's stomach. Killing them was my punishment for losing Kalara, Annette said if I didn't do it she would..... I guess she is asleep right now isn't she?"

"Yeah." The fact he was holding raw cat hearts in his hands didn't faze him he knew full well the type of punishments their step-mom gave.

"So, you come over here every night to jerk off on her couch?" Annette was egging Todd on. Jenniffer silently wished Annette wouldn't have said that, everybody knew Todd got violent when provoked and her body was hurting enough from all she had been through.

Astoundingly, Todd didn't hit her, instead he said "Go home Jenniffer, I don't need this shit right now, it's late, I'm tired, and you have no clue what you're talking about. Annette is worried the man who took Kalara will come for her too. She asked me to keep watch." he turned to leave but then caught a good look at Jenniffer's iridescent colorful eyes. "Wow! What's up with your eyes? They look cool. Are those contacts?"

Jenniffer marveled at hearing Todd's question and was surprised he didn't know about her eyes already. Being in the background, listening, gave Jenniffer a pretty good idea of the real reason Annette had asked Todd to be there and he was the one who had no clue. Annette needed a guard for her sleeping body while her mind was out possessing Jenniffer's. She wished she could take control of her body and march into Annette's bedroom just to see what Annette's body was doing or if it was even there. Clearly Todd believed he was talking to his sister and not his step-mom, why hadn't Annette told him? Then Jenniffer heard her own voice speak again, totally controlled by Annette. "Yeah, expensive contacts. By the way, does Bill still work on cars?"

"Yeah, why?"

"Can you tell him I'm going to bring this car over to him tomorrow night, it's running a little rough. It'll be after dark when I get there because I have to work all day in Tulsa."

"So this lemon is yours? You got rid of the corvette?"

"Yes."

"Man alive Jenniffer, you are stupid. I would have bought it from you, you should have talked to me about it. I wonder if we can get it back...."

"What's done is done, just talk to Bill for me, OK?"

"I though you didn't like him. Why would you want his help and drive all the way out here? I'm sure there are mechanics in Tulsa who could help you."

"There are, but I know Bill. He does good work, and I don't have a lot of money."

"I'll never understand you Jenniffer. You know he still has a thing for you, do you really want to deal with that?"

"Yeah, I know he likes me. That's why he'll take care to do it right. Hey, one more thing..." Jenniffer reached up and pulled out some of her red hair by the roots and handed it to Todd. "Give this to Annette also." Then Annette made Jenniffer's body get in the car and drive away. Todd noticed that the car sounded fine.

Jenniffer's body arrived back in Tulsa, she picked a fluffy dandelion puff before going in. Once inside the cat-free apartment, Annette prayed a quick prayer in Jenniffer's voice "Great Spirit, hear me, your daughter, Annette. Use this puff to stop Jenniffer from revealing my possession spell to anyone. Just as the little fluffs drift away in the wind, let her voice do the same should she try to speak of it. Just as the seeds break away from the stem, let her fingers, toes, and teeth do the same should she try to write it down." Then Jenniffer stuffed the whole puff into her mouth and swallowed it down with water. Annette laid Jenniffer's body down only a short while before dawn, there was no trouble making it fall sleep, it was exhausted.

When dawn arrived back at Annette's house, Annette's mind went back into her own sleeping body which stirred awake slowly with a smile on her face. Annette felt refreshed, her body was safe and rested from a full night of sleep, and ready for her trip to find Kalara.

When Jenniffer woke that Monday afternoon, she was hysterical. Annette wasn't in her head anymore but the damage was massive. Jenniffer remembered all of it, she bathed, but no amount of water could wash away the filth that her body had been through. Annette hadn't even used condoms with those men! And her cats...... Jenniffer's body shook and she sobbed until her bath water was cold.

She called her boss, but when she tried to speak about the long night her voice faded to a whisper and then fully stopped. Her boss was saying "...hello?....Hello?....HELLO?..." until she changed her thoughts and could speak again, but the call did no good and she lost her job.

She didn't know what to do, even though she was in total control of her body, she was powerless against the evil medicine woman – how could she fight her? She wondered if it would happen again that night – and she was sure it would, Annette had said as much when she told Todd she'd be over at Bill's. Bill of all people! Jenniffer wanted to throw up. He was definitely punishment for her, he gambled at cockfights, he even raised fighting roosters, he made minimum wage as a mechanic, and he didn't care at all about the finer things in life. Engines, hunting, fishing, and cockfights were all that mattered to Bill. His body smelled, it was repulsive. Jenniffer felt defeated – worse than defeated, she felt conquered, she was a slave with no hope or self-esteem.

Late that afternoon, Jenniffer tried to undo the car trade she'd made, she'd been foolish to think she could run from her step-mom. And she really did love the corvette, that was one area she agreed with Annette and Todd on. The way Jenniffer saw it, if she was going to be defeated she could at least have a good-looking car to be defeated in. The car dealer laughed in her ear and said it had already been sold.

The apartment was dead without her cats, she missed them. Her aches were great, it stung when she urinated, and so she just laid down with a small hope that maybe she would sleep the whole night through and not witness anything - maybe nothing would happen.

But something did happen, she woke up. It was only 7:30 PM. For a brief second Jenniffer believed she was herself and tried to stand up to go get a drink of water, but she couldn't move. If she was able to move, she would have just sighed a heavy sigh of resignation for another night of surreal movie watching.

Her voice said "Good Evening sweet heart, are you ready to be a good daughter?" and her body got up, made itself beautiful, and drove to Bill's house wearing a black, low-cut mini dress.

Needless to say, Bill was happy to see her, even happier when she paid. Jenniffer hated every minute of it, no condom, he was still greasy and dirty from work, and his bed was crumpled with old sheets. Jenniffer was still sensitive enough to feel Bill's ego unnaturally drop when he finished, again she didn't know where it went; it didn't go to her. She was thankful though, Annette allowed her to sleep the rest of the night, even if it was in Bill's arms.

The next morning, Bill slept in with her, they woke late in the morning, Bill's boss wasn't even mad when he called, he actually congratulated him and said he'd see him tomorrow. Jenniffer noticed that he was oddly tired, he didn't even want to crawl out of his dirty bed, whereas she couldn't wait to get out of it. She jumped up, taking the sheet with her to cover up her nakedness.

Bill leaned up "Come on baby, one more go, but why don't you ride on top? I'm kinda tired."

"You are a disgusting pig. How can you lay in that mess?"

"Ouch! What happened to the sex kitten that needed me so desperately last night?"

"I wasn't myself......" Jenniffer's voice faded to nothing. She moved her mouth, trying to fight it, but nothing came out, she was angry and wanted to cry but there was no way she was going to shed tears in front of him, and she sure didn't want him comforting her. She didn't need comfort, she told herself she was stronger than that. Jennifer mentally cursed Annette and redirected her thoughts. "I'm hungry, what do you have to eat?"

"Bread. Bring me some with coffee, it's instant, it's in the cabinet by the sink. You'll have to let the sink run for a while though to get the water hot."

She laughed in indignation. "Forget it, I bet the bread is moldy. Besides, you should be serving me breakfast in bed."

Bill wasn't smart enough to be offended. "That's cool, whatever it takes Hon, come lay back down, I need some more of you." His eyes tried to see through the sheet. "You are so beautiful. Your eyes are like rainbows, and I didn't think it possible that you could get any prettier, are those contacts?"

"No, they're not, it was a very expensive surger...." again her voice stopped cold, instead she said "I'm outta here." She didn't even hesitate when he asked her to stop, she grabbed her black mini-dress and walked out. Jenniffer wanted to cut out her beautiful eyes, she'd rather be blind. She looked in Bill's smudged bathroom mirror and touched the windows of her eyes, trying desperately to pull a contact from them.... but they weren't contacts. Maybe she should gouge them out, maybe that would stop the nightmare... Annette would pay for this somehow, someday she would pay.

Chapter 7

Kalara replayed that kiss over and over in her head, wishing they would have talked more about it. It was not over by any means. She would get to the bottom of it. He had been gone so long she was sure he was avoiding her rather than hunting. Obviously the kiss was more than a moment of weakness for him. All she needed was a few more words with him.

She wrapped herself in her bedding for warmth and decided to go look for the water she had heard splash. She grimaced as her still-healing feet pressed into the floor. There were rocky walls in the distance and a high ceiling overhead. The cavern had very little moisture and was well lit, being nothing like a dark damp chasm that other caves are. Dappled beams of sunlight bounced off crystals in the walls and magically illuminated the whole cavern, making the light's point of origin impossible to trace.

As Kalara slowly made her way across the lair other rooms became apparent. She took one careful step at a time until at last she entered a new, smaller room and found the water she was looking for. In that room there was a sprawling glassy lake that filled most of the chamber, the other shore couldn't be seen. Where she stood on the shore was a stalagmite pedestal that had a bowl sitting on it full of what looked to be ice cubes. She touched one but it didn't feel cold or wet.

The surface of the water rippled as she stepped into it. Her skin turned to goose flesh, but despite the frigid temperature she lingered. She tossed her blanket and robe back to dry ground wondering how many days had it been to cause the grime that she felt. She washed off as best she could without chilling herself to the bone.

The lake was shallow where she was but further out it looked like it dropped off suddenly into murky black ink. Ravanan must have jumped in, but looking around, Kalara couldn't see any water puddles from where he would have gotten out. He wasn't in the lair or else he was being very, very quiet.

The next antechamber she came to seemed to be a storage room for crystals and metallic rocks of various shapes and colors. If she would have had her memories back she probably could have named each one she found there; a geologist would call it a treasure room. Piles of rocks and crystals were everywhere, some were plentiful, others held just a few. There was also several stalagmites in the room, each had been topped off smooth and served as a display pedestal for solitary crystals. Kalara figured she shouldn't touch anything and after a long look she moved on to investigate elsewhere.

Kalara followed the walls of the cavern around, venturing into some of the openings and tunnels although most were uneventful and terminated a little ways in. In the far back corner was an adjoining room that had terraces and ledges at various heights, it was void of any crystals or rock piles. It would be a perfect place to lay down for a nap.

She felt bad using his bed but here she could sleep on a different ledge every night until she found the perfect one. The more she thought about it, it did seem like it was a good idea, and she would be out of Ravanan's way. With her mind made up and her body worn out from walking and climbing, she made herself comfortable on one of the lowest ledges.

Soon Kalara was deep in sleep. Her dreams took her to a crowded place. Faceless people were everywhere all holding bags, she was lost among them. One of the bags contained her memories; all she had to do was find the right one. Occasionally a stray arm would reach out of the crowd and Kalara would bite the arm off and then look in the bag. It was never the right bag though. The people didn't notice or care that she had blood on her face. She was a monster with no name. She kept walking, pushing through the crowd, but Jenniffer was everywhere she went, blocking her way. She would have to eat Jenniffer. Kalara grabbed her roommate's arm and was about to dig in when out of nowhere Ravanan the Azure Wizard appeared. He killed Jenniffer with his crystal blade then licked it clean. All the people vanished except for him and in his hand was a blue star sapphire that held her memories; it was more of a star than a blue gemstone. He held it up to her and asked "Do you want your past back?" He dangled the glinting gemstone just out of her reach, toying with her, then he swallowed it. He dramatically pulled her to him and said "Take it from me if you can, you know where it is." It was in his heart, she had to go to his heart and she knew the perfect way...

....Her hands glided over Ravanan's skin, thanking him for saving her. His hard body felt superb even as he laid there not helping her find her memories. Her inner thighs rubbed against his hips as she arched her back and danced on his slick length to find the ultimate pleasure. Leaning in close, enjoying the wet heat, her hands rubbed his chest as her fingernails grew into long, black talons. She lightly pinched his nipples, making him groan with pleasure. If she would stay with him just a little longer now, he was almost there; he felt really good -and then at his pinnacle she dug her claws deep into his chest ripping it open to pull out the blue star. But instead of a blue star the black tip of a nose horn shattered his spine from underneath, followed by a massive dragon's head that burst through and exploded his ribcage. The dragon's eyes were sharp and sneered at the human carcass it had just ripped into two bloody halves. Chunks of meat and bone flew off his long snout as Ravanan the Malefic Azure shook his head. The dragon climbed out of the blue wizard, smashing underfoot what remained of the frail human corpse, and prepared for the final lunge that would slice her to shreds and swallow her. She turned to run from the gnashing teeth with Ravanan stretching his long neck to nip at her as she ran. Ravanan took giant steps quickly gaining on her, she could feel his crackling aura on her back. Soon the explosive storm would overtake her. There was nowhere to hide and she couldn't out run him so in a final act a bravery she stopped and turned around to face her killer.

The great blue dragon didn't strike; instead he stared at her. Unblinking, he held her with his fierce and calculating eyes, she was unable to scream or move. The blue lightning of his aura was zapping at her skin and the smell of rain was on the air. Rather than a pleasant and invigorating scent it was a foreboding smell – warning her of the impending electrical doom that would befall her. This was it, he was going to fry and eat her; she braced herself for the killing jolt.

Ravanan lowered his bloody head to her height and bared his teeth, snarling. He was so close to her she could feel the steam in his hot breath and see the fine lines on his black horns. All he had to do was breathe fire and she would be dead. Kalara was terrified, staring into his eyes, seeing her reflection, but her reflection wasn't standing before him.....

.....her reflection was reclined on a rocky ledge. She refocused her eyes, blinking, and it dawned on her that she was awake now and really staring into the terrible eyes of Ravanan in his true form. He was unnervingly close and if he did choose to breathe fire she'd be incinerated. She could have reached out and touched his muzzle – he was so close, his head was bigger than her twin bed in Jenn's apartment; any nerves she had wilted with fear.

He had been watching her sleep and had also been inside her dream. Kalara's breathing was quick with fright. Taking in the ozone smell of a rainstorm – she realized he must have just quieted his menacing aura because even though she didn't hear or see any sparks the lingering scent in the air gave him away. Ravanan was angry.

Laying there, frozen with panic, she wondered what he was mad about but was too afraid to ask. In the dream, Ravanan's face was covered in human tissue and blood; now it was clean, there was no blood smeared on it where the Azure Wizard had been torn in two.

Ravanan didn't flinch a scale, made no sound but for the heavy rush of air as he breathed.

Her heart was racing in the uncomfortable silence. She felt hot from his dragon breath. She didn't think she'd done anything wrong, after all he did tell her she was free to walk around and he hadn't chained her up.

'If he'd wanted to hurt me he would have.' she told herself.

Kalara was shaken and upset by her dream, she wanted to talk so she could stop thinking about it and break the tension of the moment. She sat up and spoke with a quivering voice. "Ravanan – you're back. I looked around some, I found the lake and crystal room. I didn't touch anything, there were some really nice looking crystals in there."

"So you found my wizard's alcove." his voice filled the cavern and rang in her ears "Why didn't you make your bed there if you thought it so nice?" The edge in Ravanan's deep voice was still there, sharper than before. He was definitely upset and not happy about finding her where she had fallen asleep.

"I didn't want to disturb anything. This room was empty so I moved over here to get out of your way."

"Of course it was empty!" The edge in the terrible blue dragon's voice burned away to become an anger that had been brewing in him for days – ever since they had returned to Black Blade.

The air around him began to sizzle and spark and Kalara's hair starting lifting. "How interesting you chose to sleep here. Wouldn't you agree it is strange that you went right to my empty treasure trove? Why? Was it possibly to fetch your lost memories? Did you hide your mind in here after emptying my treasure? That is why you wanted to distance yourself from me wasn't it? So you would have time to come over here to retrieve yourself. Or perhaps your thievery spell misfired and traded your life of memories for my treasure; that was one spell you should have nailed – knowing you'd die trying to fix it."

Kalara was fully awake now and in utter disbelief at what she was hearing, "What?! You're not making any sense!"

"And still, you have no past. This is why I can't trust you. When I left to find you my treasure room was full and when we got back it was empty. Now I wonder, who would have taken it? Who knew I was gone? My snares and traps were flawless but if another dragon had months to sit and think on how to pass through them while I was gone..."

His anger-induced electrical field was raising her hair and his words were echoing off the walls like bullets, Kalara thought it best not to speak.

".... And you, little Kalara, are going to help me get my treasure back; just like you helped that dragon take it from me. Who is he? Or did you somehow manage it alone and find a way to be in two places at once – one by my side and another off at a seer pool ready to banish me?"

His words were full of malice; they stung her worse than the sparks of his aura that were noticeably getting bigger.

"But I don't..."

He cut her off "....know anything? Of course you don't. How convenient for you. But it'll come back to you with my help and I will discover your role in the heist – do not doubt that! You will welcome death when I am done with you. The need for your lost memories is the only thing keeping me from ripping you in two so let's work on getting those memories back – shall we?"

He roared and reared up to almost reach the ceiling and transformed himself back into the Azure Wizard. Walking up to Kalara, Ravanan angrily cast *"EVOKE TABLE"*. A jade-inlaid table and chairs appeared between them, the finely crafted wooden pieces matched his bed and were undeniably from a Mayan artisan who died long ago. Fingers of lightning were dancing on the old wood as Ravanan beckoned for her to sit down.

Kalara was scared. How would she ever get out of this? She honestly didn't know anything about his treasure and wanted him to believe her. "Ravanan, I'm sorry this happened to you. But how can you think that I had something to do with it?"

"I can't say that you didn't. Your departure from the territory was suspicious. Perhaps your total memory loss is a camouflage attempt, an impressive one, if not risky. And of all places to store yourself, how did you even know you'd find your way back here?" He wickedly hypothesized and emphasized his previous order for her to sit, as he sat down as well.

Kalara gingerly sat down, afraid that the old chair would snap and then all the lightning would converge and course through her body. Trying to be lighter than she was in the chair, she asked "But what about this table? Why didn't the thief take it as well?"

"This is not treasure, it is a useful thing that some human put its precious time into to make pretty for a king. It wasn't even protected with traps." the blue wizard said as he reined in his aura with a mastered control. The lightning obeyed him, even down to the minuscule paths it took as Ravanan artistically toyed with the positive and negative charges in the air around him.

Kalara's eyes fearfully watched the arcs of lightning dance back and forth, it wasn't natural for electricity to waltz. Her fear turned to intrigue "How are you able to control it so well?"

He sneered with an evil grin and with his eyes he indicated for her to watch his hand. He drummed his fingertips on the table, just as he had done in the mall when she met him. Her eyes immediately locked onto the working tendons on the back of his strong hand, their rhythmic movements nearly hypnotized her just as they had before. Why did he have to be so perfectly handsome? But then she noticed the lightning bolts had become one, maybe a foot long, and it was jumping and skipping across the table like a rock skipping over water in perfect sync with his fingers, over and over the bolt kept repeating the table dance. From watching the display Kalara understood the extreme power she was next to; it was like a dial, with a little irritability a static charge surrounded Ravanan and it could grow into lightning full of anger and malice if he wanted.

"But how?"

"I've worked with my electrical aura since I hatched over two thousand years ago, I ought to be good."

"Can you do the same with fire? Or Water?"

"Now that is the real question isn't it? All dragons know color determines primary force, blue is electricity, purple is ice. But can a brown dragon who is naturally a master of heat and lava excel at electricity? If he has cast enough electrical spells, then yes, but it would always drain him more to control electricity than lava, unless he had only focused on electricity his whole life in which case it would come easy to him, like second nature. Whereas since lightning is my primary, it costs me nothing but a thought."

"But how exactly are you doing it?"

Ravanan was not in the mood for teaching and his bolt doubled in length. "Inside my aura I charge the air wherever I want to, I can pinpoint it." Then Ravanan pointed the bolt to walk to Kalara, he held it still, aimed directly at her eye, she could feel the natural moisture in her eyes start to tickle.

She froze where she was, unblinking and not liking the display. "OK! Please, how can I help? What can I do to show you that I had nothing to do with this?"

Ravanan ran the lightning bolt backwards away from Kalara and it hit the far wall behind them with a loud bang. He smoothed his hair back down after the charged aura was gone, took a breath to quiet himself, and put his plan to work "I want to know what you

experienced for the past few months, every detail. Leave nothing out."
His blue eyes penetrated her soul.

"I may not remember every day – there were a lot of confusing
ones and many slow ones."

"Just start with why you were that far north."

Kalara knew that answer. "I was confused and lost in a jungle in
Brazil and couldn't remember anything. Annette found me there. It
was so kind of her to take me back with her and keep me safe, I didn't
care much for the airplane ride though. She is the best medicine
woman for her tribe, she let me stay with her and made this ring of our
hair to protect me." Kalara held up her hand for Ravanan to see.

At this he interjected "Kalara, you no longer need that ring, I'm
your protector now. Give it to me and we'll find out its true purpose."

Kalara handed him the braided ring and felt a shred of hope form
in her heart, maybe he was trying to help her – better than Annette
ever had.

Ravanan studied the ring and asked her "So it was a *woman*?" The
way he said it was peculiar as if he hadn't expected a woman, he
seemed to make a mental adjustment.

"Yes, her name is Annette. But I think she grew weary of dealing
with me and found a roommate for me to stay with. You see,
everything she tried to recover from my memories had failed, I don't
think she is used to failure. After that I didn't hear from her much. My
roommate was Jenniffer. She really didn't like me and I bet she is glad
I'm gone."

"So you moved to that city where I found you?"

"Tulsa, not that I got to see much of it. Jenniffer thought it was
too dangerous for me to get a job or leave the apartment for any
length of time. I had to persuade her to take me to the mall the day
you found me."

Ravanan tucked the ring in a hidden pocket. "I need details. If I
could see what you saw, hear what this Jenniffer or Annette told you,
we could possibly figure this whole thing out. I'm going to cast Union,
I'll need your help."

Kalara could see the conflict in Ravanan's eyes, he wanted to help
her but at the same time he was ready to blame and execute her. The

only thing she could do was what he said to do. At least she was more receptive to his spells after the whole Anti Blood episode. She found him so desirable, she simply couldn't imagine her former self wanting to steal from him. "There is not much to see, Ravanan. I'm so messed up. I know I am. Do you really think you'll see anything important that I haven't already told you?"

He moved his chair closer to her, "I do. It can't make it any worse can it? All I'm asking is to directly know your memories, better than if you tried to put words to them. All you have to do is say 'Union' and keep trying to remember the early days with that dragoness named Annette. Try to think of everything you saw and where you went. Go slowly."

"Say the word 'Union'? Is that it? Will I be casting a spell?" Kalara was getting excited.

"Yes, you will be. You don't have to be that strong with magic for the symbiotic spell to work since I'm doing the majority of it. Just simply say 'Union' and be wanting to share your thoughts with me."

Kalara timidly reached out for his hands, giving him her trust. "OK then, *UNION.*"

Ravanan cast *"UNION"* and *"SCRIBE"*. Immediately he slipped into Kalara's body that was looking for her lost meal in the forest. Ravanan recognized the forest he was in and began to search for his food. It had been right there before him, he had the perfect shot. How could he have lost it? The frustration of losing prey nagged at him. He never lost his target. What had happened? The memory began to pass away into a black visage until another memory rose in Kalara's mind.

A dark-haired woman named Annette was convincing him to go with her and before long he was walking to the airport restroom carrying cloths to change into. He didn't want to do it, but it was what Annette recommended so he wouldn't look out of place. He even remembered how odd it felt to physically remove the cream robe with his hands instead of charming it away. He looked down and saw his feminine human hands pick up the jeans to put them on. He then gave the beautiful robe over to Annette.

As the memory faded, another black visage brought Ravanan to the next image. A strap was holding him firmly to a seat, then the airplane took off in a forceful start. It wasn't anything like the flying he was used to with all the jarring and bumpiness.

The next black visage brought him to where the airplane landed. He was walking down a long tunnel in Kalara's body. And then on a long car ride that was headed towards the morning sun, he saw oak trees, green fields, and tasty cows. The ride ended at a lone cabin in the woods with large rocks guarding it. There were many rocks, positioned like seats around a central great stone altar.

Ravanan heard Annette say "You'll be OK Kalara. It's just jet lag. It'll wear off soon and you'll feel fine. Here is a trash can." After some uncomfortable feelings, he uncontrollably expelled corn broth. What was that liquid trash? He was so hungry. He heard himself speak in Kalara's voice "Annette, don't you have any meat?"

Annette answered over her shoulder while doing something else "No, we'll go to the store tomorrow with Todd. This is all I have for now."

He watched with sorrow as Annette took his cream robe from her travel bags and hung it behind a door. It didn't belong there. But he trusted that Annette knew what she was doing and let her do it.

The sad memory faded and a black visage later Ravanan was in the sweat lodge behind Annette's house again. This time Annette had brought Todd to help and learn. Surely this would be the day when his past would come back to him. Todd used wood from a bodark tree to make the fire especially hot. Throughout the ceremony the hot fire kept popping sparks everywhere. The sage and sweet grass was really fresh, the red-tailed hawk was alive, and the steam was made from boiling the water Todd collected from the seasonal spring down in the ravine. They prayed to the spirits of the earth; and once again he didn't know the chant so Annette had to coach him through it. The steamy lodge filled with a heavy ash cloud and a splintery voice spoke 'Stay away from me Acama, stay lost and don't ever come this way again'. By the end of the long ceremony, nothing had changed except he had a sore throat and was coughing up blood caused by the microscopic glass shards in the ash that he had breathed in.

After the sweat lodge memory, there was another black visage and he was sitting at a table allowing Annette to cut some of his long hair.

She needed it for a special ring of protection. It wouldn't be ready for a few days and he'd just have to wait for it. But it would be well worth it. Then he was elated when Annette gave him the finished ring in the following week, however he did notice that there was considerably less hair in the ring than Annette had taken from his head.

After another black visage passed Ravanan was saying good bye with Kalara's voice, he was being loosely hugged by Annette and he tried to return it but Annette made it difficult. He sat alone at a table in a crowded mall, his one small bag of clothes was with him it was all he owned. Ravanan recognized that place as the place where he took Kalara to eat when he had found her.

Then a red headed woman, tall and thin but emotionally tough, looking concerned, came up to him. She spoke in a throaty voice "Hey, I'm Jenniffer. Looks like you could use a roommate."

The spotty memories faded to nothing and Ravanan pulled away. He now owned the memories as well, having magically scribed them to his mind, they were a perfect copy in every detail. Kalara woke as if from a trance "Did I do it? Is that what I was supposed to do?"

"You did fine. We're on the right path." He told her. "Now let's go look at this ring."

As they made their way to the wizard's alcove Ravanan said "Kalara, I know now that it wasn't your idea to go north – it was Annette's. I want to know who Annette is."

"I told you that. She is a medicine woman for her tribe. She is wise and greatly respected."

"Who said she was wise?"

"She did."

"So she steals from her Acama under the pretense of helping. Maybe her version of wisdom can be seen in holding her Acama captive instead of killing her." Ravanan became serious. "Annette has ulterior motives and I get the idea that dragoness doesn't want you to remember anything. She wasn't helping you."

After they entered the wizard's alcove Ravanan walked over to a stalagmite pedestal and retrieved a small, bluish-gray gemstone cut like a disk. He treated the chamber full of rocks as a human treats a kitchen full of ingredients. He walked over to another stalagmite that displayed a single mineral shard bigger than his hand. It looked like thousands of translucent sheets pressed together giving off a black color. As he flaked off one of the brittle sheets that broke into the size of a lemon slice he asked "Do you remember the spell to reveal an enchanted item's function?"

Kalara didn't remember anything, let alone spells. "Not really..... no. Does that surprise you?"

"No, I was just checking, surely being involved with things you used to do would help you remember. This thin sheet of biotite, along with a crystal of iolite, will show us the ring's true purpose." He then walked onto a raised area near a rock that made a perfect table. He reached into his sapphire robe, withdrew the braided ring and placed it on the table.

Kalara was listening and trying to catch anything he might let slip. "..."things I used to do "....Was I your helper here in your alcove?"

Ravanan laughed as he carefully set the biotite on the table. "No, Kalara, you could do alchemy by yourself, dragons don't need helpers." He placed the ring on the top of the flat mineral and finally balanced the iolite crystal over the braided ring. "All minerals have certain defining properties. Minerals like these change what is seen when rotated a quarter of the way, they are most helpful to see hidden things."

Peering into the surface of the blue crystal Ravanan cast "*REVEAL*" as he carefully rotated the iolite and the biotite in opposite directions. He was motionless, watching the little window to learn the ring's true intention. In the window screen of iolite he could see Kalara casting a spell on the left, a bell ringing in the middle, and watchful eyes on the right.

Immediately the blue wizard grabbed his minerals, stepped back, and breathed a jet of hot blue flame on the ring, incinerating it and blackening the rock's tabletop. He turned to Kalara, "That ring was how you were being watched! It must have alerted Annette when you sensed my aura and discovered your magic for the first time in the mall; it must have detected the change in you and because of that I was dismissed. Annette didn't want me to take you away!"

"Annette? You are saying that she was watching me and banished you?! That is not possible. She isn't like that, she is nice." Kalara couldn't believe it.

"Not only that, I'm saying she is the one who cursed you and caused your guts to fall out. That ash cloud in your memory was her doing. She does not wish you well."

"Ravanan, you're wrong."

He shook his head. "You amaze me with your trusting blindness. There are many dragons in the world and each one uses magic, Annette included. That ring was a threat we didn't need."

Even though the light in Black Blade Lair was dimming, Ravanan wasn't ready to stop for the day. "I still need to know who this dragoness is and how you're connected to her. Did you meet her while doing Acama work? Maybe you knew her from your past. Why did Annette feel the need to watch you? Why did she take you up there? If she was protecting her Acama why would she send you away from her and tell you to stay lost? And why would she want to keep me away from you? I will find out. My gold is gone and I will kill both of you to get it back. Now how do I find her?!"

Kalara shook her head and cried "I don't know. I don't remember how to get to her house."

Her impotence would not become his. Ravanan sighed and went on "There has to be something inside your head that will reveal her and help me find her. Perhaps if you heard her full name it would spark a latent memory in you. From your memories we've looked at, her dark eyes indicates she is possibly a brown dragoness and living in Anarchelos Vya. Annette the Mighty Copper, does that title or the name Annette of Anarchelos Vya sound familiar to you?"

Kalara looked down, "No. I think her name was something like Annette Sixkiller. I thought you didn't know her, how do you know her name then?"

"I don't know her, that's why I'm asking you."

"But you said Annette of Anarchelos Vya like you know her."

"You told me her name was Annette. All dragons choose their own name and are known by their color and where they hatched, therefore

Annette would be from Anarchelos Vya, or as a human would say, the center of North America. Of course I'm assuming she didn't migrate from her hatching ground."

"OK, so why don't we just go back and search for her like you searched for me, since we know the area where she lives?"

"Because we can find her faster if you could remember anything about her. It took me nearly a year of daily searching to find you, I don't wish to repeat that. Now let's try again. What if the smoke and ash you experienced in that ceremony was her aura instead of a spell? Then she would be a silver dragoness but dark enough so that her human eyes would still appear dark at first glance. Do you remember the title Annette the Mighty Silver? What about Annette the Silver Enchantress?"

Kalara shook her head and the look on her face was negative.

Nothing could lessen Ravanan's drive to find his treasure, "You don't remember... Alright, we'll find your past to find her and then we'll get my gold. There are more memories you have that I need, let's get back to it."

Seated once more at the Mayan table the blue wizard told her "I need you to rethink of every moment from the time you entered that mall to when we were flying away."

"If you think it'll help, but you were right there with me, wouldn't you already know the same things?"

"I do, but not from your perspective. I need to be sure I didn't miss anything, maybe you saw something that I didn't."

Raising an eyebrow in doubt, she took his hands in hers and cast "*UNION*". Ravanan followed firmly with "*UNION*" and "*SCRIBE*". Drawn into Kalara's mind, Ravanan was agreeing to meet Jenniffer for dinner and then they parted once inside.

He was looking for anyone he might recognize and then he was being followed. Suddenly he couldn't move and saw himself approach in a casual stride, casting Calm.

After a moment of black visage, he felt the enticement of his own aura from across the table and the powerful drawing command issued from Kalara's blood as it awakened and busted through her mind block. It was like looking in a mirror for Ravanan inside Kalara's memory as he admired himself, feeling very much like Narcissus of Greek myth. He felt Kalara's body become aroused, he admired his handsome and smooth-skinned, excellently-morphed human body and longed to run his fingers over his fine muscles. He plotted how to accidentally touch him and feel the throbbing pulse in his veins. He was nearly panting at the wonderment of how hard, stiff, and bony his wrist must feel, it had to be a perfect indicator of the magnitude of his member and he pictured what he looked like at full potency, it was a beautiful thing. They were both salivating with desire, but her body was being held back by her politeness. He didn't want to be tamed and felt a deep twinge of pain from Kalara's self-imposed denial. Her weak rejection worked against itself, he had to have her, there was no stopping that now, not now that he knew her deepest feelings.

After another black visage, he was following himself, feeling and seeing more than ever before. As they were headed towards the exit, the mall suddenly grew dark with black smoke that had come from nowhere. Out of the darkness the smoke curled into iridescent blueish-green eyes, big as dinner plates, they hauntingly crowded in the air. Hundreds of the malevolent eyes were all around them, watching, seeing everything they did. There was nowhere they could run or hide from the menacing eyes. Ravanan saw himself up ahead, saw himself turn around and come back to shield Kalara; and then he watched helplessly as Kalara's protector vanished, instantly ripped away. He was in turmoil. What would he do now? How would he ever find his past? The shoppers around him were mute and irritatingly bland, just like his existence, he hated them. He tried to fly away from the cattle but was unable to do so. He was trapped! The rainbow eyes were all around him, mocking his defeat, they saw every move he made.

He couldn't fly and dragons weren't real, his heart sank at the thought. Outside of the shared memory, Ravanan heard himself whisper 'Magic isn't real' in unison with Kalara and tears of despair rolled down his cheeks, but the audible distraction did not sever the Union spell. The gloomy memory continued. 'Magic isn't real', he'd been forced to say those words too many times and they were in direct conflict with what he wanted to believe. The life he wanted couldn't be real though, there was no proof, he couldn't fly and the self-proclaimed dragon named Ravanan was not there, which meant he'd made the whole story up in his head. Terrible thoughts entered his mind as the silent, iridescent eyes drove him towards insanity. Amidst the evil peacock eyes, sadness and confusion ate away at him, he could never escape - it was a slow implosion with no end.

The memories crashed at the never-ending sadness, there were no more thoughts to know, he felt as though he'd experienced them a million times over. The blue wizard came out of the union spell shuddering with emotion. Ravanan ached for Kalara's plight.

They were clutching each other's hands so tightly that Kalara's nails brought his blood to light. Ravanan tried to pull away but she was in so much distress she wouldn't let go. She was clinging to him as if he was the very core of her sanity.

"IT HURTS!" he yelled and tore his hands from Kalara's clawed grasp using reserves of strength that surpassed the usual amount of force needed to break a hand hold, falling more into the category of battle.

His blood seeped freely and he didn't care. Ravanan had never felt such troubling thoughts before, it changed his perceptions of her, but for better or worse he did not know. He leaned back in his chair to clear his head. He could tell she was seriously confused and afraid; that her coherent and peaceful demeanor was but a thin foam over the troubled waters beneath. Whatever spell Annette the dragoness had cast on Kalara was a mess of a cruel spell, the effect of it was catastrophic. The only thing that protected her sanity was the complexity of her dragon mind; the spell would have scrambled any human mind into soup. Just looking at the damage threatened the foundations of his sanity as well. He never wanted to visit the raw nerves of his psyche again, it was a disturbing place to be where even his mind could get lost.

Kalara hadn't recovered yet. He had to shake her out of her trance, yelling "Wake up! It's only a memory you're seeing – nothing more!"

She came alive crying "Oh Ravanan, come back! Please don't leave me like that again, I couldn't handle it. Please!" She gasped for each breath.

"I won't. I couldn't do that to you." He reached out to her, stroking her hair, comforting her and taking her into his arms, thankful he was there for her and that he was sane. "I'm here, I'm right here, you're safe." He held her a little tighter just to be sure they were both real and in their right minds, the warmth of her life blood gave him much needed solace.

Ravanan was visibly moved by the passionate memories and knowing how she felt about him. He had felt her desirous aura – which was nothing new to him, he could have fought that, but in that Union spell he had experienced her body's lust from her point-of-view, had felt the memory of her wetness coming down and her body temperature rise, it was too much for him. She wanted him and he knew exactly how she wanted him. He couldn't dismiss it, the duel effect of his and her desirous memories combined to further enhance his own. His fingers combed through her dark hair and found her beautiful jaw line, touching her not only comforted Kalara but himself as well. More than just longing, he needed to feel her, needed to know their bodies were real, that their lives were not imagined. He cupped her face in his hands and brought her lips to his, they locked but Kalara was still crying, her salty tears fell on his cheeks.

She broke the kiss, trembling "I can't stop seeing those eyes, those terrible eyes. There were hundreds of them, horrible, all around me, pushing me to insanity." She cried. "Why didn't I notice them before?"

He looked into her scared eyes and softly asked "Was that the first time you'd seen them?"

"Yes. They were pure evil!" There was raw panic in her voice. "I tell you, they were evil, I know it! They came from nowhere!" Kalara twisted her hands "That is what took you away from me wasn't it?" She wiped her tears from her violet eyes and covered her wet nose and mouth with her small hands, shielding herself. She didn't want to think about them. She hated those eyes, her breath was quick and shallow.

Her torture cut Ravanan to the bone, he rubbed her arms to calm her down as he told her "Yes it was." It was all he could say, feeling that even his simple answer was adding tons of weight to her shackles of pain.

Ravanan felt bad, he hadn't realized the slow awakening of her magical awareness kept Kalara from seeing the dark spell of eyes when it happened and so he hadn't blocked his memory of it from her. He hated that he was now the source of her agony. He gently took her hands into his, uncovering her wet lips, he had to explain "The spell took both of our memories and gave us a stereo view of them. I *didn't know* you hadn't seen that rather crude Seer spell when it happened, it was my memory you were seeing. If I'd only known I would have spared you the pain of seeing it."

Kalara raggedly replied with a tear-roughened voice "Those eyes took you *and* my hope away, leaving me all alone! I was alone!" She shouted and cried. "I thought I was losing it, that you weren't real! I was losing my mind!"

Her head dropped into her hands that were wet from crying and she didn't care, not bothering to wipe them dry. More tears escaped as she feared Ravanan was only a figment of her imagination even now, her chest heaved with heartache. As she sobbed the very walls of Black Blade Lair trembled with her though she didn't notice it. There was a power in her that was fresh, young, and untamed.

"I'm real...... and I'm right here." Ravanan quieted her with a tender embrace. He saw the lair quaking from her uncontrolled power and he needed to calm her down. He knew what her dragon blood was capable of and yet he only saw her broken heart and her delicate feelings as he held her in his arms.

With her head nuzzled in his neck, he breathed in her sweet flesh, savoring it, reveling in the subtle nuances of her. Kalara leaned into him, feeling his steady breath heat up her skin. She was still too far away, he needed her closer. He took her hands in his and brought her to his lap, so she straddled him.

Soothing her, he quietly stared into her eyes for a long time, taking her away from her fears. Kalara was his mirror, she was unblinking and silent. Ravanan loosened the ties on her thin robe and moved his hands inside, cradling her back, and began softly touching her sculpted spine. He let out a long breath at how smooth and soft her skin was. The slow patterns of his fingertips on her delicate skin were actually runes of relaxation that felt so good to her. Each stroke of the letters took his hands further down her spine. He focused on each vertebra, pushing the tension from her body. Once all the way down, he started back up with a small pull to bring her in close. She could feel him hot and hard under his velvet robe which only added to the intensity of the moment. His full attention was on her and his lips were softly brushing her neck as he massaged between her shoulder blades, pressing her chest into him.

Continuing upwards, Ravanan brought his hands out of her robe and finished pushing the last of the stress from her spine as he moved up her neck. Then he cradled the base of her head, rotating it to stretch her neck muscles and expose her tendons – kissing and sucking them. Her body was pliable under his care, she moaned with relaxation. With his amazing hands he brought her parted lips to his, rubbing her supple cheeks with his thumbs as he did. Her lips were so soft he couldn't stop kissing them, she tasted so sweet, and with profound tenderness his tongue went deeper. Her soft hair draped across his face, dazing him, making him push even further into her and forcing all stress to leave her body.

It had been so difficult to not ravish her all these past days; but to experience her wetness in that memory pushed him beyond his limits – it threw him over the edge and he could resist no longer. Her tongue worked like magic, and from the way her hips moved he knew her desire was higher than ever. He needed to feel her softness stretching around him as he pushed to find her hot heart. Just this one time he would give in; the woman before him was still Kalara, or at least her body was, and he had to have it – it's what he was built for. Somewhere amidst the kisses he cast *"EVOKE BED"* and took her up in his arms. With an urgent vigor, he carried her over to the bed and laid down with her, stroking her hair and pulling the dark tresses from underneath her. She was remarkable. Her violet eyes and feminine body were mesmerizing. Her arms enveloped him and she grabbed a handful of his hair, bringing him back to her warm, wet mouth.

Ravanan whispered into her ear "How could I ever leave the one I so desperately want?" then his sapphire robe disappeared, revealing his full masculinity. He pushed her robe off her shoulders to see her perfect breasts, and ran his fingers over her newly healed stomach, smiling at his handiwork. For a fraction of a heartbeat, a shadow of sadness crossed his face when he remembered seeing her stomach bloodied and tore open and the worry that had risen up in his throat that day, it was an image he wouldn't soon forget. His greatest fear was losing her again. Now there was not a scratch on her, no scars. He lowered himself and kissed her beautiful belly, happy she was right there underneath him.

His fingertips followed a careful trail up to her ripe nipples, finding all her secret nerve endings along the way, he made a point to visit every one, sending chills over her whole body. He cupped the fullness of her breasts with his hands and kissed them everywhere, from the bulging sides to the underneath and then to her deep cleavage in the middle. Time slowed.

Somehow between his romantic kisses and her light quick breathing the rest of her robe fell away from her small frame. He moved his hand down and she quivered with anticipation. His touch caused her back to arch and he felt her body come closer to his manhood. He couldn't hold back any longer, the length of his body overtook hers, sending warm tingles all over causing her to flush with heat. Ravanan caressed her as though she was made of the finest crystal and treasured each movement with her. His long black hair fell across her skin as he reached up and held her wrists. She could smell his delicious scent as he took control over her, she was his.

As their love became more heated and needful a wide ring of indigo fire erupted around them, the flames scorched the rock floor and lit the lair, matching the fire they felt inside them. The ring of fire was so large Kalara could not feel its heat from the center of the circle, it was beautiful to behold. The wall of purplish-blue flame was taller than her and was sealing them off from the rest of the world, inside the flames there was only the two of them. The crackling sounds of the firewall roared louder with the growing intensity of their feelings, until together they held their breath, frozen in the moment, his love flowed into her. She never wanted the night to end, never wanted him to let her go, and he didn't. Embraced, they found sleep. His rising chest and strong heart comforted her. She had never slept as soundly as she did that night.

The first pink rays of dawn filled the lair, making it appear purple from the protective blue mist as Kalara began to stir in her dream. She was out hunting. The human she was aiming for had found a tree to hide behind. Her bow vanished and Kalara advanced, moving around trees and vines. The thrill of the hunt far outweighed her hunger pains. It was like a dance as the prey skittered from one hiding place to the next with Kalara keeping up at a perfect distance; until the prey entered the black open maw of a giant tree. This was it – there was no escape. Kalara licked her lips with excitement and called forth her green bow as she got in position like a cat hunkering down to pounce. She was really going to enjoy this meal – such hard work was rewarding and feeling the panic of the prey, nothing was more fun. She could almost feel the hot gooshy flesh in her mouth already. It wouldn't be long now. She took aim, then just as she was about to release the enchanted arrow, Kalara woke up.

Ravanan was in bed beside her, beginning to stir himself. He woke with her and Kalara started to tell him about her dream but he brought her in close and said groggily "It's easier to show me."

Kalara snuggled against his chest "You mean the Union spell?"

"Yes."

"Alright then," Kalara snuggled into his body and cast *"UNION"*.

Ravanan softly cast *"UNION"* and *"SCRIBE"* and *"DREAM AND SLEEP"*. He felt Kalara's body go limp in his arms and he rested himself.

The dream ended the same and jerked them both awake.

Ravanan stretched with a reminiscing look on his face, he chuckled. "That bow is such a dreadful thing, a wicked little bow of death."

"It's real?"

"Of course it is, it is one of your most treasured weapons."

"You're telling me that dream is real? That I'm a killer?"

Ravanan smirked as he got up and cast *"DRAPE SAPPHIRE"*. Then he said "That is one way to say 'dragon' but it's such a harsh word; a word more fitting for humans I think." He pulled his long hair out of his robe and sat down on the bed. "There is no way to know if the dream really happened or not. It seemed straight forward enough, and hunting dreams are very normal. I know that bow is real enough."

Kalara reflected on how in the dream she had been savagely hungry for hot bloody flesh. Disgust filled her mind but there was also a wild intrigue. She could understand being that hungry, enough to want to eat raw meat – not human meat, but raw flesh of an animal, she could see that. But she'd rather not get that hungry.

Ravanan could read her unguarded thoughts so easy that he nearly nodded and laughed. He caught himself before he did and smiled instead, "Let's go get your bow, it may be just the thing you need, to feel its delicate carvings and jewels. Holding it once again may bring everything back to you."

Chapter 8

Todd had a quiet morning, it was his first full day as Annette's stand in. No visitors had come yet but he was ready, and he kept reminding himself that some days no one would come and then others there wasn't enough time in the day to help them all.

He thought back to the day before. In Annette's hasty departure, she had instructed him to remain at the house and carry on with the needs of the tribe. She trusted him and he would not let her down. It hadn't taken her long to pack and she barely even looked at him. He mentioned Jenniffer's odd visit in the middle of the night and she hardly even acknowledged it. Todd dismissed her non-reaction because he knew she was only thinking of finding Kalara.

Todd helped Annette pack when he could, but mostly he just watched and thought about the glorious time they had shared only hours earlier. She acted like it hadn't even happened, and that was probably for the best since it was obviously part of a ceremony. As Annette got in the car to drive away, she gave him the typical half hug and motherly peck on the cheek.

He simply did not understand what Annette saw in Kalara. The girl was loony at best and a waste of time. Annette never talked about *how* she had found Kalara only that it was in Brazil. To Annette, Kalara was intriguing and an enigma to be studied, as if Kalara held some great power, but Todd didn't see it. Nothing compared to the power of Mother Earth, he knew this. Nor did he understand why Annette kept her distance from Kalara. She was as harmless as a rabbit. All in all, Todd ignored the girl and was glad when Annette asked Jenniffer to take the girl instead of him having to do it.

Todd was just finishing up the composting when Jenniffer raced into the driveway. She marched over to him with a quick step full of purpose, but they were small steps because of her tight mini-dress, "Is Annette in the house?"

"No, she left. What's up with the dress?"

"Don't ask. How long will she be gone? I need to talk to her."

"I don't know, she left to go get Kalara."

"Great." Jenniffer rolled her eyes "Where was she?"

"She didn't say where, she just took off yesterday."

"I wish she'd just let Kalara go. Who really cares about her anyway? – the purple-eyed freak!"

"Apparently our mother does and you should be really sorry you let her get away."

"I'm more sorry than you'll ever know." and Jenniffer meant every word.

Todd closed the gate to the compost pile before commenting "Annette was really pissed about it. She kept searching for Kalara and going to the sweat lodge to meditate, I even had to help her out in the middle of the night."

Jenniffer gave him a strange look, afraid he had helped in the possession spell. "Tell me you didn't help her.... no you couldn't know...... Wait, what night are you talking about?"

"Night before last."

"The same night I saw you up late in the back yard? And you two... did what precisely?"

Todd picked up his tools "Like I would tell you, I'm not even sure myself what it was. Besides, you know what happens in the sweat lodge is sacred and not to be openly talked about."

She followed him to the tool shed, "You're right, I don't want to know what you do with Annette. All I'm saying is that it would be impossible for Annette to have done anything with you that night because she was....." Jenniffer's voice dried up at trying to discuss her body possession, it really was her dirty little secret.

Todd laughed "Cat got your tongue?"

Tears welled up in Jenniffer's eyes. "That's not funny!"

Todd wasn't totally cruel, he could see Jenniffer was really bothered. "Hey don't cry. I just got done burying your cats. Their spirits were properly released."

Jenniffer wiped her eyes "Thanks Todd. What about Seven?"

"It's probably best you don't know. So anyway, what were you saying about Annette? That night she was doing....what?"

"I can't talk about it."

"Right, so you can grill me all you want, but when I ask you something it's off limits."

"Yeah, pretty much. So I wonder when Annette will be back."

"Like I know. It shouldn't be too long, how far away could Kalara have gotten?"

"I'll call her, I've really got to talk to her."

"Fat chance, she left her phone here."

Jenniffer started walking back to her yellow car. "Can you let me know when she gets back then?"

"Will do. How did it go with Bill? Did he fix your car?" Todd smiled teasingly.

"Don't even go there." Jenniffer got in her lemon and drove away.

At sundown, Jenniffer was considering the pros and cons of cutting her eyes out while sipping a soda at the mall when she felt Annette's presence join her, Annette pushed Jenniffer's consciousness to the back of her mind. Jenniffer felt her body walk through the mall, her eyes were roving for any suitable male. Annette found one, a rich-looking kid with a credit card. After procuring the cash, they fucked in the men's bathroom, the boy seemed really tired when they were finished and Jenniffer knew he had given Annette more than he knew. Even though Jenniffer had hundreds of extra dollars in her purse from the job her spirit was crying but her face didn't show it. There had been no condom, no romance, and for all she knew a young man would never be the same because of her; it wasn't who she was and it wasn't how she wanted to live but she didn't know how to stop it.

After leaving the mall, Annette drove Jenniffer's body back out to Bill's house. Bill was happy that she had returned and tried to get her in bed.

Jenniffer was surprised to hear herself refuse his advances, "No Bill."

"Aw, come on! Why did you come back then?"

"For you." she smiled coyly, "We did have fun last night didn't we? I want you, but why don't we make it more incredible? I've got a great idea, but we have to wait to have sex until tomorrow night, can you wait that long?"

"I guess so. What is it?"

"We'll need your best rooster."

Bill looked puzzled. When Annette told him what they were going to do, he opted out.

Jenniffer could only watch and listen in disgust, she felt her face turn sour as Annette expressed her displeasure. Bill had made a poor choice, Jenniffer wondered if it would be his last. Her voice said "I thought you wanted me."

"I do, but what's wrong with the way it is now? What you're talking about sounds really gross."

Jenniffer unbuttoned her dress and showed him what he was missing. "If you want this ever again then swallow Mother Earth's gift of the rooster. Otherwise you can wait and hope for the trailer trash around here and I'll take my fine ass back to Tulsa. When you change your mind go talk to Todd, I know he has done it and he can go to the sweat lodge for you to get your ancestors' approval. The sooner you do, the sooner we can be together."

The next morning Bill knocked on Annette's door, Todd answered, "Morning Todd."

"Hey Bill."

"Did you just wake up?"

"Yeah. How about some coffee?"

Bill followed Todd into Annette's kitchen. "Where's Annette?"

Todd mumbled she was on a trip. When Bill brought up the gift of the rooster, Todd gave him his full attention, "How do you know about that?" Todd said sharply.

"Jenniffer told me last night, she said we were over unless I ate the nads of my best fighting rooster."

"No way! She slept with you?!"

Bill nodded as if he owned the world.

"You're kidding, right? There is no way in hell Jenniffer would sleep with you, she hates you!"

"Well, there you're wrong."

"Seriously?"

"Seriously."

Todd was confused. "There is no way...." He could hear Jenniffer's words in his head.

"Yep, we would have done it last night too if this hadn't come up."

"You're lying. I saw her yesterday and she made it plain how she feels about you."

"If she wasn't with me then how else would I know about the gift of the rooster?"

"I don't know. She couldn't have told you because she doesn't know about it. You know she gave up our ways a long time ago, she don't believe in it. Annette said something to you didn't she?"

"I haven't seen Annette since last winter when we cleaned up her trees after the ice storm."

Todd was at a loss as to what to say. How did Bill know? Todd knew Annette well enough that she would never gossip or talk about someone's spirituality. And there was absolutely no way that Jenniffer could have known about it.

Bill filled in the silence "So it's true then? You ate a rooster's balls?"

"Look, I'm only telling you this because you are my best friend, but yeah, I did. It was a ceremony my ancestors wanted me to do. It is part of my vision quest and Jenniffer shouldn't even know about that. We don't go around talking about our spirit guides, that's private stuff."

"Well, she knows and now she wants me to do it."

Todd said nothing.

Bill took a swig of coffee and noticed Todd's biceps. "Have you been working out without me?"

"No. Looks like it though doesn't it?" Todd smiled proudly and flexed his upper arms. "It's the gift of the rooster, came on pretty fast too."

"So it's been good for you?"

"Oh hell yeah."

"And all you did was eat them? That's it?"

"Well, Annette was with me, but she didn't do or say anything special."

"You think I should do it?"

"I don't see how it would work for you. I mean, I was told to do it by my spirit guide, I had a dream about it and all. If I were you I wouldn't do it unless the ancestors tell you to. It was pretty gross."

"I bet, I almost threw up when she was telling me. She seemed pretty sure about it though. When I told her I didn't want to do it she looked very unhappy with my decision. I think I'll lose her if I don't."

Todd couldn't believe what he was hearing, he knew beyond any doubt how his sister felt about his best friend. "Look, I know she is my sister and all, if you want to be with her that's your business, but is she really your type? You and her don't match and personally I think you could do better than her. Think about your drum group and your cockfighting, are you willing to give all that up?"

"No." Bill grinned. "She is so fine though, you gotta admit. I'll get her to come around. She wants me, I'm telling you she's hot for it."

Todd shook his head "I still can't believe it. What was it she said to me that one time?" Todd searched through his memories, "Oh yeah, I remember.....she said she was repulsed by you."

"Well, she can't get enough of me now. She was all over me!"

"You sorry dog, you're making this shit up aren't you?" Any second Todd expected Bill to say 'Gotcha!'.

"No man, I swear it! She said she'd give it up again tonight if I'd do this right now, this morning. I got to do it, man. Will you help or not?"

"I don't think it'll work."

"Who cares if it works? If I just freaking do it, and you tell her I did, then so what if it doesn't work? I'll still get laid. I can handle it, come on."

Todd was skeptical. He wondered how the hell Jenniffer even knew about it. Taking the gift just because someone asked you to weakens the spiritual impact and the sacrifice of the rooster. "I don't think so Bill. Besides, I'm not Annette, I wouldn't know what to do for the whole thing to work. Why don't you wait until she gets back? Talk to Annette about it, she can tell you what to do."

"What am I supposed to do until then? I don't think Jenniffer will wait very long!"

"You got a hand don't you?"

"Come on, I'm doing this with or without you. Jenniffer seemed to think you could talk to my ancestors for me in the sweat lodge, that you could do it by yourself, she didn't even mention Annette!"

Todd bristled at the challenge. "Of course Jenniffer would say that I could do it, she hates Annette."

Bill got up from the table "Well, I'm leaving then, I can manage on my own."

Todd stood up too. "Alright, fine. If I can't stop you, I might as well help. What kind of friend would I be if I didn't? There ain't much to it, and like you said, what does it matter if it actually does anything or not?"

"Thanks man."

"Don't mention it. You go get your rooster and I'll start up the lodge."

The two best friends were seated in the steam-filled lodge. Todd sang an opening song to the winds of the Earth, bidding them to listen. They shared the pipe in all seriousness, for even though they were both wild bachelors, would-be-warriors for their tribe, unattached and free to explore the whole world, both Bill and Todd were reverent, deeply spiritual, and they followed the elders' stories and teachings.

All the smoke was rising as it normally should, the small fire crackled, Todd was quiet, he couldn't help but remember the other night when he and Annette were there together and the heated passion they had shared. The truth was it was all he could think of when he was awake. He missed her and wished she'd return soon. Todd hoped he wasn't doing something wrong, it was his first ceremony, he worried that maybe Annette would disapprove, thinking he wasn't ready to lead an ancestral ceremony. He did the best he knew how, he did it for his dearest friend, following the trusted steps Annette could do in her sleep – she was so good at them.

Todd had aided his step-mother so many times in the lodge he could hear her voice praying and chanting in his head, but none of those ceremonies came close to matching the other night when he realized Annette could speak with the voice of Mother Earth, that it had always been her, the voice in the cloud – she was so in tune with the spirit realm; before that night he'd never known a human voice could sound so unearthly like that. It was that wondrous voice Todd longed to hear again, that voice of breaking glass, it was the voice of Mother Earth that resonated from Annette's body and it was the same haunting, piercing voice he'd had sex with the other night. He knew when Annette was speaking with the shattered glass voice she was communing with the ancestors and the Earth herself, and he was to show reverence, but he couldn't help but be drawn to it physically; and he had been right to feel that way, the Great Spirit had even commanded him to do so. Speaking and acting through Annette, it was his duty to give himself, the best way to honor the spirits and to show his respect was by giving Annette his love and his very body. He was hers, no matter what came their way, he would love and defend her until he died - they were mated so deeply that wedding rings were not needed. Their mating only proved what he'd known for so many years. He lived only to serve Mother Earth and the ancestors who spoke through Annette.

Todd prayed "Ancestors, Great Spirit, please draw unto me." He waited in the cool air of mid-morning that Mother Earth had brought to the hill. Bill waited with him, anxious but silent. The ceremony was not Bill's first, for he also followed Annette's medicine and worshiped Mother Earth. Bill's spirit guide was the brown earth snail, and true to the snail he was slow but sure of his path, and he always found his way to the very end. He made his way and left his trail behind for others to follow. There was a certain strength in the snail, a strength that was constant and yet grew with him, only old age or a predator could take him down. He was slippery and had a good defense. It wasn't too bad to be a snail.

In real time, it had only been a few heartbeats, but in Todd's mind it had been an hour. Finally the smoke dropped in the air becoming heavy with ash, Todd could taste it as he excitedly called out, "Bill, what do you see?" In eagerness, he wiped the sweat from his brow.

The morning sun penetrated through gaps and holes in the structure, dimly illuminating the small lodge. Bill saw the dark cloud as it billowed and grew, it overtook Todd and it was now swallowing him as well. Bill had been intently watching, he was proud of his friend, the ancestors had chosen to descend upon Todd, Bill rejoiced in knowing it was Todd's first time to call the ancestors down around him. Bill answered him, "I see the cloud of Mother Earth, she has... hid.... hidden... you" his voice broke up in a fit of coughing Bill moved to the doorway and breathed through the narrow gaps in the wood planks, trying so hard to be silent and listen, not disrupting the ceremony. It was no good, he had to exit and shut the door behind him as the cool morning air greeted him.

Back inside, Todd spoke with a steady voice "Ancestors of Bill, my friend, I've humbly come to you on his behalf, Bill would like to receive the gift of the rooster, do you allow him to?"

From outside, Bill had recovered from his coughing, he could hear nothing and saw the smoke pushing out of the crevices in the lodge coming towards him, driving him farther away from the lodge. He could only watch and wait at that point.

Todd waited too, his heart was racing, excitement poured through him, he was actually doing it, a ceremony on his own – and he had no problems breathing the ashy air. There came a tingling sound, barely audible, it grew slowly until Todd recognized it for what it was, the Great Spirit. Todd mouthed the word 'Unbelievable.' The voice that he loved was going to speak to him! It was sharp, grating to his nerves, it was millions of tiny shards of glass being stirred together at once, all wanting to hurt him and yet at the same time wanting to communicate. Mother Earth spoke inside his head "Pay your offering before speaking to me."

Todd fumbled in his medicine bag, his mind raced. What to offer? He couldn't recall Annette ever having to offer anything. His hands were shaking as he felt around the bag's meager contents, everything in there seemed inadequate for Mother Earth he had nothing for her. A feeling of dread came over him because he had failed. He wished Annette was there, he didn't know what to do. Why had he been so foolish to think he could perform an ancestral ceremony alone?

Maybe, he thought, he was supposed to leave an offering on the altar out in the front yard. He tried to get up and leave the cloud-filled lodge, he tried to uncross his legs to stand, but something heavy, or rather – someone, sat on his lap, a naked woman materialized from the smoke, her legs around him, her face only an inch from his. Todd was startled, happy, and perplexed "You can't be Annette, who are you?

"Pay." Her sweet breath carried hot dust and glassy splinters that blew into Todd's parted lips, parching his mouth.

Todd chose to pay. He pulled his shirt off over his head and lifted her light frame off and over to the side of him. After removing the rest of his clothes, he sat beside her and ran his hands over her skin, making sure of the payment type she had intended. He was totally amazed that such a spiritual moment would contain such a carnal act. Annette had never mentioned anything sexual of any nature to him, she had never warned him or prepared him for this, which was unusual for her because she had always over-explained things and was very descriptive in her teachings.

The thick ash cloud veiled her, it was easier for Todd to determine if she was Annette by touching her. As his hands glided over the woman and squeezed her breasts, felt her neck, waist, arms, and face the more he realized she wasn't Annette. Todd studied her form and felt between her legs, her reaction and body language wasn't what Todd thought Annette's would be if he'd tried that with her. He leaned in and smelled her long dark hair. The other night had been so heated and passionate that he hadn't taken the time to enjoy her, he had assumed the woman was Annette, he'd *wanted* her to be Annette. He searched his memories and when he really thought about it, he knew he had been wrong about her identity, he didn't know the woman he had laid with. Todd replayed the memory again, both times the mysterious woman had appeared out of nowhere. Then Todd reclined with her, he mounted her luxurious body but did not enter her just yet, instead he caressed and kissed her face while he recalled how their heights had matched up when laying down the last time, it was identical to how they were right now. With his feet at hers, he compared their height difference to the height difference that would be between him and Annette, this woman he was about to enter was definitely not Annette. It was the same woman both times and it wasn't Annette. Who was she then? He wanted to see her face but the cloud was dark and thick, he could only make a rough guess of her features, they seemed perfect.

He thought more about it. With a gasp, Todd backed away and his eyes grew wide with a strange notion of the impossible. He had never considered it before, it couldn't be. Did he even dare to think it, to believe that Mother Earth could become a human? The naked woman before him had to be the embodiment of Mother Earth herself! He saw it all through new eyes and a whole new level of understanding entered his mind, he was a changed man.

When he backed away and sat some distance from her, the woman said nothing. Then Mother Earth moved and knelt down in front of him. Her delicate hands reached out and cupped his jaw line, again her dusty, razor-sharp voice commanded him "Pay."

Not that he needed to be told a second time, but Todd paid her then. There was a power that came from within him, his rooster implants were working at peak performance now and Todd was stronger than he was before. Pleasing her was easy, he had so much more to give. Over and over he pleased her until he was empty. He rolled off of the Goddess of Earth, exhausted, too tired to talk, too tired to do the one thing he had paid to do, it was ironic and he would have laughed had he not been so winded. He was hot and tired; true, the purpose of the sweat lodge was to sweat, but never had he been so vigorous and worked so hard during a sweat lodge ceremony, he would give anything for a glass of ice water and a cold breeze.

Todd did manage to at least say, "Please Spirit, can I see you?"

Todd figured he'd have to wait, the Great Spirit of Mother Earth wasn't bound by time and wasn't controlled by any mortal. But there was no wait, the ash cloud opened up between them, looking very much like a miniature hurricane with a well-defined eye, and he was gazing upon the most beautiful Native American woman he had ever seen. Inside the eye of the storm the air was still and cool, it was exactly what he'd wanted, along with the naked woman before him, in all her glory, Mother Earth cared for his comfort.

All desire for Annette dropped from his mind, there was only Mother Earth. She was stunning and his profound longing for her filled every corner of his heart until it was overflowing for her. She said nothing and did nothing to cover her nakedness, she only watched him with her dark steel-gray eyes. From that moment Todd knew he'd never marry, he was utterly captivated. Then he remembered who he was looking at and closed his eyes tight "Forgive my boldness Great Spirit!" he cried out.

The splintery glass shards of her voice spoke "Go now, tell Bill he has my favor." then her voice quieted to nothing. Todd opened his eyes but she was gone and the cloud was quickly dissipating. He missed her already and was scheming how he could invoke her presence again. He wiped a tear of sorrow from his eyes, sad for her departure, and put his clothes back on.

Bill was waiting on the back porch, when he saw Todd's disheveled look of sweat mixed with ash and his stumbling drunk walk, he ran to him "What happened? You were in there for over two hours! Did they talk to you?"

"You have the ancestors' approval."

"Alright, let's do it then!" He slapped his friend on the back then wiped his muddied hand off in the grass. "Thanks Todd, you're awesome. I bet you're glad to be out of there, you look like death."

Todd was moving slowly as they headed for Bill's truck to get the rooster, "I think I'm going to like being a medicine man." he confided in his friend. He didn't say anything else about his encounter with the Great Spirit and after helping Bill, Todd went to bed.

Chapter 9

Ravanan led Kalara to a back corner of the lair, she had been there the day before but it was void of any interesting cave formations or tunnels so she hadn't lingered. Even now as they approached, it was very common looking to her.

He stood in the shadow made from a slightly protruding rock that was somewhat taller than him. With a small movement, he quickly wet his fingertip with his tongue then touched the dark side of the rock while casting *"REVEAL"*. The shadow of the rock changed into a narrow crevice of the same size, it easily fooled the eyes. They would have to turn sideways to even fit in there in human form and there was no way that a large dragon would even notice it.

Ravanan turned to Kalara and cast *"STARLIGHT"* on her and then also on himself. Both of them were now emitting a soft glowing light.

"I seldom come down here, to keep this section lit up would be a waste." he explained then climbed inside.

Kalara nodded and eased herself in, following Ravanan who was already a few paces ahead and ducking for a low-hanging rock that was ahead of him. As they followed the jagged turns and slopes of the path, Ravanan told her more about the bow they were going to see.

"I remember it took you a few years to get the bow right and more than one trip to the Hawaiian volcano because your spell kept ruining the crystals. You had to find the most pure olivine sand grains, the kind that only occur on that rare green beach.

His voice echoed in the tight-fitting tunnel. "The bow had to be green' you said, no other color would do. No other mineral would do, the bow had to match the forest. But olivine? It's such a brittle mineral, the enchantment to make it resilient was the most difficult part of the whole weapon. But once you had thought it up you wouldn't rest until you made the thing."

Kalara was anxious to see the bow, amazed it was real. "So why do you have my bow?"

"I brought your things here while you were healing, thinking you might want them."

"Thank you for that. You didn't tell me I owned anything, I wish I could remember. What about my lair? Why didn't you take me there?"

"My anchors take me to my lair, not yours. You were getting hurt every time your body reformed at each anchor, I needed to get you somewhere safe as soon as possible. As soon as I find a way to make you safe from Annette's curse and we have got your hidden memories back, you can leave the protective mist of Black Blade Lair and go do whatever it is that you Acamas do. Until then you are my guest and you can relax. I'll take care of you just as I have been doing." He turned and smiled affectionately at her.

They eventually came to a vaulted room, Ravanan focused his attention on a hanging formation near the center of the ceiling and cast "*STARLIGHT*" on it. It began to glow with bright light and simultaneously their light spells dimmed away. He said "This is the wardrobe chamber, it is full of useful things."

The new light illuminated a weapons cache in the center of the room. Rather than quantity, the collection seemed to be based on quality as if they were meant for a quick death. The only exception were two ornate wizard staffs with crystal finials and looked to be more for display than anything else.

The weapons were perfectly laid out and in excellent condition. Kalara recognized one of them, a dirk with a transparent blue blade, it had to be Bolt the one Ravanan had evoked to drain that cow's blood for his anchor. Some other interesting ones were an amethyst-encrusted dagger and a glowing-white leather-bound set of six razor sharp curved swords that were double-ended and resembled a gentle S-shape, from sword tip to sword tip they were twice as tall as her, maybe more, all twelve blades were identical, the bright metal was etched with runes, and yet there was no handle in the middle to wield them, she couldn't figure out how to hold them without getting cut, nor could she understand why have six when one would do just fine.

"How do you hold them?" she asked, gently running her fingertips over the six double swords.

"You don't. They float." Ravanan admired his craftsmanship. "Hexdeath is a weapon of theory, I was bored when I made it. It hasn't even been used."

Next to Hexdeath was an empty place where something small was missing.

Kalara was astonished at the measurable wealth in the chamber, "And you don't protect this stuff?"

"Why would I?"

"These weapons look costly."

"Yes, they are nice tools but that is all they are."

"Ravanan, I don't get it, why didn't you just place your treasure down here? Then it wouldn't have been stolen. No one could ever find it."

He laughed at that idea. "You really think my treasure would be sitting in open view?" Ravanan asked her. "This chamber and passageway isn't the only one in Black Blade. The passageway we just came through is a fraction of the length of the one leading to my treasure room, it lies deep at the base of this mountain. The chamber you found was my display room, a perfect, three-dimensional picture of each of my treasures, stunningly lit from all angles, while the real treasure was supposedly safe down below. Once it was stolen, the display room had no treasure to display."

Kalara felt embarrassed by her amnesia-induced ignorance, "I'm sorry, I didn't realize."

Ravanan turned away and took a second, longer glance at the cache.

His face went white.

"It's not here." In shock he looked around on the floor for her Green Pack or any sign of trespassing. "Your Green Pack isn't here, the bow is gone! Everything else is here except that bow."

Kalara was only mildly concerned, she didn't understand the gravity of the situation. "Maybe you put it somewhere else."

Ravanan dismissed her theory and continued to pace the floor. "You don't get it, the tools down here stay down here unless they are summoned directly to us. Then they return to their storage place when given permission to do so. See?" He paused for a heartbeat but said nothing, and then the Mayan table and chairs appeared against the wall. "We don't create things from nothing, first we must find or make them and then enchant and name them. Only the dragon who named them can evoke and dismiss them." Ravanan looked at her "You need to cast Evoke Green Pack. Say it just like that."

Kalara was apprehensive, "Do you think I'll be able to?"

"Try it" he urged.

Kalara concentrated on seeing the bow of her dreams, then cast "*EVOKE GREEN PACK*" but nothing happened.

They both looked disappointingly at each other. Then Ravanan said "I don't understand, that bow should come to you no matter where it is currently. If it still exists then it should come back to you since you made it."

Kalara turned from him, not wanting to think about her failure, and walked over to the table to sit down. She was deflated. However, Ravanan would not give up and kept thinking about her green bow. Then his eyes lit up, "Kalara, what if your dream wasn't just a dream? What if your mind is trying to resurrect your past for you – showing you pieces that fit together?

"Listen to me, from the union spell we know you were found by Annette, you were lost in a jungle, a real jungle that I recognize I've been there too. You had somehow lost your prey, then you were stuck searching for it. That is odd because prey don't escape from dragons and why would you get lost in a jungle that you have hunted in your whole life?"

He paced the floor some more "Then in that dream you had, you were hunting in that same jungle – I know it was the same because I know that tree." he grinned at Kalara "Although it's smaller in real life. You were about to release an arrow, and then we woke up. Maybe you never got to release that arrow because Annette stopped you."

Ravanan took a seat near her. "Maybe Annette did something to you that shut your mind down. Do you realize what this means?" His voice raised pitch with excitement. "Annette didn't kindly take you up there to protect you, she trapped you and took your bow – that's why it's not here. She broke your weapon and dismantled it for parts, that is the only way it would not have returned to you. Kalara, you were taken against your will! Before that you were quietly hunting, nothing evil in your thoughts whatsoever. You didn't steal my gold....Annette did."

Kalara crinkled her forehead and replied "Ravanan, you don't know that for certain. I can't see her taking your gold and besides, I know for a fact that she is broke. The tribe has to support her and help with the bills. She doesn't care about money."

Ravanan answered back flatly "EVERY dragon cares about wealth."

She ignored him and worked through it in her head. Had Annette been so evil as to trap her? No, Annette had been trying to help her, she even said so. She quickly revisited the scary eyes that had looked down upon her in the mall, they didn't look like Annette's eyes. Could it be possible that Annette was behind her amnesia? There was no way, Annette cared for people, she birthed babies and healed the sick she wasn't evil. She liked Annette. The medicine woman had helped her when there was no one else. True, Annette had been unsuccessful in finding Kalara's past, but what if it wasn't possible to get her memories back? Or was Ravanan right and Annette secretly wasn't trying that hard to help? Kalara didn't know what to think but she wasn't ready to blame someone who had helped her so much. She would just have to get Ravanan to see it her way.

Kalara replied thoughtfully, "Ravanan, think back to those eyes that were watching us and sent you away, they were full of colors – those weren't Annette's eyes, hers are brown."

"She has my treasure. I'm sure of it." Ravanan answered solidly.

Kalara could see that she wasn't convincing him, giving up the argument she went back to glancing around the room. Aside from the weapon rack, there were chests, cabinets, and a basket of amulets that were not as much priceless treasure as they were enchanted tools that were jumbled up in a loose pile.

She also saw display cases. Each glass case contained an outfit, masculine in appearance; all were neatly hung and pristine. The most ornate of the cases was embellished with sapphires on all the edges, but it was empty, signifying it must be where Ravanan kept his sapphire wizard robe that he was currently wearing. She noticed his blue shirt and jeans in another, she casually commented "Oh, I see the clothes you were wearing when you found me – are they enchanted also?"

Ravanan looked at his blue shirt and jeans, he was half distracted with thoughts of killing Annette but he answered anyway. "The jeans intensify the mind blanketing effect while the shirt amplifies the heartbeat of my target to single it out in a crowd." Ravanan replied – bragging. "Targeting spells are the most fun, to craft a spell centered around the sound of a racing heart..." He stopped himself as the thought occurred to him that Kalara might not be quite ready yet to hear about those gruesome details.

Then Ravanan's thoughts about targeting turned back to Annette as an idea formed in his mind. He went over to Kalara and helped her up. "I've got it. You are an Acama and you can summon Annette to us right here in this room! Kalara you have got to do this, for me, for us. Bring her here and I'll deal with her."

Kalara was hesitant. "I can't. There is no way I can do that."

"Yes you can, just try."

"You said yourself that I'm not ready to be an Acama." Kalara could not see it. "I've only just begun to feel magic work again within me. I'm not ready."

Ravanan would not back down and his excitement was mounting. "Kalara, listen to me. You're right OK? Being an Acama is beyond you right now, but you still have the ability to summon dragons."

"How do you know that I do?" Kalara asked.

Ravanan looked into her purple eyes "You have something that the four of you put inside your bodies. I don't know any more about it than that, but I'm sure even if you are morphed, it's still there. Why wouldn't it be?"

His reasoning made sense the more Kalara thought about it, although she didn't know what could be inside her – she felt nothing odd or extra in her body. With an eyebrow raised she asked him, "And you really think I'll be able to bring Annette to me when I couldn't even summon my bow?"

"I do."

His excitement made her want to try it. "Well how do I do it then?" she asked.

Ravanan stepped back a little and coached her. "Just think about Annette, *target* her. Think fully about her, everything about her, then speak out loud and order her to come to you. Expect Annette to appear. Use whatever words you want, your blood will know your will. This shouldn't be hard because it is a basic thing for Acamas to do – you used to do it. You would say 'Come here whoever!' – and say the dragon's name instead of whoever."

Kalara was quiet for a moment, thinking. She was an Acama – or so he said – she ought to be able to. But then she wavered and shook her head. "I'm sorry Ravanan." The failure to evoke her bow to her was clouding her mind.

"Kalara please." Ravanan was easily reading her thoughts about the bow. "I told you, Annette must have destroyed your bow. That is why it didn't come to you. You didn't fail to evoke it, the bow you made no longer exists! You must move on and stop thinking about that; it is in the past now and has no effect on what you are doing now. You will not fail in this, your magic is in you. You felt it when you made me kiss you. Just recall how that felt to you."

She breathed deep. "OK. I will try it, but I will need to relax right?"

Looking around the room she noticed a bare spot where the bed must go and thought about relaxing with Ravanan. A smile crossed her lips "Why don't you bring the bed back........"

Kalara forgot all about summoning Annette when her eyes froze on the back wall of the long room. There were more display cases back there, all glass – the same as his – except they contained feminine clothes, *her clothes* – they had to be.

She walked over there with Ravanan following. Holding her breath, she walked around them, looking at the different outfits she had worn throughout a two thousand year history. She marveled at them. There were two empty cases, one of them was like all the others and was probably for her healing robe, but her eyes were drawn to the other one, it was made from carved ivory and jeweled with luminescent fire opals. Kalara froze while she searched her mind to figure out what outfit was supposed to be hung in there – it had to be the cream robe that Annette had taken, the same one she was wearing in her dream. Her heart sank. That had been her robe. What enchantments did it have? She reached out and ran her fingertips over the bright fire opals, thinking, wishing she could see through the haze in her mind, it was a special robe, if only she could remember more about it. Her white robe..... Aggravation built up at the road block of her amnesia. Why couldn't she just remember?

Not being able to remember anything more about the robe she turned in frustration to Ravanan and asked "What do you know about that cream colored robe? The robe that goes in this case here..." she pointed "....These are my clothes, right? You said you brought my things here."

She looked at the clothes some more, thinking and trying to put the pieces of a puzzle together. Ravanan was watching her, listening to her mind work it out, he didn't answer her right away to give her time.

Kalara's mind followed an old trail of thought, a trail that she hadn't known since before her amnesia. She slowly asked, "Why were you the one to come find me? Please tell me. Don't avoid it anymore, tell me the truth, I'm ready."

He took a breath, "It would seem you are going to make yourself ready whether your mind is ready or not." Ravanan paused regretting last night, he hadn't intended to complicate her mind more than it already was. "I was chosen by the other Acamas because I lived the closest to you. They asked that I find you and, if required, kill you." Ravanan smiled at his smoothness.

But his smoothness might as well have been sandpaper to Kalara as she looked at the centuries of dust on the top of the glass display cases. She could feel in her heart that there was more to it, whether it be her magical alertness or simply woman's intuition, his story wasn't right. "You're lying. These cases look like they were put here centuries ago...."

She ran her fingertips over the top of one and they became coated with the soft gray dust.

"....and why would you bother to bring the empty ivory one? I'm thinking my stuff *belongs* here. There was something between us before wasn't there? How else could last night have happened so easily?"

Ravanan was quickly trying to circumvent the upcoming disaster, "Kalara, you're confused. Affection between dragons is complicated because of our auras. You have been all over me ever since I found you, it has confused you into thinking I'm attracted to you but really you are attracted to my magic, you can't help it. It's difficult for me to continuously resist your charming aura, last night shouldn't have happened. There is nothing between us."

Kalara exploded with anger at him skirting the truth. "I'VE HAD ENOUGH OF YOUR LIES! WHY WERE YOU SENT FOR ME INSTEAD OF SOME OTHER DRAGON? WHO ARE YOU TO ME?"

In her anger the air around them instantly turned cool from Kalara's aura although she was too upset to notice it.

But Ravanan did. He had been able to detect her warm aura all along since he'd found her, and only now in her anger did it turn cold, punishing everything around her with a fierce onslaught of an arctic front. The frost aura of a purple dragon was magnitudes colder than the aura of dragons born in cold climates; and though rare it was just as deadly a tool as his lightning was.

Kalara's cold anger stole Ravanan's breath and caused his human skin to raise goose bumps. Instantly his aura released its bio-anti-freeze into his blood for cold protection as it had done for him so many times before.

His eyes begin to tear, there was hope that Kalara was finally making progress, maybe this is what she needed to have happen. Even within her arms' reach and bone-chilling magic Ravanan could have fought Kalara but he couldn't fight himself anymore. He had to answer her. His teeth wanted to chatter but he wouldn't let them, if he was going to tell her it would be with clarity and a solid claim.

Ravanan locked gazes with her "I am your mate."

Kalara was still as a statue.

She heard every word and her heart was proclaiming itself the victor. Her heart raced. She had been right in her desires and suspicions. He was hers, all of him, his muscles, his scales, his magic, his long flowing black hair that could twist up into black horns, he was her mate! The room warmed up with her elation and smile.

Somehow, deep down, Kalara's mind had remembered her lover even in its addled state. Ravanan wasn't lying, he was hers. In every sense of the word he was her mate and would never leave her.

Kalara took hold of his hands. "Why didn't you just tell me when you first found me?"

Ravanan sighed and went back to the Mayan table, he found a chair and sank down onto it, Kalara eagerly followed, although it was obvious that he did not share her excitement.

"Imagine how I felt," he implored her "Not knowing what had happened to you, my dragoness, Kalara the Mighty Amethyst, my own personal Acama, my most precious treasure. I had to find you, even if it was only your bones in the ocean, I had to know where you were so I could grieve. I searched for you non-stop from the moment I knew you were gone, I would never give up. And then I found you, alive, only you were no longer the dragoness I loved...." Ravanan paused in silent grief.

He found his voice again, "....You were a fragile, ruined hatchling of a dragon who could get herself and all of dragonkind killed by humans. To know that I might have to kill you to uphold the law that you agreed to enforce; to have to kill one of the only four living amethyst dragons, I ached for your plight and you never even knew it!" He spat the words at her. "You were so wrapped up in yourself, lost inside your own mind, that you couldn't even notice my remorse.

"But then to be dismissed after finding you," his eyebrow raised, "I thought you had set a trap for me, found another mate, a better dragon and had devised a plan for my undoing. I decided then and there on that hill that you would both die. I would drag you back to Black Blade Lair so that I might extract the location of your new mate from your hidden memories and hunt him down, just as I had hunted you. I would find him easily enough, after having cast detection spells continuously for almost a year.....I'm pretty good at them." Ravanan dryly smiled at her before continuing, "Two things didn't make sense to me though – why was your mind taken from you and why you were injured at that anchor?

"Regardless of my concerns I carried your limp, wounded body into our lair and what did I find?... Not only had I lost my mate, but now my treasure was gone as well. You can't even begin to understand in your state just how much our treasure is worth; and locked within your hidden past was the key to getting it back – it still is," he smirked at the thought. "So even though I hated you and was going to kill you and your new mate I had to heal you first and get your memories back to find my gold."

Ravanan leaned back and propped his feet up on the table with a sad smile on his face. "But now I know from seeing your thoughts, none of this was your doing. You are a victim just as I am. Annette of Anarchelos Vya is to blame for all of our grief and I will enjoy killing her immensely."

Ravanan became distracted with thoughts of Annette. His eyes unfocused as he considered various spells and attacks he would use against the vile dragoness. The battle would need a lot of pre-thought. He needed to study her more and be sure of her strengths and favorite spells. His attack would be swift and perfect......

From the corner of his eye Ravanan noticed Kalara repositioning herself in the chair, waiting for him to go on. The motion jarred him back to what he had been saying, he pushed Annette from his mind and continued.

"I didn't want to tell you about us because as you currently are, you are not my mate. You have none of her memories, memories of us, things we have done, treasure we have mined, and even the little humans we have made deals with throughout the years. You think you are a human! You even think like the food we eat. You don't remember anything from our lives! It hurts to remember our history when I am the only one who does. Every time I say anything about our past it doesn't even faze you. You are a stranger to me and I feel like I am the one who lost everything.

"You don't act like the Kalara I know and love. My Kalara would already have killed Annette and brought our treasure back to Black Blade. Kalara the Mighty Amethyst was a powerful dragoness, independent, and she wasn't scared of seeing my dragon base form because she was a dragon! She understood why *our* treasure was important, what it meant to us. My Kalara was as powerful as me, her magic was great. We were a team that could not be beat.

"No," Ravanan's voice cracked with emotion, "you are not her and I'll not ask you to pretend to be her. I knew if I told you you'd feel obligated to be with me and that is not love, there is no choice to it.

141

Kalara reached out to him, "But last night....."

"Was one last flame." Ravanan cut her off and pushed her hand aside. "I admit you are quite beautiful to look upon. You look like her human form, but I don't feel any connection to you other than that. Making fire with you last night was different than it used to be. As I said, you don't act like Kalara. You didn't even recognize the runes I drew on your back!"

At hearing that Kalara had to interject. "That doesn't matter – I can learn! I want you. I choose you."

"You forget I am not human. I'm only in this lesser form to make you happy. You may want this human form of me but I don't want to be with a weak human no more than you want to be intimate with a dragon." He got up to leave the wardrobe chamber.

"Don't say that!" Kalara said, rising to stop him by flinging her arms around him.

Ravanan didn't pull away and allowed her to hold him but he didn't hug her back. He knew nothing had changed in her. She was accepting him, showing him that she was willing to stay with her captor. It disgusted him. Her wet eyes told it all, she was volatile and emotional, acting just like the herd. He knew she wanted him in human form, and was frightened of him when he wasn't the human of her desire.

Mistaking his silence for change of heart, Kalara said earnestly "I am still me. I can learn how to use magic again and you know we're attracted to each other. We can help each other get through the pain." She ran her fingers up his chest, feeling the softness of his velvet robe and then circling behind his neck.

He closed his eyes and felt her touch then took in a breath of regret, thinking to himself that she didn't even touch him like she used to. She was foreign to him.

Ravanan peeled her delicate arms from his body so that he could hold her hands in his. Catching her tear-stained gaze he told her, "But I don't want to be with you like this. You are not the dragoness I love. Yes, your magic is getting stronger, but your identity is still lost to us. You are seriously flawed. I mean look at you, you move and love like a human.... and you don't even want to eat bloody fresh meat!"

Ravanan's response did not thrill Kalara, in fact it had the opposite effect; she became hostile and vehemently opposed to him. The air turned cold. It was obvious that he was still reading her every thought.

Kalara backed away from him, her eyes were full of hurt. She couldn't understand how Ravanan could be so mean and uncaring. The air grew colder with her every heartbeat and it sparkled with floating micro-crystals of ice. Never before had Kalara felt so angry. She was aggravated that she'd forgot to block her thoughts from him and that he felt the need to bring it up at that exact moment.

Everything about her became an arctic rage, even her skin tinted to an ice-blue. Kalara noticed that Ravanan's hair was gathering frost, everything was, the floor, the wardrobe cases, even her. The ice crystals seized up as water molecules tightened and grew.

It was at that point Kalara realized she was making it happen. The tingling and popping of hardening ice crystals was a forbidding warning as the temperature continued to drop. As the air dried out to zero humidity a gratified satisfaction filled her heart – the entire lair seemed to be holding its breath for her – waiting. The noisily growing ice crystals was anything but peaceful – and the sound was quite possibly the quietest battle cry every heard on Earth.

Kalara's anger climbed to new heights of empowerment. She burst out with a furious rage "YOU DON'T KNOW HOW TO LOVE ME – OR HELP ME! And I don't want your help anymore! I don't want anything from you, including this!"

She wretchedly tore away the black healing robe that Ravanan had given her and bunched it up in her hands; it crackled and froze stiff from her anger. Using more willpower than brute strength Kalara forced the robe into a ball, moisture from her palms fed ice into it. It was the weirdest feeling as water from her body started to freely seep out of the pores in her hands to soak the robe and freeze it solid. With a growing thirst and a boiling anger the black ball grew denser as it filled with all her rage. Her wrists felt strangely numb and yet ticklish as they became conduits with her body water flowing quickly through them.

Then suddenly there was a wild pain of a thousand needles pricked inside her muscles as they crossed the threshold into severe dehydration. The pain was so intense it cut through her anger, she knew she had to stop or die. With her heart pounding hard to pump her thickened blood, Kalara hurled her frozen masterpiece at the source of her pain.... Ravanan.

Unimpressed by her careless use of magic, Ravanan easily caught the ice ball and set it down gently to avoid damaging the precious robe inside of it. He hadn't stopped her or dodged the frigid projectile. Just as before, he was protected with his bio-anti-freeze – it was a talent he had developed long ago from being her mate.

Kalara was now seething mad. She was fed up with Ravanan. How dare he casually catch her ice ball with his hands like it was a damn game!

Vile hatred was in her eyes "I don't want to have anything to do with you!"

Kalara marched her naked self over to one of her display cases which contained a sleek black outfit that would hug the body and not get in the way of a sword fight. She looked for a way to open it.

Ravanan watched Kalara gliding her hands over the case, unsuccessfully looking for a latch. He said flatly "The case doesn't have a door."

She glared at him for his know-it-all advice, then being sure to accentuate each word she hatefully replied "I... don't... need... one."

Ignoring the tingling in her arm, Kalara made a fist and thrust it through the chilled glass, shattering it. She was dizzy.

With her weight against the case, she closed her eyes to keep the room from spinning and donned the black suit. She was full of rage, needed to get out of that room, away from him, and she needed a drink of water, desperately.

On her way out of the chamber she looked over at him and cruelly said "Maybe you should have just killed me in that mall." Then she entered the pitch black tunnel.

Chapter 10

Driven by her severe thirst, Kalara wandered farther into the dark crevice, knowing that soon she would be in the main lair and could get a drink in the seer pool. Even with all the twists and turns in the darkness she found navigating a whole lot easier without that black robe catching on everything. That is not to say she didn't scrap herself on the jagged corners of rocks. She had just hit her shin on a rock and could feel it already bruising and swelling against her tight pants leg as she stumbled over another.

Progress was slow in the total darkness but Kalara kept her hands on the walls to keep going in the right direction and avoid disorientation. Her head was pounding with dehydration and the path was going up and down, turning narrowly, but she kept climbing and would find her own way out just as Ravanan was making her find her own way back to her past.

Kalara's mind was on one thing and it wasn't the dark tunnel she was in. Ravanan's rejection of her after the incredible night they had shared was really bothering her. She was having a hard time believing he felt that way about her. He sure didn't seem upset when he was on top of her - or holding her all night long! How could he be so cruel? His words stabbed at her heart – 'you make love like a human'. What the hell? He knew all along about her amnesia – what did he expect from her? It wasn't like she was keeping it from him. How could she not act like a human?

It saddened Kalara to know he wouldn't touch her again. Her unrequited love caused big tears to well up in her throat - it hurt to hold them back but she didn't want to cry over him, she couldn't cry anyway because she was bone dry. Her throat felt like it was bulging and her tongue was swelling. Her dry mouth reminded Kalara of wasting her body's water just to hit him. All that effort and he caught her ice ball like it was nothing!

The chilly subterranean air did little to cool her rage. Why wasn't Ravanan more willing to help her? She wanted the same thing he wanted, only she wanted it right this minute and he seemed to not be rushed at all – as if time had no hold on him. His cautiousness and attitude only made her that much more angry.

Hitting yet another rock with her forehead, she uttered words of wrath and the dry tears broke free of her control when her headache began pounding even more. It worried Kalara that though she was crying there were very few tears to show for it; it had to be because of the dehydration. She rubbed her itching face where a salty tear had escaped from her eye and continued on, but her other hand slipped when she leaned on it to climb onto a rocky ledge. She fell to the dirty cavern floor, banging up her knees.

She sat there, not caring anymore, resting. She was mad at everything, the dehydration was one thing, but to be rejected, which in turn was because of the main problem – she didn't know who she was. She was mad at whoever was responsible for it, if anybody was. Maybe her amnesia was an accident. She wasn't ready to blindly blame Annette for doing this to her. No, it was something that just happened. She must accept that and so should Ravanan.

The fact that she desired him from the moment she saw him spoke volumes. She felt like she was his mate. Last night was the first time she had been with a man. Kalara caught herself – dragon - that she could remember. He should want to help her and do all he can to get her memories back.

Kalara had to admit that Ravanan was right – she was uncomfortable next to a dragon whose mouth she could crawl into. She remembered that dream where he tore through his human chest and she shivered with fright from thinking about it. No one could understand what she was going through. Her total memory loss was an accident and a disease; a terrible disease without a cure and even her rescuers didn't want to help her.

She could only rely on herself so she forced herself, on her tingling arms and legs, to get up again. She kept feeling the walls to navigate through the complete darkness. On the way down to the wardrobe chamber she didn't recall seeing any other paths, there was only one way. She had to be going right she told herself.

Bam! She hit her head hard against a low ceiling, she felt blood trickle down over her right eyebrow. She paused a long moment to collect herself after that. She didn't remember the passageway being this long. She needed light, if only she could cast spells. Maybe if she calmed down and relaxed then she could cast a spell of light. Maybe that was the key to spell casting, she had to be relaxed to feel it flow from her just like Ravanan had said.

She hated it that Ravanan was always right, it got under her skin. He was so perfect, so good at everything he did, so good-looking - and he didn't want her. Her anger, coupled with dehydration, was making her heart work hard and fast, keeping the newest gash on her head open and draining blood. There was nothing she could do about the wound, she was forced to accept it and actually started to like it because it gave her something else to focus on other than him.

Enveloped in darkness, blood dripping, Kalara carefully lowered herself to the ground. Blood was running into her eyes, she wiped it out, getting her fingers in it. Then she delicately felt the severity of the gash, not caring that blood was all over her hands and fingernails. The sharp rock had snagged her skin, she tried to reposition the jagged flap of skin over the wound. It didn't cover it completely. She patted the skin down, winced at the pain, and more blood oozed out. Kalara enjoyed feeling the hot blood on her hands, it signaled to her she was still alive. She wiped her hands on her neck and chest to warm her skin and then relaxed her head against the cold cave wall. She just needed to wait a bit for the gash to stop bleeding then she could continue on to get a drink of water. It couldn't be that much further.

She sat there quietly in the pitch black passageway. There was solid rock all around her, Kalara felt small next to the cool walls, she was so useless and ineffectual, especially against a mountain. Even her hot blood that was now dripping onto the rock didn't warm it a fraction of a degree.

She needed to keep all the blood she could – it had water in it. Kalara felt with her fingers and located the cold bloody spot on the rock wall, then collected as much of the dripped blood as she could and sucked it off her fingers. Aside from the twangy iron taste her tongue danced in the wetness of the cool blood, but there was nowhere near enough to quench her thirst.

Kalara wiped the wet rock again, trying to get more of her spilled blood, wanting to get it all back. Then Kalara resorted to licking the dusty and slightly muddy rock. It was her blood and it was all she owned. She had nothing, not even the clothes she was wearing for they belonged to Ravanan's mate, the Mighty Amethyst, not her. The bloodied Kalara sitting in that rock crevice owned nothing and the darkness around her did nothing for her self-worth, she was rough, ruined, and lost.

As angry as she already was, Kalara got angry with herself for feeling like that. She refused to wallow in self-pity any longer and found something else to occupy her heart, the rigid, cold, uncaring feeling of rock. In the darkness of that mountain the rock never changed, it couldn't be hurt, it had nothing to lose, couldn't be affected, it simply was there. Just as she was. In the quiet dark Kalara stopped thinking and simply listened. There was nothing to be scared of, no animals and no people. The cool air hung about her. She rested her head against the wall, the rock didn't move, didn't breathe, it was just rock. She reached out and ran her hand along the wall. The mountain didn't care that she was touching it. Kalara made a fist, hit the ground hard.... the rock didn't care and neither did the darkness. Kalara waved her hand in front of her face, not seeing it.... only the briefly passing body heat gave away the action.

Kalara wasn't just in the dark anymore – she was becoming part of it. Perhaps it was delirium brought on by her dehydrated state, but her thoughts were clear as a bell to her and in that moment a seed of identity was born. The black cavern air wasn't just touching her skin, it was inside her, filling her with its cold nothing as she breathed it in. Darkness and cold, the void in the rock, all of it was the definition of nothing. She had nothing, was nothing, and any empathy she may have had just took on the feeling of nothing.

In the stillness of the cool dark air she felt every bump and scrap that the cave had given her. Her little jaunt back to the main lair had changed from a short hike to a troubling ordeal and then to an oppressive journey. She knew she couldn't stop there, her mouth had never felt so dry. Water. Beautiful water. Surely she didn't have much further to go. She was going to have to fight, continue on. She wished

Ravanan would have followed her and cast starlight on her, but no, she would have to do it alone. She didn't have him. Maybe this is what he wanted, for her to leave him and get hopelessly lost so he wouldn't have to deal with her, just like Annette who sent her away to Jenniffer's apartment. Kalara didn't appreciate it, she was growing tired of being cast aside. Ravanan wouldn't get off that easy. He brought her to Black Blade and he would have to suffer the consequences of doing so. She would make him listen, make him help, and if he didn't, then she would make him give her the killing blow. He couldn't get out of facing her or let her die in a dark fracture of rock from dehydration.

Kalara stood up again and slowed her pace to that of a snail, feeling the ceiling and the walls; using her toes to feel the path beneath her. With nothing to see, she tried to attune herself to the acoustics of the cave. It became a game to her, one that she wasn't very good at. She even managed a smile at her opponent, but the cave was a relentless foe and struck her left temple with a hard stalactite.

The passageway would have spun for her if she could have seen it. She reeled from the pain, stumbling. Was she seeing stars? Maybe it was sunlight. Maybe they were moving comets, or maybe the stars were dancing to a well-choreographed ringing gong in her left ear.

It wasn't the hardest of hits but it was at a delicate spot, it made her breathing speed up faster than it already was. Kalara sat down again, ready to give up. There was no way she was getting out of there. She wanted to rest but knew better than to take a nap; that would destroy her sense of time. At the moment, she knew she had to be close to the end of the corridor. It hadn't taken her that long to travel through the tunnel with Ravanan. How much further was it? She hadn't been in there that long had she? But just as tossing and turning in the middle of the night warped time, so did the utter darkness and Kalara lost all track of it. If she fell asleep, it would not be good but the temptation to sleep was heavy on her. Her left temple was throbbing with pain and her left ear was ringing. She had a feeling her vision was blacked out too but there was no way of knowing.

Kalara told herself she would rest but not sleep. She concentrated on the heartbeat she plainly felt in her left temple, her whole head was pulsating in rhythm with her temple. She wouldn't sleep but had to lay down as the strain from having to remember which way was forward was tiring her. Kalara laid down in the narrow corridor that was barely wide enough for her body, she made sure to have her head pointing in the direction she needed to go and her feet toward the way she had come from; that way, just in case she nodded off, when she woke she'd be headed in the right direction.

The cold, hard bed she had made reinforced the fact that tons of cold, uncaring rock surrounded her. She just needed some rest. She wouldn't sleep, she would make herself focus on the pain to stay awake. The pain reminded her of when Ravanan had lifted the glittering mist and her body was attacked. At least now her bones weren't broken and she could move everything. Kalara reached up to feel the gash above her right eye, it hurt when she touched it, it was swollen. The wound was crusty, that was good -she could breathe a little easier now, although she strangely missed having her fresh hot blood to comfort her.

Then her mind said "What? Wait a minute, you don't want to feel your own hot blood."

Kalara was thankful for the conversation, she answered back in agreement. "You're right, feeling your own hot blood is bad, very bad."

"Yes, bad." Her mind replied and then showed her pictures of her multi-hued guts spilling out of her stomach; and it put the noxious smell of her guts in her nose then said "*That* was bad. You are nowhere near that bad off right now. You'll be fine, just some cuts and bruises – nothing a little sleep won't cure."

"NO" Kalara cried out, "I can't go to sleep, I need to go to water."

Her mind sang sweetly to her "In sleep you can dream of water." That was the last thing Kalara heard as she drifted off.

The deep sleep ended, Kalara opened her eyes. She was blind! Her vision was black, her body ached laying on the cold hard floor – why was she on the floor? She heard absolutely nothing. Normally Seven the cat was getting into something loud and breakable or else his hooks-for-claws were getting caught in the carpet loops – but not this time, what was he up to? It was too quiet. Was it time for Jenniffer to come home? She blinked her eyes and still couldn't see.

A few heartbeats of panic later, she remembered where she was. How long had she been asleep? She couldn't swallow, there was no spit in her mouth, just some dirt. Her hands felt dirty, her face and chest also. She had crusty eyes. Her body was stiff with pain, it took her a while to stretch and work the kinks out. Did her hair have mud or blood in it? She was thirsty, so very thirsty, her tongue was swollen. She laid her head back down in quiet thought.

The truth was she didn't know who she was and no one cared about it but her.... and that was alright. She would help herself, her whining was over. Her foolish lust of Ravanan's hard body was not helping her either. At least she was alive, hearing her raspy breath attested to that. But no, she was more than 'just alive', she knew where she was and how she got there which was a good way to be. She knew magic was real, it was the only way she could be where she was instead of in Jenn's apartment. Even if she couldn't do what other dragons could, she could do more than a human, she could detect auras at least.

She craved water. Fighting the cave to find water would mean her death. Even though she felt a new strength in the darkness and wasn't scared of being there, she still needed light to get out and get to water. Wanting light more than water, she spoke out as best she could to make an audible voice and cast *"STARLIGHT"* nothing happened. She went through her thoughts again. Ravanan seemed to always know where he wanted the light to go, she hadn't told her blood what to light up. She would have to be very specific about what she wanted. She wanted light more than anything, she wanted herself to be lit up so she could walk, it had to last a while until she got out of the cave. Again she cast *"STARLIGHT"* and she blinded herself with light that was glowing all around her. "OW!" she yelled and blinked, waiting for her eyes to adjust to the light.

Kalara tried to get up, but she was light-headed and dizzy. She would have to wait for her body to recover from its exertion at having cast a new spell for the first time, but she was so dehydrated she couldn't wait long. Her body was dried out, she pinched the back of her hand and the skin stayed mounded up. Kalara knew she was in a bad way, but having light now made all the difference, she'd be able to go straight to the seer pool and get water.

Finally Kalara stood up with her body glowing. Her head was going to explode, she had to shut her eyes and lean against the cave wall for a moment until the feeling passed. Her balance shifted and she toppled, she couldn't maintain it and crumpled back down. But at least she was still glowing.

She was famished too, there was a pit in her stomach, Kalara didn't know if it was because she had cast a spell or because she had been knocked out for no telling how long. Giving her heart time to pump thick blood to her head, she got on her knees and crawled towards the main lair, not wanting to delay any longer. She kept crawling, lighting the pathway before her, afraid that standing up would pull the trigger on her head.

Kalara crawled as quick as she dared. She had done it, cast a spell... and she would get out of the crevice. Casting a spell was monumental, it signified many things and was the start of something new for her. She wasn't a human. She wasn't helpless and could no longer be held captive. She could work out her own way to find her memories. She would get strong again. The tunnel was well lit by her spell and she could see beautiful formations that adorned the walls. It wasn't long before her sensitive nose picked up the savory aroma of pizza. Was she dreaming? No, she was not. It was pizza, up ahead. She followed her nose and kept moving forward over the slopes and turns until she exited back into the wardrobe chamber. There was the weapons arsenal, she stopped where she was, rolled over onto her back and cried without tears. All that work and she was back where she'd started. She heaved with loud, dry sobs.

Ravanan heard her crying and rushed over to pick her up. Kalara passed out as she heard him cast "*ANCHOR*".

Kalara woke up later soaking in the warmed seer pool. She felt weak.

Ravanan was sitting nearby at the table. There was a fresh goblet of water and pizza, a whole glorious pizza, toppings and all. She cried and cried. The crying made her head hurt which made her cry some more. Kalara couldn't talk, all she could do was cry between gulps of water. She didn't want to talk, she just wanted to recuperate.

The pizza practically dissolved in her mouth she was so hungry. Ravanan let her eat in peace. Kalara ate until she couldn't stuff anymore in.

Then she finally found words, "This is so good, where did you get this?"

"This is my territory, I've got anchors all over. You said you wanted pizza, so I went to Manaus and got you one. It got a little cold waiting on you to come out of there but it's not bad is it?"

"Oh it was fine. Why did you allow me to run off into the dark like that?"

"First off, you wanted to go in there. Secondly, you told me you didn't want my help. Besides, I couldn't see you to know where you were. Then after a minute or two when I knew the tunnel was where you'd gone, it was too late to find you. I couldn't detect you to bring you back or target you to give you light – it's that shadow suit you're wearing. You called it Naught because it masks your aura and body from dragons, humans, and animals alike, but it also severely dampens the effectiveness of your verbal spells.

"I was that good? To enchant something that even you can't see?"

"Yes, you had only made the difficult piece some hundred years ago to take advantage of the humans' first world war. It's very high level and the amethyst enchantress of your past isn't going to be happy about the holes you've made in it."

"But why would I make something that hinders magic?"

Ravanan looked sad that she would ask such a ridiculous question but yet had a reminiscing smile about him. "That wasn't your goal with Naught. Your goal was to be invisible and to make an unnatural enchantment like that, to stop a beating heart from pumping blood and auras or breathing lungs from telling the world their alive, to literally remove all the flesh from the visible world, is to also accept the fact that it dampens the ability to affect the outside world with magic. After all, that is the goal, to not let the world know you are there.

"You loved to hide amidst your prey and then primitively assassinate your target with their own weapons. The more restrictions you put on yourself, the more fun you had."

Ravanan's words reflected how much he missed his mate. After a moment he added, "You'd rather starve than take the easy pickings in Manaus. That's probably what got you into trouble to begin with."

Kalara didn't feel any closer to her former self after hearing that. And she was in no mood to hear about Ravanan's turmoil. "But couldn't you have maneuvered the bouncing beams of sunlight to light up the passageway for me?"

"But then you wouldn't have cast your first spell." Ravanan smiled, "You sound tired, I'll leave you alone to wash up."

By the time she finished her bath the lair's magical sunlight was beginning to fade with the day. Kalara agreed to wear the healing robe again after finding out it belonged to her and Ravanan was not responsible for its revealing style. He helped her put it on because her many scrapes and bruises ached her so.

As they watched the lair grow dim Kalara reflected back on the day "I realized something in that crevice; it is that I can only count on myself. Annette tried to help me. You are trying to help me. But really it comes down to just me. I have my magic now and if nothing else I can build on that to get my memories back. I know you also want my memories back and any help you can give I appreciate, but I don't need to keep asking you about it; waiting for you to do something. I can try to fix myself in the meantime."

"Yes you can." he answered her. "But I also feel like it's time to get your memory back. So let's begin in the morning after you've rested. I'm satisfied with the clues we've found in your recent memories, unless you held something back from me which I don't think you did."

The blue wizard stood up from the table and Kalara scooted over to make room for him on the bed. Instead of going to her, he walked far enough away to undo his Morph spell. Kalara watched Ravanan's robe disappear and saw his hair grow upwards into long twin horns when he released himself back into the dragon that he really was. The gigantic cobalt-blue dragon arched his back and stretched out his wings as if he'd been confined for months and flicked his tail to curl it around his clawed feet.

The immense dragon before her was magnificent to behold and she felt a hint of envy that she couldn't leave her human form behind like he could. She had, however, heard his unspoken statement loud and clear. He would not repeat last night.

Kalara rolled over to face away from him and hid her disappointment that Ravanan had chosen not to share her bed.

She was done with being vulnerable to him and returned her mind to the crevice where she'd found strength. No longer would she allow herself to be hurt. She didn't have Ravanan though she wanted him desperately. He was untouchable, mated to her elusive past. He wasn't hers. And so, deep within herself and far away from Ravanan she buried her desires, hiding them in the dark void of her heart.

Kalara didn't even shed a tear over the matter. Deep inside the darkness was the only place remaining where she felt safe from heartache. The dark crevice would be hers, she would claim it and no one could take it from her, she owned it, she had lived it, and the bumps and scrapes on her skin proved it. No matter where her body was, who she was with, or whose clothes she was wearing, none of it really mattered because she was at home with herself. The darkness of that corridor had filled Kalara with a cold nothing and that darkness was part of her now; giving her strength, protecting her. She had immersed herself inside the uncaring rock and could not be parted from it because it echoed how she felt. The dark part of Kalara was more than independence, it was cold indifference.

In that peaceful void Kalara felt relaxed, able to cast and craft spells – that was all there was left to do in her life. The newly formed dark crevice in her core would be her training ground to work on spells, slowly building off of the one she knew, Starlight.

It didn't matter if she was tainted as Ravanan said, she was the only one of her kind, not human, not dragon; and she might never get to change so she would gladly wear the banner that separated her from all other beings. Driven there by his rejection and anchored there by her sorrow, Kalara embraced the darkness.

Ravanan swung his great head over to her, it was the same size as the bed she was on. He was trying to read her thoughts but he couldn't – not even a hint of an aura change. He could still sense her aura, but beyond that there was nothing but silence. All he frustratingly knew was that Kalara wasn't dead and her aura was fully charged.

He had gotten used to knowing her feelings and he hated asking but he asked anyway "How does your head feel?"

Kalara didn't move or speak, it was as if she hadn't heard him which was preposterous because he hadn't whispered. He craned his head around to see her eyes in the darkening lair, they were closed but he knew she wasn't sleeping. Ravanan let it go, realizing that she was blocking him, and it gave him hope that his mate would return to him soon.

The next morning, early, Kalara woke to a maelstrom of high winds and cold rain. She was in the eye of the storm with only an occasional spray of rain hitting her and her body was pressed down magically to the unmoving bed that was still inside the main chamber of Black Blade Lair. She peered through the storm to see Ravanan the Azure Wizard standing safely outside of it, he was controlling it. She waited to see what would happen.

Nothing happened. The winds died away eventually and Kalara felt the release to move.

Ravanan walked over to her "Do you remember anything?"

"Should I?"

"I chose to try that spell first since you were sleeping. I knew it was a long shot, but I had to try it." Ravanan looked eager. "My theory was that the rocks you've called home for two thousand years might hold some impressions of you. If they did listening to them would require you to be very calm since they live slowly. Did you feel anything at all?"

"No, not a thing other than cold water spitting on me."

"Well it was only a theory."

After Kalara had eaten her breakfast of boring cooked steak, Ravanan took her back to the bed. "What are you doing?" she asked him.

Sitting behind her, he answered "Preparing you for your past. I'm going to make sure you are relaxed for the spell to have full penetration. I know you don't like it when I calm you with the spell so I won't, I'll do it with massage." He braided her long dark hair, sometimes his fingers brushed against her skin.

Kalara couldn't deny that she enjoyed his attention, but she refused to let it show. She retreated again into her crevice to shield her desires from him. As he worked her hair and touched her skin, beckoning her to relax, her body was now prostrate on the bed and her finished braid spilled out on the bed beside her like a snake. Ravanan pulled her robe from her body, revealing her naked flesh, and began to rub her back. Her loose body melted like butter and she noticed that the patterns his fingertips made on her spine were the same as when he had been true to his heart the other night. The relaxing runes worked their tranquil magic on her. She was comfortable and didn't resist him in the slightest way, so comfortable in fact, that she was beginning to drift off to sleep. In those drowsy moments she heard Ravanan cast "*RESTORE*".

She didn't feel any different after his spell. Ravanan laid down beside her breathing with exertion, he was worn out from having put so much effort into the spell. In the long moments that followed she drifted in and out of sleep. As they both laid there resting he asked "Well, did that do it? Do you feel anything? Remember anything?"

Half asleep, she answered "No, but I do feel good."

Ravanan turned onto his back and stared at the ceiling.

Kalara looked over at him then fell back to sleep.

When she woke up around mid-day, Ravanan the Malefic Azure had just returned from hunting, his scaled belly looked quite full. Kalara was proud that she felt his aura at full strength at two striking distances away from him. He tossed a seared jaguar leg to her and then morphed back to the Azure Wizard while heading off to his alcove, deep in thought.

Kalara gave him time to think, feeling that he must need it, and chewed a few bites of her lunch. Then she got up and went to the wizard's alcove to find him. Ravanan was at the dais studying a green crystal, he was visibly upset. Kalara asked "What is it Ravanan? How can I help?"

Ravanan threw the crystal over to its pile and answered "I can't find a suitable mineral for what I need."

"Why do you even need crystals? Isn't your magic strong enough?"

Now it might seem that question would have upset Ravanan but it didn't. He plainly answered "Sometimes the properties of crystals are a tool to help our blood manifest the spell we want by amplifying it. But sometimes there isn't one. It would seem that no crystals exist for what I have planned."

"And what do you have planned?" Kalara could tell that Ravanan was reluctant to proceed without a crystal.

He regarded her offer to help "Perhaps if *you* were to cast a spell of remembering, your past would come back to you. I know you don't have the expertise needed to cast such a spell..... but I do."

He came closer to her, "I don't want to control you. You must believe me when I say that it sickens me to even consider manipulating you. You're my mate, or at least you were, you are not idle prey to be driven to its own death. But I could cast the necessary spell through you, using your voice and your blood. I was just hoping a mineral could take the burden rather than me... it could have been a simple crystal that you willingly pick up and it releases a one-time-only binding spell to control you and cast the spell through you. You're so defenseless, I would hate myself for taking advantage of you."

Kalara said softly, "It's not taking advantage of me if it's something I want you to do. I want you to do whatever it takes to get my memories back and I want to help however I can. It's either control me or kill me, right? So control me then. What do I need to do?"

"Alright, just like this morning you need to be relaxed. Relaxing isn't necessary but it helps for better spell penetration and we both want this to work. Don't even get excited about it working, just think about the massage I gave you, feeling my hands on your skin. You want your heartbeats to remain low and steady."

Ravanan was speaking gently and cast his spell. "*I'LL BE CONTROLLING YOU*, I don't want you to speak or help me in any way, got it?" He led her by the arm as they walked over to sit down at the table. While they were walking he suggested that they practice first to get her used to being controlled. Ravanan was so good at casting the high level spell that Kalara didn't even notice he had already slipped into her mind, perfectly matching her own will and pace to make her body walk. He was a master at mimicking movements, pretending that he wasn't there inside her mind. He hid his presence from her and mirrored all her small movements exactly.

He sat down across from her, leaned back to relax and cast "*ARMOR*". There was a level of uncertainty about what would happen when her memories returned and Kalara the Mighty Amethyst discovered that he was controlling her. He needed to be prepared since he was linked to her mind. With his transparent coat protecting him, he said "I won't hurt you."

When Ravanan finally did reveal his dominion to her, the shearing effect was unnerving to Kalara. She felt his will shift and slide off the rails to run alongside her own. Even though her will was still running the race she saw it for what it truly was; he was right there, matching everything she did, copying her. Who was controlling her? It was tearing at the connectivity of her mind. Even though she was yielding to him her primal, basic existence was still fighting – but it had to give way or else the stress would tear her body asunder. The only thing he had done differently was to lift himself away from her, showing her his will, revealing who the real power over her was; it was disturbing. Then his will overtook hers, beating harder and faster, until his was the only one on the track; and just that easy, Kalara had become a spectator in her own mind.

Kalara was calmly sitting in the chair trying to be still for Ravanan. Then her arms raised up. She feared she'd disobeyed. She hadn't done that, she was being still but she did it anyway and her arms stayed lifted. Her arms felt heavy as her fingers began to remove the braid in her hair. Ravanan easily took her tight braid apart as if he were doing it with his own hands. The movements were smooth and deft, they would fool anyone into thinking that Kalara was intending to undo her braid. It felt weird to be touching her hair, feeling it flow through her fingers when she wasn't meaning to. She watched him from across the table – it was all she was able to do since he was in full control of her. He sat there with an involved look on his face, staring at her.

As she was watching him, unable to move her head, Ravanan took his eyes off of her to look down at the hem in his robe to flick some dirt off the otherwise pristine sapphire robe. Kalara wanted to scream "What are you doing?!" He should be concentrating on her. He held her very life in his mind, this spell was a whole lot more important than keeping his robe perfectly clean. He was obsessed with that robe!

In dismay she realized that line of sight wasn't even needed for him to control her. With a dead quality, her arms came down after pulling the remainder of the braid out. It didn't stop there. Ravanan then made her hands fluff her loosened hair and drape it beautifully around her. Her body was numbly following his orders. She was nothing more than a puppet.

Kalara felt herself stand up, turn to face him, and then her eyelids closed. This upset her because she couldn't see what was going on. She saw nothing but pitch black. Not that the darkness bothered her, it strengthened her. But this wasn't simple darkness. Kalara was trapped so tightly that she couldn't make her eyes open or lungs breathe, even her connection with her newly found magic was severed. Being trapped inside her own head bothered her a great deal. The not knowing what was happening, the wondering......

All Kalara could do was think......

'DON'T LEAVE ME LIKE THIS!' Kalara wanted to scream. She feared he'd left. Couldn't he have at least opened her eyes before he did?

Nothing was happening, was the spell of remembering over? Maybe the spell didn't work and now Ravanan was going to finally kill her. She couldn't see or move. Of all the ways to kill someone, why did he have to trap her in the dark? She wanted to cry, to feel wet tears flood her eyes but couldn't even do that. What was he intending by this? At least he could have had the decency to let her see until her last breath. It was so dark.

She waited, trapped. Fright overtook her as she remembered that darkness in the shopping mall, how it had descended, and trapped her with those iridescent eyes, eyes that took Ravanan away from her, leaving her alone. They were everywhere around her, watching her without sound. Would the eyes return this time? What if the eyes had returned and she didn't know it? Did the eyes take Ravanan again? Is that what happened to him? New panic washed over her mind. She began screaming and fighting but somehow knew she really wasn't. Oh how she wanted to cry and scream out! She would be stuck like this forever – it was maddening. Was Ravanan alive? She'd never know because her eyes were shut!

Once again she was left to wonder if she was making all of this up. Maybe she was. If only he would say something to let her know this was really happening to her..... Could she still be at the shopping mall curled up in a ball, alone inside the fantasy world of her mind? It had to be, she knew magic wasn't real.

Kalara listened but heard nothing. She was losing her grip on reality; laying on the floor in a coma was most likely the case. She couldn't call out, she was helpless, an insane human screaming silently at the world, trapped inside her own body, in debilitating darkness.

Kalara's eyes opened suddenly. She was now seeing the chair where Ravanan had been sitting but he wasn't in it. Where was he? Kalara was trying hard to stay sane and not panic. Had she made all this up? Ravanan wasn't there. She couldn't move. Maybe all of what she was now seeing was still in her head. Where was he? He should be there. Had the eyes come and taken him away? Maybe she had never really left the mall and was laying there rigid with insanity. She didn't know what to believe. Had Ravanan ever been sitting there? Was he even real? She couldn't hear him. If he was real, she didn't know where he was. He said he wouldn't leave her so why did he?

Then she spoke, actually heard her voice cast *"COME HERE ANNETTE OF ANARCHELOS VYA!"*.

She didn't feel any new auras appear but her mind was reassured from the spell at least. Could she even feel auras while being controlled? She wished she knew. Obviously Ravanan was still controlling her and must be near her somewhere even though she couldn't see him. Kalara was relieved, at least she wasn't insane and the horrible eyes hadn't taken him away again.

Ravanan currently reigned in Kalara's mind. Though upset by the failed summoning spell, he continued on and did not release her. Ever the opportunist, he had more than one agenda while controlling her and wanted to try everything he could. In all of his long years this was the first time for him to ever control another dragon, it wasn't unlike a human mind, stronger willed perhaps, but then he had never bothered to really examine what he saw before he ate them. In truth, he felt wrong controlling Kalara even though he had her permission to do so, that perhaps somehow he was violating her, and more so violating an ancient code of millions of years ago. But he wasn't aware of any such code and he doubted that any dragon would know of it – if it existed at all.

The longer he maintained the control spell the more it reminded him of exploring new land. A side effect of the spell was that every detailed thought Kalara was thinking, even if she was trying to hide them, would be known to him for as long as the spell was active. Unlike the union spell where he had experienced her memories as if they were his own, this time he was listening to all of her thoughts as they sped along, giving her mind and body instructions.

He analyzed the amazing processes that she had just worked through as a meticulous psychiatrist would, fully listening but yet detached. He was stunned at how quickly her mind degraded towards insanity, it was absurd – more of Annette's doing no doubt.

Kalara's mind was still muddled and delicate as the day he'd found her. She was full of fear and her emotions easily flared up at anger, fear, doubt, sexuality, or anything else. She had an unnatural worry of being trapped and he knew it was Annette's fault. Kalara's most basic awareness was that she was vulnerable and entrapment was her greatest fear. He wondered to himself at what horrible magic Annette must have used against Kalara.

Ravanan wanted to help and let Kalara know that he had shut her eyes to give him time to hide in case the Mighty Amethyst decided to attack him when she awoke, that way she couldn't target him first. Ravanan sent his words directly to her mind that he was only protecting himself and assured her that he would not allow her to be trapped again.

He saw inside her mind that the normal state was an unsteady mix of fear and aimless wandering until she found her past. He saw Kalara's mental image of herself stranded on top of a precipice, walking around looking for her identity. She was stuck. The precipice was cut off from the world by two deep crevices, one was a calm, cold black while the other was dreadful with a dark tumultuous storm about it – and he knew that Kalara had almost fallen into this one moments ago when he got up to hide. Both were bottomless, both were traps.

Ravanan mentally joined Kalara on the precipice. He was standing in the center of the tiny platform, fighting the blustery wind that all tall places have, but Kalara was as far away as she could get from the dreadful darkness and standing right on the edge of the larger chasm. It was a chasm so big that it could swallow a mountain, it was incredibly dark. There was simply nothing there and one would fall forever it seemed through an endless cold night.

Little did he know that Kalara had already visited the dark nothing and that she had carved out a hidden staircase leading down to the abyss so she could go there any time she wanted to. He couldn't have known about it since she wasn't actively thinking about the newly-formed darkness in her, all of Kalara's energy was focused on standing on that tall precipice trying to find her memories. Nor did Ravanan know that he was the one who had pushed her to build the hidden staircase.

It was odd – Ravanan noted – that Kalara had no fear of falling into the great void, she was favoring it. He had to agree with her that it was much nicer than the other violent chasm.

After he came to be by her side he could hear haunting whispers of delusions and doubts coming from within the violent crevice. And if he looked just right he could see large iridescent eyes trying to rise out of the darkness and hound Kalara but as soon as they emerged they faded to nothing. It was a horrible darkness indeed. Ravanan hated those eyes ever since the other day when he had acquired Kalara's version of their shared memory. He glared at the rising eyes, refusing to shiver. They were flat and reminded him of a bird feather.... a peacock feather to be exact, and not the eye of any dragon he had ever seen. Perhaps, he considered, it was a mask that Annette was using to confound Kalara.

He needed to help Kalara cross over the chasms, it was the only way, if he could help her over then maybe her identity and memories would be on the other side waiting for her. Why didn't he think of this before? Maybe controlling her and being inside her mind was what he needed to do all along – one could hope.

With the wind whipping his long hair about, Ravanan extended his hand, she grabbed hold, and he pulled Kalara back to the relative safety of the middle of the mental precipice. Ravanan meant to take off and fly her across just as he had in the shopping mall. He took flight but lost her hand and Kalara never left the ground. He returned to her with a quizzical look. How had Kalara done that? And then Ravanan remembered Kalara couldn't fly.

Ravanan sent her a strong mental message that he was in total control of her and he would make her fly.

"Let me fly you across." he told her.

He tried to take off again and the same thing happened. It was no use, her feet would not budge from the rock. Sure, he was controlling Kalara and could have really flown her body across the lair but apparently a mental exercise to change a dragon's mind was not possible.

In a desperation attempt Ravanan mentally released his human form inside her mind and was now his normal dragon self-towering over her. He hated to grab her with his talons, knowing Kalara was scared of him already – 'what would that do to her?' he wondered. So he lowered his head and did something then that all dragons detested, he let the tiny human Kalara climb onto his back. She climbed up and sat between two of his spikes.

'Thankfully, all of this was only mental imagery', Ravanan consoled himself.

It was awkward, he would never do this again in a mental state or in real life – he was not a beast to be controlled. He took off and easily crossed the void then landed. But the moment his talons clicked on the ground the new land became the pinnacle again with chasms all around.

Ravanan was dismayed but Kalara didn't appear to be surprised at all. Again he took flight, Kalara still clinging to his blue scales and black spines, and again they landed back on the tiny precipice. It was the oddest thing because he was flying straight and saw the goal, but when he got there the land all looked the same, just barren rock until he landed.

Flying her around wasn't working and Ravanan had had enough, he reached around and picked her off his back and stood her back on the ground. He looked across the chasm to the expanse beyond – her memories were out there and there had to be a way to them.

Then he thought of another idea. He would teach Kalara to fly, give her the *memory* of flight by implanting his own memories in her mind, his best memories of their first mating flight, because during that time both minds are closely linked out of necessity. The boundaries of who was leading whom as they flew through the air were blurred and he could easily make Kalara believe they were her own memories she was seeing – they practically were anyway. Mating while flying was the ancient way, more dramatic than on land and a whole lot more difficult to do, however it was not nearly as sensual as it sounded without the many nerve endings of the frail human body. Regardless of all that though, it was a ritual for those dragons who held true to their kind and never before was Ravanan so glad they had followed tradition when the memory of their bonding flight might recover her lost memories.

Inside her mind Ravanan told her "I know what I said yesterday hurt you. I'm sorry that I did but you must understand I am hurting too. I remember so much about our lives together, your life, even your precious creme-colored robe that you asked about. Don't you know I made those fire opals that were on that robe the day we met? You watched me do it."

He replayed his memory of when they crossed paths for the first time, they were both hunting in human form and a territory fight ensued. Ravanan survived her frigid aura by using a fire armor that nearly suffocated him. But he lived long enough to spark her interest and cause her to drop the attack.

Then the young Ravanan kept her interest by taking some quartzite from the lair that he was building; using fire and lightning to break the piece of rock into silica dust, he then fused it together again with water, resin, and his own blood. The end result was a pile of glowing fire opals which continued to glow as he placed them in her open hands.

Kalara promptly put the beautiful orange-red cabochons in her satchel before flying away from the black ledge. Ravanan immediately took off in pursuit. She was trying hard to outpace him but he was gaining on her and cutting short every impressive move she made. The more she tested him, the more determined he became. He'd nearly grabbed her a couple of times before catching her foot which caused them both to laugh. His grasp was solid, then another, and another up her body, until finally he got her to slow down.

The memory was vivid, and complete, so much so that the real Kalara could feel the images' auras, they made her smile at the frivolity of it all.

Embraced and hovering, a devilish grin spread across the young Kalara's face as she floated in his arms. Then Ravanan saw her eyes deeply for the first time, they were purple...... he couldn't believe what he was seeing.... was it even possible? His heart skipped a beat at their beauty and in anticipation at how majestically-hued her scales must be.

Both dressed as human natives, their backs were bare, Kalara's hands found Ravanan's shoulder blades and followed their curves, toying with him as they hung in the air. Her touch awakened his senses all anew. He knew her thoughts and what she would have of him. The enchantress was testing him, wanting him to drop his human form to see how good of a flier he really was.

The pace of the memory slowed down as they both began to release their human forms (Ravanan wanted her to fully experience what morphing was like).

The young Ravanan mirrored her morph with his wing bones emerging and pushing past her fingers. His back was strong, hers was too under his hands, and together they shed their delicate human skin. Time was slow, each stage of the morph was distinct. Each bump on their spines became spikes, their wing bones widened and powerfully extended as their torsos did also. Soon his arms did not encircle her. Emerging in front of him was an amethyst dragoness of pure beauty. He was stunned that there was such a thing as a purple dragon and Kalara took that chance to kick away from him, flying once again and breaking the mental connection.

They were both now back to their true forms and he could not allow her to get away, ever. He could sense her come-hither-if-you-can-aura, and it intrigued him to obey. He was covered with her pheromones, smelling them, enticing him, he knew she was young, alone, and would soon be his, and besides, she had chosen to keep his fire opals.

He pumped his wings as hard as he could. That Mighty Amethyst dragoness would not best him. She was giving him a good flight though and putting him through all the moves. All he now lacked was a small distance, the temptation to cast a spell and skip the lag entered his mind – but no, he refused to cheat, not on this, not on such a grand and spectacular dragoness. He would win her fairly and with pure raw strength, magic would somehow cheapen his victory. No, he wouldn't use it unless she did first. He pumped harder and focused on her purple wings, trying to predict her path. She was using the updrafts, soaring and rolling, enjoying the pursuit.

He gave her time, watching her, learning her. Finally seeing his chance, Ravanan pumped his powerful wing muscles harder and faster than ever and closed in on his prize. With a viper's quickness he grappled her, using his larger weight to take her down. Now they were falling, falling so fast it took his breath away (even down to the pain in his hurting chest, Ravanan planted his remembered feelings deep inside Kalara's fragile mind).

The purple dragoness wasn't helping him fly and he wouldn't let go of her. As close as their bodies were, they were still very separate dragons in flight. The ground was getting closer, the tree canopy no longer looked like smooth green velvet. This was the final test. Would she agree to join him? It had to be now or it was over.

With her next breath the young Kalara opened her thoughts to him and they curved off the fall together. Her mind was racing with the daredevil fall, she had enjoyed every heartbeat of it.

Flying fast over the jungle with Kalara under him, Ravanan captured her neck, entwining it with his and taking control of her path. The rhythm of her purple wings was synced up with his as their minds worked together to fly. The rush of air against them was exhilarating and Ravanan knew that Kalara could feel it in his memory.

In that moment he gave Kalara the feeling of flight, the most basic of gifts, it was something that even hatchlings were capable of, but not her, not until now. Ravanan wanted to give her the full experience of flying, the physics of every wing-beat was important. He did not fast-forward through a single turn, wanting her to know how the muscles felt as they flexed and worked with the wind. In every detail Ravanan etched it to her brain cells, ensuring she would absolutely not forget this important memory of their lives together.

Minds melded, wings beating and bodies turning the same way in the air, flying together they started to head back, it would be a long and hard flight back to Black Blade Lair, *their* lair.

Ravanan was thoroughly enjoying himself as all memories are full of emotion and salted with embellishment. This was the closest he had felt to Kalara in a while. It was hard to stop the memory replay but he forced himself to, fearing to continue on with such a powerful moment of their love – the memory of which would undoubtedly cause him to lose the control spell connection.

He was sure he had been successful in the memory transplant from the rapid firing of Kalara's neurons. The historic notion of flying was so strongly embedded in Kalara's mind that he could even feel the phantom muscular spasms of her body in flight.

Still controlling her, Ravanan was sure any time now the old Kalara would return to him. He was ready for it.

"So do you understand now why your loss is so hard for me?" He asked her from inside her mind. "You've got to feel that Kalara, I can sense that you do feel it, those feelings were so strong that even your subconscious mind still remembers them."

"Now," Ravanan instructed Kalara as he once again mentally stood with her on the narrow piece of land, "You will fly beside me over these chasms to get your past back."

He held out his hand and she took it.

They took off together, making progress over the darkness below them. Kalara was doing fine. They came to the other side, the vast expanse of barren rock that promised her memories and hovered there.

Ravanan said "This is it Kalara. All you have to do is land, just step down. Your identity is here."

She stepped down. The moment she did they were once again on the narrow pinnacle.

Surrounded by the dark chasms, Ravanan was at a loss. He was glad Kalara couldn't see his body because a few tears escaped from his human eyes. In frustration, he mentally grabbed her hand again and they took off flying straight up, leaving the whole scene behind.

Though the attempt failed Ravanan still held hope for Kalara.

"Don't focus on what didn't happen." he said to her. "Just relax as you have been doing."

He collected his thoughts about him. There had to be a reason that his spells were not successful, he only needed to find it. He reaffirmed his control over her by walking her in a circle and feeling relieved when she did.

Not deterred, Ravanan addressed another of his agendas, finding his gold. He knew somewhere in her muddled mind must be a road map to Annette. Looking in her recent memories, he realized he hadn't had Kalara show him where Jenniffer took her to stay. He did that now by instructing Kalara to think about it and go in every room. He saw very clearly the small apartment that Kalara had been living in. It was made with cheap human-made materials that easily fell apart, not lasting more than a few decades, nothing like the strong rock of Black Blade lair.

Then Ravanan instructed Kalara to leave the apartment. She did, even turning around to show him the door that had the number 208 posted on it. There was an outdoor staircase that she went down.

Now he was getting somewhere with her. Ravanan made note of the trees and topography. Kalara even looked behind her at the style and color of the apartment complex, tan with green trim.

Then he told her to walk to the mall where he had found her – here the road map fell apart. The landscape and buildings all tended to look the same, typical and nondescript. The wonder of being inside a car was apparently more exciting than driving through the outside world. Some buildings were remarkable enough for Kalara to remember, but for the most part she hadn't cared enough to observe where she was – which was very uncharacteristic for a dragon. Eventually Ravanan gave up and told her to stop.

If only he knew where to look for Annette. She had to be somewhere in the middle of the continent.

Kalara's body started walking to the middle of the chamber, just like Ravanan did when he wanted to morph back to his base dragon form.

Then she heard him say "Oh, we almost forgot, I know you don't want that robe ripped in two when you shed your tiny human form." She felt the ceremonial healing robe leave her body to be stored once again. Now she was naked, even though she couldn't look down to see her skin she still felt the openness and cool cavern air on her most private of body parts.

She was walking, not of her own volition but willing all the same. She was trying very hard to stay calm despite her anticipation. It was going to happen, after a year of waiting, she was going to find her past. Ravanan must have observed her thoughts because she heard him cast "*CALM*" on her. Her heart and breathing immediately slowed down, and she didn't mind at all because it was for the best, she wanted this, desperately.

Her body arrived at the destination point, and almost immediately she heard herself cast "*REMEMBER EVERYTHING FROM MY LIFE*".

Nothing happened. No memories, no past, they weren't there. The whole spell had been for nothing.

Her world was quiet.

Kalara felt Ravanan walk out of her mind which made her feel even more empty. She had nothing he wanted, not even hope. She was truly alone. There was nothing inside of her, not even a person, she was hollow.

It hadn't worked.

She ran, not caring where, she just took off and ended up at the seer pool. She was crying and fully expecting to die soon, it didn't matter, nobody knew her or what she was. What she was didn't even have a name, she was a grotesque mishap that reeked of humanity.

Ravanan came near her at the water's edge and she braced herself for the killing blow. She bowed her head and pulled her hair around to the front, exposing her neck.

Without looking up Kalara said "I'm ready. You don't have to say anything, just get it over with."

She was hurting so bad she let her tears fall without wiping them, it didn't matter for soon she would be dead, her human body was motionless with sadness.

Had Kalara been even remotely sensitive or aware, or had looked at him, she would have seen his tears, his pain. Ravanan was in as much agony as her.

Ignoring her, he released his sapphire robe back to the wardrobe chamber and jumped into the seer pool, swimming deeper with every stroke until he couldn't be seen. He didn't return.

Chapter 11

T odd was worried for his step-mom. Almost a month had passed
since she had left to get Kalara. He couldn't call her because she
had intentionally left her phone. If only she had said where she was
headed maybe he wouldn't worry so much.

The needs of their people continued though, and Todd was glad
that he had stayed behind to help his tribe, or rather, he was glad for
any opportunity to visit the sweat lodge and pay an offering to speak
with the ancestors. The tribal elders didn't like it though because he
was so young, they forbade anyone from referring to him as a
medicine man or going to him officially for their needs even though
everyone knew Annette's special connection with the ancestors was
also in him. His medicine worked, even his healing salve and chant
worked, but like all of his various medicines and tasks it came with a
price he was happy to pay. The drawback being he had to pay first
every time before he could work his medicine, making his patrons
have to wait outside of the lodge. It would be exhausting and
impossible work without the stamina that came from the gift of the
rooster and a high protein diet.

Todd had always had a high sex drive, just as much as any other
guy, if not slightly above the norm. But as often as the Earth was
taking his seed, his lifestyle was not sustainable without the extra
testosterone. Sometimes the thought would cross his mind how very
peculiar his spiritual calling was, to have sexual relations with the
Great Spirit, sometimes several times in one day, was unbelievable,
but his ancestors had known what was expected of him and had given
him a way to cope with the task; a drain that would surely destroy a
regular man. And as with any beneficial situation, the one receiving
the benefits did all they could to minimize drawing attention to it and
risk losing it, in other words – he didn't talk about it. Todd didn't want
it to end and was giddy with happiness, to question it would be folly.
The Great Spirit was blessing him, his muscles were bigger, his mind
was sharper, his medicine was powerful, and of course there was the

pleasure of knowing he was giving himself to the most beautiful being in the universe, life could not be better for him.

But one thought kept nagging at him, how had Jenniffer known about the gift of the rooster? He also found it odd that his sister was with Bill at all, it didn't make any sense.

One morning he decided to find out and went over to Bill's house. Sure enough, Jenniffer was there and he had woken them both up. He waited outside the front door and he could hear his sister being her usual grumpy self, she never had been a morning person.

Footsteps thundered to the door.

Bill opened the door, his cheek was red from a slap and fresh fingernail tracks. Todd didn't know what to say so he just nodded and walked in. Bill went to the bathroom and Todd was left standing in the living room. Jenniffer bolted from the bedroom carrying her high heels and purse, making a beeline for the door. "Good morning Jenniffer, sleep alright?" Todd grinned.

"Go to hell Todd. Go straight to hell."

Todd followed her outside, "Did he hurt you?!"

"Yeah, his morning breath is vile. The disgusting pig should have killed himself instead of trying to be in my world."

Todd held her arm to keep her from leaving. "Seriously, are you alright?"

Jenniffer huffed, she rolled her iridescent-blue-green eyes and glared at her brother "No, I'm not fucking alright!" she began to cry.

"What did he do to you?" Todd demanded.

"Nothing."

"Then why are you crying?"

She only shook her head and looked away.

"What the hell? What is wrong with you?"

"It's Annette. She..." and then Jenniffer dropped what she was saying and hung her head.

His heart skipped a beat "Annette?! Is she here? Why didn't she come to the house first?"

"No, I haven't heard from the bitch." Jenniffer tried to wiggle free from his grip.

Todd wanted to slap her for calling their step-mom that but he didn't. But neither did he release his vice-tight hold on her arm. "Then what are you blaming her for? Tell me what is going on! You look horrible, like you haven't slept in days."

"Todd, I want to tell you, but I can't, I just can't. Now let my arm go. I want to leave." She was frantically trying to pull away like a raccoon caught in a claw trap.

"Fine!" Todd let her go "Just tell me this, do you like Bill or not?"

"Hell no!"

"Then why are you sleeping with him?"

Jenniffer didn't answer him, she slammed the car door shut and sped off, kicking dust in the air and leaving deep tracks in the yard.

Todd found Bill in his kitchen and took him by the neck. "What the hell did you do to my sister?"

"Nothing, I swear!"

"Yeah, she said the same thing and I don't believe it. You raped her didn't you?"

"Come on Todd! You think I'd do something like that? I mean, I know you two aren't close or anything, but I would never harm her, she's your sister. I love her."

Todd shoved him hard "Like hell you do! What did you do to her? Is it the gift of the rooster? Has it messed you up? Tell me what you did!"

"I woke up. It's like this every morning. I wake up looking into her pretty face, watching her sleep. That's all – I swear – I watch her sleep and then as soon as her rainbow eyes open and she sees me, she slaps the snot out of me and storms out of the house. She is so different in the mornings! At night, everything is great, she's happy, I'm happy, then the sun comes up. If she wasn't so hot and I wasn't so freaking horny all the time I wouldn't be with her. I mean she is a pussy cat at night, but man alive, daylight comes and you'd think I was bedding down with a man-eating tiger. We ought to call her Dr. Jekyll and Ms. Hyde."

"No kidding?"

"Like I'm gonna lie to a medicine man... or my best friend for that matter."

"But it doesn't make any sense."

"I know, I can't figure it out either."

"Well, when did she start being this way? Was it after you took the gift of the rooster?"

"It has been this way all along with her, ever since I looked at her car."

"There was nothing wrong with it was there?"

"Nothing. I figured it was just a way to get me in bed."

"Yeah, I thought the car sounded fine when I heard it. Can you believe she got rid of her corvette? What is going on with her?"

Bill shrugged.

"Look, Bill, you are the closest thing I have to a brother and I want to believe you, but I can't. I know my sister and she don't like you. And just because she ain't my favorite person in the world doesn't give you the right to hurt her. I know what I saw and it doesn't look to me like Jenniffer wants to be here. So why was she? How did you get her here?"

"She drives over here."

"You're telling me that my sister drives for over an hour so she can fuck a guy that she can't stand? Something isn't adding up. Don't you find it odd that she went from hating you to wanting you? I do, and I think somehow you are making her do it."

"Are you calling me a liar? I told you, we love each other. We are SLEEPING TOGETHER! Don't you get it? Now I told you all I know, why don't you go talk to her about it? Better yet, if you don't believe me, then get your ass over here at night and watch!"

"I just might do that."

"Great. Enjoy the show. Maybe you'll see her tramp stamp, it has my name on it."

"Shut the fuck up!" Todd drove his fist into Bill's cheek.

"That was a bad idea" Bill said as he wiped a trickle of blood from his mouth and reared back with a tight fist. But he didn't get the chance to throw it because Todd was quicker and didn't wait for a gentleman's word exchange. Punch after punch came at Bill's face, there was no time to defend against Todd's fury, however, the fist fight was in Bill's kitchen and he knew the path of retreat would take him over the dog's water bowl and to the knife drawer. Bill acted the punching bag and back-stepped strategically over the water trap, letting Todd trip in it.

Todd looked up from the water puddle to a serrated blade. Bill wielded the knife out the back of his fist with his arm drawn across Todd's chest. "I don't want to fight you Todd" he warned. But Todd was getting ready to lunge, fueled by twice as much testosterone as a man should have.

"Too bad!" Todd knocked him down and pried the knife away. The punching resumed, with every hit Todd said his words "Leave. My. Sister. Alone!"

"NO!" Bill roared and with a mighty strength he flung his arms wide, grabbed Todd by the shoulders, then launched Todd across the floor. Once free, Bill scrambled outside. Todd followed and was surprised at the door as Bill planted his foot in the small of Todd's back and kicked him into the yard. "Get your ass outta my house! And don't come back until you know I'm not lying!" The door slammed and locked. Todd started to break the old door down then thought better of it when he heard Bill cock his gun.

Todd drove out that afternoon to see Jenniffer in Tulsa. He knocked on the door "Jenniffer? You home?", he waited "I went by your work, they said you got fired. Why didn't you tell me? Come on Jenniffer..... Open the door."

"Go away Todd."

"No. We need to talk."

"I don't want to see you."

"Fine by me. I'll just yell really loud. WHY ARE YOU SLEEPING WITH BILL?"

She didn't answer.

"WHERE ARE YOU CATS JENNIFFER? LET'S TALK ABOUT THAT!"

That did it. Jenniffer opened the door "Shhhhhh, everyone will hear you. Don't say it please." she said as she went back to the couch where apparently she had been sleeping moments before.

Todd joined her in the living room. The apartment looked fine considering Todd hadn't been there in over two years, the only thing wrong or missing was her cats. "Jenniffer, I didn't come over here to fight. I'm worried about you. I can be nice if you can."

Jenniffer gave a laugh "Did I miss something? Is it Christmas already?"

"Are you alright? I didn't know what to think this morning. I mean, look at you..." he paused to take in her rats-nest-hair-do "It's like you've just given up trying to be pretty."

"Todd, you don't have a clue what I'm going through. Just leave it at that."

"How can I – when obviously something bad is bothering you? Is it the cats? I know that must have been hard for you, I'm sorry you had to do that."

"It's more than that."

"What then? Why did you lose your job? And why were you over at Bill's last night?"

"I can't tell you because Annette won't let me."

"Oh. Don't worry about that, I won't tell her you told me. What is going on?"

"No, you're not getting it, I am not able to talk about it, even though I want to."

"OK then," Todd looked puzzled ".....let's talk about Bill."

"Jeez, Todd, what is there to say? I hate your friend, you know that." She grabbed the remote, quickly losing interest in the conversation because she knew it was going nowhere.

Todd kept on at her. "How do you know about the gift of the rooster?"

Jenniffer looked a little lost at first but then remembered "Oh, yeah, that. Boy that is really gross isn't it? Did you really do it?"

"You didn't answer me, how do you know about it?"

"Can't really say." she tried to focus on the TV.

Todd was getting nowhere with her. "Why do you go over to Bill's? If he is abusing you then stay away from him." He ignored the TV and noticed a tear falling down her face. "Oh, that's it! I'm gonna kill him. The son of a bitch."

Jenniffer turned to him "No Todd, don't. It's not him. I hate him but he has nothing to do with this."

"You are not giving me anything here. What am I supposed to do? Sit back and watch you get raped?"

Her face was wet with tears, "He isn't raping me. He's not making me do anything. It's all me and I don't want it to be. I don't want to be with him."

"Then why are you?"

Jenniffer was quiet. She'd had many days to think and plan when she wasn't trying to catch up on sleep. She looked down at her coffee table where there laid her make-up mirror, fresh clean towel, a paring knife, and a big spoon. The trash can was waiting next to the table to receive her eyeballs if she could ever muster up the guts to do it. She wanted to so bad but every time Jenniffer got ready to pluck out her eyes, knife in hand, she froze in a panic the fear of pain was too great. Todd hadn't even noticed her make-shift surgery table, it was all perfectly normal for their little messed-up family to have knives lying around.

In all her planning though, she'd been riddled with emotional shock and stress, unable to think properly, and hadn't considered going to Todd for help. He'd never been her first choice for help because she knew he was close to Annette. Annette, the bitch, oh how she hated that woman.

Annette was continuously on her mind throughout her bizarre but regular day, every day she would wake at Bill's mid-morning, drive home, bath, sleep some more, sit on the couch, then at sundown Annette caused her to go sell her body for a while until she drove out to Bill's to finish the night. The days were running together to the point where she was nearly a zombie and the calendar date no longer mattered.

She wondered if she could trust Todd now, she knew he didn't know about her possession and she wondered what he would think about it if he did. She remembered the dandelion puff curse, she hadn't tried to write it down because she didn't want her fingers to break, and she knew she couldn't talk about it either. What would Todd do if he found out? Jenniffer wondered what Todd was doing now without

Annette around and guessed that he was still as loyal as ever to their step-mom.

"Let me think", she was trying to clear her thoughts and begin a new plan, but what seemed logical to her was skewed by her irrational thinking.

"Alright." Todd waited.

An idea came to mind. Jenniffer reached out and took the knife in her hand and held her breath.

"Jenniffer.... what are you doing?" Todd was apprehensively inching backwards, he didn't know whether to flee or grab her.

She would do a test and she knew that one possible outcome of the test would be that she would finally dig her eyes out of her skull. It all depended on what her brother's reaction was. Maybe he really knew about her already and was just being mean to her. It could all be over so quick, the possession curse would end. She could be free, he could watch her do it.

As Todd watched, Jenniffer reached up and delicately placed the point of the blade to the corner of her eye.

"Stop!" Todd scrambled into action. "What are you doing?! Stop!" he reached over and grasped her hands. "Jenniffer, what are you doing?!" he pulled the knife from her hands.

She didn't fight him but she wasn't relieved either, she had wanted the other outcome.

"They're not contac....." her voice faded. Jenniffer's fingers went to her eye and held it open and leaned in close for Todd to see.

Todd was stunned. Her blueish green beautiful eyes were real, the irises had a three-dimensional depth to them they captured the light and reflected an iridescence that was a perfect match to peacock feathers. "Whoa! They're real! How did you get them to look like that?"

Her lips shut and she warned him that she couldn't talk about it by shaking her head.

"Jenniffer, come on, surely you can say something. You're scaring me. You don't like your eyes? How did you do it? I think they're awesome! But I'm taking all your knives now, you know that don't you?"

Jenniffer wanted to say something but knew that no words would come out of her mouth until her thoughts changed. It was hard to stop thinking about it, her intense hatred of Annette was what fueled her and kept her going. She thought about the curse and possession so much that she worried she may go mad from that singular thought. Jenniffer turned back to the TV in an effort to think about something else. A loud infomercial came on the air then, breaking her concentration for a moment, as they are so good at doing.

After the commercial she looked at the clock to see how much longer she had until the sun went down, then she spoke. "Follow me in your car. Let's go to a movie right now, but stay away from me and only watch what I do afterwards. No matter what, don't talk to me."

"Alright, I've got time. But why can't we talk or sit together?"

"Because I can't!" She angrily stood up to get ready, wiping a tear from her eye.

Todd noticed the top edge of a tattoo when she got up, it was hard to miss. "Hey wait a minute, did you get a tattoo?"

Jenniffer froze where she was with her back to him. She sighed and then dropped her jeans just far enough for him to see a wild tramp stamp, it said 'Bill's Parking Space' underscored with an oil spill like what would be seen in a mechanics garage, there were deer antlers also, and it was bordered with camouflage and flames.

"Oh man Jenniffer. You do know what that says don't you?"

"Don't remind me."

On the way out the door Todd confiscated all of her knives.

Jenniffer walked out of the theater when the movie ended, Todd followed her discreetly. He watched her target a man who had just seen the same showing, he was alone. Todd saw his sister escort him outside into the night where she used her yellow car for an office. Never once did she look Todd's way and he was in total disbelief at what he saw. After a while of steamy car windows, the man got out and she drove onto the highway to head east out of Tulsa.

Todd followed her all the way to Bill's house, he hung back and actually parked on the highway, then he hiked through the woods and crossed Bill's yard under the cover of night. Todd saw Jenniffer's yellow car in his drive, she was already inside. He stood under Bill's bedroom window and got an ear full of the lovers. Bill had conveniently left his curtains pulled back, there was no mistaken, Jenniffer was having a lot of intense fun with his best friend. Todd felt very weird having seen what he did and quickly left, not able to explain what he'd just witnessed.

Todd couldn't rest, he checked the clock and saw it was early still. Using the excuse of hunting, he drove over and banged on Bill's door a mere four hours after he'd left them.

Finally, Bill answered "What are you doing here?"

"Telling you you're not lying."

"Come on in then." Bill offered him a beer. "It's too early for coffee."

Jenniffer appeared at the doorway, a dirty sheet wrapped around her. "Todd?! What are you doing here?"

Todd looked over at Bill who was trying to come up with an answer. It was obvious Bill was worried he would be slapped.

Todd answered quickly for them both. "We're gonna go hunting, wanna come?" he smiled. He knew Jenniffer hated killing innocent animals.

"No, y'all go on."

"Well, alright then. Bill, go get dressed already, we're probably missing that big buck."

Bill jumped up and happily left them alone.

Jenniffer yawned, "Well, I'm going back to bed."

"Hey sister, you're up. Let's talk."

"No, I'm tired. You should be too."

"Can I ask you something?"

"No."

Todd got up and stepped in her path. "Sister, I just have to know, how did you know about the gift of the rooster?"

"What?" her eyes avoided him, "Oh, yeah, you helped Bill with that didn't you? Thanks."

"But how did you find out about it? Did Annette tell you?"

"Yes, she did, she thought it could help Bill and I. Now good night Todd."

He blocked her attempted detour. "But it's so gross, why did you go along with it?"

"It's not that gross, you did it, and besides, Bill needed help."

"But I thought you hated Bill. So why are you here?"

"He's good in bed." she smiled and evaded him.

Todd let her go, he was more puzzled than ever.

On the way to their favorite hunting spot Todd apologized to Bill.

Bill was easy to forgive his best friend. "No problem. You see what I mean though? She was all over me."

"OK, OK. No more visuals please? I just want to figure out why."

"What? You don't think I'm good enough for her?" Bill asked defensively. The extra testosterone in Bill's blood was affecting his sensitivity.

"Settle down, I didn't say that, you're better than she deserves, but I just want to figure out why Jenniffer is lying and hitting you every morning. Don't you want to know too? Better to find out now before y'all get married instead of ending in divorce."

Bill straightened his jacket, "I guess you're right. What did you think of her tramp stamp? I designed it."

"Yeah, I thought so, it has everything you love on it."

"She makes it look good too."

"Come on, man! No guy should have to see his sister that way."

"Alright, alright. Let me know if you find out anything."

"I will, don't worry. Until then, why don't you stop sleeping with her?"

"No way. I'm sorry, but no way."

"You idiot, I mean after your fun, send her home. Or better yet, why don't you start going to Tulsa, then you can leave afterwards and no harm done?"

"Oh, I guess I could do that."

Todd was anxious to get to the sweat lodge that morning. After he'd paid his sexual offering to the veiled goddess he reverently knelt and asked "Great Mother Earth, please fix Jenniffer before she hurts my friend."

The tingly voice shattered and spoke "The rooster's gift protects him, do not worry for him."

"Great Spirit, if he is fine, then what of Jenniffer? Please fix what is wrong with her."

"She is not broken."

"She is not happy during the day." Todd returned.

"Rightly so. Your sister hunts at night, and during daylight she wishes she was hunting."

"She doesn't seem to be longing to hunt."

There was no answer. Todd feared the ceremony was over. "Great Spirit, please, how can I help her to be happy?"

There was no answer. The smoke began rising normally again and faded into the daylight. He knew the ceremony had ended.

After a quick lunch and a healing rub for Ms. Whilamer's arthritis, Todd went back to Tulsa and to Jenniffer's apartment.

He knocked lightly on her door. "Jenniffer, it's Todd again, can you open the door?"

The door opened.

Jenniffer looked a mess "Well? Did you follow me?"

"Yes I did. Can you talk about it now?"

"No."

"Alright then, listen to me while I talk. I saw you last night with Bill."

"Oh, Jeez."

"I'll ask you again, Do you like Bill?"

"No."

"What? I can't help you if you are going to lie to me. I saw you with him, not that it was something I wanted to see. But yeah, you were on top, you were happy – I think. Do you at least remember what I said to you this morning when I came to get Bill for hunting?"

"Yes, you asked me to go with you, then you asked about the gift of the cock and why I was with Bill."

"Yeah, and you said he was good in bed. You also didn't seem to care that we were going hunting to kill an animal which is odd. So why were you there?"

"I told you I can't tell you."

"Fine. Then what can you tell me?! Can you explain how you knew about gift of the rooster?"

"Annette kinda told me."

"I find that hard to believe."

"Believe what you want to. I knew it was too good to be true that you would help me."

"Jenniffer, come on. I'm trying to but you are making it difficult, just tell me why you are different at night. Why are you whoring around?"

Jenniffer ignored him by turning back to her TV with a face of stone and beautiful eyes that were full of tears.

"Whatever." Todd grabbed his truck keys out of his pocket. "You are screwed up in the head, you know that? If you won't talk to me, then at least meditate and reach out to our ancestors, tell them your problems and maybe they'll send you a spirit guide to help you." He walked to the door, "One last thing – stay away from Bill." He shut the door behind him.

Chapter 12

I t felt good to leave his tears in the seer pool so he wouldn't have to know their sting. The cold water shocked his system but not as much as that spell's unexpected failure shocked him. He was devastated. Why didn't that spell work, especially when so much was pending on its success? Kalara's words echoed in his ears, *'You don't have to say anything, just get it over with.'* He couldn't do it, the thought of taking her life caused his stomach to knot up, he felt bad enough without her having to say that. The water took his tears but it could not wash away the image of her standing at the water's edge, exposing her lovely neck, waiting for the killing blow. He hated himself for loving her still. No matter how hard he tried he could not tear Kalara from his heart. Ravanan wanted to forget ever finding her alive.

He had placed so much expectation on that spell, wanting to bring his mate back to life, that when it failed Kalara died all over again in his mind. It was too much to relive, his chest quaked in sorrow and the chilly subterranean water offered no solace. She was gone, dead to him, and she had been for nearly a year. He shouldn't be broken down and weeping, but he was. Even as he felt his aura kick in and take over his breathing, he swam deeper, he continued to shed tears.

It was difficult to have her body back but not his mate, and seeing her constantly reminded him of his loss. They had done so many things together, shared a history that spanned two thousand years, there was a familiarity and a history there that the woman currently staying in his lair just did not have, but he did.

Ravanan knew the flooded cave shaft backwards and forwards, and though he didn't need light to navigate he cast *"STARLIGHT"* anyway for comfort. He was tired of constantly being reminded of her fate which was worse than death, tired of the oppressive sadness in the lair, he longed to be out and in the bright daylight, free and away from things he could not change.

He could not fix her. He had put everything into those spells, they were powerful, and so rare that he'd actually felt faint from the depletion of his magical blood when he cast them. It wasn't a lot of blood but he could feel the loss all the same. He even felt the drop in Kalara's blood when that final spell was cast through her by his mind control. The spells were sent out, why didn't they work? They should have. She was calm, unguarded, no defenses, no armor, and she was willing. His other spells worked on her, so why didn't these? It was true the spells were not efficient or well-practiced but they still should have worked, his blood loss was testament to that. It went against the very principle of magic and there was no reason for it.

She trusted him, believed he would help her, she needed him and he let her down. He felt flawed and less than the dragon he thought he was, he wasn't good enough to undo her damage. He failed to find her past and seeing her would only make him remember his failure. No, he wouldn't even gaze upon her. He didn't want to be near her, but he couldn't bring himself to kill or imprison her either, the only thing he knew to do was leave. She didn't need his protection now that she was home and under his blue mist. He didn't have to be there. She was safe in Black Blade.

Kalara's reaction to the failed spell had been to run from him he was sure, he knew she thought of him as cruel and that he didn't love her, she was ignorant enough to mistaken his irritation of having to constantly teach another dragon as hatred. He could still feel her aura, it was powerfully sorrowful, yearning and calling out for him, it pained him not to answer it but he had to get away from the hurt.

He would be beyond her siren call when he entered the main flow, already he could feel the current begin to pick up speed. He couldn't shake the ruinous feelings of not being able to help her. He hated failure. He hadn't failed in a task in over a thousand years, defeat was unknown to him. To be unable to solve the one problem his mate had was eating him up.

Even though he knew his mate was gone for good, Ravanan could not kill that woman, not yet. He wasn't to that point and he didn't know if he would ever be. But if that horrible day did come he would be the one to end her life, not the Acamas. He feared that day would come soon. Acama business was so random and unpredictable. He knew they would find out about Kalara's condition, it was only a matter of when. All one of them had to do was summon her and when she didn't show up they would come calling. She thought he wasn't in a hurry to recover her memories, but she couldn't be more wrong.

In his efforts, he had done the unthinkable, used his prime spell of manipulation on Kalara, he'd treated her like a lesser being, a mere human. He controlled her mind as he had countless times on prey. He knew what his spell did to the mind, he crafted the damned thing! He knew how it ripped the mind away from the spinal cord and unplugged it from the very core of feelings and signals and yet he did it anyway – at her request.

Invariably, death was rewarded quickly to his victims so there was never an issue of long-term effects but if one were to be left alive such as she was, he knew the tear would take time to mend and he surmised she'd have a tremendous and lengthy headache with possible irrevocable mental scarring.

As the pressure of the water increased, so did his anger. He hated himself for controlling her, even though he'd used it only as a last resort and she wanted him to do it, he shouldn't have, he was just so desperate to bring his mate back from the dead. He cursed himself for listening to her sweet, enticing, persuasive talk. In all his life he never could resist her and he knew it wasn't her aura or magic, it was just her, there was no magical defense against love and it was maddening. To listen to the reasoning of a dragoness, especially one that is a step away from insanity, instead of following his own common sense was idiotic and he hoped nothing bad would happen to her mind because he had walked inside her head.

He realized that the chances of getting her memories back were slim, but if somehow he found a way, what was she going to think after she finally woke up from her amnesia and she remembered he had laid with a lesser being during her absence, taken advantage of her frailty. What was he to do? How could he know whether to take the ruined Kalara to his bed every night or stay away from her?

Ravanan tried to think more on what his mate would want, he marveled that after two millennia with Kalara he wasn't sure, it felt like he should know her better than that. The topic of 'what if you lose your mind?' had never come up. Ravanan wondered if any other dragon had ever suffered the same fate. He hoped his mate would understand his dilemma if she ever came back, but if she wouldn't forgive him he'd at least be happy her mind was restored and then he could focus fully on working things out with her, provided she didn't try to kill him.

Then Ravanan considered something worse, what would she do when she remembered he'd walked inside her mind, controlled her, treated her like livestock and severed her neurons? He contemplated that she might hate him because he had done that to her.

In all ways things were grim, he was alone and with no treasure, nothing to show for his life.

He entered the main water course then, with its large tunnel and fast moving current. He allowed his human body to transform back, becoming once again the magnificent blue dragon that he was. He didn't hate the human form but he didn't love it either, it was merely another tool in his arsenal. One thing he didn't like about using a human body was its easy manner of turning sadness into all-out crying, that was one thing he didn't need. But it was the one thing he felt like doing.

He heard Kalara's sweet voice again. '*You don't have to say anything, just get it over with.*' She was ready to die. He wanted to roar in upset. He felt the water pick up even more speed, there was no turning back from its pursuit of sea level and freedom. He could see the familiar faint light up ahead. He was ready, more than ready. Heartbeats later he launched like a bullet from the top of the waterfall, beating his powerful wings to soar out over the jungle and dry his cerulean blue scales with the warm sun.

His waterfall was far below him now, splashing into mist and flowing out to join the larger river, Ravanan bellowed a mighty roar and flew free, hearing the non-sounds of the quieted and fear-stricken creatures of the jungle. He favored the wild panic of his aura accompanied with a good, throat-clearing, fierce roar and longed for the places such as this where he could get away with it. Today however, even his Dragon Fear was not enough to make him happy.

How would he ever find Annette? As much as he wanted to kill her, he could not deny she was interesting. The silver dragoness was cunning enough to trap an Acama and smart enough to break through the protective wards on his treasure chamber which he had thought were impenetrable. He'd love to know how Annette trapped Kalara, she had to be a powerful dragoness indeed. But even with all that power why would she want to bring the wrath of all dragons down on her? What made Annette want her Acama's treasure anyway?

Their treasure, Ravanan pictured it in his mind. If Kalara could see it, the material history that recorded their love, maybe then her memories would return. Ravanan did a quick review in his head, seeing again the many etchings, sculptures, and outright acquisitions they had made and claimed. He chided himself then, knowing that Annette would have erased all his work to make her own meaningful art. He took a sharp breath out of anger at the thought. Even if Annette had melted all of it, it didn't matter to him, he wanted it back, all of it. He would craft it all again from his memory. He did it once and he knew he could remake each piece.

He went back through all he'd learned from Kalara's weak mind but there simply wasn't enough pieces to track Annette down. He was going to have to resort to the lengthy and slow method of search-under-every-rock just as he had done for Kalara. It would take a while and that was alright with him, he wasn't ready to be back at Black Blade lair any time soon. He would see and smell everything, somewhere was a clue, somewhere he would find Annette, force her to cure Kalara, then kill the wretched dragoness and take back his gold.

With a new day came a better mood. The untamed jungle was alive with color. His rain forest was among the most beautiful in the world, maybe not quite as breath-taking as some of the islands he had seen but this was home. Fed by steady water, the land steamed when it wasn't raining. The grand Amazon River was a source of life, the many floods over the years decorating and sculpting the river basin. He rather enjoyed the catastrophes and seeing how humans responded to them. Every century there always seemed to be 'The Big Flood' that took out human dwellings and provided him and his kind with cover that allowed for great feasting without detection. Natural disasters always made the perfect explanation.

Days went by with no clues but it was good to be outside and away from the lair. The many smells across his territory, from flowers to humans in Manaus, were soothing to his aching heart; he knew they would do wonders for Kalara too. If only he could take her out of the lair for a while. But the sight of her broken body still hung in his mind. It was so sad to see her that way, the unexpected nature of the attack, he couldn't dare let that happen again, not even to try an odd spell that may not work.

Kalara would feel better to get out of the lair for even a short flight. Ravanan questioned how healthy it was to stay cooped up all the time. Each day when he dropped off her food she was the same. He would always bring her food despite his broken heart because he could not kill her. Using the anchors, he was quick about it, masked and invisible – he could not deal with her anymore.

The first time was the hardest, seeing her sleeping that early morning, he just had to get close to her bed, and she just had to be wearing the black robe that he loved, even in her sleep her aura was powerfully wanting him, he had reached and lightly touched her shoulder, he couldn't help himself, but she started to roll over and he vanished. She had called out to him even, but he couldn't answer her back, not yet, maybe never.

The hurt was always there, every day. Finally after a few days of delivering her food and secretly seeing her, he started just drawing anchors each time and sending the food by itself.

Time went on for Ravanan. When he approached his northwestern lands he detected the recent scent of another dragon, he took a second, longer inhale then cast *"ARMOR"* and landed. He felt prickly with alertness, awakened with wide eyes, an intruder!

"Too long." Ravanan spoke under his breath. He knew his mistake, he had been gone for months from his land and then after his return he'd been too concerned with staying near Kalara and the lair, leaving his borders undefended, another lapse in wisdom on his part.

The dragon would regret coming into his land, Ravanan wasn't ready to lose any more than he already had; and he was more than ready to take some answers from the young one.

Before he set out he paused and adjusted to his surroundings. There was a burbling creek some distance away and he was on a small game trail that led to the water. The birds and monkeys near him were going about their day, insects were being slowly sucked of their life by larger insects, and an anaconda had just attempted slithering onto his right wing talon but was unnerved by the invisible armor of air that he was wearing and turned back when half of it' body was hovering a few feet above Ravanan's scaly skin.

The human Manupaco tribe was nearby, he hadn't visited there in a few years, but now was not the time to hunt food as he was set on a course. He moved on through the trees, sometimes through flooded marsh land, splashing and squishing as quietly as possible, determined to track down the one scent that was pungent in his nares.

He heard a movement, the sound was too close to be a dragon because he felt no aura. His great head turned to get a visual and then he cast *"I'LL CONTROL YOU"*. The young warrior was carrying his prey back to the village but he turned instantly and began walking on an intercept path with Ravanan's. In those moments Ravanan read the warrior's mind, to learn that lately there had been more death, and heightened fear of the evil spirit called Kanaimi that lurked in the mountains.

Any other time as their paths crossed Ravanan would have shut his jaw around the man and continued on – but not this time. The tribe was wounded by a foolish young dragon and it needed to recover.

The encroacher had fed frequently on the Manupaco, to the point of increasing their fear. The young fool sealed his fate by being too flashy and open. He would suffer even more for his actions. For even if his mate wasn't an Acama Ravanan would still have been a strict follower of Dragon Law, being very careful to keep all traces of his presence away from man. He even went so far as to use his aura to remove his footprints. He was a careful and vigilant shepherd over his humans. This dragon would pay.

Smelling the forest around him Ravanan sneered and curved his lips, the intruder was young, his scent brash and reckless, arrogant. His body was ready to attack as he followed the trail to the mountains west of the city of Boa Vista. If the scent could be trusted the intruder would be an easy kill.

Ravanan passed out of his territory and into land that before now held little interest for him. The weathered table-top mountains in the Guyana Highlands of Brazil loomed over the jungle, wreathed in clouds. He knew there was a pair of ancient dragons living in one of the mountains but they had never intruded into his lands before and he never bothered them, always keeping the bulk of his hunting to Manaus. This scent he was following didn't smell like them. Their lair was not far and it was a good place to start looking.

His first guess was right, the young dragon's trail led straight to the lair that was located inside a tepui, which was a Brazilian mesa. Near the center of the table top was a hole so wide that three dragons wingtip to wingtip could not span it. The lair was old, formed by rain over the eons, falling into a crevice, widening it, grain by grain. It looked bottomless, a small river was falling into it, endlessly trying to fill it up. A whole ecosystem of mosses and ferns were draped on the wet walls, afraid to descend into the darkness.

From behind lone boulders Ravanan watched the lair for days to learn the daily schedule of the intruder. There were very few trees, the lushness of the forest was not up there on the mesa. The rock was barren, bleached dry by rain, something like a giant bone of the earth. Ravanan searched the whole countryside looking for secondary exits and he found none. All of his movements were slow, methodical, and during the information gathering only two times had he actually been close enough to sense the aura of the dragon. The young brown male hadn't sensed him, as Ravanan stayed completely hidden.

Ravanan suspected for some time that through his exhaustive searching for Kalara his aura detection range had increased. This intruder had given him the perfect chance to test his theory. His detection limit was now nearly three striking distances, while the brown dragon could only detect at the normal two. Ravanan judged by the male's size that he was maybe a century old, no more than two, probably still without a mate, but definitely looking for one. Ravanan had yet to pick up any sign of a dragoness nearby.

Ravanan didn't need to interrogate him to know what he'd done. The brown male had to have bested the ancient pair and took their lair and treasure with his youth, treasure he didn't deserve and Ravanan's gold was now with it. Those ancient dragons didn't just die of old age, there were well-known spells to counteract that. Sometimes, when a dragon is very old, a fight to the death is welcomed, he couldn't see how a young one could win without the battle being given to him, especially against two time-tested dragons that fought perfectly together. It was an esteemed class of dragons, where you could count on the other dragon to always get your back, it was like single-minded and strategic fighting with two bodies because the connection was so great. He and Kalara had been nearing that level of pairing until she forgot everything. He choked as tears rose in his throat from yearning for the past and swallowed hard in an effort to clear his mind.

When he was sure he knew everything there was to know about his opponent, Ravanan began preparing for battle by making an anchor of retreat should things turn for the worse; it was more out of habit than it was doubt of success. Ravanan waited for the night to deepen, thinking by tomorrow night he'd have his treasure back and a whole lot more.

Chapter 13

It was a sunny afternoon in Manaus, Brazil, a cab pulled up to the travel agency and let Annette out. She entered and was greeted in Portuguese by a woman behind the counter.

Annette showed her a picture of a cliff. "I want to climb this" Annette said perfectly in Portuguese, just like she had practiced it.

The travel agent looked at the picture then back to Annette, pausing. This was the first time she had been asked about *that* tepui – everybody knew to not bother with that one. The gray mesa, like others, had a waterfall but unlike others this one had a most unusual scar on one of its cliffs – a black blade of hardened magma that cut across its face, rising at an angle and ending half-way up. The dark gabbro rock was stark against the pale quartzite and at its tip the narrow black sword formed a ledge. It was no good to go to that black, evil rock.

The agent pulled out a brochure to point to the five day jungle tour she offered instead, the tour would at least take Annette near there.

"No." Annette said straightly, it was one of the ten Portuguese words she knew.

The woman smiled and said something else Annette didn't understand.

"No." Annette pushed the brochure away, making sure it was understood that she didn't want the tour.

The woman held up her hand and picked up the telephone. After a short conversation she gestured for Annette to have a sit and handed her a cola to drink while she waited.

Before long a man arrived, he looked to be the owner.

"I am Eduardo Kern, I speak some English can I help you?"

They went to his office and Annette showed him what she wanted to do and what she was willing to pay. The arrangements were made to depart the following morning.

Her tour guide knocked at her door. Annette opened it.

"Good morning, I'm Jeremy, your guide."

"Thanks for coming. I am so glad you speak English."

He chuckled and smiled warmly. "You picked the right travel agency, luckily I work for a couple of them. There aren't a lot of English-speaking guides willing to climb, most just want the jungle and river jobs."

He picked up her bags and she held the door open for him.

"So you're from America?" he asked "I am too."

"I'm from Oklahoma. And you?"

"California. But I got the chance to work down here so I took it."

They talked more as they made their preparations and boarded the helicopter. As they neared the tepui and Annette saw the black sword for the first time, a lump in her throat made her realize what she was about to do.

After being dropped off they prepared for their climb in the rain.

Jeremy had his concerns about the locale but the money she was dishing out was enough for him to proceed and his boss to sign off on the climb – it seemed strange to Jeremy that his boss accepted, he suspected more than money was involved.

It was becoming evident that she was a natural hiker and accustomed to nature. The woman listened and obeyed everything he asked of her. It was a good thing because he needed to concentrate. This particular tepui was largely off limits as a dangerous cliff, of course everyone in Manaus knew of it, but none would speak of it – there was an ill-feeling that came over those that did.

He was good at climbing, really good, but not one to brag, and he gladly accepted the job that his boss could hardly even speak of.

Just moments before he took hold of the rock Annette stopped him so they could pray. She did the oddest thing he had ever seen when she began to chant.

Her short song ended then she said "Take off your gloves, let me see your hands" and she began taking off hers.

"Whoa." he moved back, "What is this? What are we doing? Time is wasting." For him, this was a break in routine and an invasion of his expertise and authority.

"This won't take long, but we can't go until we are blessed. You have made all your preparations now let me make mine."

Jeremy knew he couldn't argue with the person paying for the trip. And he needed her full attention during the climb so he let her carry on and took off his gloves.

Annette reached into her pack and took out something wrapped in plastic wrap, and unfolded it. It was a whitish cream. Using a bunch of feather tufts bound with leather string, she dipped the hand-made brush into the cream, it was gooey.

She dabbed it on his palms and her own, saying "Let us climb with ease like the lizard, fast and sure."

The tour guide felt a warmness from the stinky goo and made to wipe it off on his pants.

"NO!" she warned. "Put your hands together and rub it in, like this" Annette showed him.

It simply smelled something awful. "What is this stuff?" he asked.

"The Great Spirit's gift to us, lizard and frog slime" she answered.

They reached the black ledge without incident and Jeremy set up their tent for the night, wanting to get this job over with.

Annette rested with her beer and pipe, looking out over the jungle far below, her woods seemed like a freshly mowed lawn compared to this place. She was glad he hadn't made a campfire, the forest was better without it.

"Pretty cool isn't it?" Jeremy grabbed a beer and sat down, "makes you want to stay up here forever."

"Don't you know how to be quiet?"

He didn't say another word.

The stars were beyond counting. The forest wasn't quiet. It was a perfect night. There were growls and such but nothing could frighten Annette, no thing and no one except for Kalara. And the fear she felt of Kalara cut deep into her core. Her thirst for power ran a close race with that fear, she would have whatever it was that empowered Kalara, it was real, and it was different than hers.

The actual fear she'd experienced so long ago didn't last that long though, it was for only an afternoon when she'd first met Kalara. After that initial meeting Kalara had become a docile and dazed lamb while Annette now struggled with her desire for more power and also wanting to flee from the dangerous woman at the same time. Finally the simple memory of that terrifying day, the haunt in the back of her mind – *knowing it had been real* – won out and Annette had to distance herself from Kalara. She'd secretly study her from afar, pulling on the mystical resources of Mother Earth more than ever before. Then, thanks to Jenniffer, Kalara's secret power was lost to her, but not for much longer now.

Annette fought her fear and recalled that day over a year ago when they first met, trying to find something, anything in the memory that might help her out tomorrow.

It was the last day of her first rain forest trip. The vacation was her first time to get a passport, Todd and Jenniffer could take care of themselves finally and it was high time for her to do something big for herself. She had decided to do some last minute poking around the forest just outside of Manaus. Having said her goodbyes to her old school friend who unfortunately had to go to work, she confirmed her flight's departure time and mounted her rented dirt bike.

She was glad to soon be leaving the humidity of the Brazilian rain forest behind. It had been the trip of a lifetime, made possible by her friend from the local junior college of years ago. Her tribe was happy for her and promised to look after her animals while she was away for those two weeks. Todd said he'd even pick up her mail and newspaper for her. She could just relax and enjoy herself.

After a few hours of walking around she had managed to find a few useful roots and stones. Up ahead were some eroded boulders at the base of a mountainside; they would be a great spot for lunch and to find some mushrooms.

Making her way through the dense trees, she became aware of a presence.

Pausing to listen, Annette decided to play it safe and be watchful, but not giving in to fearful thoughts. She had grown up in the woods of northeast Oklahoma, the forest didn't frighten her; it never had.

She recited to herself 'Animals are more scared of us then we are of them' she knew it was true. 'If humans just respect their territories, they'll leave us alone or run away.'

Annette continued on through the jungle, yet the feeling of something near her increased.

Her head itched with sweat. She couldn't see any animals around. Just herself alone with the mossy trees. The big rocks were just ahead, maybe another two hundred feet.

The non-sound of someone alert for any noise she might make caused her concern to grow even more. It was the sound of nothing and something at the same time. Fear crept in, unwelcome, but there all the same.

Suddenly the jungle seemed to become a little muted, as if all the colors were running together into a pale green wall. There were no indications of an animal, no color variations. It was unusually quiet, the monkeys and birds had ceased their calls.

Annette tried desperately to put a sight to what she knew had to be there, somewhere near. It must be watching her. She looked but saw nothing.

The big rocks were just too far away. She settled for a bush instead. 'Can it see me in here?' she wondered as she held her breath, trying to not itch her tingling scalp.

'No, this cover is no good.' she took off again.

The game of cat and mouse continued. She glanced over to her right and saw an old tree with a hollowed out trunk.

Heart pounding in trepidation, Annette wiped the dripping sweat from her brow while weighing the distance versus the risk. After working up the nerve to expose herself she quickly ran a few feet away and squeezed herself inside the tree to wait it out.

'It'll pass by and go on.' she told herself.

The vibrant green of the jungle returned.

'I'm no threat to you.' she wished she could tell it.

'It. What was it?' she wondered. Wouldn't it be a jaguar or anaconda? No, a snake wouldn't wait to attack like that. It was probably a jaguar but she thought they hunted at night.

Time passed. She listened. She cursed the humidity with her mind, her fine hairs were sticking to her forehead and neck. Her fingers numbly played with her buffalo bone ring though it gave no solace. Her view from inside the tree showed nothing but brilliant green tropical rain forest. In the far distance she could still see those big rocks. Nothing happened still.

'I'm OK. I'll wait a bit more. Oh thank you Mother Earth! Thank you for sending your creature on elsewhere far away from here.' she prayed.

She peered into the sweltering forest once more and saw nothing. Annette shifted her weight to exit the tree. But just then a new feeling of sweaty dread shook her heart.

It was still hunting her, watching her from the tree cover. Hidden by the graying trees it had moved to get a better view of her.

'Where is it?' She froze, trying to become smaller, transparent to the world. 'I have got to stop breathing, stop my heart. I've got to become a lifeless rock' she desperately told herself. This animal intended to cause her death.

Now her hideout seemed brighter than the gray forest around her. Light was pouring out of the tree's crevice she had barely fit into, beaming into a forest that should have been lit from the midday sun.

'Where is this light coming from? Turn it off!' Annette silently panicked. 'If I'm going to survive this, I've got to work fast.' There was no time for a pipe ceremony, no time for praying to the four directions of the earth.

'Great Mother I need you right now!' she prayed, 'I need you to work this instant.' Thinking up a confusion hex, she clumsily retrieved four sage-and-tobacco-covered dried cat hearts from her medicine bag.

The terror was mounting. Annette was worried that she had never performed instantly before; worried her magic would fail. She gripped the cat hearts with fury. Squeezing the terror from her eyes she entered her trance thinking of nothing but total confusion and she broadcast that command with all the power her mind could muster. In a final heroic moment self-preservation pushed the thought beyond her skull and out into the world with a sonic boom.

Time passed once more. Stiff from standing in her trance while crammed into the tree trunk, the Medicine Woman woke slowly to the hot afternoon sun.

'Did it work?' She wondered, listening for anything, any clue that might say otherwise.

The jungle birds were noisily going about their day, according to them there was nothing wrong.

Rubbing her neck, Annette remembered the time. 'Oh damn! My plane! I've got to get out of here right now. Is it out there? I've got to get going!' she exclaimed.

She listened once more but didn't notice any hint of that terrible animal. Her confusion hex must have worked. The exciting thought of her medicine skills working and getting stronger gave Annette a renewed vigor for the walk back to her dirt bike.

After leaving the tree she loosened her vice-tight grip of the dried cat hearts, now moist and gummy from her sweaty palm. She realized now just how much Mother Earth shared with her. The spirits of all creatures sheltered her, bringing her ever closer to the Spirit World. Nothing but a Prayer of Thanksgiving would do. She dropped the cat hearts to the forest floor and wiped her hands off on her jeans. Annette pulled her pipe from her pocket, packed and lit it. With tobacco smoke encircling her she began to bury the instruments of her spell; returning them to Mother Earth so that one day she might use the cats' spirits again. With a prayer of thanksgiving she started off.

Walking just a few yards, Annette paused when she saw a woman with dark long hair looking in some bushes.

The woman was intent on her search and not aware of Annette standing there. The fair woman was wearing a creamy satin lined robe. The robe's lace and orange jewels were sewn into vague symbols that resembled letters of an archaic alphabet, Annette could not decipher the runes, nor recognize even the type of language it was. The cream colored robe was adorned with intricately carved ivory cabochons inset with distinctive luminescent fire opals, she had never seen their like.

Annette wondered what the woman was doing and why she hadn't noticed her before. Maybe the woman saw that dangerous animal about to attack and scared it away.

She walked up to the woman. "Hello? Hi. Did you see a wild animal a moment ago? Did you scare it away?" Thinking the woman probably didn't know English, Annette kindly smiled, spoke slowly, and used lots of hand gestures to expressively indicate, "My name is Annette. AH NET. Did you scare away a wild animal a moment ago?"

The woman looked up at Annette trying to discern if she was a friend or threat, she watched Annette's every move. Apparently deciding on friend, she spoke. "No, there are no animals around here. I was about to eat a snack and I lost it. Where is my food?" The woman's violet eyes hauntingly bore into Annette's.

Annette assumed the woman was lost and traumatized. "Well, you must be hungry, let me help. We'll look for your snack together."

Annette looked on the ground and in the same bushes the woman had been looking at and saw nothing. She gave up "I'm sorry I don't see it. Look, it's going to be OK. I'll help you. Here, take a drink of my water." While the woman took a drink Annette continued "I've got a bike just over that hill, I can take you back to Manaus if you like, we will get you some food there."

"Manaus? OK. I'll go there."

"Well let's go then." Annette scanned the trees one last time for the wild animal while the woman gave a last glance for her snack. Not finding anything, they took off; never seeing the green shiny bow camouflaged by the forest floor laying just a few yards from where they were.

Once back to town Annette found a restaurant with a patio and tables. "Let me go get us some food at the order window. I'll be back."

Annette brought some fried chicken and water back with her and sat down.

It was just a bit odd how unfamiliar the woman was with the normal way of things, she was dazed and muddled.

"So, what is your name?" Annette prompted.

"Kalara of Kynasteryx Ravyx"

"It's nice to meet you Kalara, I'm glad I could help you get back." Annette had never heard a name like that but she accepted it as a regional thing.

As they began to eat, Annette felt a subtle change in the air. A shift that maybe Kalara didn't need rescuing back in the forest.

A strange feeling came over Annette like when the last warm breeze of the summer blows by on a cool autumn day, she shivered.

With each bite Kalara seemed to be enjoying it more and more.

Trying not to stare, Annette stopped eating when Kalara started biting her chicken bones in half. With each crunch and painful-looking swallow the strange warm feeling increased in Annette until she came to identify it as a spirit energy growing from Kalara.

The sickening sound of the bones breaking and popping sent a new horror straight to Annette's brain.

Aghast, Annette realized Kalara was the one hunting her. It was the woman sitting in front of her who had dimmed the forest and made the inside of that hollow tree glow. She was going to eat her!

Wide eyed, Annette jumped up and backed away, stumbling over chairs, not daring to take her eyes off the woman.

Kalara quizzically watched her and asked "What is it?"

Shear panic kept Annette from answering. The feeling of being hunted again prickled the hair on the back of her neck. What was Kalara planning by this deception? She must get away, fast......"Oh shit! Oh shit!" Annette worried aloud.

She carelessly, stupidly, brought this monster into town; foolishly believing she was helping her. What kind of place is this? Shaking her head in disbelief, Annette spoke out with tears "I've got to get out of here!" Turning, Annette fled down the street and around a corner.

She kept running down another street and made two more corners to evade Kalara. Finding a doorway, she ducked in and held her breath, waiting for the air around her to glow again.

Waiting for what seemed like an eternity, nothing happened and the feeling of dread dissipated. 'She didn't chase me. Maybe she went after someone else.' Annette thought.

Rubbing her well-worn ring, Annette relaxed and cursed herself for being so ridiculous. She needed to think, so she lit up her pipe and tried to attain normality again. Soon the smoke was thick in the air. She was better than this, she didn't need to run. Her skill as a medicine woman protected her back in the jungle. She had won against Kalara, confused her, and she could do it again.

Whatever spirit had been aiding Kalara, it felt powerful. Aside from herself, Annette had never known anyone who was blessed enough to give off such a dynamic spirit energy. She must learn what she can from the Spirit that Kalara prayed to.

Annette resolved herself then and there to figure out Kalara's mysterious power.

Wondering how long the confusion curse would last, Annette snuffed her pipe and doubled back towards the restaurant. She checked the time, dusk was setting in and soon she'd need to head to the airport. Kalara was still there across the street, not hurting anyone or making the world gray. Annette couldn't think of any words to say as she drew near.

Cautiously, Annette stuck her hand in her medicine bag and closed her fist around the store of dried cat hearts. Keeping her hand on them, she circled around a couple of tables to approach from a better direction.

Kalara noticed her and looked up "What happened to you?"

"I, I must have had a reaction to the chicken. It wasn't very good. Probably under cooked and laden with some Brazilian disease. I hope yours was better than mine."

"I thought it was small and dried out."

"So you are OK now that you are back in Manaus? Can you get home from here alright?"

"Yeah, I feel good. Just needed some food I guess. The thing is I don't quite seem to remember how to get home. Isn't that odd?"

Annette bluffed her reply. "No. Not at all. Your body was in survival mode. I've read where the mind can play tricks on you especially when you're hungry. You'll continue to have memory loss until the chemicals in your brain balance out again."

"How long will that take?"

"I don't know."

"What should I do then?"

With all the cunning of a smiling fox Annette smoothly answered "Well, I normally would look after you since I'm the one that rescued you. Rescuers really should make sure their ward is safe before leaving them. It's the right thing to do. You were in trouble when I found you and now you're in more trouble of a different sort here in the unsafe city with nowhere to go at night. One could actually say I'm the reason you're currently in trouble. I really thought by bringing you back to town you would be safe again. Can you not think of anyone to stay with until your memory returns?"

"No I can't. What happened to me back there?"

"I didn't see anything happen to you. You were like this when I found you. I'm sorry to say I can't stay with you, I'm leaving the country in a few hours. I'm sorry, I really am."

"I could go with you. Wouldn't that be better than staying here alone with so much danger?"

"I suppose you could."

Annette let the memory pass. It was time for action. The loudest and darkest night settled in around her as she prepared for tomorrow. She didn't bother trying to be quiet and the beam from her flashlight hit everything around. Soon it would be dawn and she would be ready. She rustled through her pack, holding the light with her chin to find her latex gloves. Jeremy woke up and squinted at her.

"Be careful for the edge."

"Got it." she mumbled.

Before dawn Annette had the fern located and had her gloves on. In the back of the ledge, against the wall, she held a plastic bag with a bit of water from the waterfall in it and the little crystal. She sat there facing the pale quartzite wall but keeping one eye to the east. She carefully withdrew the rock fragment from the bag and placed her other hand on the fern that she had already weakened for fast removal.

She waited.

Jeremy asked "What are you doing?"

"Quiet! Turn away from me. DON'T LOOK AT THIS WALL! I mean it. Don't piss me off!"

She waited and heard the rock climbing guide roll over.

"Good. Now close your eyes until the sun comes up. DO IT!"

Jeremy closed his eyes. 'What a weirdo' he thought to himself.

The dawn rays gave their soft light, the mist was there. Annette closed her eyes, pulled the fern away and placed the crystal in its hole. Then she felt the rock wall, it was still there.

She waited with her hands against the wall.

The sun was fully up. It had been an hour or more and the wall was still there. Annette peeked. Nothing had changed. "DAMN IT!"

She stood up and dusted off her butt. "You can get up now. Open your eyes, let's eat." She moved over to the tent area.

"This is the craziest adventure." Jeremy said under his breath as he wiped the sleep from his face. He couldn't wait to tell the guys.

"Please don't bite my head off, but what were you doing?"

"A test, nothing more."

He noticed she didn't look at him, but kept her eyes on that rock as she sat down.

"What do you think that rock is gonna do?"

"It's going to disappear."

Jeremy rolled his eyes and wondered what was in her pipe.

Another couple of hours went by and the rock wasn't fading away. Annette just kept watching the wall, her back to the forest. Jeremy couldn't figure her out, most people would be enjoying the view. He started packing up.

Annette didn't turn her head to say "We aren't leaving."

"One night, that is what you paid for lady. We need to start heading down now so we don't miss the helicopter."

"If you try to leave you'll find out that smelly cream is not the worse thing in the world."

Jeremy kept packing. He half-jokingly threatened, "If you don't come, I'm leaving you here."

Annette started chanting.

"Now don't do that," he pleaded nicely "come on, we've got work to do."

When the cursing chant ended Annette lit up her pipe and inhaled deeply, then pulled the pipe from her mouth. The smoke started curling upwards and Annette caught it between her fingers. She began wrapping the enchanted smoke around her pipe and then laid it down on the black rock.

Then Jeremy's gear attacked him. He screamed in shock as it started wrapping tightly around him. The ropes took him to the ground, immobilizing him. "What the hell!??!?!! Let me go!"

"Do you understand now? I said we're staying."

He nodded, "Yeah, sure."

"That's better." Annette said. She picked up her pipe and released him.

She was frustrated. Annette knew the Great Spirit was allowing her to find Kalara, the rock should have opened up. It was time to do something different.

Annette put on her latex gloves, took Jeremy's tent and cut a large piece from it to resemble the wall before them. She then wadded up the thin piece of tent fabric and dropped it into the plastic bag that held the water from the waterfall. She wasn't sure why that particular water was needed but Mother Earth had been specific about it.

The plastic bag holding the small piece of fabric became the center of the circle. And there in the rain, high above the jungle on the black ledge, Annette began a ceremony of blessing. With Jeremy's sudden and unplanned conversion to the faith of the Great Spirit, they both danced and chanted around the bag.

When the ceremony of blessing was over, Annette grabbed a chocolate bar and had Jeremy melt it while she smoked her pipe. They had to wait for the rain to stop anyway. When it finally did the sun was low and they went into action.

Jeremy started drying off a spot on the wall and then Annette, still wearing her gloves, removed the little fabric "wall" from the plastic bag and used the chocolate for glue to stick it to the real rock wall in front of them. Then they both sat there cross-legged, facing the rock wall. Jeremy handed Annette his climber's chalk and she dusted the tent fabric wall with it.

Most oddly, Jeremy noticed, there was only one little spot on the fabric that the chalk would stick to. Annette took out her pocket knife and cut the chalked spot almost completely out, leaving a small section intact to be a hinge. With her gloved fingers, Annette carefully pulled the spot, swinging it open like a door.

Immediately the corresponding area on the quartzite rock wall vanished.

"Here Jeremy, hold this open with your gloves on."

He hurried up to put his gloves on with eyes wide open and did as she said.

Annette jumped up, gathered as much of their equipment as she could and raced to the doorway. Once inside she said "Come on, hurry up, I'll hold it open. Grab everything, even our little wall!"

Jeremy had never moved so quick.

Chapter 14

Kalara didn't know how long she stood there naked at the seer pool. However long she stood there, she tripled that time after she sat down, staring unfocused at the blue mist around her.

She was empty.

Why didn't he kill her? He was done with her, she knew it. She had felt his thoughts as he walked out of her mind, out the lair, out of her world. He didn't hide his feelings from her, why would he? He didn't care if she knew his thoughts because he wasn't coming back.

Sitting there reminded Kalara of all those days she had sat trapped in that apartment knowing less than she did now. And still, at this moment Annette was trapping her with that evil curse. Perhaps it would have been better to not know what all Annette had done to her and taken from her, but one good thing did come from it all – Kalara knew now without doubt that magic was real and she could use it.

Why did Annette target her? Did she want Ravanan for herself? Kalara could have gotten angry about it but what was the use? And continuously thinking about him or her brought nothing but sadness. She had to let those thoughts slide off into the abyss of her heart and move on. She was done with thinking about Ravanan and Annette. It wasn't an easy thing to do, to stop thinking about him and how much she missed him, but with a cold determination Kalara berated herself into submission.

Without anger and sadness distracting her Kalara became keenly focused on how her body felt. Her head ached from being walked into by a will other than hers, the base of her skull throbbed particularly bad which was a little worrying to her.

The human skin she wore was cold from being naked in the cool cavern air but at least she was alive. Never again – Kalara vowed – would she freely present her neck.

She stood up, brushed the dirt off her back side and thought about wearing something; not that it mattered since she was alone but it would feel right to her. She was naked and cold, she needed to cover herself.

The healing robe would have been best for her headache but Ravanan had failed to tell her its name. She tried anyway, mentally retreating to her dark crevice, she visualized it on her body and cast *"DRAPE HEALING ROBE"*. That wasn't it, the name was wrong and it didn't appear.

Kalara sighed, "Why couldn't things be easy?"

She picked over the meat left on the fire and then went to the far back corner of the lair where Ravanan had stood by the rock. Kalara did exactly what she saw him do, licked her finger, touched the same spot he had, and cast *"REVEAL"*.

The spell worked and the crevice appeared although it did make her feel tired as though she'd just climbed many flights of stairs. She guessed the reveal spell would work because if the Mighty Amethyst had kept her stuff with his then she ought to be able to access it with her saliva.

She quickly stepped into the darkness since she didn't know how long the doorway would stay open and cast *"STARLIGHT"* on herself. Her body lit up the dark corridor and she made her way to the wardrobe chamber to get that robe.

The lacy black robe was sealed tight in its case. Kalara remembered back to when she was there before and broke Naught's case. With confidence she made a fist and punched the glass; it didn't break but it felt like her hand did.

Was the robe's case different? She didn't think so, it looked like all the others. She stood there in thought while her knuckles reddened. What was different this time?

One thing was that she wasn't angry. As she replayed what happened before, she realized it must have been her aura that had helped her. She stared at the glass, thinking about how to turn her aura cold. She wanted to break the glass and not hurt herself again.

She needed coldness and ice.

Without any more effort than that thought Kalara began to hear the faint crackle of water vapor hardening into ice, it was a very satisfying sound as the world turned cold. The air turned chilly and yet she felt fine, not cold at all. Her aura was helping her. The happiest of feelings washed over her heart.

She punched the frozen display case and shattered it, grabbed the ornamental robe and shook the broken glass out before putting it on. As soon as Kalara put the lacy black robe on she began to feel less pain from her headache and hand. The robe was amazing, even if it was thin and intimate.

Before Kalara left she visited the weapons rack. She ran her fingers over the weapons, admiring them. Bolt was still there and next to it was the amethyst inlaid dagger, it had to be hers by process of elimination. Kalara picked it up and admired her craftsmanship. The piece fit perfectly in her hand, becoming an extension of herself. Each faceted jewel on the hilt glinted in the starlight spell that had dimly illuminated the room. The dagger was a fine blade, she wondered what its name was. There were so many things Ravanan hadn't told her, this was another one. Kalara set the blade back in its place and went to bed.

The following morning Kalara awakened when she thought she felt a touch on her shoulder. Ravanan's warm aura was there. She opened her eyes and turned over but he she couldn't see him.

"Ravanan?" she called out. There was no answer but she did see her breakfast at the fire. Kalara did not say his name a second time.

She took her food into the dark crevice to eat it. Lit with her light she spent the whole day exploring the tunnel and mapping it out in her mind. It was the center of her home and the furthest she could get from him, she was going to learn it well.

The next few days there was food each morning when she woke but Kalara never sensed his presence. Sometimes it was pizza, sometimes it was the leg of a cow, but it was always warm.

Kalara always took it to the dark crevice to eat in peace away from the memory of him. Food for her became a sad reminder and it was an upsetting way to start each day. But she was determined to not let him bother her with his elusive manner. Being in the tunnel helped her, the cold rock was familiar and she got to the point where she didn't need or use the light spell while eating anymore.

213

The notion that she had conquered the darkness lifted her spirits also. She was going to be alright. Even her head finally stopped hurting.

There was a lot to practice and it seemed she was eating constantly as she pushed her magic to the limit each day, working on duration and intensity. It became easier to use her aura to make ice. The seer pool was an infinite source of water and before long she was making icicles crash into the rocky walls.

What was hard was trying to warm up her bath water, but soon that came to her too. At first she cheated by blowing through the flames of the cooking fire that she'd built near the seer pool but after a while she was breathing fire just like Ravanan. She discovered that breathing fire was highly variable, depending on the shape of her lips and amount of air she gave it.

Kalara was depending on her aura more and more, trusting it to chill the air or help her breathe fire. She had come a long way with it and began thinking of experimenting with the more difficult magic of verbal spell casting. Sure she was already able to cast reveal and starlight, but other spells were necessary if she wanted to continue to grow.

Freely casting verbal spells at whim was a bit daunting. Kalara was anxious that it wouldn't work so she went back into the dark tunnel where she took every meal. In the comforting darkness she found her way past the cave formations and rocks to the certain stalagmite that made a nice chair. She could even see the orange crystal in her mind although there was no light to see it.

Kalara warmed her chair slightly with flame-breath and took off the black healing robe, letting it fall to the ground and pushed it aside with her foot. She reached out to lean and relax against the formation and breathed deeply.

She was as peaceful as she was ever going to get. The dark void was silent while it waited to hear her voice. Kalara thought about Naught. Naught. Naught. Naught.

"DRAPE NAUGHT", she cast.

The torn and filthy shadow suit covered her skin. She did it! With relief and a smile she sat down. Kalara hugged herself and ran her hands over the tight outfit. Yes there were some holes in it but it felt so good. It was hers and she knew the name of it!

She had really messed Naught up though. Kalara put her hand on her knee and could feel skin. She examined every rip and tear carefully while eating another couple of slices of pizza, thinking on the enchantments of Naught. Although she didn't feel any different she was invisible right now – even though there was no one there to not see her. It was amazing to think there was magic in the very fabric of Naught, that she was touching magic when for so long before this she had been thinking that magic didn't even exist. She needed to fix Naught.

Remembering the downside of Naught, Kalara took it off and folded it up in her lap. She breathed deep, drawing strength from the nothing around her, and visualized all the mending that Naught needed.

Kalara cast *"REPAIR"*. Before her eyes, Naught's fabric healed and even the snags were smoothed back to pristine condition. There was still some dirt, but no snags.

After that all she wanted to do was sleep.

The next couple of days were mental exercise as she stood in the wardrobe chamber draping Naught and letting it go back to its broken case. Over and over Kalara cast drape. She was relentless and walked around as she practiced.

There was a lot of stuff in there. Not just weapons and clothing, but there were bags, sacks, jewelry, chests, furniture. And odder stuff still, like two green crystalline disks that were bigger than dinner plates, she had no idea what they were. The chamber stored everything that they could ever need to pass in a human world, wallets and money from eras and nations.

Her eyes went to the special ivory display case, different from all the others, set apart and empty, adorned with fire opals, part of the first treasure he ever gave her from some two thousand years ago.

She knew the meaning of it now, a tear flowed from the corner of her eye, but she knew it too late to keep him.

One of her first memories was Annette stealing the cream robe from her and she was too confused to know it was happening. Kalara forcefully wiped the tear from her face and turned away from the case. The cream robe was gone and so was he. 'Why do I even still have the stupid case?' she wondered to herself in anger. The air behind her grew cold, she dropped the temperature even colder. The old case was creaking in protest but she didn't care. Kalara took the air as cold as she ever had then kicked her heal backwards, destroying the case. The ivory busted into powder and the fire opals dropped into the dust and broken glass.

It was over and gone, her heart relaxed. Kalara was glad to have that tomb of their love out of her wardrobe. She used her aura to gather the mess and dumped it all into an empty jar, opals included.

Then she looked at the broken display cases that stood without their glass panels. Naught's case was in front of her and glass shards everywhere. She carefully thought about how many shards there were and visualized working them like puzzle pieces. She regarded the height that the many pieces must travel, and when she felt like she was ready and relaxed enough she cast "*REPAIR*" and thought of 100% of the pieces going back into the case. The shards lifted and flew into their places, it was magic! She yelled out in joy to no one but herself. The glass display case was crack free and perfect like it had been before. The spell made her tired though, she was needing rest and food.

It was the next morning, as the lair began to lighten and color pink with the dawn Kalara woke like always. She was thinking about the repair spell and how it was so tiring to her. If only she could repair herself, she paused and stared at the fire pit.

There was no food waiting for her. She sat down on the bed, suddenly really hungry. What had happened? Kalara felt prickly with alertness. She didn't feel his warm aura which meant he wasn't there, or maybe he was there and hiding from her. It was so very strange.

She hurried down through the dark tunnel to the wardrobe chamber to have a look at Ravanan's things. After casting starlight on the hanging rock formation she checked to see what was missing, thinking maybe it would give her a clue. All his weapons were there, so were all of his clothes, even his sapphire robe which had been there for days.

There was no sense in guessing why Ravanan had not brought her food so Kalara decided to get her mind off of it. She went over to her display cases and looked at other possible things to wear. Most of her old clothes were enchantress robes, some more revealing than others, but as far as "normal" clothes to wear she only had a couple of things.

Kalara decided on a purple enchantress robe that matched her attitude, which was 'ready to throw more magic around'. Since she didn't know its name she had to break into the case.

The purple robe fit her nicely, an elegant brocade overdress with bare shoulders and hanging sleeves, and a lavender under-dress that seamlessly followed her body to the floor. The back and front panels of the low-cut silk dress were fastened together at the sides by fine chains that stopped at her hips.

The golden hairpiece came next, Kalara considered not wearing it but after trying it on she loved it and how it held her hair back from her face.

"But of course it keeps my hair perfectly in place," Kalara flatly told herself, rolling her eyes, "I designed it for my own head years ago." It felt odd to go through her old outfits, they didn't seem like hers and she actually felt somewhat like a thief, worried that she would be discovered. "But by who?" her dialog continued, "myself?" Kalara knew it was an outrageous concern and made herself ignore it as such.

Kalara wondered how the robe was enchanted. She could guess at the enchantment on the hairpiece by the way her hair felt, nicely tight and pulled back, no human hands could get it so perfect. It was probably wrong to feel so beautiful.

She needed to know how her magic was being affected by the purple robe. Immediately she thought back to Ravanan casting reveal on her ring and she would have to do the same spell – she had to find out for her peace of mind.

On her way to the wizard's alcove she noticed the two green disks were missing. Kalara knew Ravanan had to have them for some reason, but she was at a loss as to why.

She took off the enchantress' robe and laid the under-dress on the table in the wizard's alcove. Carefully placing the biotite and iolite Kalara cast *"REVEAL"*. In the little iolite crystal she saw herself intent on an object in front of her, it was changing shapes very fast, there were fuzzy distractions around her but they weren't touching her. She understood, the robe had an improving enchantment where she could think and react faster, and avoid distractions to stay focused, its name was Silk.

When she cast reveal on the overdress Kalara learned it was enchanted to warn her of immediate changes and threats around her, and its name was Cerberus.

Lastly she was right about the hairpiece whose name was simple enough, Silk Hair.

Mid-day came and went, Kalara was hungry but she let it go, sure that Ravanan would bring food to her that evening. She kept practicing sending Silk and Cerberus back and then draping them again. Kalara was getting pretty good at the drape spell – feeling like practice was the only way to get better.

The purple robe still felt oddly foreign to her though – even after draping it so many times. And Kalara knew it was crazy to feel like the clothes weren't hers. "They are mine, all of them." She tried to convince herself, "They fit me! And if my old self ever comes back to claim them, then... great!" But Kalara couldn't stop feeling weird about it, despite loving the robe she needed to do something more, needed to make it hers, give it a different name, re-enchant it.

Back down to her stalagmite chair she went. The dark crevice was the only place where she felt like she could find enough power, it was where she felt her best. She sat down to plan the enchantment she would do and how to do it. Kalara felt like she needed to learn about the enchantments of other things, like those two green disks that went missing earlier that morning.

After gathering biotite, iolite, and a heavy black rock from the alcove Kalara sat down again in her stalagmite chair with everything in her lap. She figured that Silk would help her with the enchanting so she kept it on. Kalara retreated inside herself, finding the dark void of her heart, listening to the silence, and drawing from the darkness around her in the tunnel, using all her focus and aura she cast *"ENCHANT SILK, CERBERUS AND SILK HAIR WITH REVEAL TO BECOME HEED"*

Faintness overtook her and she fell fast asleep.

When she woke she was naked and in her lap was a purple pile and metal corset. Kalara was so glad that she'd left the healing robe by the chair and reached down to get it but got dizzy instead and felt out of the chair. From the ground Kalara managed to grab the black robe and struggled to put it on before going back to sleep.

Kalara was beyond famished when she rose later that evening and was surprised that still, Ravanan had not brought her any food. "Maybe he will in the morning" she told herself and went back to sleep.

But the next morning was no different. Kalara frustratingly pushed her hunger aside and walked back to the dark crevice to get Heed and check out her work.

She picked up Heed and left the healing robe by the chair again. Kalara excitedly ran naked through the blackness to the wardrobe chamber's wall mirror to see her result.

Her eyes were wide in the reflection as she held it up to her body.

Heed didn't have as much substance as Silk and Cerberus had, there was less material and a whole lot more skin. "What happened?!?" Kalara stood there shocked. She hadn't planned to change the style or cut of the dress, only to increase the enchantments.

She dropped the robe and took a few steps back, looking oddly at it. "Well," she said, "I'll know soon enough." and she cast *"DRAPE HEED"*, instantly Heed was on her body.

In the soft light of her starlight spell on the ceiling rock formation Heed sparkled with dark glints off biotite flakes and the dark metal filigree armored corset. The robe was still mostly purple but the black biotite had fused throughout the materials.

Kalara looked again in the mirror and cast *"REVEAL"*. She watched as her hairpiece morphed to add iolite spectacles over her eyes, and in the blue lenses she saw the same image as before, but now the object was defining itself telling her what its purpose was. The fuzz around her had become distinct swords and claws as if they were trying to battle her but couldn't touch her. Her hair was perfectly out of the way during the fight. Then Kalara noticed the flaw, the robe on the little figure of herself was eroded and tattered somewhat, distorting back to the raw material of the Earth, its basic form and function had moved a step closer towards chaos.

She wondered how much more enchanting Heed could take and how long it would last in its current form. The deep purple enchantress robe still felt connected and strong, especially with the added metal scrolling on the bodice and overdress. She hadn't planned for that either, the dark heavy rock was supposed to secure the fragile biotite flakes to the material but it did that and more.

Kalara smiled chicly at herself in the mirror falling in love with her purple robe Heed. It may have turned out more seductive than she had planned but she had paid real blood for Heed and it was all hers.

She designated the empty display case of Silk and Cerberus as the new home for Heed and practiced sending it back and draping it again.

It wasn't long before Kalara took notice of Naught hanging in its case - Naught was clean. She learned the display cases were enchanted to clean their contents. That display case hadn't cleaned Naught when she sent it back the first time because the glass panel was broken. After using her reveal spell she found the display cases repair their clothes also.

Kalara revealed everything and every outfit in the chamber, learning their names and learning what she had crafted and also what all Ravanan had. No longer would she be ignorant about such things. She moved on to what wasn't in the chamber, which wasn't much, just the bed (which she was sure was Ravanan's) and the black healing robe.

Kalara the Amethyst Enchantress sat down once more on her stalagmite chair. Veiled in the darkness of the crevice she held the black lace healing robe in her hands and cast *"REVEAL"*. After the iolite lenses lowered over her purple eyes Kalara peered into them and saw Ravanan kneeling beside her limp naked body to cover her bloodied chest with a monk's black robe. Then he held his hands over the robe and re-enchanted it three more times, each time the robe looked different and smaller.

She knew – the robe was his and *he* was responsible for the artfully missing fabric – but also for the superb healing enchantments that had saved her more than once. Tears escaped her eyes when Kalara heard his voice say its name, My Heart.

Kalara wailed with sadness, letting pain flow over her, covering her face with the lace robe, soaking it with her tears. Her loud sobs echoed down the tunnel, causing the rock to weep with her. The void in her heart filled with emotion as she released her feelings, holding nothing back and letting everything go.

That black robe was good for nothing but physical healing as the lace was fully saturated and could hold no more of her tears which were now wetting her hands. It was such a delicate thing.

Knowing now how fragile My Heart really was caused Kalara to worry that even the salt from her tears might erode it further into dust. Never caring so much before, Kalara took My Heart and delicately set it back in its display case, hoping the symbol of Ravanan's love would never be needed again. She didn't understand her own thoughts regarding the matter but knew that she could never touch My Heart again. Kalara repaired the case, sealing it from her grasp, her eyes looked instead to her own wardrobe where she had her old healing robe waiting should she need it.

Kalara went to bed that night drained of energy. She dreaded another day without food.

The fire pit was empty again. Kalara refused to stay trapped in Black Blade Lair forever like a starved prisoner. And it didn't help her mood any that every time she walked by the fire pit she could see the scorch marks on the rocky ground from when her and Ravanan had made their ring of fire. That night meant so much to her but to him it was disgusting, how horrible that he had been with a human!

"AAARRRGGHHH" Kalara screamed and breathed her dark purple fire high into the blue mist. She simple was not going to let him treat her like this. She was her own being now, half human, half dragon, an enchantress.

By the third day with no food, Kalara planned to leave with her weapon in hand to slay the first animal she saw. The dagger called

Cutter with the amethysts was enchanted with a sure strike to never miss her cut. She worried about her fighting abilities and the animals she imagined might be out there, none of them wanted to die and she was sure they would put up a good fight. She needed a better weapon and chose to not leave the lair with Cutter.

On the table in the wizard's alcove, the hungry purple enchantress placed several different ores in a pile then made another pile of garnets which she chose for their blood-red color. Kalara knew the enchantment and tool she wanted, but knew nothing of metallurgy save for the five minutes she saw on Jenniffer's TV which said the metal was folded. She hoped her aura would take over that part as it had when removing fabric from Heed.

Kalara took a deep breath and blew the hottest fire she could muster on the ore, separating the slag from the metal. Then she picked up Cutter and slit her finger wide open, quickly, ignoring the pain which was overshadowed by her hunger.

From deep within the dark crevice inside her, the purple enchantress cast *"MAKE SIPHON"* on the molten metal and Cutter, then dribbled her fresh blood onto the bubbling orange pool that would soon become her blade. The metal worked itself from the blood, fire, and aura she had to give it. Kalara kept draining her magic blood, each drop was like a hammer, sparks flew and the metal sizzled. She continued dripping her blood until it felt like enough and then Kalara sprinkled the garnets onto the piece. The blade was forming and Kalara felt really faint again, so while Siphon cooled Kalara laid down to rest.

Siphon was a dark dagger. The shiny black metal blade was set with garnets that gave it a bloody hue. When it pierced flesh, even the tiniest nick, it would magically sever all arteries from the victim's lungs to teleport every drop of the oxygen-rich blood and pour it directly into Kalara's hungry stomach.

Kalara woke up hungrier than ever. She looked over to the pit, no food. In her next breath she cast *"EVOKE SIPHON"* and her new blade was in her hand, she looked it over but was so hungry she couldn't think straight enough to fully admire the work she had done.

She spit on the ground and cast *"FIND THE EXITS"* on her spit and fell over exhausted from the verbal spell. All she could muster was to watch from where she lay, her spit floated up and split into two, one flew to the seer pool and the other went to a wall.

After recovering for a time she cast reveal at the wall with new spit and the wall opened into a large exit that a dragon could easily go through. On each side were massive black pillars. Kalara entered the grand hallway, the walls held sconces that blazed brightly.

As she walked carefully, Kalara thought about the blue mist that surrounded her, protecting her from Annette's evil spell. It had become such a fixture for her, and to think of it, she had never seen the lair without Ravanan's blue mist hanging in the air. She wondered how far the mist extended, trying to visualize how big that first one was that she saw him make and if it reached to the outside, she didn't even know how long the cave was. Kalara didn't know if she would be able to see the end of the mist before she walked out of it and into pain.

She had walked far enough down the hall that it began to narrow and there were no more sconces to light her way, she cast starlight and went on.

Remembering that horrific pain made her shudder. Before advancing any further she dismissed her cherished robe and cast *"DRAPE HEALER"* and a robe of blue ribbons wrapped around her body.

Kalara followed along the passageway until she came to a chasm that she couldn't hope to cross without flight.

She was so hungry, and every spell she cast was like another nail in her coffin, decreasing her life.

The drop was so deep her starlight spell couldn't penetrate the darkness. But after everything she had done lately, the purple enchantress was not going to quit now.

With eyes closed, Kalara knelt and ran her hands along the rocky ground, feeling the mud and every pebble to find strength and courage. This was her rock and it made her strong because she owned it. She was so hungry, all she wanted was food and however she had to move her body to eat she would do it or die trying. Inside her heart was the void, the uncaring void, it was part of the void from her lair, and it was a darker void than that which filled the chasm.

It was her chasm, she owned it and she would conquer it. Kalara's purple eyes opened with determination. Using her dirty hands as springs, she launched her body up to hover in the air. Old memories awakened within her, memories she hadn't remembered until now, it wasn't her identity but more like a sense, her body knew what to do and she leaned forward in flight.

The purple enchantress flew higher, enjoying it. When she reached the other side, she didn't land but kept on flying though the cave.

Until she left the protective blue mist.

The curse was upon her! She fell to the rocky ground, writhing in pain. Slowed down by Healer, her stomach skin stretched tight rather than burst open, small rips appeared and grew until they started reddening with blood. Her feet were blistered and smoking. There was greater agony still when her leg bones broke - but at least they didn't puncture the skin.

The robe was fighting the curse, her skin was mostly holding together but she couldn't go any further like she was.

"Oh please NO!" Kalara pleaded with the evil curse, hoping the rips in her stomach didn't join together and open. Through gritted teeth, she targeted her own mind and cast *"CALM"*, she could feel her heart slow down. It would be OK if she could just conquer the pain.

Kalara had fallen in mud. She grabbed a handful, cast *"NUMB ME"* on it and rubbed it on herself, feeling faint from the spell. There was so much pain she was whimpering. Was leaving to find food worth it? She wondered. Maybe she should just die right there and Ravanan could find her dried up body a century later when he finally came back. Ravanan. Just thinking up his name sent her into anger. She was not going to die because of him or Annette. No, she had to continue on, she must.

A major battle of magic was happening inside her and it felt like it was tearing her up. She was running out of time to live, to retreat and try to enchant more items would kill her from the drain of blood, every spell she cast was eating away at her and knowing that fact was all it took. The purple enchantress packed on more numbing mud, and when she felt the pain lessen a little she forced her tired body into the air.

Flying her broken body wasn't as difficult as it sounded due to the nature of magical auras, muscles weren't involved much. Her legs hung limply as she tried to not stretch her taut stomach for fear her guts would spill out.

It wasn't much further before Kalara saw daylight for the first time in a long time. There she was, looking out over the great rain forest – it looked so calm from up where she was. The black ledge, warm in the sun, felt good to her.

If only she wasn't broken and numbly hurting she could really enjoy it. The sun quickly warmed her body, dried the mud, and increased the smell of her oozing, burning feet.

Trembling and tortured, Kalara looked for an animal. There were none except for a small lizard sunning itself. She threw Siphon at it and the black blade connected. There was so little blood in the lizard. Kalara crawled over to it and ate the whole thing, bones, scales and dirty sharp toe nails.

The day was marked with horrible pain as she laid there hunting on the tip of Black Blade ledge. She felt queasy from the magic fight within her and vomited which opened up the worst of her stomach lacerations. It may be that she would die from eating.

An unfortunate bird landed for a minute to rest on the black ledge and soon its blood was digested by Kalara. She didn't know where the body was or else she would have eaten that too.

Far down below was a chorus of monkeys, she'd heard them all day and finally decided to try for one even though she couldn't see them. Before she threw Siphon, she touched the garnets on the blade, asking them to find the target. In a delirium, Kalara did the best she could with targeting and threw Siphon at the squealing monkeys.

When Kalara felt her stomach fill with monkey blood she managed a smile, and quickly flew her broken body back to the safety of Ravanan's blue mist.

She landed back near the fire pit and evoked Siphon, overjoyed at seeing her tool return to her.

Kalara rubbed her agonized skin and thought about her day. Siphon was a pretty handy little treasure, but as far as leaving to find food, there had to be a better way. She didn't know when she'd feel like doing that again but feared it would be soon. With a full belly of blood the purple enchantress found sleep.

Chapter 15

Time melted into one long nightmare for Jenniffer. Every day she woke in the high afternoon and cried until sundown, not eating, just dreading the night. She didn't want to eat, she wanted to die but couldn't bring herself to do it. Annette and Bill shoved what they could into her mouth, from chocolate covered strawberries to cold American cheese slices swabbed in margarine and washed down with whiskey. Her body was a wreck and her mind was trapped in it. She felt perpetually dirty.

The clock was her enemy, counting down to when Annette would enter her. Nothing could stop her, sleeping, praying, laughing, reading – nothing could trump Annette's forceful entry into her mind. Every dusk Annette would say 'Good Evening' in a most loving way and wipe the tears from her iridescent eyes.

She was too tired during the day to accomplish any housework and finding a respectable job was out of the question. She was too scared to pluck out her eyes for fear of bleeding to death, and now Bill had a key to her apartment and was considering moving in and finding a job in Tulsa. Bill didn't seem to mind the nightly tricks she turned either, he was always ready for her when she got back late in the night. She was always sore between her legs. Her life was very bad. Todd hadn't called on her again after he'd left that one day and her friends from school stopped calling because she dropped out of college. She wanted help but was too distraught to look for it.

The first few nights Annette had said some words to Jenniffer, small talk, but that was no longer the case and Jenniffer was glad for the silence. But lately, the eeriness of the silence and routine that Annette put her body through was its own kind of torture. More than the disease and pain that her body was inflicted with, was the bizarre quality of being a machine. It was like Annette went to work every night but instead of operating a piece of heavy equipment or driving a tractor, the evil woman climbed into Jenniffer's body to work another shift. It was a task, and Jenniffer wondered how Annette could get any joy out of it.

One afternoon, when her eyes were bleary from sleep, Jenniffer's ears picked up a TV commercial for one of the local Native American tribes, it had the iconic flute music that was actually a soothing melody.

Her mind jogged back to what Todd had said about the ancestors. Annette's medicine and curses always scared Jenniffer, making her want to turn and run. She'd been foolish to think she could run from it. Now she was saturated in the dark magic, imprisoned and tortured inside her own body.

The flute music grew loud, signaling the end of the commercial and then it too ended. But it lingered in Jenniffer's ears.

The tribal medicine was real, Jenniffer knew that for sure. And since it was real then what was to stop her from talking to the ancestors? Long ago, Annette had wanted to teach Jenniffer about their heritage and blood. Surely Annette thought Jenniffer capable. Perhaps if she tried, the ancestors would bless her and undo Annette's hideous curse on her, and in her prayers she wouldn't be revealing the possession spell because the Ancestors must know about it already. Maybe Mother Earth would take pity on Jenniffer. She could try at least, there was nothing stopping her but Annette.

Jenniffer checked the clock, there wasn't enough time to drive out there before sunset. Her prayers would have to wait until tomorrow.

The following morning, instead of rolling over and sleeping more, Jenniffer sprang up, ready to pray. Bill was passed out beside her. She still didn't like him, but he was becoming a regular fixture in her life and she'd stopped slapping him at least. He was actually becoming more fit, leaner, bigger, probably working out at the gym.

She had to admit, Bill had a stamina that other men did not. After the many men Jenniffer had pleasured, she knew something was up with the gift of the rooster. The odd removal of the men's sex drive and ego was diminished when Bill climaxed, the fire that Annette pulled from him didn't take such a large toll on him. Sure he was wiped out afterwards and slept a deep, extended sleep, but he was able to bounce back from it and wanted her body just as badly when he woke. She also noticed Bill ate mainly red meat and very little else, she was sure Annette had cursed him also, but at least his curse was an enjoyable one.

Jenniffer left him asleep and drove out to the hill. During the drive she was trying to recall how to summon the ancestors so she wouldn't have to get Todd's help. Better yet, she decided to not even use the altar or sweat lodge for fear that he would find her. Jenniffer parked at the bottom of the hill on a side road and made her way through ditches and woods to the natural spring where she played as a young girl.

The spring was small since the winter hadn't brought them much rain, there was more mud than water in it. The old fallen log she used to walk across had decomposed into a soggy slick mess that would surely break apart if she tried to walk across it now. For a while, Jenniffer just sat on her favorite rock and pulled her jacket around her, the winter was mild and the warmest part of the day was approaching.

It felt good to be there, it was the one place where she had been able to be alone and play without Todd being mean or laughing at her. Trees were all around her, it was quiet.

She couldn't remember how Annette summoned the ancestors, and she couldn't remember what sacred items to use, not that it mattered because she had none. She didn't know any songs or chants. It didn't even make sense to her why songs were needed in the first place – surely the gods or spirits would accept normal speech like a prayer.

Jenniffer remembered all the things and games she used to do out there. It was her private world back then, she could be anything and anyone, even Queen of the Amazons with her secret treasure. That old pretend treasure box she kept...... that was it! – her secret treasure chest! She could use it for an offering.

Eagerly, Jenniffer hiked over to a leaning tree she used to climb, it was leaning more now with the years. She cleaned the leaves away from the trunk and began to dig under the rocks at its base. It was still there, Jenniffer wrapped her hands around the plastic jewelry box and opened it to find a quartz crystal, some crinoid fossils, and a dingy ring with a plastic jewel.

She placed the crystal and fossils on the decayed log back at the stream, and said quietly "Ancestors, will you let me honor you with this treasure of the earth? Can I talk with you?" then she sat back down on her rock and waited to see if anything would happen.

It wasn't long before the sky grayed, it seemed to Jenniffer that the forest grayed slightly as well. She checked the time, it was nowhere near dusk. Everything seemed muted with a fog. From behind her, a non-existing window shattered, startling her.

Jenniffer looked around but didn't see anyone or anything. The glass shards from the shattering window kept falling and then she heard the clinking sounds form into words that she could identify. The other worldly voice said "It is enough."

Jenniffer stood and turned around to see a beautiful Native American woman, clothed in a gray silk robe studded with polished hematite and gray gemstones.

Before she realized how jaw-dropping dumb she sounded Jenniffer asked "Who are you?"

"I am the voice of your ancestors, I am Mother Earth."

"Really." The flat, disbelieving tone in Jenniffer's voice could have brought the clouds down to earth. "I didn't know you were human. Who are you really?"

"I'll forgive your disrespect just this once." the woman's voice was shrill and full of razors.

Jenniffer said nothing, either she'd see who was fooling her or she was about to be severely punished.

The woman said nothing.

The stare-down became a waiting game, a game that Jenniffer was happy to play, she'd had many years of training for it and was prepared to win. With each passing minute, Jenniffer was becoming increasingly suspicious that the woman was indeed somehow Annette, though she looked younger and prettier than Annette ever could. She refused to say another word, she wouldn't flinch, and she stubbornly waited for the woman to act first. If the woman kept on waiting, Jenniffer set in her mind that she would observe what happened at dusk, then the truth of Annette's possession spell would come out.

She didn't have to wait long. The Great Spirit of Mother Earth spoke in the same shrill nails-on-a-chalkboard voice "The ancestors have seen your insolent heart. You have not honored your ancestors in many years, why should we now honor your request to stop the spell of a medicine woman?"

Jenniffer became concerned, the woman standing before her knew about the evil spell. Either Annette was excellent at disguises and could change her voice or it really was Mother Earth reading her thoughts, she ought to be prostrate licking dirt in humbleness.

After some careful thought she chose to test the woman further because it probably was Annette.

"Because the possession spell is beyond cruel; it is wrong." she answered. "I will change my ways, I see now that the earth and the ancestors care enough to give audience and hear my words, surely the ancestors would welcome another devoted follower. I will not stray and I will honor the Great Spirit always, knowing that Mother Earth leans towards kindness rather than cruelty."

"So you would listen to and follow your medicine woman?"

Jenniffer clinched her jaw at the abhorring thought of learning from Annette. "No, I will follow the ancestors and listen to Mother Earth directly."

"You don't like your medicine woman?"

"Please, Mother Earth, I can't like someone who has hurt me as much as she has."

The woman smiled but with a voice like broken glass, it was difficult to show mirth "You think I'm her."

"I'll know for sure at sundown."

"You can know now." The woman uttered some unknown words that were highly distorted with the splintery shards. A mirror appeared in her hands, she extended it to Jenniffer.

Jenniffer took the mirror and looked at her reflection, her eyes were brown again. She did a double take and then fell prostrate to the ground and kissed the leaves on the forest floor.

"Thank you, thank you, thank you Mother Earth! I'm yours, always, willingly yours."

"Then rise and be mine, *MY VIXEN*."

As Jenniffer rose her mouth felt funny and a queasy feeling washed over her, her stomach was momentarily in knots and she fell down with dizziness.

Her sinus cavities felt hollow and cold with air as if she had just eaten wasabi or hot mustard. Her mouth hurt, she touched her face with her fingers, only to notice then that her palms and fingers itched like mad as tiny barbs emerged from her skin. A new purpose filled her being.

Jenniffer grabbed the mirror again with her barbed grip. She inhaled carnally as she examined her new teeth. Though she still looked human she knew she wasn't. She was better than human. She had fangs, lots of long fangs, still the same number of teeth but they were very, very different teeth. Her whole jaw had been reshaped to contain them and it was narrower. Her incisor teeth were slightly smaller, pointed and sharp to penetrate skin, her bottom canines were vicious solid points, and her upper canines were three times their former length and were now translucent, hollow needles for envenoming prey.

Her taste buds had been re-wired to desire something other than food and venom sacs developed below her sinus cavities. Her endocrine system was now enhanced to trigger stronger reactions to her sense of smell, especially targeting the exquisite odor of testosterone. Just the memory of how a man smells was enough to make Jenniffer wet and her mouth water.

Her thoughts were singular, not for blood, but a primal urge for men. The desire to bite was strong within her, causing her to run her tongue over her teeth. Her venom would travel in men's bodies, riding the strong currents of sexual tension that made them rise and flush with heat. Her venomous bite wasn't an ugly discoloring, flesh-rotting poison but a tiny, erotic, clean wound that would change their ejaculation, making it not only give semen but also all their testosterone forever.

The Vixen spell took hold and settled into her, the pain subsided, her body had changed. All she wanted was to bite and feel a man give her what only a man can give. Jenniffer liked the predator she saw in the mirror, although she wondered how could any man want to look at her. Even as she thought about it she watched her main fangs fold up and recess into the roof of her mouth. Her barbs retracted and her hair smoothed as if she'd spent hours in a makeup studio to look naturally perfect. Her face assumed a gorgeous shape, the monster was hidden inside.

With a velvety voice Jenniffer purred "Thank you".

Mother Earth's voice shattered on the wind "Go hunt."

Chapter 16

S unrise was moments away, soon it would illuminate the flat-topped mountain that towered above the canopied jungle. A circlet of clouds graced the regal mesa and veiled monolithic boulders found on top that were testaments to a former frosty summit. The lone giants were scattered about as they waited on time to finish breaking them into dust. Some were bigger than others, and behind one of the largest Ravanan was crouching with folded wings, covered in deep shadow, the blue of his scales made him all the harder to notice. If one stared hard enough, they'd see the air around him shimmering from his long-lasting air coat armor, aside from some mental protection, it was an insulator against heat and flame-breath, making it a good defense against a brown dragon's heat attack. Piled next to him were five dead bulls just in case the battle ran long.

He was waiting for sunlight to spill over the edge of the abysmal lair. From his vantage point he couldn't see the fern-covered walls but he didn't need to – he knew the occupant would emerge up and into the trap.

The warm rays of morning would set the bait for Ravanan's trap, it was invisible to the eye and covered the opening like a net. It had taken a while to enchant the air and rock with the crafty spell that would mimic the wrath attack of a green dragon's aura. But the time spent was planned for, as well as time to recover any exerted aura. Yes, Ravanan was quite ready to pounce.

Pink and purple hues colored the eastern sky, giving Ravanan's watchful blue eyes a hint of Kalara's beautiful orbs. The corners of his mouth curled in silent anticipation, his massive chest expanded and waned with slow, quiet breaths.....

As predicted the brown dragon rose with powerful wings towards the brightening sky. As he shot out of the ground the trap covered him like a cloth of acid. Now as he climbed higher he was drenched in the corrosive liquid, his scales began smoking and dissolving. His eyesight was gone in a sizzle. Instantly enraged, the dragon's aura heated and fused the rock ledge of the lair into hardened glass, a lethal attack of terrible heat that caused all nearby vegetation to burst into flame.

The blue spectator watched from behind his boulder. From his safe distance Ravanan quickly followed up the acid trap with a hold spell to give the acid time to eat deep into the brown dragon's thick scales. The smoldering dragon was now suspended in the air, the only thing that moved was the rising fumes from his body.

Ravanan was about to throw a lightning bolt when his blood curdled. Poison!

A chill ran along his spine as the poison worked its way like splinters between his scales. His aura instantly lit up with electrical charge in a knee-jerk reaction. He was so angered by the surprise poison attack that the edge of his aura was well-defined, a perfect, bluish, opaque sphere of electricity with a blue dragon at its core.

Where had the poison come from? There was no way the brown dragon could be responsible, he hadn't even seen him to target him, and Ravanan knew the hold spell was still active, despite his waiver in attention. He was so thankful he had added a duration to the hold spell, it would continue to hold while he dealt with this new foe.

There had to be another dragon nearby, a red dragon most likely, and his armor was not prepared for that. He looked around wildly but saw nothing. Was the poison from a spell or an aura? He didn't sense any dragon near him so it couldn't be an aura attack which meant that he couldn't be certain of the attacker's color or how best to defend himself.

One thing Ravanan did know for certain was that he had to deal with this problem quickly. Poison wasn't instant death, but death was a sure thing unless he could get antivenin. The more movements he made, the less time he had and he needed time to find the dragon behind the attack. Ravanan commanded his aura to slow the poison in his system, trying to buy himself more time.

An invisible dragon, it wasn't near him, Ravanan knew this only because he could sense that his aura wasn't hurting the mystery dragon, but he wished it was. Conserving energy, he commanded his aura to drop the arching lightning.

The need to quickly finish the fight became urgent. Battling two dragons was never good, he needed to even the odds. Taking a deep breath, Ravanan held his calm resolve. He would not fail. He could not fail, his territory was at stake. He cast *"BOLT"*, causing a tremendous bolt of lightning to shoot from his pointed talon and explode into the acid-covered dragon. The air cracked loudly from the intensity of the spell. His enemy's body convulsed from electrical shock, Ravanan knew death was near, two more unprotected hits would stop the heart.

Then from the same invisible source Ravanan was hit with red flames of dragon breath. It had no effect on him because of his heat-shielding armor, and it revealed the hidden location of the poisonous problem.

His attacker had made a foolish mistake. Ravanan turned, feeling the poison drive nearer to his heart, his veins were now throbbing and his muscles were starting to feel tight as swelling intensified. The fiery breath wisped away and Ravanan saw who was responsible. Before he got to his target though the red-robed enchantress, flying backwards away from him cast *"SILENCE"*.

Ravanan cursed a muted rant at her.

She had been within his aura and he hadn't detected her. She had been unaffected by his shocking aura because she was covered entirely in an armor of salt water, looking very much like a raindrop of blood, even her head was covered. Salt water was an excellent choice of armor, appropriate for fighting a blue dragon as it was effective against electricity. The particulate matter in the water acted as a Faraday cage by forcing Ravanan's crackling lightning web to pass harmlessly over her. And all the while her vile poisonous aura was hurting him just as bad as any fire would, more so because it was inside his blood, permeating throughout his body with each heartbeat.

Ravanan could only assume that she had crafted her robe for invisibility and hadn't been in the area long enough to leave any signs of her presence or else she had been staying in the lair with her own reason for not leaving it. Either way, there was no way he could have known of her presence in the area.

With no voice and a useless aura he approached, breathed his blue fire back at her but it extinguished as it hit her water armor. To be able to hurt her Ravanan needed to cast a verbal spell or start a physical battle which he knew would speed up the poison. He cursed himself for giving her the opportunity to take his voice with the silence spell and he hoped she was young enough and her spells were so low in level that they wouldn't last very long.

"Release Kianthyx." she commanded. "You are trespassing and have no right to be here. Release him and leave!"

That wasn't going to happen. Only a few select times in his life had Ravanan retreated, this time, battling amateurs, wasn't one of them. Even though the pain was building and his mind was working double to keep focus on two dragons Ravanan wouldn't give in to her demands. Instead he raced with a powerful thrust towards the red enchantress, he may have been muted but words were not needed for ripping a body in half.

With every beat of his massive wings the poison was acting faster, it was already bruising his delicate wing skin and blackening it. Flying was making his heart pound hard against his rib cage.

The red-robed enchantress became alarmed when she saw Ravanan coming at her. In disbelief at his determination she dismissed her robe and let her little human form go before he reached her. Her water armor had expanded and thinned with her, her entire red dragon body was covered by the coat of water, and it did nothing to hide her serpentine shape base form. She was a diamid, her slender body, mirrored feathered wings of two pairs – one over the shoulders and the other over the hips, and pronged horns all spoke of the land across the water. But that was not all her body revealed, Ravanan could see she was about to give an egg as she snaked through the air.

Ravanan hesitated. He knew what he saw was true, there was no hiding an egg bulge. Her pregnancy changed the battle instantly for Ravanan even as he chose to charge on. She never should have entered the fight.

Her mate, Kianthyx, still hung in the air above the hole of their lair, blinded and mad. He worried for her and their egg. As the acid dissolved its way into his ear canal, Kianthyx the Malefic Copper could barely hear their battle before going deaf. At the moment he was not at all as regal as his title suggested - the self-proclaimed king was bound and helpless. Like Ravanan, he too was hoping the spell holding him would end shortly, until it did he was as good as dead and unable to help his mate. He wanted to fight, wanted to protect his egg and her. He could feel his attacker was outside of his aura and there was nothing he could do to stop the fight. He could only painfully remember those last sounds he had heard, the last sounds he would ever hear.

The chase was on, the red dragoness was desperate to keep the upper hand, she looked behind at Ravanan and cast *"CALM"*. His heart relaxed from the spell, but his will did not change.

With a quiet energy Ravanan continued to close the distance between them. His menacing body flew through the air, his wings were pumping fast. The eyes of the red dragoness grew wide with fear.

Her heart sank as Ravanan strengthened his pursuit despite his weakening aura. Silent and deadly, he was set on a collision course, he was foaming at the mouth and fighting the convulsive forces welling up inside him, but he refused to stop. There was malice and determination in his cerulean blue eyes that calmness only amplified. He would not tolerate careless thieves intruding in his home. There was no escape for the young dragons, not even her continual poisonous aura would stop him.

As Ravanan had hoped, her low level silence spell ended quickly; in her youth and panic she forgot to renew the spell immediately. That was all the time Ravanan needed. He felt his voice come back and with his next breath he cast *"I'LL CONTROL YOU"*. Immediately he made her aura stop pumping poison into him. But because of her egg he did not attack her with his deadly lightning.

It wasn't enough that he owned her now, he needed to grab hold of her. Ravanan grappled her in the air, his powerful muscles were more than enough for both of them. His body plunged through her water armor even as he commanded it to mist away. The red dragoness was smaller than Kalara, lighter and younger. Even with her egg she was svelte and nice to hold, it had been so long since he'd flown with a dragoness, and never one as slender as her. Ravanan tightened his grip and wrapped his long neck around hers.

From inside her mind he learned the red dragoness' name, Ishida of Nikhadelos Dialo, finally a name for those diamid horns, feathered head crest that flowed like tongues of fire, and the long whiskers from her snout.

Ravanan landed with her, far from the dangerous heat of her mate's aura that was baking the mountain. By walking inside her mind he mentally examined her body, experienced and felt the egg growing inside of her, it was nearly ready. He placed his black talons on her soft underbelly, touching and feeling her scales, feeling the heat of the egg, loving the object that her red scales protected. It was life, a dragon egg, the most precious symbol of dragonkind was so close to him, only separated by her scales and flesh.

Knowing Ishida's egg was safe, he bit down hard on her neck but his fangs didn't puncture her tough hide. She may have been young but she had already hardened her scales like most reds do to block any remedy-seeking bites.

Ravanan was desperate, his stamina was gone. His blood was not able to clot and it started to trickle from his eyes, nose, and ears as the poison thinned it. It hurt to draw breath and his thoughts were drifting towards rest. His control over her wavered as the poison was disorienting him and making his eyelids heavy. He needed to get the antidote of her flesh. His bite would have to be from her belly, the only semi-hard place on a red dragon and his teeth hurt already from the first attempt.

Ravanan laid Ishida on the ground and was about to strike again when he felt a stinging pain and heard a quiet SLIPH! as one of his back scales lifted and sheared away from him. The brown dragon was free from the hold spell and had hurled a cleaving disk at Ravanan.

The razor of Kianthyx was coming again when Ravanan lost his control spell over the red dragoness.

While still prone on the ground, Ishida cast *"SILENCE"* on Ravanan for a second time, putting as much duration to the spell as she could and armored herself again with water.

All Ravanan could think about was taking that bite, he would get it no matter what it took. To not bite her was death.

SLIPH! - another scale was gone. Ravanan roared and tackled Ishida with more force than speed. The ground trembled under the two fighting dragons. They wrestled but she was no match for Ravanan's size, he pinned her and sank his fangs through her water-covered abdomen and carefully away from the egg before letting go and taking flight.

Flying hurt so bad, and Ravanan's breathing was wet with blood, even his vision was red. SLIPH! – he kept going as his third scale fell away.

He was muted and still holding her flesh in his mouth. He kept low and struggled to get away. Ravanan heard her cast a spell and then an envenomed spear lodged into his exposed back. He recoiled and dropped even lower. As he searched for a large enough boulder to hide behind he noticed she was no longer looking at him and instead was moving towards Kianthyx.

The once-brown dragon was armored with bloody mucus to counterbalance an acid attack. The blinded thief believed he was battling a green dragon and was still defenseless against shock – Ravanan's trap had worked! He needed to strike Kianthyx now before he learned the truth but there was no way he was going to get close enough to use his lightning aura and he still was under the silence spell, so casting was out of the question.

A new pain grabbed Ravanan when the enhanced neurotoxin took effect from the spear. By the time he landed his body was in spasms as the poison confused the muscle. After several failed attempts he reached and tore the spear from his back then broke it in two. Still holding the meat in his mouth, he laid down to rest and wait until he got his voice back, hoping he wouldn't bleed to death before the silence spell ended. Closing his bloodied eyes, he listened with his ears and aura to know how far away the pair was, it was all he could do.

His diaphragm and lungs were seizing up and threatening suffocation by the time the silence spell ended. With little time to spare he targeted the meat in his mouth and cast *"ANTIVENIN"*. Ravanan swallowed with relief. In that quiet moment of peace he cast *"EVOKE ALOE EYES"* Dark green crystal lenses covered his eyes. The faceted gemstones weren't minerals but crystallized aloe Vera gelatin that emitted a faint green glow as they deadened his pain and made new blood for him. He was going to be alright. Soon the poison would be gone, he just needed to rest while the poison battled inside him. He hoped he had the time to catch his breath before they came for him.

While quickly eating his bulls, Ravanan considered using his anchor and coming back another day to finish the fight but he knew as time went on that Kianthyx would find a way to regain his sight. He had hurt Kianthyx badly and needed to finish the job before the dragon recovered. He was exhausted. But at least seeing everything in hues of green was a comfort to him. He would finish this fight now and get his gold back, he may be weak, but his enemy was too.

His rest was brief, they were coming. Ravanan felt them enter his aura, it wouldn't be long before they found him. They seemed to be headed straight for him as if they were smelling him with enhanced senses. They knew his location now, so there was no reason to try to keep quiet. He charged his aura full of spidery lightning. It was no good, he could feel that his aura didn't harm either one of them.

He didn't want any more poison, he had to protect himself with a better armor. The one he chose was a more difficult armor to cast and wouldn't last nearly as long as the simpler air armor he was using but it was better. He whispered, *"AIR BARRIER"*. The whitish bubble covered him, it was noticeable, but that didn't matter, he was safe from heat, poisonous air, and projectiles so long as they didn't understand the tight molecular bonds. It was such a delicate armor and if one knew the right way they could restructure the air molecules and bring it down. He hoped they weren't that schooled.

Still laying down, he felt the approach of their warm auras.

Then he saw little poison needles fly past and flick off his armor. He needed to move immediately. With every heartbeat he could see the ground getting brighter as it heated up; Kianthyx was with her and rage didn't even begin to describe the emotion that Ravanan felt coming towards him. The ground kept getting hotter until it began to melt. Somehow Ravanan's hiding rock didn't seem big enough as it too became gooey with lava. He was lying in a puddle of orange lava conserving strength. The aloe eyes were helping, but not fast enough for any major spell or battle.

Using what little strength he had left Ravanan resorted to using a weapon and cast *"EVOKE HEXDEATH"*. Six brilliant blades appeared and hung in the air in front of him. He untied their leather binding which set the blades to spinning. He hated using weapons, but in this case he needed to, there shouldn't have been a second dragon to fight.

The severely acid-burned Kianthyx came around the melting rock first.

With a flick of his wrist Ravanan pointed Hexdeath at his foe's neck, their white enchantment easily passing through the brown dragon's armor. The blades pricked the neck radially and sank deep as all six tips came together with a metallic ringing inside Kianthyx's neck. Then moving like a wheel the blades went to work, one after the other they sliced through it, clean and neat.

Ishida roared in protest when she came upon the stunning death of her mate and the gleaming sword collar that was killing him.

His brown head spun and toppled to the ground. As with all dragons, the body and severed head faded away with his burial spell to reappear at the bottom of the deepest ocean trench to be erased from the Earth.

Ravanan's vicious blades returned to him, circling him, awaiting a task.

Ishida froze for only a heartbeat, looking at Hexdeath. She opened her mouth, inhaling to either breathe fire or cast a spell but Ravanan cut her off with grave words.

"I don't like being forced into a corner." The command and force in his voice was more like a spell than a simple statement. With another flick of his wrist Ravanan sent the blades to her, dazzling and gleaming in the morning sun as they teased and sliced through her water armor. Hexdeath threatened her egg, her life.

Ishida had to think. She dropped her aura, seeing that it wasn't hurting the blue dragon, and changed some of her water armor to ice only surrounding her ribcage and torn-open, egg-laden abdomen.

Casting silence again would not prevent her death. She was smart enough to know that the blue dragon didn't need a voice to command those horrible blades. By the time she cast any offensive spell the blades would be slicing her up. If she tried to flee, the blades would follow, lunging at him would also mean falling onto the blades. Ishida wondered to herself how to gain the upper hand, and she studied the odd white bubble around him, looking for a way to make it fall apart.

Ishida started to speak but again the blue dragon cut her off, only this time it was with a spell.

"SILENCE!", he yelled.

Then he rose up and walked out of the cooling lava puddle he was in.

In her quieted world, Ishida backed up, rethinking her attack plans without the heat aura of her brown mate to help. She wouldn't mourn a fool of a dragon that she had only known for a season. She should have trusted her first opinion about the brown.

Re-seating himself on dry ground and knowing his armor was about to end, with a foaming mouth and bloody face Ravanan spoke to Ishida calmly, his blades still ready to strike - "You hurt me to the point of death, you know this don't you? I imagine right now you're plotting how to finish me, the dragon who murdered your mate. If I wasn't so weak right now, things would be different, but as the situation is not in my favor and my blood is fighting your poison, *I NEED TO CONTROL YOU.....*"

Ravanan really hated doing that to Ishida again so he decided to not reveal his presence in her head. Before controlling Kalara, he had never wanted to control another dragon. It just didn't seem right. And now here he was doing it again. Why? And why did he feel like it was his only option?

The first time with Ishida was to save his life, but this time he could have done something different to her. Yes he was good at control spells, an expert of experts, but he shouldn't treat his own kind like cattle. Kalara was one thing, she was ruined anyway, but this..... Had he changed somehow? Perhaps he just didn't care anymore. And he had to admit that controlling his enemy was the easiest, most-rehearsed choice at the moment.

He had Ishida fly him down to the lair. Once at the bottom he knew full well that it wasn't the actual lair, but merely the bottom of the hole. After his body healed up he would go exploring to find his gold and get some answers but for the moment he needed somewhere safe to rest away from humans and especially away from Kalara.

Chapter 17

The seer pool within Black Blade Lair screamed in pain when its glassy surface became painted with the visage of the door opening.

Kalara had been in the main lair when a sharp pain stabbed her right breast. She ran at the sound of torrents of water splashing.

"Ravanan!" she yelled, thinking he had finally returned with food. She could see bright light coming from the seer pool chamber as she ran to it.

When Kalara arrived at the seer pool it was a storm of commotion. Ravanan was nowhere to be seen. She didn't know what was going on. All she could do was watch the water splash around vehemently as she rubbed her chest to soothe the strange pain. It wasn't from hunger, she knew that at least, and the pain seemed to be lessening. She didn't know what had caused it. And yet the water continued to splash on....

It was dark after the rock wall closed behind him, Jeremy had a moment of worry. It had all happened so fast when he wasn't sure it even would. There was no time to think about it but now he was thinking it was probably a bad decision to follow his client through the odd door.

Annette was the first to grab her flashlight.

"Annette, we're not equipped for spelunking. You should have mentioned something yesterday about this. I have *never* done this."

"We have ropes and lights, we're fine." She started whistling.

Jeremy stood there, running his hands over his pack, there were too many zippers on it.

Annette kept whistling and he was getting annoyed. Finally he found his flashlight.

"What are you doing?" he demanded.

"Calling bats. Now be quiet."

She wasn't the best whistler.

Jeremy could stand it no longer, "I can help. I'm a better whistler than you."

"I'm not whistling, I'm calling bats."

Before long a little bat fluttered furiously around them. Annette kept whistling and held her finger out for a perch. The bat landed. Quick as lightning Annette grabbed it in her hand. The bat squeaked in protest. Annette offered some spit to Mother Earth for the bat and blessed the bat's spirit.

It squeaked for the rest of its life, which ended a minute later at Annette's pocket knife. Then she knelt down to use the rocky ground as a cutting board to cut off the bat's ears.

Jeremy said nothing, but there was shock in his eyes. He wondered if there was anything Annette wouldn't do.

Annette held the little bloody furry ears in her hands and said a prayer "Great Spirit, hear me, your daughter, Annette. Use these ears to bless your children as we navigate this cave. Protect us from falls, crushing rock, water and bad air, anything that might keep us from our goal. Let us be as the bat in your dark worlds."

Annette handed an ear to him and said "Eat this." Then she placed the other in her mouth, and started chewing.

He didn't think twice about it and tossed it in.

Just as the Great Spirit foretold, the journey through the rock was daunting, it was pitch black and the cave wouldn't end. The further from the entrance Annette walked the more her fear grew and Jeremy was not helping to calm that fear. When the Great Spirit said Kalara would be inside the rock Annette thought that meant Kalara lived in a cliff dwelling similar to ancient Native Americans of the Great Southwest, nothing like this dark hole - it was unexpected.

The cave kept going deeper inside the mountain, where people don't live. Why would Kalara be there? Annette was glad she had packed extra food and water (thinking Kalara would need it), even when Jeremy had told her not to because the extra weight would hinder their climb, and now he was thankful too, even apologetic – repeating 'if I had only known'.

He was a full believer in the Great Mother Earth now and was going to make a fine student. Annette thought about how Jeremy and Todd would get along, 'probably not very well' – she answered her own thoughts.

She looked Jeremy up and down, he was a good ole' city-bred white boy, you could tell by the way he used his equipment, he was fighting the environment instead of living with it. She could almost hear Todd laughing.

"How could your friend be in here?" Jeremy asked her during a rest break.

Annette had no answer for him. It didn't make sense but she trusted the Great Spirit and knew she was on the right track.

She had to be right in this. Of course Kalara was in there somewhere deep inside or else that rock wall wouldn't have been a doorway. Kalara was near and she would find her.

Like the doorway, the traps Annette found were unnatural, they were more than just subterranean hazards, and the energy coming from them gave further evidence that Kalara was there and that her spiritual gifts had returned to her. Annette could only imagine how Kalara must be growing, remembering her past and regaining her blessings from the spirits. She wondered just how powerful Kalara could be, she prepared herself for the worst, always keeping in mind that horrible day.

That night they settled down to sleep. Annette's body found rest. It had been so long. She actually dreamed real dreams, the type of dream that tells you you're getting enough rest. When Annette woke she knew Jenniffer was dead. In the dark cave a smirk crossed her face as she thought, 'it was fun while it lasted'.

Solving Kalara's traps only made Annette's thirst for power grow stronger. Yes, she was able to get past them with her spiritual blessing and ingenuity but how much more could she learn from Kalara? Or even learn from that man in the blue shirt who was with her? – Annette thought about him for a moment – she was sure that he had somehow helped Kalara regain her memories, though it was odd how he had just disappeared while she was watching in the peacock pool. She wondered if he would be with Kalara now and if he also shared a strong connection with the spiritual world, he had to. Annette's heart skipped a beat in excitement.

The pair of spelunkers came upon a sheer drop, a chasm with no apparent bottom. Their flashlights were not strong enough to penetrate the strange blue mist that had been hanging in the air for some time now. Annette tried a couple of times using different ideas to throw light down the hole but nothing worked.

Although it was odd for her spells to fail it wasn't unthinkable. She knew there were those few times when nature was not willing to bend and this had to be one of them. Thankfully they had Jeremy's expertise. They safely descended into the hole and hours later they were climbing out on the other side.

It wasn't long after the big chasm until they approached a grand hallway. Flashlights were no longer needed as there were strangely-convenient sconces on the walls that flickered brightly with flame, welcoming them. Annette knew she was close now, and her fear-laced eagerness grew with every step.

The far wall was guarded by two giant black pillars in each corner and glittering blue mist filled the chamber.

Annette squeezed the fear from her heart and pressed it into the dried cat hearts in her hand.

Jeremy kept walking towards the nicely lit room. "Wow, are you seeing this??" he asked her.

Annette spoke out "Jeremy, stop. Don't go any further just yet."

He listened and turned back, glad for the break and sat down to rest.

The hallway was big. The pillars were big. There was a lot of black floor to cross, there had to be a trap somewhere. Annette studied the gray walls, they were not black and were weeping steady drips of water which was a little odd considering the lack of water in the cave until this room, and also the fact that there were no water stains or cave formations where the water landed on the ground, it was as if water spigots had turned on when they entered and like a giant fountain in some grand hotel, the water magically vanished to come out again on top.

The flaming sconces were high up, thirty feet or more, carved from black rock and hung on the gray walls with what looked to be decorative little jagged lightning bolts.

Annette remembered that horrible day of being hunted and watched, that is how she felt now. The level of fear she was feeling was great, the cat hearts were not working. And she knew..... Kalara must be on the other side of the far wall.

She fingered her braided ring of Kalara's hair. It would be her protection although she had never had the chance to test her work. Annette had imbued the little ring with the blessings of the Great Spirit to counter Kalara – should she attack again. Annette didn't know what to expect, but if Kalara tried anything she'd be safe. Making that ring had been one of the first things Annette did after taking Kalara home.

With trembling hands, Annette made a little ceremony to Mother Earth. She was nearly out of tobacco but this was important, she smoked half a pipe only. On the floor in front of her she dealt her peacock feathers, chanting, then spoke softly, "Oh Great Spirit, show me the trap that awaits." the feathers remained feathers and no iridescent pool formed.

The peacock pool's failure meant something was going on. Annette looked over at Jeremy, and he was looking at her for answers, but she had none to give.

She had an idea and took out the piece of tent that was their doorway along with a small dream catcher she had packed for when she met up with Kalara just in case things didn't work out. She handed the tent to Jeremy.

"Take this, let's be fast." she looked around at the sconces, "You need to go first and place it like you saw me do and then pull the little door open. I'll come then and make sure to grab the real door when it appears. Don't forget to grab the little tent door as we leave."

Jeremy took off at a brisk pace, tent doorway in hand.

Annette couldn't be sure in the blue mist but Jeremy's body seemed to somehow glow.

Now she was sure he was glowing brighter each time his foot landed on the black floor. Right when she was going to tell him to come back, Jeremy started to say "The floor, it's gotten...."

Jets of water and lightning flew to Jeremy, becoming charged ice that clung to his clothes.

"colder." he forced out through gritted teeth. It was his last word before the ice jetting from the wall spigots covered him completely.

Annette was wide-eyed. She took a deep, horrified breath before tucking her little dream catcher in her pocket in relief that it hadn't been her.

The seer pool water was still splashing around wildly, Kalara had no idea what it meant. What she did know was that merely running to the seer pool had tipped her hunger over the edge.

Kalara constantly wore Healer now to combat her hunger and exertion, but the ribbon robe could not make food from nothing. She dreaded going outside again but walked over to the exit. Some things just had to be done even if she didn't want to do them, it didn't help putting it off because it only made her weaker and that much closer to death. She needed food.

If only Annette's curse didn't wound her so badly.....

Kalara found herself thinking more and more of Annette lately, everything was that woman's fault. There was nothing else to do but think, there was no food, she couldn't practice her magic, hating Annette was all there was. Kalara angrily spit on the wall and cast *"REVEAL"*.

The barren rock floor was not comfortable to sit on but Annette was tired of standing. She was stopped right there and had no idea how to proceed. The sound of water dripping off of Jeremy's ice resonated throughout the chamber.

Then Annette felt a cold wave of air move around her and the water seized up again. There in the quiet room something had changed and she hadn't done anything to provoke it. The blue mist still hung silently in the air, not frozen. Annette turned her head to look down the grand hallway. The drips of water had frozen to make little icicles all over the walls and ice sheets were on the ground. She trembled knowing something was happening that she didn't cause.

Annette peered across the grand hallway to notice the far wall was now gone and walking between the two giant black pillars was Kalara coming towards her. She stood up, teeth chattering.

"Kalara!" she cried out, "I've been worried sick about you!"

Kalara, dressed in a sultry blue ribbon robe, looked over at her with an angry stare that quickly turned to shock. *"EVOKE SIPHON"* she heard Kalara say. Before Annette could contemplate what that greeting meant a little black blade materialized in Kalara's hand which she then threw at her.

THUCK! The dark blade Siphon landed in Annette's shoulder. "What the hell?!" she exclaimed looking at it then back to Kalara who was still walking.

Annette pulled out the dagger and threw her dream catcher at Kalara.

The dream catcher hit Kalara but it fell away pitifully without working its evil curse. They both watched it fall.

Annette couldn't believe what was happening. Why wasn't any of her magic working?!? She felt a little faint but wielded Siphon up to use against Kalara.

Despite the freezing air, that oddly warm spirit energy was growing in Kalara, just as it had in Manaus. Annette threateningly held the dagger a little higher, "That was a bad thing to do Kalara! I didn't want it to be like this." she warned.

Kalara smirked. *"EVOKE SIPHON"*.

Annette's eyes grew wide when the blade vanished from her hand to reappear in Kalara's.

'How was that possible?' Annette wondered, but not for long as the room started spinning and she dropped to the cold floor.

Annette tried to calm her speeding heart. It was so cold. She was laying on the floor and heard Kalara's footsteps come closer to her head.

Her pulse began to slow and her body felt heavy with an odd feeling like she wasn't getting enough blood.

Beat..... beat...... beat..... beat..... like the ticking of a clock winding down. She had no strength left to fight and she felt oddly dry and very cold as she opened her eyes to see where Kalara was.

Kalara startled her. She was right there, looking down at her. "Why are you here?" she calmly asked.

"uhhhugg" Annette attempted to answer.

"Can you not talk? That won't help me. You see, I've been having these dreams lately." Kalara sat down out of Annette's reach. "I was hoping you could interpret them for me. In my dream I'm always hungry and have lost everything and then you show up – bringing me food. Now what do you think that means?" she asked with a wicked smile.

Annette tried to answer again with a weaker "uhhhugg". She could see Kalara and she could hear the bitch talking, but all she could think of was getting a hold of Kalara and killing her before her magic did any more damage. Why was it so cold?

Beat..... beat..... beat..... beat..... it was getting slower. Annette worried she may be dying, trapped like a bug in a web, but it wasn't possible, the blade had hit her shoulder, it wasn't a mortal wound. She just felt so weak and Kalara looked stronger by the minute. There was nothing she could do, not even a cursing chant.

The end of her life wasn't supposed to be like this. Not this soon. How was it possible? Little Kalara was taking her blood somehow. What evil magic was in that blade? Without touching her, she was killing her. Each pump of her heart was tugging at her throat, the back of her neck, her chest, her legs and arms – all were begging her to just give up.

"Give up." she heard Kalara say.

Those last drowsy moments were quiet. Hot blood oozed from her knife wound, trickling down her shoulder and into her armpit, feeling wet, each spurt less forceful than the last, her powerful heart was draining her dry. Annette could feel her blood warming her skin while at the same time not sending continual warmth to her core. Where it should have been warm in her bones, now she felt icy-cold, chilled, and then even colder as her blood froze on her shirt.

She suffered. Kalara demanded. She cried-or rather yielded dry sobs. Her body hurt. Kalara laughed. She cried harder. She had no choice but to submit, every heartbeat was going to Kalara. And because she cried, her blood was flowing away faster, draining her..... Annette hated it that she was helplessly giving Kalara *her* life. She hated her.

She.... hated.... her.

Annette could see her left arm from the way she had fallen, its veins now looked like deathly purple rivers. Little black lightning bolt patterns – zigzagged across the back of her hand.

Beat..... beat....... beat......... beat........... her blood felt loose and watery. Her eyeballs hurt with too much pressure. The world around her grew dim. Annette wanted to scream, one last time to make a noise, somehow make an impact on the world around her, but it was no use, sleep was easier.

Then Annette stopped looking through her opened eyes.

Her soul was quiet as it lay there listening to how death sounded. All of her rich life blood, and now only drops remained. Moisture had left her. She was so *dry*. The vanishing, thickening blood was sticky on her shirt and skin, it was the only blood that Annette couldn't give to Kalara's vampiric thirst other than the blood that had run from her tear ducts and orifices.

Annette's soul knew it was over and was anxious to leave. The body was still performing its muscular work, using up that last bit of energy, her heart was still weakly pumping just as a snake's heart will pump for an hour after its head has been cut off. It was a sad, quiet time while her heart pumped out the last drops of beautiful red blood, draining her veins completely.

So cold. So thirsty. So dry. So hollow. Annette's soul shivered uncontrollably, cold and afraid to become a timeless non-rock of the Earth, a helpless observer of time barely attached to the body. Annette hated to leave the beauty of the Earth and the fun of life, but then again she wanted to get as far away as she could from her cold, dry corpse.

The pulse throbbed like a slow engine, ticking, heavy – slowly, ticking each second away like a century, counting out these most irritating moments of her life. She wanted to die, end the torture – every moment, they were dragging her down like weights when she wanted nothing more than to float away.

Beat....... beat........... beat.

Strangely, her soul both wanted the last drop to stay and also to go, she mourned it. Annette's soul would forever know this moment as The Vanishing, when that last drop left.

Then everything in her body went silent.

Annette's soul lifted and saw something forming around her in the blackness.

The something became a room, it was colorful like the green and blue Earth. There were flowers and a gentle waterfall in the corner that flowed out to nourish an ancient tree living in the center of the room. The carpet was green grass, the ceiling was sky blue with golden sparkles for stars. It was beautiful, the opposite of chaos, it was everything that made sense in the world and she could stand on it, knowing.

No sooner had the room formed when there came to be a spirit near the water, some would say a saint or angel, others would say an emotionless government employee who looks up your numbers on a table to find the value assigned to you, and yet a few others would call it a judge. Whatever it was, it looked at her for a time of counting.

In an instant the spirit knocked on the wood of the tree to declare the decision and then a doorway opened off one of the walls. The spirit vanished. The Room of Deciding was disappearing behind Annette and she was being pushed to and through the door.

The hallway remained dark as her soul went further into it. Nothing was behind her. Then in front of her she saw a spot so dark it looked like a black hole. The spot was so black that the tunnel she was in became noticeable.

Annette had heard of the evil some called Hell, she'd never been sure about it until now when floating further in she began to hear faint moans and screams of torment, they were coming from the dark, far away but they revealed the chaos and sadness of the black hole. Just hearing the sounds of so many hurting and lonely souls horrified her, she wanted no part of it.

But there was nothing she could do because her soul was being sent there. The Nothing behind her was growing larger and pushing her away. There was nowhere to go but forward.

Terror filled Annette's soul. She shouldn't be going towards the negative energy of that black hole. Countless times she had been through smudging ceremonies, her soul was clean, purified, this wasn't right. And it wasn't fair, she shouldn't have died there in that cave away from her tribe and land. They could have helped her soul find its way, and said the proper prayers to send her to her ancestors.

The voices were louder now, the black hole was larger. Some were calling out "hello?" while others were whimpering, but none were joyful.

Annette's soul heard something then. Was it a voice or a wind of Mother Earth? She looked behind her at the Nothing that was pushing her but instead saw a faint light in the distance. There was hope, there was another way to go.

YES! She'd always heard about this, the on-going argument if it was the way to Heaven or if it was the final trick of the brain as it died. There was eagerness that finally she would find out which way it was. After her whole life of waiting, it was finally happening. Her happy soul remembered the distant smell of burning sage and rejoiced.

She turned and started moving towards the light. It wasn't white light, but instead it had a faint black light quality which she'd never heard anyone describe before.

Although she was making progress and the ultraviolet beacon grew larger while the sounds of screaming souls grew quieter, her phantom extremities began to tingle with ugly numb pain like the nerve endings were trying to reconnect after being cut off from oxygen-rich blood. The tingling was maddening, Annette's soul tried to shake off the pain but it wasn't helping. It was almost like her body was waking up.

Not only was she tingling, but her soul felt weighted down with lead, making it harder to reach the light. The tunnel had been long before but with the added weight it was going to take forever to get through it. That did not matter though, she would advance for eternity just to avoid the black hole; she didn't even want to look back at it. Annette continued to float on laboriously, but happily at the chance, nothing was going to stop her from moving away from the black hole.

The path to the purple light seemed to stretch on forever with the pins and needles pain and added weight. Maybe her body was coming back to life. She couldn't hear a heartbeat though. Annette's soul wondered if she should be going this way, but decided she should when she remembered the sounds coming from the darkness. (Not that she could have turned back anyway because her soul was unknowingly being gently tugged and pushed.)

She didn't understand. Things weren't right, that much she could feel, the light should be white, not purple, and she shouldn't have a dead weight body caging her soul still. She thought maybe she wasn't alone. Her soul spoke out "Mother Earth? Great Spirit? Where am I? Are You here?"

There were no acoustics in the tunnel, her voice did not echo and fell flat in the air.

Mother Earth did not answer.

Annette's soul was truly lost, the only thing she knew was that she didn't want to go to the black hole, it terrified her.

Maybe all of this was a dream. She was getting closer with each step, a few more and she would be out of the tunnel. Her body had to be waking up now because she was light-headed and the painful tingling was all over her arms and legs. She was dreading those few remaining steps because the tingling was going to be severe. Up ahead she could make out shapes, lights, the tunnel was opening into a purple hallway with purple flames high on the walls above her.

Then it hit her, she had died in a hallway, laying in front of Kalara. All of a sudden she didn't want to go any further and turned around back toward the darkness.

Annette's soul stopped where it was. No, not darkness, she didn't want to go there, anything but there. Even if the tingling grew worse the closer she got to the purple world, she would suffer it. She didn't want to take even one step back towards that blackness. Was there no other choice?

If she ventured out into the world of purple, what would be there? She paused and strained to hear sounds from where she stood just inside the tunnel. There was no sound. So Annette took another cautious step.

Now she could see what was outside waiting for her. There was her cold body with sunken skin. It looked leathery like it had been tanned and preserved. It was laying where she had left it. It didn't look inviting but rather used and shriveled, and much older than she was.

Then her soul took another step and felt cold. Two more and she would be out. Another step.

"AAAAAAAAAAHHHH!" Annette's soul screamed at what she saw, even her body's mouth opened and let out air. It was a dragon, a giant purple dragon looming over her dead body.

The dragoness was now looking at her dead body with her head cocked to the side, she had noticed the air pass out from the lungs.

This wasn't Heaven, it was Earth and she was in Brazil. But why was there a dragon? Was this a dream? Dragons weren't real, everyone knew that.

In that instant, Annette's soul wanted to hide inside the tunnel, but taking a step back would bring her closer to the darkness and she most definitely didn't want that. And she couldn't stay in that spot because the darkness could maybe suck her in.

She wanted to cry. She didn't want to move, but her body was wanting to. It wanted to walk around and make the nerve pain stop. She didn't know what was going on, so Annette's soul just went down to her knees and cried in dry sobs. She could hear her voice crying without tears and groaning, it strangely comforted her in this weirdest of times.

Opening her eyes again, the tunnel was gone. Annette recognized the spot where she was, it was where she had died in the cave. She looked around in the purple light for her dead body.

Except the light wasn't purple anymore. And there was no body except for the one she was in, it was kneeling on its knees now before a giant purple dragon.

She looked down at the clothing, it was hers. The sunken and dried-looking hands were hers, they looked like some of her dried cat hearts. Why didn't they have life in them? She was even still wearing her ring of Kalara's hair though it was looser now. She felt for a pulse at her neck. There wasn't one. She screamed and it came out breathy.

Then she noticed the dragoness had lowered her head to right in front of her. She screamed again and put her arms around her head, preparing to be eaten.

But the purple dragoness didn't eat her. Instead, with Kalara's voice the dragoness said "You don't have a pulse, you're dead."

With trembling hands, Annette tried again. The dragoness waited, and Annette waited. She pressed her fingertips harder against her leathery stiff neck. There was nothing. This had to be a dream. She fell over and curled into a fetal position, wanting desperately to wake up.

The dragoness chuckled. "Oh you are still kicking, don't worry about that. I've preserved you. You've been mummified, caught between life and death. I couldn't let you slip away and die now could I? So I did what I had to. Care to guess who your master is?"

Annette shook her head, refusing to believe, and mouthed a silent NO, a terrified NO.

"It's me, KALARA." The purple dragoness shouted.

All Annette could say was no. "NO NO NO NO!" She didn't know where Kalara was but she wasn't looking at a woman.

The purple dragoness spoke more "I could have eaten you, finished you off, but I didn't, your blood was quite enough to please me. And now you are going to serve me. You cannot harm me. If you go against me, it'll be darkness for you, you'll see nothing, and I *know* you don't want that. The only way you'll see light, the *only way your world will brighten up*, is if you do my bidding."

Annette tried not to believe the dragoness. She envisioned her preserved self-standing up and chanting a curse against Kalara. With her thoughts came the darkness, flooding the room, haunting her with horrified voices of dark torment.

It was enough. Annette didn't want any of that. She knelt again "Yes, dragoness." she spoke in fallen tones of miserable acceptance.

"Why did you call me that?!?" Kalara demanded.

"Because that is what you are."

"No. I. Am. Not. Thanks to you!" Kalara stood there, teeth clenched hard with fists balled up and a steely stare of fresh anger. There was so much to what her new mummy said that it disturbed her. It made Kalara think of Ravanan's rejection, it pained her. "DON'T

CALL ME THAT! I AM YOUR ENCHANTRESS! GOT THAT? Enchantress, call me Enchantress. Do you understand?!? NOW SIT DOWN!" Kalara spun away from the mummy so fast her deep purple armored robe Heed swirled about her legs.

Annette shivered and lowered her dried head "Yes, *Enchantress.*" It was all so very perplexing to Annette. Clearly that was Kalara's voice but it was coming from a giant purple dragon. And somehow when the dragon was mad the air turned colder. She herself was dead and deep inside a mountain far from Oklahoma. She sat and watched her enchantress move over to the lifeless body of Jeremy.

Kalara cast *"MUMMIFY"* on Jeremy's body and then collapsed in exhaustion

The mummy watched as another of her kind was born, all moisture from Jeremy's body rose from his skin and orifices into a cloud that slowly expanded into the air of the grand hallway.

His body did the same odd silent scream and then clumsily rose into a kneeling position.

Jeremy groaned in a low, raspy voice, deeper than he had before, then he screamed again at seeing the purple dragoness.

"Stop screaming."

"But you're a... a.. dragon. You're not real."

"I am an enchantress and I am *very* real." The dragoness looked angered at his mistake and Jeremy the mummy felt the chill of it.

The terrible dragoness sat back. "I preserved you into a mummy."

"Oh NO WAY!" Jeremy moaned as he looked at his dried hands, he knew it to be true. His skin still had its tan color, but it was now marked with dark purple veins. He felt his hair, it was still there and looking good. "This can't be happening, it can't be. Dragons aren't real. This must be a type of heaven or hell, or maybe, maybe.... is this a dream?"

"No its not." Her great head came down as she looked closer at him. "You're not Todd, who are you?"

"Jeremy DeHay, tour guide."

"Fine. You will provide food for me until I can hunt on my own, Jeremy."

"No! You did this to me!" The silent darkness fell over him immediately and caused him to scream again in worry. "I want to go back!!!!!!!!!"

"I said stop screaming."

"But what happened?!? What did you do?" he whimpered in the dark.

"Like I said, I mummified you. And when you go against me there will be nothing but darkness. Now go get me some food."

Jeremy remained on his leathery knees in the darkness and cried without tears. He didn't want to be there, he had been quite happy with death. "Please release me!"

His enchantress yelled "NO! You *will* bring me food! I want animals to eat twice a day, no, make that four. This is your task and you will not be able to break it. Consider it your payment for immortality."

"I don't want immortality and I don't want this!" Jeremy the mummy spoke out from his darkness.

Kalara narrowed her eyes "I have given you a better life than you had before. Your body is dead – it can't die again, all pain is behind you and like a plant you will keep on living. The only thing that can destroy you now is fire and it would be a slow death I think."

"No, please no." Jeremy pleaded even as he saw the truth of it. Light returned to his world. He saw Annette. "All of this is her fault. Use her! And let me go."

"I will use you until I no longer need you."

Jeremy hung his head.

"Your body should still be able to move fast enough to hunt and I can enchant it should you need more."

"I'll need more." Jeremy was quick to say as fast as he could with his slow, dry voice.

"OK. Fine. I need some food first. When you return I'll have this door working for you." Kalara turned away and started walking back to Black Blade Lair dragging Annette with her.

Chapter 18

The desk of Dr. David Wilson was covered with his research notes. The afternoon sun was lighting the room. He had just come back from refilling his water glass and was getting back to his latest research paper.

He typed ".... and the results of this study are promising, showing greater efficiency in the blood stream's transportation of testosterone" he deleted it.

Documenting his findings was the worst part of his job but it was necessary. With no less than eighteen published articles covering his hormone research, he and his colleagues were on the forefront of testosterone therapy.

Dr. Wilson continued typing his thoughts, oblivious to the invisible presence in the room with him. She was devouring his every thought as his most avid follower.

The truth was that the person who was secretly with him had logged more hours in Dr. Wilson's presence over the past few months than anyone else had. The reason for this was that in his field of study it went undisputed that he was the best, the most studied, most creative, and a top researcher, grant money sought him out.

She knew him better than he knew himself, she saw how he did his best thinking after lunch and the hour leading up to playing racquetball. She even took her research to his bed, posing as his wife. And anyone that stood in his way, rival or reporter, she artfully removed them and if that didn't work, she ate them.

Dr. Wilson's invisible shadow not only gleaned from him, she helped where she could. Hidden, resourceful, a reminder of past ideas that might help on the current problem, she did all she could to contribute. She needed his curiosity to further her own research, she had the memory but not the creativity. Learning from her own spells and pets, she would report her findings directly into his mind and listen for how he processed the information. It was exhausting but rewarding work, and her efforts were starting to pay off. She felt great and could fly faster, further than she ever could before. The steroids were working.

Her efforts were also making their mark on his world of laboratories and campuses. In the months since she arrived, his peers had taken notice that his already impressive career was really taking off. With jealous eyes they applauded him.

Chapter 19

Bill took a drink from his cola and went back to work. This particular car was giving him grief, he hoped replacing the starter would take care of it. The bolts were far down in the engine and they weren't budging. Reaching as far as he could he pushed with all his weight on the wrench – they didn't budge.

After spraying some WD-40 and waiting a bit he tried to loosen the bolts again. Looking at him you would think he was mad, and possibly he was, he was totally focused on a bolt when finally it gave way and he busted his knuckles on the dirty old engine. Now he was mad.

He yanked out his hand to suck the blood off his skin and looked at the damage done – it was already throbbing. He wondered why he was even working at the garage when there were other easier jobs out there when Jenniffer came walking up.

She looked like dessert and a smile spread on his face. "Hey hey Gorgeous!"

Her smile made him forget all about his bloodying hand. Blood dripped onto the oily ground as he looked and saw her old red corvette. "Oh WOW, you got it back! How'd you do it?"

Jenniffer replied "Oh it wasn't hard, the guy actually begged me to take it back."

Her response seemed a bit weird to Bill but he was more concerned with her daytime visit, that was something she never did, and especially coming to the garage. It was unheard of.

Bill wiped his hand off with a rag. Jenniffer's eyes were pinned on him. Things began to rise up inside. Then he noticed her eyes were no longer the beautiful rainbows of color. "No contacts today?"

"No. I got tired of them." she said as she came in for a hug. Jenniffer cuddled her face against his skin like a cat. "You smell terrific."

Bill let out a laugh "Don't lie."

"No seriously, you smell amazing" her nose went behind his ear then her mouth found his neck. "You taste even better." she licked the salty sweat off his skin.

Bill looked around for his boss. "I'm glad to see you – after you not coming around the past couple of nights. You OK?"

Jenniffer leaned against the car he'd been working on, "I feel terrific. I had to go do some stuff, like getting my car back and all. But I've been missing you. Can you stop for the day?"

It was a struggle to unlock the door with Jenniffer's hand down his pants. He finally stopped trying and turned around to taste her. Their lips pressed hard and parted so their tongues could twist. It was one of *those* types of kisses, the kind that is clearly a preview of things to come.

The rotten wood porch wasn't going to stand for their heavy action though and they both knew it. To his surprise Jenniffer was able to open his door without missing a tongue sweep. She was awesome that way and it only made him want her more.

Bill shut the door and threw his keys to the coffee table, hot on Jenniffer's heels. He let out a whistle when she removed her shirt to reveal a new bra.

"Damn girl! Come here and let me see that."

She winked and then took off running for the bed.

The short chase stoked the already bright red coals in Bill's pants. He caught her at the bedroom door, kissed her and ran his fingers along the black bra. "Nice!" was all he could think to say. Breasts had a dumbing effect on him. With greased-stained hands he touched her neck and shoulders, kissing her all the while. A little bit of automotive grease got on her skin, it was no matter to either of them.

He pushed her against the wood paneled wall and held her wrists high. He just could not kiss her hard enough nor get enough of rubbing his face on her chest. Jenniffer's legs wrapped around his and he carried her to the bed.

"You know what a new bra means." Bill said as he took off his clothes.

"Do I?"

"You're fixin to", then he mounted her from behind and used the bra as a handle. While he was plunging into her he could see her beautiful red hair fall across her long back. He visualized the new bra cutting into her cute breasts, making them bulge as he tugged on it. He could just picture them jiggling as he rode her hard.

Jenniffer moved off him before he got to explode inside her. "You think I'm gonna let you get me that easy?" she played with him.

"What you got in mind?" he asked with a smile.

"Your cock." She turned over and started licking him.

"Oh Jenn!" he let out as he laid back into his pillow. "I thought you hated this."

Between kisses she teased him by breathing her warm breath on his tip. Then Jenniffer smiled deliciously saying "Surprise" before running her tongue along his length and then taking him in her mouth.

His hands found the back of her head and he pushed her onto him repeatedly. Her red hair was everywhere, he loved every silken strand that moved over him.

She worked herself free of his grubby hands and sat back on her heels "My goodness you're in a hurry. Don't be." She moved to get between his legs and pushed them apart. "I'm gonna make you feel things you've never felt before. I'm going to make you cum so hard you'll be changed forever."

"Oh yeah?"

"Yeah." she whispered as she found his balls.

"Ooooo careful there!" he lightly pleaded with breath held.

Her lips were like the smoothest satin against him. She was good. Very good.

"I had no idea."

"Shhhh."

He could feel her hot breath as she quieted him. Damn she was an artist! He enjoyed her work very much. A tingling sensation traveled from his toes to the back of his head. The pleasure he felt as her wet tongue found his hidden areas made his eyes roll back in ecstasy.

Jenniffer took her time, feeling the moment. The hotter she got the more the little barbs on her palms rose up like goose flesh.

With the kissing and caressing going on Bill didn't notice the barbs on her palms that held him firm, it wasn't enough to puncture the skin but just the right amount to secure the prey. If anything the barbs awoke his skin even more.

Then when he was fully into it with head thrown back and her numbing saliva all over him, her needle-like fangs dropped down and Jenniffer struck like a snake, they sank deep into his balls.

Bill felt a slight and quick pressure that thrilled him even more. She was right. He felt like he could never achieve this feeling again. He loved it. He loved her!

The rush of venom through her fangs caused her to orgasm. Bill wasn't far behind and Jenniffer collected every drop, purring as she lapped up his cum. She was a very clean and thorough monster after all. His cum was her reward while the testosterone flowed out and vanished to be awarded to her maker.

Within days Jenniffer had increased her social network considerably. From university grounds to mega churches she roamed. There were so many men and she wanted them all, not giving another thought about Bill. She lived for the night time and was always on the lookout for a guy to fuck. She hunted them and bedded them, the tougher the guy the harder she worked to have him. And in her wake across NE Oklahoma many men were left ruined and weak, their spark was gone. Size didn't matter, nor color, nor marital status, nor job or education – only their ego and bright eyes that signaled confidence were needed to attract the vixen. Jenniffer took all of it from them, they would never recover.

Her favorite marks were policemen, they really got her barbs to itching, wanting to grasp their cute asses and thighs. Rare finds were ball teams where she'd move from player to player, she could ruin a team within a week – then the coach wouldn't know how to pull them out of their losing streak and shortly he too would become weak and uncaring.

On a Saturday trip to Tulsa Bill and Todd went to the gun show at the fairgrounds. As usual the parking lot was a mess with cars but one stood out, Jenniffer's red corvette.

Todd saw it first. "What the hell? There's Jenn's Old Red! We ought to go get it back!"

"She did. I guess you haven't seen her lately."

"Nope." Todd replied. "So she got it back. First smart thing she's done. What is she doing here? She hates guns."

"No clue. I haven't seen much of her."

As they entered the crowded Expo Center Bill eagerly scanned for his girlfriend. There were so many people – he didn't see her.

Jenniffer was following her next victim, a camo-wearing guy. They'd already played the eye game. What made this guy fun was that a woman was hanging on his arm completely oblivious that Jenniffer was already stealing him away. The guy was doomed when the pair parted for a bathroom break. She overheard where the couple said they'd meet back up.

She took off behind the woman and actually held the bathroom door open for her. Once inside she took the stall next to the woman and waited. When the woman sat down Jenniffer vaulted over the wall. The woman screamed but that didn't matter because the vixen had already grabbed her hair and was biting her face. Jenniffer felt her venom pulse into the woman, satisfyingly removing the competition.

Seconds later with fangs hidden Jenniffer was checking her beautiful self in the mirror while the woman slept, slouched over on the toilet and turning into a vixen.

The camo-wearing guy arrived at the designated meeting place, smiling kindly to the red headed bombshell that was near. He was soon to be her sixth trophy for the day.

Jenniffer wasted no time. She befriended him and started slowly moving towards the door as they talked. Her voice was low and sexy, forcing him to keep inching forward to hear her. It'd be a quicky, the exit door opened to trailers that the vendors had brought their wares in. She had previously found one unlocked. Then she spied Bill and her brother – curiosity grabbed her because their musky smell was more exotic and stronger than all the other men in the place.

The vixen quickly grabbed her victim's arm and pulled him to the exit, using him as a blind to hide behind.

He was nice to have. She'd picked another awesome cock. Emerging from the trailer the vixen adjusted her clothes and made her way back inside to follow that wondrous aroma.

There she was! Bill's heart leaped in his chest. He made his way to Jenniffer with Todd in tow. "Jenn, hi! How are you doing?!?" he asked her.

Todd had a smile for his sister but it was colored with raised eyebrows "...and why are you at a gun show?"

Jenniffer went right into Bill's embrace, smelling him. "I'm good..... better now."

Todd kept his reservations alive. "I saw your corvette parked outside."

Clearly Todd was a third wheel. The magnetic pull between the vixen and Bill was heating them both up. Jenniffer mumbled something about walking around and the two headed off into the crowd.

Todd set off the other way to find the bullets he needed. That was really strange, Jenniffer being at a gun show and she got her car back. He'd get the rest of the story later in the car ride home. And she looked so hot – Todd hadn't ever noticed before or else she'd gotten prettier. It wasn't right to be thinking that way. He got his head into something else quickly by looking at a booth swarming with salesmen.

In the unlocked vendor trailer, their hot breath was making it steamy.

While undoing Bill's pants Jenniffer commented "What happened to you? You are more amazing than ever!"

"What do you mean? I'm not different. And I could ask you what happened. Where have you been? You haven't returned my phone calls, you're never home...."

Jenniffer had her arms around his bare waist, kissing his chest. "I mean you are freaking hot! Look at you! And you, you're... you're not empty. But you were empty, I know. Ah..... – I don't get it but that doesn't matter. I need you. Now!"

Todd ended up driving home alone since Bill, The Endless Fountain, took off in Old Red with the vixen.

Chapter 20

R avanan finally woke up feeling better. He blinked his eyes and stretched his scaly blue body. He had been in his healing sleep long enough that his scales were mostly healed over. But during that time of recovery he still had to keep Ishida controlled which prolonged the healing process that much more. He wasn't sure how long it had been.

He desperately needed food, which made him think of Kalara – how long had it been since he'd fed her? Ravanan immediately left to find the closest meal he could, not wanting to get so far from his prisoner that it would break his connection with her mind. He set up an anchor and sent Kalara her part of the meal, knowing she would be as hungry as he was.

Only then did he look ahead. He had a lot of work to do with this new lair and its treasure.

Days later, after countless meals and endless blood-consuming enchantments and all the while maintaining his control and sleep spells over Ishida, Ravanan kept at least two striking distances away and tossed some dead humans at her, hitting her snout and waking her up.

Ishida checked that her egg was safe, noted that the bite out of her belly was healed, and then attempted to fly out of the hole. With a 'thud' she hit an invisible barrier over her head; it was as she suspected, she was imprisoned.

She targeted the blue dragon and cast *"SILENCE"*. But was startled to find the sound waves of her spell were visible blue threads that fell down to the ground to be fully absorbed by it. She blew fire but Ravanan was out of reach and beyond her aura.

The red dragoness quickly snatched up her food and stared at her enemy.

Ravanan was watching her too, trying to discern any indication of intent from her since she was hiding her thoughts, and of course hiding thoughts was normal and expected. What wasn't normal was being blasted by the deafening emotions of Kalara, that was not typical dragon behavior and it wasn't fun knowing every single thought she had. This was much more fun, actually refreshing to him to have to pay attention and figure out the mystery.

Ishida cast *"EVOKE SPEAR"*. And again her spell turned into blue thread and fell at her dark red talons. Then there came a list of spells *"POISON" "FIREBALL" "DIE" "SLEEP" "STOP MAGIC"*. All turned to blue thread and fell.

Then she bent her head and looked at the ground. It was nothing noticeable, just dirt and rock. Targeting it, Ishida cast *"STOP MAGIC" "END CURSE" "RETURN MY SPELLS" "NULLIFY"*. And again her words became blue thread falling down. The pregnant dragoness quieted herself with a meditation pose and closed her eyes.

Ishida stayed in that pose until the following day then quietly she cast *"AURA TAKE ME TO MY BROOD ROCK"*.

She didn't leave or disappear, but Ravanan did notice her eyes seemed wetter, any more wet and a tear would possibly fall from them.

Ishida had only one last idea, *"VANISH"* - but that did no good either.

It was another three days before she made a noise, she roared. Loud and long, her roar echoed and traveled up into freedom.

Ravanan only watched.

With good feelings of a small triumph, she targeted him, casting *"SILENCE" "EVOKE SPEAR"*. But her spells only became falling blue thread.

Angry, poisonous gas filled her aura, "What have you done?" she spat the words out. "Trapping my spoken spells?"

Ravanan consoled her from across the chamber "At least you can talk, be glad for that."

He continued to feed her well, keeping her body healthy for the egg. While she kept her indignant silence, Ravanan was meticulously going about, discovering the new lair.

Finding the lair's entrance was easy since the hole was left visible. Ravanan descended into its depths. He cast *"STARLIGHT"* and began the tedious search for traps, knowing his patience would be rewarded.

Just as it was in his lair he knew somewhere near him was a short anchor to skip over the treacherous passageway but he also knew that the short cut was keyed to the dragon who placed it there. It would be easier to suffer every trap rather than attempt to decipher the magical doorways that Kianthyx or that ancient dragon had crafted. At least he would only have to walk it once and then he could make his own anchor later.

The cave system was wet and with many tight squeezes, the ancient pair had to have been dabbling in rock growing as the formations didn't look natural to Ravanan's studious eye. Rock bedding planes were interrupted, the color of the rocks didn't always connect, and he noticed at least once that a fault line was oddly terminated. It just didn't look right.

Nearly at the onset of his trek he cast *"MORPH TO ANACONDA"* to make navigating the gauntlet easier. His anaconda spell was convincing with the exception of his blue eyes because no matter the form of the body the eyes are directly attached to the nature of the individual and cannot be changed.

The path was riddled with numerous slippery ledges and turn-backs, each were traps within themselves. Slithering through the hazardous subterranean climb Ravanan gained an appreciation for the pair of master rock sculptors and he was already redecorating Black Blade's entrance inside his head. The small water ways and waterfalls were always splashing at the worst place possible for anyone trying to cross them and then there were the steep drops and rises. He was learning and exploring with wide eyes, not that Black Blade was lacking for high quality traps but he was always looking for ways to improve it, and what better way to improve than to review what 7,000 year old dragons had done.

He found his first magical trap. It was a loop-back trap and he discovered it when he felt the subtle phase-out of his body as the trap moved him back to its beginning. He had this same trap in his own lair, it was easily foiled by a simple spell of stability.

After passing through the trap and seeing new cave formations once again Ravanan came upon a chamber. It was small and he could tell it had recently been widened to accommodate two dragons. There wasn't much to the chamber and he could see where the cave continued on the other side. Kianthyx must have set up camp in the room, unable to get past the next trap. That little fact made Ravanan even more alert.

There wasn't much to the make-shift lair. Their wizard's alcove was greatly lacking. He could see one corner contained their wardrobes, beside them were their tools and weapons. He took a closer look, seeing if there were any useful ones he didn't have in his collection. Ravanan saw up close the razor that shaved off his scales, he hated that one. Of everything there the razor was the most unique but even that one he could reproduce from memory with no need to study it further.

Ravanan slithered around the chamber, following the walls and using his snake tongue to investigate. If there was something to find it most likely wasn't in the middle of the room. On the other wall was what he was looking for when he bumped into an invisible obstacle. He stopped and raised up his anaconda head to look above him and all around, sensing no traps he decided to change forms.

While not a lover of the human appearance Ravanan saw the value of it and at the moment human hands were needed. He cast 'MORPH TO HUMAN", seconds later he was naked and erecting his human body by pushing with his hands up off the cavern floor.

He dusted his hands off before casting "EVOKE TOOLS"; then his bag of minerals appeared in his palms. He opened the pack and took out his iolite crystal, and then biotite, pulled off a flake of the black mineral and dropped the rest back down inside the bag. Ravanan held them up to his right eye then rotated them while looking intently at the invisible thing on the floor.

A small chest materialized before him. He thought about traps and cast the reveal spell again to check the chest. He could hardly believe that there was nothing protecting it other than the invisibility spell, but then again they were young dragons. He knelt down and opened it carefully. The chest was partially filled with gemstones colored clear and red. They were small sizes but beautiful none-the-less and now they belonged to him. Ravanan allowed himself a moment to visualize what he would make with the little gems - that was the most fun part of getting new treasure.

Again he opened his tool bag and took out a small crystal of rock salt. Adding one of the red gemstones, he put them in his mouth and held them in his tongue. Using his aura, he could taste it, the salt enhanced the gem. The red ones were spinel, not such a rarity but their color was bright. Next he grabbed one of the clear gemstones. From the fire-like sparkle he was pretty sure they were diamonds but did the same test to be sure.

Diamonds and spinels, three hundred of each. A good start for a dragon, and in his case, a small restart.

Ravanan sealed the tiny lair with his own enchantments then moved on deeper into the ancient cave, looking for whatever trap had bested Kianthyx.

A short way further and he came upon a corridor connecting nine passageways of various sizes and shapes. Going largest to smallest as a guess he took a step towards the biggest tunnel and the room filled with a dark cloud so magically dense that it broke his starlight spell. He stood there and after getting the room cleared he noticed all the passageways had changed places. He headed back up to rest and figure out a plan.

The next day when Ravanan came back from hunting he brought no food for Ishida. Most of the day was gone before she finally spoke out "No food today for your prisoner?"

"No. Not until I get some answers."

"I won't answer. Soon my egg will be gone and then I'll be dead by your hand."

"Why do you say that?"

Ishida scoffed, "I know my egg is the only reason I'm alive. Don't think I don't know that you have also set a killing curse upon me."

"You're wrong about that. *That* won't come until after I have what I need."

Ishida laughed "I don't believe the words of a Naga! Especially when I can feel the enchantment in my head. The base of my head still hurts!"

Ravanan wasn't laughing though and he wondered about the pain in her head. "Tell me Ishida, why are you here in Kynasteryx when your brood rock is in Nikhadelos?"

Ishida quickly answered "I am fleeing from the Naga, this is their egg." Her eyes were wide with astonishment that she said that.

Ravanan asked "How long were you mated to Kianthyx?"

"A little less than a season." Again her eyes were wide. "Why am I telling you this?" she yelped.

Ravanan's voice was calm as always "Because the enchantment you feel in your head forces you to answer me truthfully, it is not one of death. And it will cease when my aura gives it the signal that I have all the answers I need."

Ishida asked "Is that all it does?"

"Yes"

She was amazed, "That must have been most difficult to do."

"Yes," Ravanan nodded, "My last interrogation was impromptu and rushed. Not so this time however. I've had time to build it right."

Ishida relented "So feed me then, let me nurture my egg."

After the meal Ravanan asked her "How much longer until the egg is ready?"

"weeks maybe."

"Well hopefully I won't need you much longer and then we'll see about that egg." Ravanan advised, "Now about your treasure, is any of it stolen?"

"No." she rubbed her neck. "We mined it freely and won some in fair battles."

Ravanan paused at Ishida's answer. His treasure was not there. Yes the ancient lair had other treasure which would soon be his, but of his and Kalara's treasure he still hadn't found it.

"Do you know who took the treasure from Black Blade Lair?" Ravanan used his aura to paint a sparkling blue image of the Black Blade cliff near Ishida in the air.

She took a good look at his art work, "No. That place is foreign to me."

Ravanan was becoming sad with every "no" he heard. "What part did you play in trapping the Kynasteryx Acama?"

"None. I didn't know she had been trapped."

"Who took her?"

"I don't know who bested the Acama."

On any other matter Ravanan's manner was cool and kept but on these topics his nerves were fraying and his frustration was starting to show. Ishida noticed. She spoke up "So you thought we had stolen your treasure. That is why my mate is now dead and I am soon to be."

Ravanan said nothing.

She didn't mind him ignoring her because she knew she was right. Ishida played with her long, ornamental chin feathers and kept talking "I never met the Acama here, I take it she meant more to you than simply acting as your communications channel to all of dragonkind – possibly your mate? Or are you just that heroic to lead a search for any dragon gone missing?" She smirked.

He was silent and turned away from her. But his actions only fueled her further.

"I've never had a use for the Acama, the one over Nikhadelos, what is his name? Oh yes, Kadd, he sure doesn't help much with the Nagas, of course who would want to deal with such vile dragons? – it's a wonder that they still hold with Dragon Law at all. It causes me to doubt that Acamas are even useful to us."

Ishida continued uninterrupted. Her tail was playfully twitching like a whip and she was purring with satisfaction "Now that I think about it, you are most likely not a Naga, because I am still alive and my egg is still in me. And you were so careful to not bite into it when you took my flesh – you shouldn't have been able to do that you know."

Ravanan turned his head around to face her, wanting to put an end to her game, "You're right, you'll probably want to improve the hardness of your scales before you battle again."

If Ishida was simmering from that statement she didn't let it show.

Seeing she had no response Ravanan decided to go in another direction "Why are you carrying a Naga's egg?"

Ishida answered "I was arranged to mate with a red Naga and right after I did he got into a fight with another dragon and I saw my opportunity to get away before he could trace me."

"But why leave your mate? After all you chose him knowing he was Naga."

"I did not choose him. From the moment I hatched I was bound to a red – him; it is their way. Never left alone for seventy five years; I was always watched and when they band together there is no way to battle with all of them and their collective knowledge. I could be Naga, I suppose you could say I am a Naga since I came from them, but as time went on I felt differently about humans and did not agree with all I saw going on. It is a bad thing to hatch in those lands. I couldn't openly relocate, it was only from my inherent memories did I believe there was another way to live."

Ravanan recalled her wet eyes the other day when she tried to return to her brood rock. "So you don't want to go back to Nikhadelos?"

"No. Only to avoid death would I consider going back to the Naga."

"How do you know he won't come find you?"

"He thinks I'm dead."

Ravanan wasn't so sure, "What is his name?"

"Somen of Nikhadelos Xylo the Malefic Garnet"

"So how did you convince Somen you died?"

"We were in our mating flight, necks entwined, he quickly completed the bond. Then I saw my way out, a young black dragon who was minding his own affairs, seemed to be hunting. I took advantage of my mate's primal mood and flew in a path to get us within the aura of the black dragon. Timing my magic was essential, I told my aura to target Somen from the black dragon, a ray of sickness and fatigue – a black's basic attack and it appeared to come from him. It worked, I feigned getting hit with the main blast which theoretically would kill me, they fought, and I vanished."

A silence fell over them then as they both followed their own thoughts. Ravanan couldn't help but see how she used a different color attack to meet her objective just like he had with Kianthyx. From there he ventured to consider another future for himself.

278

The following morning Ravanan admitted to Ishida "I've come to nine passageways."

Ishida knew then that the blue dragon had bested all their crafted traps and wondered to herself if there was anything he couldn't do. Somehow she felt small all of the sudden, he was bigger than her and he now owned her treasure. But she would never let her ill feelings show, after all she had almost killed him with her poison.

"And what will you do?" she asked.

"What all did Kianthyx try? I know you couldn't have done anything because of the egg."

"He tried an air bubble that filled the room, but his bubble was weak. He wanted to send lava down each tunnel and whichever one didn't fill up had to be the one, but I told him that plugging the holes was the wrong thing to do. He tried placing his light spell on the rock, that didn't work. Then he also tried just walking into them with the darkness but soon gave up. There may have been others but that is all he told me."

Ravanan said nothing. He left the hole to hunt and think.

Later that day he was ready to try the trap again. Standing in the small corridor, Ravanan cast *"SONAR"* and waited to hear the sounds come back. He cast the same spell several times to be sure. It was the smallish one that was two to his left with two jutting out rocks, that was the correct tunnel.

Before he moved he cast *"AIR BARRIER"* with a bubble as large as he could make it which turned out to be larger than the room he was in, the bubble extended a ways in each tunnel.

Then he took a step, the bubble held tight against the blackness but the passageways still moved. So again he cast the sonar spell to check, the location was still right although the opening was different. He took the path without hesitation, solving the trap.

The path narrowed and so Ravanan morphed to an anaconda again. Slithering over the ground, the next trap he found was a water trap, its inky black surface hinted at unknown depths and had been intended to ward off humans, he could smell how the water had been laced with fear. He slid in, immune to chemically-induced fear, the narrow passageway narrowed before shrinking even further to become a tight fit. His aura took over his breathing as he continued to squeeze through and down, as the tunnel led him at a decent angle of descent. The lower he went through the submerged tunnel he could feel the acidity of the water increase. Ravanan had an idea about what was ahead of him and before going any further he cast *"WATER BUBBLE"* to seal the existing water around him, preferring to swim in a pH of six as opposed to a pH of one.

The tight channel finally opened up to an acid-filled chamber, the acid was dense and harder to swim through than normal water.

Ravanan recast his starlight spell to be brighter. It was a great trap. Had any human done the impossible and reached the room, they'd have melted before they found the exit, because there were four of them, and he was sure that only one was the real exit. His water bubble armor of pH six was slowly burning its way around the edges of his scales but he still had plenty of time left before taking any real damage from the weak acid.

He looked up to see that there was no air captured at the ceiling. As he searched the ceiling further, he saw a large selenite gypsum crystal, it hung neatly in the center of the ceiling, and was probably used for illumination, but without upkeep it was dark. Ravanan targeted the crystal – his first maintenance spell of his new lair – and cast the longest-lasting and brightest starlight spell he could on it without using up too much of his available magic on this one trap. He grinned as much as his snake lips would allow, happy with his spell that would last for half a decade or more. Now that the chamber was lit up again he noticed an illusion caused by the light.

Then he understood the beauty of the water trap, the ancient pair of dragons had sculpted a mirage lens in the crystal, promising air and an escape from the virulent acid, luring strong explorers away from the chamber exits and giving the acid more time to eat into the marrow of their bones. Created expertly by the ancient dragons the light bounced off of other crystals to give the alluring image of a dry ledge above, safe from the acid bath if only the explorer could hurry and swim to the mirage.

The chamber was beautiful with golden walls, piles of gold were at the bottom all of it fool's gold and the source of the sulfuric acid bath.

Ravanan turned his attention back to the four exits, they could go a long ways before terminating. They needed more thought, more time than he could spare; so he left back the way he came. Once out of the murky acid Ravanan allowed his water bubble to collapse, there was a slight scalding to his scales but nothing that wouldn't heal with a little time.

Ravanan slithered back into the first room where Ishida was imprisoned and let the morph go. He was deep in thought. He considered pinging each exit and using sonar but dismissed the idea because he couldn't be sure that the dead ends didn't have air trapped at the far end which would give him a false positive result. He also considered growing a tentacle to explore each exit but abandoned that idea because he knew his bubble of water around him couldn't stretch very far before becoming too thin to protect him.

He'd swim each one of the exits if he had to. He would not fail. He'd had too much of that lately. A trap wasn't going to beat him. There had to be a way in and he was not going anywhere until he solved it. There had to be tons of treasure down there, it was practically calling to him.

Ishida watched Ravanan come back from the depths. She had no idea that he had already gone beyond the trap that stopped Kianthyx.

As a red dragoness her poison was potent, but her most hideous venom was injected into her words. With all the surety of the world she said "I knew you couldn't do it. You're not that good. There was going to be something that stopped you, no dragon alive can break into that ancient lair. Those dragons were old, nearly 7,000 years."

Her words definitely rubbed Ravanan the wrong way and his aura defended him at once – he wasn't guarding it as he constantly did when he was around Kalara. If felt good to relax and let his aura out. But now sparks ignited into a spiderweb of lightning and for his three striking distances, Ishida was covered with electricity.

At once Ravanan realized what he had done and was at Ishida's side checking the egg. In panic mode Ishida's aura erupted into a red cloud of poison.

"NO!" Ravanan roared as his blood curdled. Fighting himself, he quieted his glowing aura that was trying to outfight the poison for fear of more damage to the egg. "NO! NO! NO!"

With a grimace of pain he cast *"CALM!"*

Ishida was burned and shaking, but her and her aura were calming down.

Ravanan took her to the ground and bit her stomach. Their bodies were so close, she was in his grasp and in the tackle Ishida's fang nicked his wing. She laughed in the most peculiar way as he jumped off her and retreated, leaving her bleeding and open.

From the other side of the room Ravanan cast *"ANTIVENIN"* then swallowed Ishida's flesh. He glanced at his wing, it was sizzling from her poisonous tooth.

"What are you trying to do dragoness?!" Ravanan roared at her. "Killing me will not release you! If I'm dead my enchantment will continue for yearssss!" His body seized up for a moment, he jerked in pain.

Ravanan roared loudly and shook his head trying to clear the pain.

"Release me!" she ordered.

"NO!"

"RELEASE ME!"

"NO! I said no! I will not, not until that egg is buried and I can truly fight you."

"You'll regret it." she said with an odd, hurt smile.

Ravanan cast *"SILENCE"* and let the poisonous dragoness be so that he could heal.

A few mornings later Ravanan was fishing, quietly fishing and enjoying it. By himself, away from any dragoness, his mind was working on a plan for the trap while his body was working on healing the poison damage – his wing hurt the most. But at least the egg was saved.

"Damn she is dangerous" he said to the fish. He reached his black talons over and took hold of his right wing that Ishida had snagged with her tooth. Extending it slightly, looking at it, it wasn't healing very well. There was still a black spot and dark deadened veins around the mark. He considered how he could heal it. The Aloe Eyes weren't working. His normal healing spells weren't working either. This was the first time a red dragon had actually bit him and it was the most stinging wound he'd ever received. When he was flying sometimes a nerve would catch and drive him crazy, making him turn suddenly.

What he couldn't figure out was why she laughed. Did she enjoy the shocking pain of his aura? Was she wanting him to tackle her? What kind of dragoness would want a bite taken out of her? Or what if the venom in her fangs was the worst poison of all and she knew he'd be dead in a few days from that one little black wound – it was a troubling thought. And every time it ached a fear of dying crossed his mind. What did she mean by "regret"? Perhaps she did intend on killing him after he made it through all the traps of the ancient lair. And of course he had lied about the duration of the prison, he had to renew it every full moon. Curse that egg, without it she would already be dead.

Taking his catch and a cow for emergency, he cast "*MORPH TO HUMAN*" and traveled by anchor directly to the water's edge of the acid trap. Ten fish, it was probably overkill.

It was a long, taxing process, controlling the mind of the little fish, placing it in the water, casting a water bubble around it and Starlight, and then swimming in its body all the way through the acid.

Through all four exits he did this, and each one opened up with air and a tunnel that continued on with dry ground.

But through the eyes of a flopping fish all four tunnels appeared the same after he jumped it out of the water, there were no distinguishing rocks or features – he would have to use the fish as the target of an anchor so that he could go to each of the four exits and look for himself.

With prey he only controlled them long enough to get them in place before walking out of their mind and eating them, he had never stayed to the end before. But with the fish he was forced to experience their little deaths as he made the fish lay there, wanting air, each one in a different position relative to the water's edge. It was a sad thing to possess a mind as it dies, even the tiny ones, and with each fish Ravanan's mood become more melancholy.

After conquering the acid trap he was drawing the four anchors to take him to each fish when he felt a twinge in his right shoulder blade.

Ravanan used two more flakes of biotite, cast *"SIGHT"* on them and held them like mirrors so that he could see what was bothering the skin on his back. He held one flake to the spot that hurt and the other he peered into closely. The poisonous wound was there, a jagged spot from Ishida's tooth, it had stayed with his body during the morph. He needed to heal that thing before it killed him. It didn't hurt like a serious wound but what if it became worse?

Concentrating more than usual Ravanan recast *"MORPH TO HUMAN"* and this time he re-painted his skin with how a flawless human should appear. Looking again the mark was gone even though he could still feel it inside him. That wound was going to have to be dealt with.

He continued on with his work, finishing the temporary anchors with the blood of the other fish and cow. His drawings made him feel like he was building a memorial to his four friends who had died except he was doing it out of greed and for reward. 'Their worth didn't match it though' Ravanan told himself. He named the acid trap 'the Hall of Fish' and traveled as a ball of lightning to each dead fish. Seeing them lay there in their death pose was not helping his mood so he ate each one he came to as he made permanent identifying marks in the schist floor of each tunnel.

Ravanan didn't feel much like exploring after that and found himself wanting to think on something else. Surprisingly what came to his mind was talking with Ishida more, trying to figure her out. She was fascinating, different from Kalara, both the old Kalara and the new. Before now he'd never spent so much time with a fiery red dragoness.

Ishida looked surprised to see the blue dragon emerging from the cave since she thought he was out hunting. And then all he did was sit and stare at her. She sat up and watched him watch her.

Time passed and finally Ishida spoke "I know you have all the answers you need and my egg is nearly ready. Am I dying today?"

"Are you so eager to die?"

"No."

"Then I guess today isn't the day."

More time went by and nothing was said. Ravanan thought she looked curious. "If you have something to ask me, then ask." he told her.

"OK, I will. You protected my egg again, I understand that, but you also chose to speed the healing of my burns and the bite you gave me – why? They weren't mortal wounds, having them wasn't hurting the egg, and they weakened me for when we battle next."

Ravanan hadn't expected her to ask that. He said flatly "I'll keep my answer until I have yours. Why did you laugh during that mess we had?"

"I found it funny that we were both accidentally hurting each other."

"Funny? Your egg was almost lost and you found it funny?"

"Yes."

He was amazed at her definition of humor and yet he was also happy to learn her poison-filled aura was accidental as was his shocking aura. "So if I were to come within your aura right now you wouldn't poison me?"

"No."

"Why not?"

"Because I don't want you to bite me again, it hurts and I have enough pain already in my head."

Ravanan stood up, thinking to test her aura.

Ishida spoke out "Now will you give me your answer?"

"I don't have to answer you, dragoness" he took a step closer "I made progress today and solved another trap, how does that make you feel?"

"I admire you for doing what I couldn't. You impress me, achieving the impossible."

Ravanan knew she was speaking truth but her words and voice were so sweet to hear that he feared a trap and stopped where he was.

Seeing that he wasn't going to answer her Ishida asked "How is this? That I am compelled to answer but you don't offer any information to me? I don't even know your name!"

"Ravanan of Kynasteryx Diamid"

"and where is my answer then Ravanan?"

"Alright, I'll answer your question after you tell me this – "Ravanan extended his right wing, showing her the black wound. "How can I heal this fang mark on my wing before I die from it?"

Ishida laughed, "You can't. And you won't die from it either, it's a scar not a wound."

"It still hurts."

"It always will." Ishida said with an alluring smile.

Ravanan couldn't help but be intrigued. As long as he lived he would be marked by the red dragoness who nearly killed him, carrying a part of her with him always.

He reached the edge of her aura, wanting to claim that wicked smile that was hiding behind her words and teasing him, to take the prize that should come with the noticeable scar he suffered by her.

"Alright" he said "I healed you again because I don't want to be the cause of your pain."

"You're already causing me pain, hurting me by keeping me imprisoned and charming me." she reasoned.

"And if I release you, you'll attack me to win back this ancient lair."

Ishida turned away from him "You don't trust me. Despite the fact that I must tell you the truth on every question you ask."

"Do you want to harm me?"

"No."

"Tell me then, do you want to fight me to get this treasure for yourself?"

"No." she stressed.

"Fine." Ravanan gave it some thought. "Do you want the treasure of that ancient pair?"

"Yes."

For some time he stood there outside of her aura, listening, trying to feel her unspoken words, seeing only her back full of blood-red spikes running down her spine all the way from her pronged horns to the feathery tuft of her tail. Her folded, feathered wings looked like an iridescent shield, only the reddish tint at their bases gave away their presence, in the air they reflected the sky so perfectly that the diamid dragons looked wingless. She was a beautiful sight. If only he could look into her wine-colored eyes..... He searched for a way to get her to turn back to him.

"What did you mean the other day when you said I'd regret it?" he asked her.

Forced by his enchantments to speak honestly but keeping her back to him Ishida replied "I said you'd regret it because I could be good for you, you know my poison is good in a battle, and your mate is gone. If we fight I know I will lose and die. Then the rest of your life you'll always wonder what could have been between us."

"So you want the ancient treasure and me with it?"

"Yes."

The silence that overtook them was heavy. Ravanan deeply considered Ishida's answers as he stood there watching her. She'd basically proposed albeit unwillingly. He hated feeling awkward. He wasn't ready to respond to her and knew he should.

It was easier to leave, to give himself time and so he left for the Hall of Fish. He set himself to trying each submerged tunnel. Three of them led on for a long ways but finally after some slippery ledges with long drops and other such karstic hazards they terminated.

The other passageway, which happened to be number two in his numbering system, was the true exit. It was broadening and soon was wide enough that he was able to morph back to his base dragon form. It had straightened out and was void of traps. The rock floor was angling up at a gentle rise and then became steeper. After changing to a sharp incline, the cave terminated at a solid rock wall of dark gabbro. Ravanan was not fooled. It was the same trick he used on the ledge at Black Blade, the spell worked on humans and simple-minded animals, and from a distance, some dragons as well.

The solid rock wall did it's best to dissuade all explorers, it was seemingly impenetrable. Already in human form Ravanan cast *"EVOKE TOOLS"* and pulled out his iolite and biotite to cast reveal on the wall.

Faintly at first, but growing brighter, he spotted the outline of a dragon breathing fire in the alignment of the crystal grains in the rock. It was sketchy but more evident than some of the constellations that humans could conjure up from the night sky. At the mouth of the dark dragon was a glowing mark of dried and aged saliva of the previous lair owners. Targeting the spot he cast a small spell *"DEW KISS"* and the old dried spit hydrated with the moist cavern air and swelled to look fresh and wet.

After the reveal spell ended Ravanan looked again at the black wall and where he had seen the fire-breathing dragon. Without the reveal spell, one would never notice the dragon and his flame breath on the wall, however now that the saliva was there and Ravanan knew the picture, he could see it and the subtle depression of where the flame breath was. It was plain as day to him, so obvious he wondered how he didn't notice it before. The jagged tongues of fire on the outline was the finest of edging work, well-defined and exact. He ran his fingers over the carving, thinking, analyzing it with critical eyes, the body of the dragon wasn't carved but was simply the grain of the rock. It wasn't recessed like the flame breath was. Something belonged in that depression, perhaps another rock, the sunken flame breath sketch was practically begging for a key.

A key. He should have known that there would be a key. He had a key for Black Blade, convoluted though it was. Ravanan ran his fingers through his hair, thinking.

The easiest solution was mud, Ravanan searched the cavern floor and found some smooth cave mud, he scooped it up and filled in the depression, being careful to fill every point and making it uniformly thick. Happy with his mud job, he blasted and baked the mud with his blue flame breath. After allowing it to cool down he retrieved his key and held it in his hands, letting his aura imbue it with natural magic to open any door. The hardened mud key glowed a faint blue as his magic sank deep into it. He then placed the key back into the rock wall and waited for it to open but it didn't budge.

Ravanan smiled. If it had been that easy he would have been disappointed. He removed the key and smashed it back to dust.

He thought about the cave so far. Where would a flat key shaped like a flame breath be hiding? It could be anywhere for miles surrounding the lair. Most of the rock of the tepui entrance to the lair was quartzite, but there was also plenty of schist and gneiss. The more tabular of the three was schist and he was standing on some of it. Ravanan did a quick reveal spell. Nothing in the tunnel lit up. There was just no telling where the key was.

He retraced his steps and thoroughly examined every flat rock he came to, walls, ceilings, and floors. He passed through passageways and the Hall of Fish, time went by.

As he searched for the key his thoughts returned to Ishida. There was no point in keeping her captive any longer, he had all the answers he needed from her. Before Kalara's mess he would have ignored Ishida's proposal completely but now he found himself considering it. And although the future was still too painful to think about he was ready to set Ishida free.

His search had turned up nothing in the tunnels. The blue wizard entered back into the make-shift lair and found Ishida staring at the wall and her new egg. She was so engrossed with putting the egg in its rock nest she hadn't noticed his approach.

Ravanan stopped before he entered Ishida's aura. "Have you got the spell worked out for that?" he asked her.

Ishida snapped her head around and saw him returning back to his base form. "I will have." she said curtly.

"At least find a rock softer than quartzite, the spell will go easier for you and the egg."

Ishida flexed her wings angrily and looked back down at the egg.

'Must have hit a nerve' Ravanan thought to himself, realizing she had been at it for awhile.

"What would you know of eggs!?"

"More than you obviously. I know a good spell for hiding them."

"Do it then." she commanded.

Ravanan took no insult at her commanding words, knowing that right now she was simply doing what all dragoness' do with an egg, they try to hide it. He stayed where he was and let the enchantment go. With a whisper he canceled the barrier above her head as well.

Ishida didn't make a move or speak.

"Bring the egg."

Ishida paused at that, "You don't intend to take it back to Nikhadelos do you?"

"No, just away from my land."

She obediently made for the exit with the egg safely in her grasp. And for the first time Ravanan noticed he was in her aura and not taking damage.

They agreed to a rocky crag that would protect the egg for the next year. Soon he had the egg inside the rock face about a fang's length in where no being would ever suspect and yet close enough so that the hatchling could break free.

Later they returned to the bottom of the hole where their camp was set up. In that familiar place Ishida resumed her spot where she had spent all her time. Either she was making a point to say she was holding a grudge for being locked up or was it a sign of complete submission like a beaten-down slave.

Ravanan let her be and continued to search for the key. Without a second thought he morphed to human and evoked his sapphire blue wizard's robe and began to scan the room with his crystals. As he did he thought about the Hall of Fish and the selenite crystal, how it looked like a giant tooth made from many layers of tabular crystals. Then it hit him – the key must be hidden among them, flat and simple. He wanted to go get it immediately but he paused to look over at the freed Ishida. What was he going to do about her while he was down below?"

Even now as he stood there his right shoulder blade twinged. He couldn't put it off any longer, it was time. He had to decide now since he was so close to his goal. This was his lair now and it held his treasure – Ishida just happened to be there too.

He wasn't uncomfortable around her and knew her desires, they weren't a bad thing. After all, he'd had them also a couple of times.

She didn't have to stay in that spot where he had imprisoned her, she knew this, having left it to deal with the egg. So why did she go back to it?

He looked over at her, seeing pretty much only her back side and whip-like tail. Her actions brought into focus everything that he had done to her: controlling her, imprisoning her, shocking her and the egg, killing her mate, stealing her treasure, biting and eating her flesh, enchanting her to have to answer only truth, and taking away her verbal spells – it all had to be done and he didn't regret it but he could see how she might be upset.

It'd be fine if she left except that he feared that Somen would hunt her down. He wanted her to succeed in her escape from the Naga, it seemed they were a growing threat. They were an unpredictable and rough group of dragons. From what Kadd said – the Naga weren't even a unified force. It was more of an idea around the whole planet, a very egotistical idea of the way that a dragon should treat all lesser species. In one aspect Ravanan agreed with them, that dragons should rule – but he strongly felt that Acama was right and didn't want to see the outcome if humans were to discover them. If the Naga did come looking for Ishida she would need help.

Ravanan let his morph go and went over to Ishida, no longer fearing her poisonous aura. She turned away from him.

Ravanan reached out with his black talons and turned her back around. He looked into her dark red eyes. "I've found what I needed, are you coming with me?"

Ishida said nothing.

"You can't keep sitting there like you're dead because you're not. You're free! Do something."

"And what would you have me do?" she sounded a little hurt.

"I would like for you to stop playing this game."

"Then you stop pretending you didn't hear my forced confession!"

He understood now. Being forced to say her heart before her mind wanted to must have really bothered her. In a softer tone he replied "You're right. I did hear your hidden desire."

"And?"

He reached out and stroked her invisible feathered wing, his claws appeared to hover above her red scales. "And just because I freed you doesn't mean you have to leave."

The two dragons were soon standing at the water's edge. Ravanan morphed to his anaconda shape and told Ishida to do the same.

"You'll need a water bubble around yourself – there is acid down below."

"Oh I've done that plenty of times."

He looked over at Ishida wondering how many times "plenty" meant for a 76 year old dragon.

"OK, let's go." He slithered into the dark liquid. *"WATER BUBBLE"*

At the giant crystal Ravanan morphed to human. Working quickly, his reveal spell worked on the twenty foot long selenite. He saw the key light up against the transparent crystal and knew right away it was an exact match down to each pointed tongue of fire. He extracted the glassy-looking key carefully and then left the acid bath to stand at the door.

Ishida didn't lag and slithered up onto the muddy shore. She looked winded as if that was her first time to transform into a snake.

Ravanan stored the key in his pack. As much as he wanted to use it he knew that he should prepare and proceed wisely. Once inside he would have to destroy the door which would take a lot of time and power – they'd be trapped until he did. So he cast Anchor and they left to collect food reserves.

They didn't waste any time. As soon as they formed outside they dropped their morphs and took off to hunt.

He already knew where he was going and shortly had several cows ready to take back with him. Ravanan piled them up near the anchor and looked around to make sure that Ishida was still off hunting. He thought about what Kalara was going to eat while he was trapped behind that door. Quickly, he enchanted a cow to make it stay fresh then sent it to Black Blade Lair.

But Ishida showed up right then, coming back from hunting in human form and wearing her invisibility cloak. She dismissed her robe and let her human form go, appearing in front of Ravanan. "Why are you sending them one at a time to the door?" she inquired.

"I was testing my spell. It works, so now I can send them all."

"Are you always so thorough? I would have figured this would be easy now, given all the work you've already done in the cave." Ishida made a mental count of the pile, there were eight - she added her two. "So we have eleven. Let's go."

Ravanan knew he had been caught. He sat down and flexed his wings to catch a glimpse of his black scar. "Ishida, I didn't send that cow to the door. I sent it to a prisoner of mine."

"So I wasn't your only one. How many prisoners do you own?"

"Just the one."

"And you've been feeding him this whole time?"

"Yes."

"Does your prisoner have something to do with the Acama and your stolen treasure?"

"Yes."

Ishida thought about what he said, she knew he had been robbed and that his hunt is what brought them together. "Well you've got plenty of treasure now, and me. Is this new life not enough for you? Instead of feeding him let's go end him and be done with it."

"Maybe later after the new lair is secured."

Thankfully Ishida dropped it and prepared to anchor back to the locked door.

Ravanan joined her at the black door. He pulled the key from his tool bag and set the flat, jagged crystal into its real home. Again he cast *"DEW KISS"*, knowing that spell may never work again to rehydrate the ancient saliva. The whole rock wall glowed then vanished. They passed through with the supplies then the wall reappeared behind them.

He worked patiently with single-mindedness to demolish the fake door and its enchantments, sleeping when he needed to and Ishida stayed out of his way. Soon his door would be there and it would only respond to his DNA. It was good to have her there so he didn't have to wonder what she may be doing.

After much time and work over many days the new door was done, he'd finished it as Ishida slept. He trusted her well enough but he wasn't about to share the door with her, it was his.

Ravanan was glad to get out of the small tunnel that they had been camped in. They both looked disheveled and worn with dirt. With stiff achiness the pair of dragons walked forward, lit with their starlight spells.

The path was steep for a while longer before leveling out, at the end was a drop. Together they peered over the ledge into darkness, the opening of a constructed hole. It was square, carved rock with smooth walls and a vertical shaft. They were beyond the cave and at the entrance to the real lair. Ravanan and Ishida grinned at each other then left to recuperate.

They returned later and were once again looking down the dark shaft. Ravanan didn't trust it and took a dead monkey from his test fodder pile (most were dead). He targeted the monkey and cast *"PUPPET"* then sent it down into the hole where four darts shot at it. Ravanan pulled the monkey up to examine the damage. Only one of the darts actually hit the small target, but where it hit looked like a mild acid and was still sizzling. More acid. One of the ancients had to have been green. He carefully removed the dart from the little monkey. It was more of a hollow shard than a true dart and possibly magnetized. Ravanan used his aura to make an electrical field for a test and the shard turned away.

"You ever seen that before?" he asked Ishida.

"I knew it could be done but I haven't worked much with it. Pretty deadly I'd say."

Ravanan agreed as he took another monkey and let it slowly descend. He could hear the pffft pffft pffft pffft of the darts as each round flew at it.

After that monkey hit the bottom he grabbed another one. He looked at Ishida "Just to be sure." he grinned.

More darts hit that monkey too. How many were there? He grabbed another one. Seven monkeys later no more darts could be heard.

"OK, grab a monkey, keep it in front of you and let's go." Trusting his aura to shield him and keeping his monkey ahead of him to trigger the trap, he jumped and floated down.

The shaft was wide and deep. During their descent light of his starlight spell revealed alcoves on all four walls. And in each one were jade and emerald dragon masks. The darts had come from the masks' mouths like shooting fangs.

He didn't land at the pile of dead monkeys and unspent darts, instead he flew away from them first. Ishida followed his lead.

"Whew. That was something." Ishida said as she cast her monkey onto the pile.

When the pair of dragons were away from under the shaft Ravanan's starlight spell went out. He recast it, "STARLIGHT" but it didn't work.

Ishida tried. *"STARLIGHT"* with no success.

"EVOKE DIAMOND STAFF" but Ravanan's trusted diamond staff could not penetrate the darkness. He pointed the staff back to where he knew the pile of monkeys were and cast *"ILLUMINATE"*. That worked although it was a dim light source.

They looked around for anything to get reference but the walls were still out there somewhere. It was just them. Ishida started to step but Ravanan stopped her. "Hold on."

He cast reveal on the floor around them but saw nothing.

"Sure wish we were back out in the sun." Ishida commented.

"I know what you mean. We need to be careful down here, the dark can play tricks on you."

"I know that." she shot back.

Ravanan didn't need her hot attitude, not when the dark seemed so heavy. He'd been at this lair so long that his nerves toyed with the idea of beginning to fray. "Let me think."

"I am. And I'm thinking too just so you know!"

"Good. Then think in silence."

"I will."

"DRAPE MASTER". A golden crown set on Ravanan's head, giving him extremely clear thought and mental armor. He targeted an acid-gooey monkey and hurled it away in the opposite direction, it

took its dim light with it. And then he took another, sending it in another direction. Ishida helped him until their known area was larger all over.

Ravanan cast *"ARMOR"* and picked up a foot to take a step.

"Stop!" Ishida yelled. "Are you sure Ravanan? What if this is a trap?"

"Of course it's a trap Ishida. What would you have me do? Stand here forever? I've got my armor on and I've cast reveal. The way is lit before me.... I'm going!"

"Just don't. Please? Not yet. Let's think some more. What could it hurt?"

He put his foot back down and glared at her. "What are you afraid of?"

"I'm not afraid. You're being careless."

"No I'm not."

"At least use a monkey first." she pleaded with him.

"Ishida. We just threw monkeys all around us."

"Oh. We did. Right."

"Get yourself together. Don't you have anything to help combat mental attacks?"

"We're being attacked?"

"Can't you feel the fear pressing on you?"

Only then as they stood there arguing did they notice the little filaments hanging in the air like dust.

"What have we here?" Ravanan pondered. "Don't let them touch you."

"What are they?"

"I don't know."

"They're growing."

"I know. Make an air barrier around yourself!"

The tiny things were now easily visible in the air and coalescing into little black puffs. Soon they'd be the size of apples.

"There's one in my bubble!" Ishida shirked away from it as best as she could and remade her air bubble to remove it.

'Let's get out of here!" Ravanan took to the air flying fast and correcting his flight every time his scar from Ishida twinged; the faster he flew the more often it acted up.

Back at the top of the shaft the pair of dragons let their air barriers go. Ravanan gasped. He'd had two in his bubble. The rotten smell of decay filled his nares. He cast *"STARLIGHT"* and turned around. "Can you see my back leg?"

Ishida stretched and lowered her head to look. "oooo. One got you. It's eating your flesh!"

"EVOKE ALOE EYES!" The green lenses covered his eyes. "How about you? Are you OK?"

"I think so."

They stayed there for a moment then Ishida took a sharp inhale and touched her neck "OW!"

Ravanan looked at her new wound and then at the air around them. The black bacterial clouds were silently filling the air with their evil fibers. "Come on!" he ordered. They found his anchor and left the tunnel.

The sun warmed their hides. The fear inducing rot came with them through the anchors and was still replicating in them but at least the delicate Black Death clouds were gone.

"That was a most deplorable trap! To feed off the body and replicate, filling the air...." Ravanan remarked in agony. Then he turned to retch again. "The other dragon had to be black!" he cursed and wiped his mouth.

"Do you feel oddly warm?" Ishida asked.

He could hear the fear in her voice "Yes. It's the sickness. We've got to cut it out."

"I know!" she perked up with an idea. "I'll bite yours out if you bite mine. Our auras and saliva should protect our mouths."

"Won't your bite give me poison?"

"Yes, but you know how to fix that." she explained.

"How do I know you're not trying to poison me while I'm down with the rot? No, I've got a better idea." He retched again from the smell and then cast *"EVOKE HEXDEATH"*.

Without hesitation Ravanan told Hexdeath to cut. He buckled in pain. The green lenses over his eyes were glowing with healing power.

Ravanan looked over at Ishida, his eyes were crazy with the fresh pain of feeling air on his open flesh. His bloody blades hung in the air. Ishida remembered those blades slicing easily through her mate's neck and now they were at hers. She winced when the six points pricked her flesh. "Please don't kill me Ravanan!"

"Ishida, I have to do this."

"Bite me instead!"

"You're not thinking right!"

"I'm not ready!"

"Yes you are." The blades went to spinning.

Chapter 21

The mummy Annette stood there in the soft light of Black Blade Lair before the Amethyst Enchantress sitting in her stalagmite throne. She was slowly swaying back and forth like a tree in the breeze. Kalara looked over her way in disgust. Annette wondered if maybe she wasn't standing exactly how she had been told to. But of course she was doing it right or else Kalara would be unhappy and the world would grow dark around her.

Annette loathed herself. She knew what she was, an undead spirit. The worst spirit of all creation. An abomination of Mother Earth. How could the Great Spirit let this happen to her most faithful? She hated being what she was to the point of anger. But what could she do about it? Nothing. And Annette, being as crafty as she was, had played out every possibility of escape – there was none until Kalara willed it, and though she hated Kalara the instant she thought of causing harm to Kalara her world went to an ugly dark – a place she didn't want to be. And so she was here. There wasn't anywhere else Annette wanted to be, other than that fabled place of light she figured was there – in the void – that place she wasn't sent to. The place she couldn't go.

In life there had been that slight mystery, of not exactly knowing what lies beyond death. In life Annette had always spoken to her tribal members with assurance of knowing (or at least pretending to know) what the spirit can expect after death. As if. Annette the mummy grumped at herself. She knew full well that her human life spent as a medicine woman was adding sparkling words to her advice to the wounded. She was paid better if her words and actions were more flowery. But in all that, there was sincerity. For good or bad Annette had always tried to help those who sought her out. It just helped to make it a bit more mystical for the Belief Factor, and the patient recovered better and faster.

Now after dying Annette had truly seen what is waiting for humans such as her and she didn't like it. She preferred where she was now, helping the bitch Kalara. And so it was that Annette took a liking to her current state. It was the Belief Factor that Annette now spent all her mind's waking energy on, it became real to her. There was a life after death and she was going to try everything to change her course towards the dark, even if it meant pleasing Kalara for the rest of Kalara's living days.

And truly the mummy's alert time was a waking energy; Annette felt it, as an undead on Mother Earth's world she took energy from the sun, or any light source, even the pretty, glowing illuminations of Black Blade Lair was enough to sustain her. She felt like a strong plant powered by Mother Earth's sunlight. Even if all her roots and leaves were plucked off, her arms, head, or legs, gone, still, the little DNA leaf nodes in her bones would build her anew. If both her arms were cut off at the elbows then there would arise three Annette Mummies to please Kalara. Whenever light shown on her Annette felt a strength of will that she could do ANYTHING.... so long as it didn't involve going against Kalara.

Annette thought back to when they first met. She had wanted Kalara's power badly. And now she knew what it was, only she had to die to discover it. She was very different now, very strong, and she was dead. Now that she had come to terms with the initial shock of mummification Annette could see Kalara's human form fully and she also saw the gigantic ghostly aura form of a dragon centered on the purple-eyed human.

She not only knew (and believed) in the Belief Factor, but now Annette knew life after death was indeed fact. Mother Earth, The Great Spirit, wanted her here. Why? To be Kalara's slave? No matter, she was where she wanted to be. Light fed her. Light alone. It was the waking energy. Not that she as a mummy or even Jeremy the mummy, could sleep as humans do, rather, they just kind of hung out, standing, sitting, or laying down. When there was no light they reserved what energy they had and always, always, thought good thoughts of Kalara. Because if they didn't a darkness blacker than black would overtake them, to the point of sorrow. It was almost exhausting the amount of mental energy Annette and Jeremy spent just keeping the happiness of Kalara in their thoughts. Kalara's happiness- that was their only goal.

Kalara thought she may vomit in revulsion from looking at Annette – the mummy looked absolutely sick with her purple-veined leathery skin, all dried and sunken in. The whites of her eyes were now a solid blood-red – and the pupils that used to be black were now a milky white, same with her brown irises which were now deathly white. It was spooky. Kalara had to look away to re-gather her thoughts.

When Kalara had reentered the lair a short while ago the first thing she noticed was the seer pool quieted its outburst and her right breast had totally stopped hurting. She wondered if maybe the seer pool acted as a watch dog or warning sound. She couldn't believe her luck to find Annette right outside her door. She hadn't thought of casting reveal on the seer pool itself and made a mental note to do that later to learn about it.

She returned to the task at hand and asked Annette "Why did you capture me and take my mind?"

Annette moaned back "I was curious about your power and what Spirit gave it to you because I wanted it too, wanted to know that Spirit."

"So you took my mind for it???"

"No, you were hunting me, somehow I know it was you." Annette's voice was crumbly. "I had to stop you from eating me so I confused you."

"And taking my memories was the only spell you could think of? To make me forget everything? Well I want them back! You will put my mind back in order. Now! Do it now!"

Without a word, the mummy Annette set to work. She oddly sat down and rummaged through her medicine pouch. With clumsy hands she got her pipe together. She looked around the lair for a time before rumbling aloud "I need some stones, good-spirit stones. There are none here, this ground is worn smooth and pebbles are gone. Where did they go? And there is no dust. How odd."

And truly there were no stones small enough to pick up in the well-worn 2,000 year old lair.

Kalara was watching all this with irritation. "Well? Get on with it!"

"I need some good-spirit stones" Annette rasped.

"Fine. Come on, I've got plenty in here." and she led her mummy to the wizard's alcove.

As the mummy got everything in some kind of proper order – it reminded Kalara of the short time she actually lived with Annette as her "guest" - the mummy sat down to chanting. Her voice wasn't as pretty as it had been in life and it was a great deal more haunting. The moans and rhythm fought each other to keep the beat, but the heart was in it. From the sound alone, Kalara felt like this spell was going to fix her.

The mummy mumbled words to her Great Spirit, smoked her pipe, and prostrated herself with the greatest of effort and humbleness.

And that was it. After all the showiness, the ceremony had ended. And Kalara didn't feel any different.

Later in her bath Kalara ruminated, 'Nothing works' she thought. She knew magic now and could work it too. She could fly, breathe fire and even create enchanted weapons! She had warmed the seer pool water herself with her fire breath, the exact same magic that Ravanan had always used to make her bath. She was not human, but a powerful enchantress, half-dragoness, whatever she was, she had magic. So why couldn't she get her old mind back?

Kalara was just rinsing when her mummies lurched into the chamber.

"What do you want?" she asked.

Jeremy was first to answer, "I brought your food, its cooking now."

Annette spoke up "I just wanted be here. We belong near you, you have life. The world is brighter where you are and I really, really don't like that darkness."

"Oh, I see. So you're afraid of the dark?"

"Yes, Enchantress."

Kalara dried off and draped Heed, her new favorite robe, she could still feel the blood loss from the drape spell, but knew it was getting easier, she just needed more practice and time.

"Do you realize your little show earlier did not fix me?" she asked the mummy pointedly.

"Yes, I realized it the same moment you did. It's like it was before I died, my medicine wasn't working then and now I am dead for it."

"But your medicine did get you inside my cave." Kalara's eyebrow raised with an idea. "Yes, that's it! The blue mist. Ravanan's.", she stopped at the name and breathed it away from her dark void. "I know why your magic doesn't work, because it's not supposed to, not in here. And once again Annette, it's your fault. You are to blame for everything!" The air turned chilly and Kalara walked over to her cooking fire to think.

Getting her memories back now would be a simple task. All she had to do was get Annette out from under Ravanan's blue mist.

The enchantress and her mummies watched the cooking fire dance around her evening meal. "Annette, how did you wound me from so far away?"

"What do you mean my Enchantress?"

"My stomach ripped open, and my legs were mangled. How did you do it?"

"Oh that. I thought it didn't work." Annette's leathery face twisted into a smile "I guess it did after all. I was trying to stop your escape with that man in the blue shirt. I used my medicine on a pelt of your essence. But you look fine to me."

"Of course I look fine! The blue mist fights your curse and I'm trapped inside of it until the curse stops. I want your curse to stop."

"I do too!" Annette was Kalara's best champion. "I need to go back home and end it."

"You're not going without me." Kalara wasn't going to risk losing her mummy Annette.

"My Enchantress, how do I do it then?"

"Let me think. And you guys think about it too."

Days passed as Kalara worked on ways to leave the blue mist safely with her mummies. Jeremy was getting better and faster at fetching her meat. He was useful, Annette however, was not. And neither one of them had come up with any ideas about the cursed pelt.

It was curious that her mummies had their way of eating too, it wasn't much though, just a handful of mud. They actually were somewhat like plants. Her mummify spell had worked great, and it should have because it had drained her to make them both.

And it was most curious that suddenly one day Ravanan's meals started showing up again. Kalara hated the daily reminder of his rejection and that she was still a prisoner and would be until that pelt was destroyed.

Kalara resolved to head north with her mummies knowing that it was going to be an extremely painful journey unless she traveled by anchor. She set herself to revealing the anchors in Black Blade Lair. She had figured there would be anchors but she had no idea how many. Every bit of the floor was covered with anchors. It took time to find anything that looked remotely like the cliff in Tulsa that Ravanan had drawn. It was no use. She didn't recognize any of his drawings. She even got her mummies to help her look at each one, but they were useless.

Nevertheless Kalara continued until one day when they were revealing anchors near the wizard's alcove, and Annette spoke up. "Enchantress, I just noticed you have geodes." The mummy held up a leathery finger to a pile of rocks & crystals.

"So?"

Annette led Kalara and Jeremy to the pile of sparkly bowl-shaped rocks crusted with crystals on the inside, there were all different colors and sizes.

"I have an idea." Annette said. "You said the anchors make you into a cloud", she picked up a white one and the soft light glinted off the many facets. As Annette held it and peered into the geode's many crystals, she could see her own reflection, her hideous reflection. She could see how the red in her eyes had blackened, they were even scarier to behold being that aged black blood color with white centers.

"Well!?! Out with it." Kalara demanded.

Annette looked back to Kalara "You could become a cloud and hide inside one of these. That way you won't be in pain and Jeremy and I can carry you to my house."

Kalara was speechless as her brain worked through that idea. How did Annette come up with it? Was it that human-creativeness that Ravanan told her about? Something humans have over dragons? She would never have come up with such an idea, such a frightening idea – to be inside a rock. Annette meant to trap her!

"No way." Kalara blurted out. Kalara's mind went to that dark place. Annette was surely planning on trapping her forever inside a rock. "Do you think I'm stupid? You mean to trap me!" Her breathing quickened and the air turned cold. Memories of those large peacock eyes hung in her head. Fear was choking her.

"No Enchantress. I don't." Annette put the rock down in darkness. She had stepped out of her Enchantress' happy light. "Please Enchantress, what can I do to serve?"

Kalara's chest felt tight and she struggled to speak "Get out! Get away from me. Don't touch me! Go. Go to the seer pool. NOW!!!! Jeremy, don't let her escape!!!!!!!!"

Her mummies lumbered off and Kalara dropped to the cold cavern floor, crying uncontrollably and surrounded by large colorful eyes watching and unblinking.

The next morning came with pinkish light flooding into Black Blade Lair. The two mummies only saw darkness and huddled fearfully together, standing with their feet drinking in the water of the cold seer pool.

Hours happened. They ate their mineral-rich mud, and light returned to their world as Kalara finally retrieved them. It was a joyous moment. Jeremy took off to hunt and Annette attended to her Enchantress.

"Annette," Kalara spoke as she bathed, "what you suggested yesterday was disturbing to me. I had to think about it. If I can craft a spell for this idea of yours, it may work but you will not be allowed to ever touch my geode with me in it. Understood?"

"Yes my Enchantress."

Kalara took a big breath in, preparing herself for what else she needed to say. She knew it was the best solution. She was going to have to trust Annette and that she wouldn't run away.

"Furthermore, I want you to start heading to your old home while I'm crafting the geode spell because I'm pretty sure it is going to take a while to get there. And then when I'm ready Jeremy and I will come to where you happen to be. I don't know how long learning this spell will take me. It may not work. If you make it back to the pelt before I come to you, do not – I repeat – do not destroy it. Instead, I want you to very carefully bring it back here to me. Where the pelt was located I want you to pour this out on the ground." Kalara handed Annette a vial of sand. "Do you understand all that I've said?"

Annette nodded, "Yes my Enchantress."

"One more thing, let me feel your hair."

The mummy leaned forward and Kalara yanked a handful out. "Now you can leave."

Kalara knew she was assigning a giant task for herself, there was so much involved, and lots of practice – Jeremy would be endlessly hunting for her to keep up her blood and she had a lot of learning to do, including learning the language of the runes Ravanan had used. She cursed under her breath again at Annette for taking her mind from her.

The idea of the geode spell still terrified Kalara even though it had been a couple of days since Annette suggested it. All Kalara could see was being trapped inside a rock. Maybe it was that terror that was slowing her work. But in any case the spell wasn't coming together and she wasn't that upset about it. Every day practicing in the wizard's alcove she would spend hours with animal blood on her hands trying to write a spell in a partially-decoded language that would place a living animal's electrical cloud in a rock (she wasn't about to try it on herself yet).

Working in terror was better than sleeping though. Her work on the geode trap was bringing back the nightmares that she'd been trying so hard to not have. She'd been doing better with Ravanan gone. But now they came flooding back, sometimes several per night. Nightmares of her trapping herself with magic and all the while being watched by those silent rainbow eyes. Sometimes the eyes were trapping her by filling every inch of air around her and closing in. There were also nightmares of Ravanan's lightning jolting the geode with her inside it, killing her for what she was. There was even Jenniffer's laughter in the darkness at a drooling insane Kalara sprawled out on the floor. Perhaps the worst though was seeing her lifeless body on the floor of her wizard's alcove while her mind and spirit were forever trapped in the rock that was red with blood.

It got to the point where Kalara refused to sleep and ordered Jeremy to keep her awake, which wasn't working out so well. Every time she'd nod off Jeremy would be in utter darkness. He would have to shake and slap her, making blind contact to wake her. There were bruises.

Days passed in torment and struggle until Kalara had the idea to let Jeremy know her sleep. She paused her work on the geode trap spell and instead crafted a spell to give him telepathy. Since Jeremy never slept it worked great. He'd wake her whenever her dreams turned bad or help her dream world to shift into something happy. He knew her mind and she had nothing to hide from her mummy. He was there for her no matter what.

Chapter 22

Annette was traveling as fast as she could. She stole a car in the first town she came to and drove till it ran out of fuel. Then she was running again until she found another car. This occurred over and over. And when there wasn't a car, she would steal a horse. But horses were harder because they sensed death so well. And in the rare times she was seen a quick decapitation by twisting off the head stopped any ruckus.

She found that she ran faster during the daylight when the sun would warm her dried skin and long black hair, so much like a plant, lush and thriving, she didn't even tire out from running.

Kalara didn't know where or how far Annette had gotten. Ravanan was still sending unwanted food to the fire pit in Black Blade Lair, Jeremy was still hunting all day every day because she refused to eat Ravanan's food and instead used the blood from those carcasses for her ink. She was finally able to transform a monkey into a cloud and back again. The next step went easier than she thought it would, putting the monkey's cloud into a rock. She wondered if the type of rock mattered and tried several – the hard geode crystals, flaky shale rock, grainy sandstone, and even the super hard rock of Black Blade Lair itself – they each made the spell a little harder or less to cast. There was definitely an art to wizards' alchemy and Kalara felt as though she had barely learned to color inside the lines.

When it came time to actually start practicing on herself Kalara was unable to proceed, not even from within her dark void, she couldn't do it. Never again did she want to feel trapped, not even by her own doing. She switched to plan B, deciding to waste no more time and travel to wherever Annette may be.

She draped her healing robe and let its blue ribbons cascade about her body. The next thing she did was to evoke a green-jeweled choker that graced her neck. (She'd found out what Ravanan's two large green disks were for, a hardened aloe vera gel meant to aid recovery and it had other specs in it also of mold and fungus, held in check by magic, and also discovered several more pieces of the odd jewelry in the wardrobe chamber.) The one she wore now was called Leaf and it was one solid piece of hard aloe gel fitted for her neck, it was big and clunky but effective.

"OK Jeremy, take my hand and be ready. All I can tell you is that we are going to travel to Annette's dried up body. Be ready for anything, but above all you must protect and keep me from dying. You must get me to that cursed pelt." Kalara then wrapped Annette's lock of hair into her and Jeremy's entwined fingers and cast *"CONNECT THIS HAIR"*.

Jeremy experienced a wash of air, a dusty smell and a waving touch all over his skin. It was a rather nice experience to feel again for that brief moment of Kalara's spell. He never got to feel anything anymore other than the dull sense of information he got from grabbing his prey, (his hunting relied more on his spirit-eyesight, and hearing rather than touch).

He loved hunting for Kalara, for that moment of contact, and though it was dull and slight, when he made the tactile connection with the wiggling animal his world turned brighter because he was hunting for her, and that numbed touch and brighter world were his rewards. To the living he knew touching was taken for granted, but to him feeling life move under his hands was a real treat. Death had taken most of his sense of touch, while his eyesight had become more of a spiritual thing.

The world of death was more vivid. Neons, vibrant yellows, stark greens, glowing blues, that was the true world, it only took death to see it, everything glowed. The spirits of all living things were giants, fully encasing the little earthen bodies they were tied to. That is what he saw of his Enchantress, a dragoness, it was her true form and she towered over him. Even the spirit of a monkey stood as tall as him. It was unnerving at first, to take down a six foot tall monkey, but Jeremy got used to it, knowing his spirit – like Annette's – was every bit twice as tall as their dead bodies. The colors shown even brighter when the light of Kalara's happiness highlighted them, the monkey's fur turned a rich gold color with gleaming white. Seeing the world as it really was caused Jeremy to know magic was real.

No sooner had Jeremy felt every hair on his body rise straight and fall again like cottonwood leaves shaking in the wind, the spell was over and they were sitting beside a surprised Annette with their hands tangled in her hair. Annette was driving a car and ended up swerving into a crash.

Jeremy climbed out of the wreckage pulling his Enchantress with him. She hadn't been kidding about the pain, now made worse from the wreck. She dropped, screaming. Not only could he hear Kalara's screams he *mentally* heard them as well and they broke his heart.

He scooped Kalara up with his strong arms which were as strong as wood from a bodark tree and yet his intent was as tender as a sprout. With a commanding voice he asked "Annette, where is that pelt? We need it!"

Annette pulled herself out of the mangled car. "Wow, ya'll just appeared outta nowhere!"

"Annette, look at her! Our Enchantress. Do you have the pelt?"

"No. But we're getting close I think."

"Where are we?"

"North of Mexico City – I just got passed all the lights and sounds." She looked at Kalara, having never seen a body shifting so. "That is something! I thought she was going to use a geode. She won't make it like this."

Jeremy frowned "She chose not to."

Kalara was delirious with pain, screaming, groaning, and shut her eyes, pressing her face into Jeremy's shoulder.

Jeremy turned to show Annette his pocket "Reach in here, I brought a geode just in case."

"Good thinking." she found it, a purple geode "Here" she gestured "Put her down."

As Jeremy did so Annette came and knelt beside her. "We gotta get her naked, she can't take anything with her."

As they worked to get the necklace and robe off, Kalara came alert with wild eyes "rrgg.. what?.. OW! What?"

Annette tried to calm her "Kalara, trust me. Trust your mummies".

Kalara's wild eyes caught hold of Annette's and made an obvious threat and also a pleading for Annette not to proceed. "NO!" Kalara yelled through clenched teeth.

The mummies' world grew dark but they did managed to get her freed of everything. Then Annette took Jeremy's hands in hers and together they placed the geode on Kalara's belly button as the skin burst open. She prayed "Great Spirit, hear me, your daughter, Annette. Put this person in this rock! All of her, in the rock!"

There was a tiny red whirlwind under their hands and then there was only the ground and the geode surrounded by a cloud of Kalara's matter. Annette immediately left the geode in Jeremy's hands.

In cold, deep darkness of disobedience Annette picked up Kalara's things while Jeremy put Kalara's geode in his pocket. The air was so cold the grass crunched under their feet.

"Which way do we go?" he asked.

"Hold on," she made sure to keep hold of Jeremy's hand in the dark and knelt down to find a pebble. She whispered another prayer and felt the pebble roll on the Earth towards her thumb, "we go this way", and they took off, feeling their way and going as fast as they could.

From inside the geode Kalara sensed nothing. She was pain-free and alone with her thoughts. The connecting arcs of electricity that was her consciousness were stable inside the quartz crystals. She was mad that Jeremy brought the geode but *incredibly mad* at Annette and hoped Jeremy would continue to protect her.

Light returned to Jeremy's cold world just as dusk was settling in.

For Annette it was nothing but cold darkness. It helped her to talk, anything to get her mind off the darkness she was in.

"You know Jeremy, I think the living can tell we're not human. I think we talk slow."

Jeremy arched his leathery eyebrow in resigned agreement "Yeah, I have to say Annette, you don't look pretty anymore. In fact, you're pretty ugly. Do my eyes look as scary as yours?"

"Yes."

"Well I think it's pretty easy to tell something isn't right with us then."

Somewhere in the night suddenly Jeremy felt a great weight and heard his pocket rip. Kalara had freed herself and was now in agony again laying on the ground.

"What do we do now?!" he screamed at Annette.

The mummies fumbled around for the robe as Kalara cast, *"DRAPE LEAF! DRAPE HEALER!"*, and ended their struggle. Then the enchantress cast *"NUMB ME"* on some dirt and rubbed it on. Between moans she ordered Jeremy to continue on.

Jeremy took off again and Kalara groaned as she bounced in his arms. The mummies ran northward through the jungle of Mexico, wishing they had a car. The trees kept hitting them in the face and arms which helped keep Kalara alert.

Kalara was relieved when the land opened up finally and the trees were spaced far enough apart as to be avoided. Occasionally Jeremy would jostle Kalara back awake to make sure she was still alive.

In the coldest part of night Jeremy stopped, he read Annette's mind and knew she needed a break.

Annette sat down. "What's up?"

"We're not going fast enough. I think she's dying."

Although Annette couldn't see she checked her for fever, breathing and pulse. "Well, she's about like I'd expect. I'm sure if she has made it this far alive, she'll live. Let's keep going."

Jeremy's eyes turned to steel "That's not good enough. I can run faster than this. I know it, she made me to run faster with magic. I have been letting her down and I aim to stop. Is this the fastest you can run?"

"Yes."

"Then we'll split up. I can get there faster than you."

"Jeremy, splitting up won't do any good – you don't know where the pelt is. Now think!"

They both thought.

Annette offered "I'll stay with our Enchantress and tell you where to go. You take the sand. I'll give you a day and then we'll join you. Here, give me some hair."

Jeremy huffed. "No. I don't like that."

They both thought some more.

Then with the uncanny ingenuity that only humans possess – even the dead ones – the mummified medicine woman had a better idea. "Let's hide Kalara here, then you'll carry me to the pelt and we'll zip back here with it."

Kalara, for as much as she could hear, apparently liked the idea because finally Annette's world brightened up.

Jeremy smiled a stretched, dried smile. He was so glad he learned to worship Mother Earth and follow her teachings. He watched as Annette chanted and placed four stones to the four directions of the earth, she spat on the ground, she picked certain grasses, smoked some grass, and sang, Annette took her time, but when she was done Kalara could hardly be seen.

In Annette's pocket was a chip off a nearby rock to bring them back. He carried Annette fast away leaving their enchantress behind, crying in the bush.

When Annette's dried feet touched her land it was sunrise a day and a half later. She was home. She took off towards the honey locust tree, keeping alert for any sign of Todd.

He could be anywhere, or maybe not here but over at Melissa's. He was most likely sleeping but some rituals and tasks required sunrise, and then there was hunting and fishing – always done better at sunrise when the critters were waking to feed. She did not want to see him, or rather, didn't want him to see her.

The place looked great, a little cleaner. Todd was keeping it all up just as she knew he would. She missed being here, it felt like a lifetime ago when her world was simpler. Even though she knew the Great Spirit was everywhere Annette still felt a special connection as she ran through the back yard, wishing she could take some time to visit the prayer stone she had made many years before. But there was no time to waste, her and Jeremy kept to the edge of the yard and used the trees as cover.

Annette stopped to listen. Yes, she heard them, Todd's footfalls on the leaf-covered grass. He was coming back from hunting, evidently not successful. She and Jeremy had just enough time to evade and hide. He looked really healthy, attractive even. The gift of the rooster was indeed a gift. She wondered how he was getting along – if only she could talk to him one last time. It was simply out of the question. Never again would she get to talk with her son, and she couldn't even shed more than a drop of a sappy tear over him.

It wasn't hard for them to hide, being plant-like helped when hiding among plants, their respiration was always low and quiet. Annette watched Todd go in the back door to the house and then they took off again.

At the honey locust tree Kalara's Pelt was still snagged on the thorns, hanging there mournfully. Jeremy had to get it off because Todd had placed it up high. Annette poured Kalara's sand on the ground and pulled out her chipped rock piece that would get them back to their Enchantress.

Then a dense cloud of smoke enveloped the mummies. Jeremy looked around for a fire. Annette quickly prostrated herself in reverence. "Oh Great Spirit!" she sighed with happy surprise. Jeremy did the same, unsure of what was happening.

The splintery voice shattered in their ears "My child."

Jeremy opened his eyes and lifted his head. He kept raising his eyes trying to find the source of the odd voice, lifting his chin higher to take in all he could see. Though the cloud was thick he was able to see the spirit of a towering silver dragoness peering down at them.

Annette still had her eyes closed. He wondered if she knew about the dragoness in front of them. He nudged her elbow. She didn't flinch except for to move her arm away. He wasn't scared. After all, he was dead, so with a silent curiosity he followed Annette's lead and lowered his head once more.

"You've returned without Kalara and you're helping her."

"Yes."

"That little animal skin won't help her. Return it to my tree."

"Mother Earth, I need it."

"Return it to my tree." Again the shattered glass voice was jagged in their ears.

Annette the mummy raised her head, looked up at her Great Spirit, in defiance she answered "No." Then with a mighty blow and no prayer the mummy medicine woman slammed her hand, chipped rock shard in the palm, hard into Jeremy's back with such force that Jeremy's tree-hard body made an impression in the dirt. Both mummies and the pelt vanished.

A shrill scream went out over the woods that morning, the few humans who were awake could not describe it later and all the forest animals heard it and ran far from the hill in a panic.

The mummies appeared at Kalara's hiding place.

"It worked!" Annette exclaimed. "I mean, I didn't have to do a ritual or sing, not even utter a prayer!"

"I'm glad it did." Jeremy returned. "I didn't know what she was fixin' to do to us." he added as he went to their Enchantress.

Kalara was in a tormented and sweaty sleep but at least she was alive. Jeremy scooped up her body to wake her.

In a delirium Kalara opened her eyes "Help." was all she could say.

Jeremy held the ugly white pelt that had some of Kalara's own dark hair on it. Annette took it and held it out for Kalara to see.

Seeing it brought Kalara to attention better than coffee ever could. She mumbled "Is there anything special we have to do to end its curse?"

"That depends on if you want to upset Mother Earth or not." she threw it on the ground.

Purple fire shot from Kalara's mouth and the pelt was no more.

Kalara laid back, feeling the power of Leaf and Healer take over the war on her flesh.

That little spot of land became their hidden camp of recovery. In the following days Kalara continued to feel better and better and was sleeping less.

Her mummies were enjoying themselves too, being out in the sun. Annette was teaching Jeremy her medicine and he was picking it right up. It never occurred to Kalara to question how Annette was so powerful, she just accepted it as she always had. Jeremy was teaching Annette how he hunted as an undead even though she wasn't as fast as Jeremy. In any case Kalara was glad for the company, even if they were undead. She noticed they needed new clothes to cover the disgusting leathery skin, that would be a task to do upon returning to Black Blade. Yes, full clothes and dark sunglasses to hide those hideous eyes.

There were cattle in the area but Jeremy feared hunting too much and thankfully Kalara wasn't requiring a lot of food for spells at the moment. The area was farmland and he remembered in Oklahoma that dead cattle were investigated immediately with guns. He'd found a nearby town and hoped to snag some restaurant food for Kalara but chose not to go for fear of getting caught. So hunting became a real game to find small animals – his success was fairly high.

In time Kalara was able to drape her favorite robe Heed. The purple looked great in the sun with all the little black shiny glints of biotite, but the dark metal breast cage was heated by the sun. This gave Kalara something to work on, making her aura cool off the air without her having to be angry to make it happen.

The curse was gone and she felt truly free. Kalara still wore Leaf for final healing but her mood was good and her thoughts turned to a total recovery. She called Annette to her.

"Yes My Enchantress?"

"Enough time has been wasted." Kalara said. "I want you to recover my memories now. Give them back to me. You ought to be able to, now that you're away from Black Blade."

"Yes. I want to. We're out of that mist, my medicine works out here." Annette thought for a moment and then grabbed an old pack of crackers from her pocket. She took one out and broke it on a rock into several pieces. Then as she carefully put the little puzzle back together again she concentrated on broadcasting clear thought and total memory recall to Kalara.

Instantaneously Kalara thought more clear than ever before. So clear were her thoughts that she knew Annette's medicine had not brought back her memories. She gave Annette an unimpressed stare.

Annette grimaced in the darkness of failing her Enchantress. "That didn't work did it?"

There was no answer and Jeremy knew to keep quiet as well.

"It should have worked." Annette went on, "What went wrong?"

"When you figure it out tell me." Kalara replied sourly. She had no idea how to get her memories back now. First Ravanan failed, now Annette herself failed. Somehow she was going to have to fix herself if it was even possible.

At night the three of them explored under darkness. One night they heard voices on the wind and moved in to investigate.

They came upon some hills that rose up from the flat land, river-bottom flood plain land – the hills didn't belong to it. Annette knew about the ancient peoples of Central America and hill-building was their thing as a lot of her own ancestors were – this had to be an archaeological site. Sure enough as they circled wide around the voices they came to a sign that read: TAMTOC ZONA ARQUEOLÓGICA Patrimonio Cultural de San Luis Potosí y de la Nación. The voices were young and laughing, speaking English. There were three of them.

A girl's voice said "I *said*, 'You shouldn't mess with that'!"

There was a boy's laughter and another said "You worry too much, it can hold my weight."

"Whatever. Don't blame me if it breaks."

"It won't. - Man! This place is awesome."

"Don't you guys feel the sacredness of this place? We should be more careful!"

"Oh ho! So now you believe in magic? Does Pastor Joe know?" More laughing followed.

"I say we sleep on top of that highest mound!"

The girl objected "Just because we missed the bus doesn't mean we get to sleep here. We should look for a phone and call Yolanda."

"Oh come on! What's the harm? It's not like we're ruining the ruins. They'll get us in the morning and we'll get back in time for class."

"Yeah. Besides, Yolanda's probably already asleep. Come on, race ya to the mound!"

Kalara backed away, she'd heard enough. "Jeremy, feel like hunting?"

"I'm ready."

She smiled "Get to the mound and take the winner."

Jeremy took off at full speed and got there in less than a minute. He could hear the student running in the night, his laughter growing louder as he neared. He was ready to lunge... waiting..... when he saw it..... a spirit in the shape of a dragon swoop down and take the guy. It was dark but there was no mistaking the spirit he saw, a dragon but it had no body. It wasn't his Enchantress either, she had a body like all living spirits did. Along this journey to save Kalara he had seen a few other dragons but they never killed humans and never got that close. This one was different. Why didn't it have a body?

The girl saw her friend vanish and was screaming about it. But her screams were cut short when she met the same fate. Jeremy raced to the last student before he vanished too.

The student screamed when he saw the mummy running towards him in the dim moonlight. He tried to fight but was no match for Jeremy's speed and strength. With ease the mummy tore his head clean off.

Jeremy brought the body and head back to Kalara who evoked Siphon to drain its blood.

"That was the second boy, a dragon ghost beat me to the winner and the girl."

"Dragon Ghost?" Kalara laughed. "I saw them disappear too." She looked around. "I didn't see a ghost but that doesn't mean there isn't another dragon here." She looked around them and tried to sense an aura but there was nothing.

Jeremy explained himself "I saw its spirit just like I see yours but there wasn't a body attached. Doesn't that make it a ghost?"

"No. There are such things as invisibility enchantments." She scanned the area again but knew she wouldn't see anything. "Come on, let's get out of here."

The mummies carried the body and head until its blood was drained and then Kalara burnt it to ash to leave no trace. She was an Acama and she would follow the law.

Kalara felt exhilarated. They followed the nearby river upstream. She wanted to fly which she hadn't done since ending the curse. So she took it slow and her mummies ran with her, watching constantly to avoid any humans even though it was night. They passed farms all the way until coming to the mountains. They feared there would be tourists at such a beautiful place and so the trio swung south over the forested mountain tops, trying to follow the river when possible but keeping to the southeastern side.

They ended up on a high mountain that was being cut by the river as it swung around another mountain to their north.

In the quiet night Kalara heard a hum, more like she felt a good vibration in her head. The sound was so subtle it could easily be ignored; but out in the middle of nowhere and with a burning drive to explore, she could not help but follow it. She got up and her mummies followed her as she flew towards whatever it was down the mountain to the southeast.

Ten minutes later Kalara found where the resonance was strongest – at a giant hole in the ground, known to humans as the Cave of Swallows.

Her mummies stood guard while Kalara faltered on what to do.

Standing on the edge of the pit she cast *"REVEAL"* when the blue glasses extended over her eyes from her hairpiece she looked to see a home, nothing more, no threats or traps, no dragon or inhabitants. "I'm going down. You need to hide here. *DRAPE NAUGHT! EVOKE SIPHON!*"

The mummies watched her body disappear so that all was left for them to see was the giant dragon of Kalara's spirit.

"I wish she would have taken us with her." Jeremy remarked – even though he didn't have to say it. He could have just put his thought into Annette's head but he still was used to using his mouth.

"Nah, she'll be alright. Some journeys have to be walked alone." Annette replied quietly and pulled out her pipe; she lit it and sat down. "I'm so glad I found more tobacco."

The pipe smoke swirled up to the stars as she handed the pipe to Jeremy.

"Well, being with her would be something to do. Waiting sucks." He took a puff. "I'd much rather go into that cave with her. I think that is the Cave of Swallows and it's on my bucket list." He laughed. "Bucket list! What should I call it now? I've kicked the bucket already."

Annette laughed with him. "True."

Jeremy looked out across the big hole "Still it would have been nice. I'm so close...."

Annette knew his mind was turning. In hushed tones she scolded him "Don't. You may still get the chance. Besides, you want to try to navigate that in total darkness? You'd fall."

"Would not. Remember who the trained climber is here."

"And what would you see?" Annette challenged him.

Jeremy couldn't argue, knowing he'd see nothing in the dark of disobeying.

Annette nodded and tended the ash in her pipe. "Do you think what you'd see down there is anything more powerful than what you see here, around you?" She looked around and beckoned Jeremy to do the same.

To the mummies the night forest was beautiful with all its spiritually vibrant colors of life. Even in a new moon they could see a lot of life happening about them and also see the glowing spirits of sleeping birds nesting in the tree tops.

"No." Jeremy admitted. He puffed and let the smoke leave his dried up lips, listening to the sounds of the night.

In the dark light of the night Jeremy glanced at Annette as he handed the pipe back to her. This was as good a time as any to tell her about his telepathy. He searched for the words to say. He didn't want to scare her by just putting his voice in her brain. He thought about their relationship if you could call it that. They were friends he assumed. More like they were soldiers who had been thrown together in service. And they were the only two of their kind.

He cared for her, yes, and he admitted to himself that in life certain thoughts had crossed his mind. How could they not? You can't stop thoughts of that nature. The medicine woman had been a beauty, everything about her was perfect, her breasts, her hair and face but now in death her rich-colored skin had leathered and receded. She wasn't juicy at all. There was no healthy life in her. Or in him. Come to think of it now, he hadn't thought about sex since he'd died. How strange. And he never even saw his dick now, never had to urinate, never undressed never pulled it out. He subtly shifted himself and - sure enough – it felt like a piece of jerky down there. He lamented the loss. Could he even do anything with it if he tried? What would come out? Dust? He chuckled at that.

"What?" she asked.

He ran his hands through his hair, the only thing on him that still looked good. "Oh nothing, just thinking how pitiful we look."

Annette raised her eyebrow and took another puff.

"Hey Annette. I want you to know something."

"Okay."

"After you left and our Enchantress was working on that spell. She couldn't sleep well."

"What of it?"

"Well, she made me able to help her sleep by letting me know her mind. And I can say things inside her mind. Yours too I think."

"Really? That is amazing!"

"Can I try it?"

"Well sure. Like I'm gonna say no to magic..... Go ahead!"

And Jeremy did just that. He asked her to hand the pipe back to him.

Annette smiled and complied without a word.

Kalara flew down the dark hole letting the reverberating hum guide her. It wasn't hard to find the spot on the cave wall where the lair's entrance was. She trusted Heed that there were no traps and put her hand forward.... and sure enough it went into the fake rock wall. She flew inside.

The hallway lit up with ice sconces in her vicinity and it seemed to go on beyond several gentle bends and dipping all the way, some places steeper than others. Kalara couldn't see the end so she proceeded quietly. She wasn't sure of the distance but it took a great deal of time and all the while the soft crystalline light stayed with her, extinguishing as she passed.

The question crossed her mind as to how the lights knew she was there when she was wearing Naught but ultimately she continued on, following the odd hum.

The long hallway ended at a huge pyramid-shaped chamber. It was lit from a bright lavender crystal high at its top and then smaller ones on the walls. The four walls were perfectly smooth. Near the top where the walls came together they were tiled with a white shiny metal, below that were gold tiles. Kalara could see markings in the gold, possibly they were pictures but she would have to get closer if she wanted to see the details.

The chamber had three rooms attached on the other walls. At the center of it was a raised dais. Taking up most of the dais was another platform of rock that rose up with a map of the world etched in deep relief on it. The map had moveable markers on it strategically placed and every continent was depicted in its whole form. Four chairs were casually placed around the map table. The alcove to her left was cold with ice in its dark corners while the one to her right felt warm. She headed for the warm alcove, it was empty of life, the whole place was.

As Kalara entered the warm alcove she saw four beds in the corner closest to her. There was more to the warmth that was radiating from the room, it truly did feel like it was healing her. She dismissed Leaf and let the room do its job.

The alcove across from the entrance passageway was a seer pool and fully stocked wizard's alcove. Lastly Kalara headed for the cold room and in it she found frozen food of all kinds, and not just raw meat either, there was everything from vegetables to pizzas.

Back in the main chamber Kalara looked over the map. She didn't know what the markers meant. She stood there wondering why no one was there in the middle of the night when most of the world was sleeping. Then she flew up to the apex to look at the golden pictures.

The light from the lavender crystal shown on the golden surface. The ceiling was a treasure in itself! All the stunning gold from four walls reflected warmly back to her. It wasn't just a vast expanse of gold sheeting but rather meticulous craftsmanship. There were obvious sections, pieces of hammered gold in a variety of two-dimensional shapes that fit together with near puzzle-piece precision. Between them there were dark grooves where the host rock shown through. Refocusing her gaze she saw the entire shape of the golden puzzle made one whole depiction of a dragon rising above others while each of the four walls told their own story of a dragon rising.

Kalara noticed each of the four dragons looked a bit different and pieced together the clues around her starting with the resonating hum that drew her to the cave in the first place. There were ice lamps in the hallway, a world map, a chilled alcove.... this lair had to be for the Acamas and at that thought she flew down to leave immediately.

Before she made it to the hallway the resonance grew a little stronger and a coldness entered the room followed by a purple dragon. Kalara's eyes widened in panic. What was he doing here? Which one was it? Her mind raced, thinking quickly she moved out of his path. She hid her thoughts in the dark corner of her heart and was so glad she was wearing Naught so she could sneak out.

The dragon looked her way. "Hello Kalara. Its been a long time. How has the hunting been here?" Tristan asked.

Her mouth fell open – how did he see her? "Why do you ask?"

He gave her a weird look. "You're wearing an invisible suit."

"Oh yeah. I forgot I was. It's so comfortable you know." She dismissed it and draped Heed. "The hunting has been good."

Now Tristan took a step closer and sat down, he was studying Heed as she was studying him. He looked way different than Ravanan. This dragon's wings were nearly invisible and he had four of them – two sets of feathered wings. He had feathered whiskers and different shaped horns that were encrusted with fashionable lines of diamonds, his talons had diamonds also in a neat row. *All* of his talons had glistening diamonds.

"Wow." he said "You've been busy lately. That thing must be full of enchantments."

Kalara was about to comment when a purple-eyed wizard entered the room wearing casual jeans with a comfortable shirt. His face was scruffy and rugged.

"Hi guys." Kadd looked around and did a double-take when he caught sight of Heed. "So." he smiled "I didn't see Ravanan outside...."

"He's not here."

"This must be pretty urgent, it's dark outside, what is it... just after midnight?" he walked around the dais, looking at the map, trying to look like he wasn't staring at Kalara.

Nobody was saying anything.

Kadd turned to Tristan and asked him something about ocean currents while they waited.

Tristan started telling him all the latest on the subject. As they went on killing time Kalara looked down the passageway again, thinking on how to leave and wondering how that Acama had seen her.

Kalara did feel the resonating hum get stronger when he appeared and still more when the second Acama showed up. She wondered if maybe she was giving off a hum too and that was how he had detected her. Kalara tried to feel the directions of the humming without staring and thought maybe she could feel something. It was such an odd thing to sense, like a vibration or phantom sound.

She had to get away and headed out towards the exit.

Kadd called out "Where are you going? I'm sure Morada will be here anytime."

"Out. I won't be long." But it was too late, as she felt another vibration and a warm aura enter the lair.

A voice came from the cave and the hum got stronger "I'm here now Kadd. I know. You beat me again."

Kadd and Tristan laughed.

Morada came in, she looked sparkly. Kalara looked at her talons and horns, they had flawless quartz crystals extending from their tips – even her spikes and fangs had them! They'd started growing at birth and in 800 years some were nearly three inches long, the ones on her fangs looked to be only dew drop size from wear and tear. The quartzicles would continue to grow as her aura melted and fused desert sand grains to them. They were beautiful.

When Morada saw that Kalara was in human form she shrugged and morphed to a dark-skinned human while walking to the table and chairs. By the time she was sitting down she was wearing her favorite robe.

The Acamas got comfortable. Kadd grabbed a drink from the chilled alcove and threw another one to Tristan who had also switched to his human form. The oriental wizard Tristan looked wise with age, his diamonds hug magically in his hair while the others were embedded in his long fingernails.

Kalara was trapped.

"So Kalara," The Amethyst Wizard Tristan began. "Why have you summoned us here?"

Chapter 23

I t was a warm humid morning, Todd had his shirt off, wearing only his jeans, his neck was adorned with his bone choker and wearing his turtle shell necklace rattle – he had painted a bull over Annette's gray snake.

He was sitting in the living room chair with his back to the big window for light, the webbed shadow of the large dream catcher was on him. Sara Jenkins was sitting on the couch beside her teenage son Eric. They'd come to Todd because she had no money for an urgent care clinic. The cut was deep into Eric's ankle, and of all things it was a shovel that he fell onto when jumping over a trench. Dirt was deep inside the bloodied cut.

Todd worked his medicine carefully, chanting as he massaged salve into the wound. His strong hands rubbed the whole ankle lightly, waking the skin and calling it to heal. He didn't rush.

As the sunlight caused the web shadow to move across his tanned back the deep cut began to close up. Sara let out a relieved breath but kept quiet for the medicine man. How was she ever going to be able to repay him? She would bring him some cooked meals and can tomatoes for him. Even give him the last two jars of her jalapeno pear jelly.

After the mother and son left Todd went for a walk down in the woods to collect a few things. It was just a sticky day, so humid! He was glad he'd changed into his swimming trunks. At the creek he bagged a little bit of the soft black mud. He also had to gather cattail and mistletoe. He knew the perfect tree to climb for the mistletoe, he'd been eyeing that batch for a while now, letting it grow large. Now it was time to pick.

Todd shimmied up the tree barefoot and took a seat on the tree limb. Then he paused to think and remember John Trickfoot's little boy with the eight warts. John and the boy stopped by last week about it. Todd had been careful to examine each wart without touching them – such disgusting things they were. He prayed to Mother Earth, thanking her for the tree in which he sat and the healing it was going to do for that little boy.

The beautiful goddess unexpectedly appeared near him "Pay."

He didn't question her. Of course she meant for him to pay right there at that very spot. Thankfully there were other limbs nearby for hand holds. This was a first and he made sure it felt like it. He took her powerfully, the branch waved, leaves and catkins sprinkled from the tree. The look in her eyes was exactly what he wanted. As usual she was quick to disappear right after but it was nice that at least this time she took an extra moment to linger before leaving. To have the approval and favor of Mother Earth was his greatest joy.

Winded, but regaining his prayerful heart, he thanked the Earth and the tree once more. Then Todd pulled out his pocket knife, seeing those eight warts in his head he began to sing and transfer them to the tree with his knife, making a total of eight distinct cuts.

In the following early morning hours Todd dreamed. Oddly, it wasn't about Mother Earth but Melissa. He hadn't thought of his ex-girlfriend in a long time. The dream seemed so real. She was sad that they had broken up, crying it up real good on the tail gate of her truck in the Walmart parking lot after work. With every tremble of her delicate shoulders she began to shape-shift into the goddess he loved. She wasn't wearing a bra and when she laid back her round breasts fell naturally against her sides. She raised her shirt and started to touch her nipples and play with herself – tempting him to take her. He walked over to her and started pulling her clothes off. He spread her legs and then woke up.

The dream was unnerving but not too much. He took care of his morning wood and felt like he was cheating on Mother Earth as he did. It was a very carnal and selfish act but he wanted it! Little did Todd know that his waking thoughts were being heavily influenced by an outside force. He wanted to fuck Melissa hard. He missed her. He missed her companionship.

A panicky thought took over him that the Great Spirit saw his dream and knew his thoughts but he couldn't help his dreams, they just happened. To be safe he went straight to the sweat lodge to pray for forgiveness but the goddess never appeared. Todd didn't know what else he could do about it.

The day's list of chores included shoeing the horses, restringing a dream catcher and making more to sell at the next pow-wow. He checked the live trap and sure enough he'd caught that opossum that was threatening his chickens so he'd have to deal with that. There were fish to be caught and beer to drink, but Todd could hardly find time to do either.

In the time since Annette left he had found out just how much the medicine woman did around the place and for the tribe. He was busy – even the elders were happy with him! And adding the fact that he'd been giving himself to Mother Earth so much it was understandable how he hadn't had much down time to be lonely. But on this day his thoughts kept returning to Melissa. All he wanted was to sit on the couch with Melissa and watch the ball game, eating chips and drinking beer.

By the end of the day he knew what he had to do. He drove to the bar where Melissa waited tables and asked her if he could walk her to her truck after she clocked out.

When he went back to fetch Melissa she smiled warmly up at him. It sure seemed like she missed him too. Her hands squeezed his bicep as she matched his slow pace. And when they got to her truck they both talked and apologized. Then she invited him over to her place.

Melissa unlocked her door and they went inside, Todd found the TV remote and started to scan for something to watch while she went to her bedroom to change. She shut her bedroom door and headed for the closet when all of a sudden she couldn't move or scream.

What came out of the bedroom a short time later was a hungry monster that was following the scent of her first target. The tantalizing smell of testosterone drew her to him. She pushed the coffee table away and knelt her naked body at Todd's feet and prepared herself to feast at the stunning factory and storehouse seated on her couch.

The gift of the rooster made for a long, wonderful night and Todd was thoroughly worn out when he arrived at his home the following morning. His pickup truck bed was full of Melissa's things – she was moving in and he was overjoyed.

In the sweat lodge later that day Todd was hosting a cleansing ceremony for a tribal elder. It was a high honor and he was going to ensure it was done perfectly but he was still exhausted from his pleasures with Melissa and hauling her stuff in all day.

The guests were seated naked outside, waiting prayerfully and patiently for Todd to call down their ancestors. They could smell the earthy sage and spice from within. Todd stilled his body and mind, chanting and waiting, pushing away the fear that he might not be able to pay The Great Spirit as he needed to, he kept one hand working himself up, imagining her beautiful body bouncing on top of him. Too soon for him the familiar ash cloud filled the steamy lodge and the splintery voice of Mother Earth spoke so intensely that the shrillness caused him to shiver in pain and cover his ears "You shouldn't have called upon your ancestors when you can't pay for it."

"Great Spirit, I can. I will."

The sharp tinkle of glass shards was the reply.

"I'm ready. Please."

"What you have done can't be undone – ever. From now on your supplications will be made in faith only, paying in the traditional ways of your ancestors."

The powerful Great Spirit left him alone in the steam.

He bowed his head and cried.

Todd then regained his composure and continued the ceremony by opening the door and inviting everyone in.

Afterwards, as they were leaving all the guests said he did a great job. Todd waved them goodbye, still in shock as he watched them drive away.

Chapter 24

Their open flesh wounds at least had scabbed over but Ravanan was anxious to kill the rot trap. And so with modified armors and toting extra air bubbles behind them Ishida and him headed back down. He didn't want that rot filling his lair. They emerged from the Hall of Fish illuminating the way as they went with his Diamond Staff and flew quickly down the Shaft of Darts and on through the last unexplored chamber, the heart of the ancient lair.

It was a well-balanced lair with a multitude of columns and nearly touching stalactites all around the cavern walls. They took no time to look around other than a quick glance as they flew to the far side. Above them was a giant labradorite and jade chandelier, though it was now dark with the death of its creator and couldn't light their way. They didn't even touch the floor that was covered in golden statues and reliefs depicting the ancient pairs' lives. A full 7,000 years of memories was immortalized in gold and jewels just below their feet. The briefest thought came into Ravanan's mind, it was that the former residents followed the *really* old way, sleeping on their gold, eating with it, and bathing in it just like birds taking dirt baths. Their photo album was their bed.

At the far wall they were going to cast the spell Solar Flare together but then Ravanan stopped them. He looked around. "We can't use Solar Flare. It'll melt everything together into one big soup of lava."

"What are you thinking? Cold flame?"

"Yes, breathe the coolest fire you can on everything and on all the air. Remember, keep it cool or else we'll ruin some things."

The ancient lair was his at last, and all of its treasure. Ravanan studied an interesting piece that stood off by a stalagmite, a gold tree set on a large disk of petrified wood that was entirely blood-red carnelian. There was a man bound to the trunk with gold wire and a circle of men around the sacrifice tree.

The treasure was massive and he should be smiling. And he was..... it's just that there was more on his mind.

His eyes came back to Ishida.

"How is your headache?" he asked her.

"It only hurts in the mornings now. Did you know that truth spell would hurt me like this?"

"It wasn't the truth spell. It was from our battle when I controlled you."

"I see. You didn't care if it hurt me."

"Not at the time."

"But you do now?"

He gave her a small smile. "I'm concerned that it's still hurting."

"Oh it's better than it was. There was a time when I feared I wouldn't ever fly again. But you don't have to give my head another thought."

Ravanan heard her words and knew she meant something else. He wished she would just say it plainly but that was too much to ask for. "I'm glad it's better." was all he could think of.

"How nice. I have your concern. But you're not happy. I can make you happy."

"Are you so sure about that? You don't know me."

Ishida reached out and grabbed the painful scar on his wing.

Ravanan howled and pulled it away from her.

She laughed. "It wouldn't have scarred if you would have released me when I asked – I could have got to it in time to heal it." Ishida grasped his wing again and looked at the dead spot. There were still a few black spidery veins around it too. "I've seen worse. You're fine."

He glared at her "I should cut it out like I did that rot."

"Why didn't you then? And stop the irritation?" She let the wing go and fixed her red eyes on him. "I may not know your past but I can give you a reason to enjoy that scar."

Ishida took hold of his arm and cast *"MORPH TO HUMAN"*.

To keep her from dangling Ravanan quickly morphed too. But before he could evoke his robe her mouth covered his member and she put to use all she learned about the job from her native land. He put his hands on her head thinking to stop her. But that idea couldn't carry through to his hands that were now running through her soft hair. As he moved his arm he felt the slight pain of his poisoned scar in his shoulder blade.

There was a wildness she possessed. Being with her was a test in wrestling, he had never cared much for the sport until now when she conquered him by pinning him with his long dark hair – he hadn't seen that one coming. The way she used her magic so subtly to mask her actions and then to embellish them with it – weaving it into her every move was definitely the way to win his heart. The more they tussled the sharper their reflections became in each other's minds, the more they understood, discovered how to please and tease each other, it was a whole new realm. Gold coins were flying and sticking to their backs. The sound of shifting metal made them both smile.

Auras changed to heat, smoldering heat turned to flame, and the flame erupted into a circle of purple fire just beyond his treasure. Ravanan caught a glimpse of the purple firestorm raging around them, it was *her* color – he turned away. He couldn't do this. Of all the dragonesses in the world he had to get with a red! There was no way he could live being reminded of her every time he was with another. He stood up and draped his robe.

Ishida stormed over and ripped his beautiful robe off him, throwing it down. She wasn't about to stop, not at this point. She ran her hands along his smooth chest trying to lure him back to her. She wasn't going to let it be this way. She started kissing his back all along his spine.

Ravanan let out a sigh and rolled his head. She was wicked with her runes, writing them with her tongue and mesmerizing him with every touch.

He was a mess of emotion. His failure, his lost love Kalara, Ishida tearing his robe and rubbing her skin against his....... he spun around while grabbing Ishida's wrists and pinned her down to his gold. He kissed her wildly, owning her, taking what he wanted – ridding himself of all the pain and frustration he pushed it into her, with every thrust he would make it disappear forever and the purple fire would be his reward.

Chapter 25

Kalara held her head high and took a seat at the table. Ravanan's words hung in her head *'they will kill you for your condition.'* The dark corner in her heart didn't seem dark enough to conceal her missing memories. She envisioned drawing more darkness from the rocks under her feet and matched their gaze, it was darkness covered by a smile.

If she was going to live another minute she had to do this. Kalara told herself she had been in the cave many times before this and that the dragons in the cave didn't want to eat or trap her, they were the law keepers, the Acamas, *her* group, and they were sitting around waiting to hear why she brought them here.

But she didn't know why; or how they were summoned. She didn't do it. It was getting uncomfortable as they watched her. "Well," she started, recalling what little she knew.

"I got to thinking how long it's been since we got together. I knew it'd be daylight for you guys so you wouldn't mind. Does anybody have anything to say?"

The Acamas exchanged looks. Morada leaned forward "Well I didn't think it had been that long. Things are about the same where I'm at. I still have Naga issues of course but don't we all?" she looked around and smiled. "No, I've got a pretty good handle on the research coming from my land."

Kadd spoke after her "You really had me going Kalara, I thought something big was up." the others agreed. "But I think it's good we're talking. I've been considering calling a meeting too - nothing's immediately wrong" he assured them "it's just the Naga in my area have been talking about ending the Law. They feel like the herd needs to be thinned out because their filth is ruining the planet. You have to agree with them on that part at least."

"You're right," said the old Acama gloomily, thinking of his infested homeland.

Kadd added "One of the most vocal is Salman the black dragon, he's immersed himself in their society and acting in their movies but every time he meets with me he cites endless numbers and facts to support his side. He hasn't requested a full meeting yet but I'm sure he will at some point. I think he is rallying support before he does."

"Well what of the research down there?" Tristan asked. (Being from the south pole, Tristan felt like his fellow brood rock dragons in that they were, in fact on top of the world looking down at the other inferior continents far below.)

"I've got researchers in all directions, there is a lot going on. For myself, I've been spending a lot of time in Nikhadelos Dialo keeping the feathered ancestor digs quiet but that Naga Xu Zheng keeps discovering and broadcasting them. He needs to be stopped.

Tristan spoke up "Remember, we're not law enforcement, we're mass communicators – that's all. Every dragon knows and keeps the Law in their own way."

"Tristan, I know that. But I can't turn a blind eye to the change I'm sensing. I fear this whole Dragon Law thing is going to fall apart."

"We need to give it time, it's only been 600 years." Tristan said. "The Naga agreed to the Law when it was made, they won't break it now."

It was clear to Kalara that Kadd disagreed with Tristan.

Morada joined in "It sounds like you've become pretty busy with keeping an eye on the research."

"I have."

"We simply need more help." Tristan replied. "Morada, what of that egg we just made, was it an amethyst?"

"No. You know I would have told you guys the moment it hatched if it had been. Shall we try again?"

"Sure." Tristan then turned towards Kalara. "And what of your little amethyst over here? Is he ready to help out his sire yet?"

Kalara was stunned but able to maintain her control over her thoughts and aura. She hastily smiled and said "Nearly."

Kadd gave her a surprised look and intervened. "No he's not. It'll be another few years at home for him, he's barely over 40. We can't throw a new young Acama into Nikhadelos, it's too busy. I'd rather recruit help."

"No." Morada replied. "This task was given to the amethysts and we'll do it alone. Even if we have to stay together and tackle one thing at a time. No dragon can fight us all at once."

Kadd went on "Tristan, why can't you come down and help, just for a while, maybe? How are things up there anyways?"

Tristan gave a stern look to his fellow Acamas "I can't leave my land. My dragons need me now more than ever, what with the cattle's recent worries over the climate warming up – their scientists are coming in record numbers. Their incessant mapping and exploring never ends! It's like they've never seen ice before and all the mysteries it has. No, it's not a good time."

Kadd looked to Morada "What about you in your sands? Maybe you could spare some time."

She laughed, "Kadd, didn't you hear me? I'm having Naga issues as well. I don't need to take on any more."

"Well we all know Kalara's busy." Kadd said emphatically.

The Acamas were quiet in thought.

'What did Kadd mean by that?' Kalara wondered, but more than that she couldn't believe she had mated with him. Who was her mate? Had Ravanan been lying about everything?

Kadd went back to his point. "Oh, and then also in Nikhadelos Dialo, you know that little area the cattle call "North Korea"?"

Tristan roused at the name "So, what is going on there?"

"Their old leader died and the son took over. Things have gotten pretty delicate and the dragons can't agree on who is doing what. There is great opportunity to eat at leisure but at the same time everything could bust wide open."

Tristan had heard enough "I'll care for North Korea, don't concern yourself with it any longer. The dragons in that area owe me, especially Jung and Mortiff. Leave it at that. But before I help I'm taking Tamtoc to Viptryx with me. He'll be safe enough, my lands are less dangerous. And then when I think he can be left alone to do Acama work I'll go handle that crisis for you."

Kadd looked away but didn't argue.

"Alright. Is there anything else?" Tristan looked around. "OK then, why don't you two go get your son" he nodded to Kalara and Kadd, "while Morada and I prepare the rite."

"Fine." Kadd stood up, ready to go then paused "Where are we meeting up? You know Vya Matros has become too crowded since we did the rite."

"Well, the end destination is my lair so how about there?" Tristan offered.

They all agreed while Kalara kept silent and nodded.

Tristan and Morada left the lair by anchor.

Kadd turned to Kalara who was still sitting down. "Are you ready?"

"No." She wasn't going anywhere except away from him.

"Why?"

"Because you don't need me for this and I've got to get back."

"Right." Kadd thought she was joking. "Let's get this over with."

"OK." She snapped then stood up. Kalara's control of blocking her thoughts was straining with fatigue. It had been a long unexpected day and she had no more ideas on how to escape. She waited for Kadd to make the first move. All she could do was mimic and not ask any questions. At least she was with someone who knew who she was; Kalara tried to keep focused on that. Isn't this what she'd been wanting for so long?

But dying because she was a half-breed was what she wanted to avoid and Kalara feared that the longer she stayed she'd accidentally make it happen.

Kadd walked around the dais until he found his anchor and opened it for them. Kalara watched the dark red runes appear and then they stepped onto them. Their lightning balls sped along to the next anchor. Kadd wasted no time in taking them through all the anchors until at last they stopped.

It was still dark and dawn was hours away. The moonlight on the countryside told Kalara they were in a grassland with only a few sparse trees. The horizon looked like table top mesas and there were lights from a few small towns. But for the most part they were in the middle of nowhere.

Kadd walked over to a gap in the rocky ground where he stopped and turned to Kalara, smiling. "You did it! He's finally gone." then he caught her off guard with a hug. Kalara didn't know what to think so she hugged him back, hoping she was doing what her old self would have done.

"I know we gotta get Tamtoc but I just had to pause for a moment now that we're alone. So Ravanan accepted it without argument?"

Kalara wondered what was going on. She kept hugging him while thinking of an answer. "Well what could he say?"

"I know.... right?" Kadd commented. He released her and took in the full sight of her. "I'm glad he took it well. He had to admit it was practically over anyway."

Kalara's skin was blushing from his stare.

"That robe is nearly in chaos. You do look incredible though. Are you trying to enchant me with it? Because it's working – not that you need any help." He winked and wrapped his arms around her waist.

By now she had a pretty good idea what her old self would be doing at the moment and struggled to quickly decide if she should do the same.

She smiled and followed her gut.

In between fervent kisses he got the words out "You're OK with doing this here?"

"What do you have in mind? She asked.

Kadd moved down, kissing her neck. "Its fine with me but I thought you may want our first time to be somewhere special or at least go to the overlook at Palmeiras." he nodded towards the mesas.

That jolted Kalara. How could they have a son together if this was their 'first time'?

He noticed her pause and she answered quickly to cover it up "I do! I do. Let's wait."

"Wait?!?" Kadd asked incredulously. "For what? We've waited 200 years. I say we go inside and tell Tamtoc to go say his good-byes while we give my old lair a going-away party." Then he led Kalara into the gap in the rock and down to the edge of a beautiful clear pool.

After a quick anchor the two Acamas were standing in the lair where Tamtoc had been sleeping and was now gone to settle his affairs. The rock was still warm.

"Finally." Kadd remarked then kissed her all the way to the furs in the wardrobe chamber. There was no stopping it now. Not that she wanted to, it wasn't difficult to love a body like his.

He held her at arms-length and twirled her around, studying her body, "I'm thwarted!" he exclaimed, "I see no way to get that metal cage off of you. You are going to make me work for this aren't you?"

Kalara smiled devilishly "It doesn't have a clasp." then she dismissed Heed.

The way he looked at her told a lot. It was far from his first time but it was a first to be with her and he was relishing every second of it. His kisses warmed her skin and made the little hairs rise up for more. She tasted his lips again and held onto his strong arms, she was no longer acting, wanting to reflect back to him how great he made her feel. Yet it all seemed bland when compared to the driving rhythm of his resonance as it joined with hers. There was nothing like it and Kalara was instantly hooked. More powerful than just auras, more than the Acama hum, it was all made stronger with the fuel of desire. It beckoned them to do more, calling them to dance harder and longer, demanding their sweat. Their energies combined. She had no idea it could be this good.

Neither did Kadd. Sure he had been with Morada, and their Acama hums had joined but it was nothing like this. The contact of his hands on her bare ankles, her feet, her thighs, anywhere he grabbed her was simply amazing. He couldn't kiss Kalara hard enough and pushing forcefully against her body was pure joy.

The ring of fire growing into licking flames was the most brilliant purple. The flames of passion grew higher and hotter. At their powerful zenith Kalara lost control of her hidden thoughts and Kadd saw them plainly but for a brief split second. He kept his eyes closed to ride the storm and then after his final thrust he rolled onto his back, perplexed.

They laid there in silence, both deep in their own thoughts. Kalara scooped up her emotions like they were money dropped on the ground, hoping he hadn't noticed while Kadd sorted his shock from the heady clouds of romance.

"We need to talk." Kadd finally said "But it's going to have to wait. Tamtoc will be back any time. Let's just carry on as before for now. Try to keep your head about you."

He knew. From inside her dark void Kalara chided herself for slipping up and wondered how much he heard. She rubbed her face to wake up.

As he found his robe Kadd asked "Do you at least remember Tamtoc and that he loves us as a human child does his parents?"

Kalara wanted to lie but figured it wouldn't work so she shook her head no.

Kadd hid his disappointment. "I'll explain it later but right now I don't need you acting strange around him. Can you try to act like a mom?"

"I think so." Kalara said as she draped Heed.

He noticed her wardrobe choice. "Hasn't that robe done enough already or are you wanting more?"

Kadd was so seductive it made her feel warm all over.

"Oh," Kalara brushed the dark purple fabric off. "It's my favorite. I feel good in it."

"Yes you do." Kadd came up behind her and held her close, she could feel his warm breath in her hair as he whispered "I know we'll talk later but for now know that I love you." His hands found her breasts. "You don't need to be afraid of me."

"OK, ok." she wiggled away with a grin. "How about this?" She dismissed Heed and draped a skirt and top.

They returned to the main lair to wait. After a couple of minutes Kalara asked "So can you start telling me about Tamtoc just until he gets back?"

Kadd gave her a smile "I can but tell me first, you really don't recall *any* thing about us?"

"No I don't."

"OK then," His purple eyes opened wide in disbelief. "We'll get to that later but for now I'll start with our son. You know dragons have never been attentive parents. As hatchlings our auras protect us so there is no need to get involved. Before now no dragon has ever given thought to his heritage. But Tamtoc is different. He is *so important* to us and represents 500 years of trying. You placed his egg in your lair to guard it as you do with all your Acama eggs, Morada does this too. When he hatched and you saw he was purple you summoned us immediately.

"The four of us brought him here, my old lair, and we stayed with him for weeks. We laughed and cried with him and from the start he was taught family terms for us. So he has Uncle Tristan, Aunt Morada, Sire, and Mother. You can see how this is different; a different dragon for a different age of dragons. It's new for us. We don't know the future implications of being parents to him but how bad can it be if it works so well for humans?"

"What did I do with my other hatchlings?"

"You let them fly away."

"Oh." Kalara looked down. "Well how often do we go see Tamtoc?"

"Not so often anymore. But he doesn't mind when we do."

She tried to think how to act around her son. "Do I hug him or kiss his cheek?" Kalara remembered watching Annette with Todd.

"You have before, mostly when he was younger. I'd just be calm and natural. You don't have to do anything. Do like you did with me" Kadd winced to himself, "Act the shadow and let him make the fir...." he stopped. "He's returned."

Tamtoc appeared before them. His black horns reached high from his amethyst scales to extend into the dark ceiling beyond, they were shiny with youth.

Kalara felt so small. It was something she was going to have to get used to.

"OK, I've taken care of my business here." Tamtoc looked at them both. "It's nice to see you both at the same time and without Ravanan. Does this mean what I think it does?"

"It sure does son." Kadd wrapped his arm around Kalara's waist, pulling her close.

"That is fantastic news!" Tamtoc lowered and brought his head to them.

Kadd sent a strong message right to Kalara's brain to mimic him as he rubbed Tamtoc's purple snout with his human hand.

Kalara felt the warmth of Tamtoc's scales, they were slick and hard. As they embraced her hand was brushed by Kadd's. The family hug felt a little odd and was a first for her, but at the same time there was also an enjoyable love between them.

Kadd ended their embrace as all men do, its universal. "We should head out. Are you two ready?"

And after a trap inspection they left by anchor for Viptryx.

Kadd's last anchor placed the three of them in Tristan's grand hallway, it put Black Blade's to shame. The temperature in the room was warm and it dazzled with sparkles everywhere. The walls were white mica schist adorned with columns of glossy black tourmaline. At the top of each black crystal was a golden sun. While Kalara took in the grandeur Tamtoc morphed to human and draped some comfortable sweat pants and t-shirt.

Tristan's mate, Vritra the Gold, greeted them at the entrance. "Tristan and Morada will be here tomorrow since they have to travel without anchors. I've prepared a feast for you while you wait, and you can rest here as well" she turned her golden head to Kalara. "Tristan said you've been up all night on business."

Kalara noticed that Vritra had the same two sets of feathered wings like her mate. Feathered wings were so different to look at, she tried not to stare. Vritra also had diamond studded horns and talons. Her horns were big, bigger than Tristan's were. Kalara wondered how old she was.

Vritra led them across the main chamber, it had a gentle river along one wall that had been worked into stepped waterfalls. "We are pleased that you will be staying here." she said to Tamtoc. We've located a lair Tristan thinks you'll like. It's not as close to a magma chamber as ours is but it's still good."

When they crossed the room she stopped and gestured towards the table for them to sit. "Tamtoc, I've heard you don't eat humans. Good. We don't either. We hate them, filthy things." Vritra spat the words out like poison.

The table was spread magnificently with toothfish and penguin waiting for them. There were even vegetable dishes and bread, Kalara could not believe it. The feast was fit for even the pickiest of human kings.

"Don't get used to this Tamtoc. If you're going to live here and convince these dragons you are an Acama you won't be in human form much if any. Your parents know, this is the best and cleanest fishing village in the world. Humans don't belong up here and you'll do your own fishing."

Vritra gave a final look at the feast. "That about does it. I'm going for a swim and leave you alone."

Kalara heard the golden dragoness mumbling to herself as she left "Disgusting human form! I don't know why every dragon down there likes doing it so much."

Kadd took the opportunity at dinner to prepare Tamtoc for the rite. The love he had for his son shown in his purple eyes.

"We've told you the rite will be painful, but it won't kill you – and you'll have all four of us here to keep that from happening." Kadd said.

Tamtoc nodded.

Kadd went on "I want to also make sure you understand exactly what we are doing."

"OK...." Tamtoc said with apprehension.

"We will be re-creating the impact inside your heart for the rite. That meteorite nearly ended all life but it also brought magic to us. You know this. Even before you hatched we knew this day would come. The four of us did this same rite to become stronger, able to carry out our duty to all dragonkind. By doing this you will be able to cross the door into the Acama lair, you will give off a low resonance that only we feel and look for. You will add to our power, five is better than four in a fight, and your individual magic will increase. You can live your life as you please but know that you will be forever bound to uphold Dragon Law."

"Sire, Uncle Tristan says we only share information on research to keep humans from discovering us. We're not the police."

"I know what he says. And he has a point. But we're not just a telephone either. He sits up here, well-hidden from humans, thinking that every dragon will hide like he does, but that is not so. He'll find out soon enough when he comes to Nikhadelos."

After dinner Kadd left the table where they were sitting and dismissed his robe. Kalara watched the man she'd made fire with release his human form. His hair flew up into horns and his wings spread out. Kadd roared freely just because he could. "It's been a while." he chuckled.

He lowered his head to look at Tamtoc with true tenderness in his eyes. "Son, learn all you can up here. I know you're going to be fine. You've got to know that I tried to get you more time but Uncle Tristan wants to start training you now. And really, you're doing this now because of me. The work I'm doing in Nikhadelos has grown and I need help, but I didn't want to take you there yet, I wanted him to come. I need his age and knowledge. Your Uncle Tristan is a fighter, an old salt from a harsh land. He is not limited by his 4,000 years, instead his age gives him power."

Kadd flicked his tail. "Well, I'm sure you'll get an ear-full from him about our differing ideas of the role of Acama so I'm not going to squander this short visit on it."

"It's OK Sire, I've been around the globe a couple of times starting my treasure. I've spent time with humans, watching them. I've got a pretty good idea what our job is."

"I know you do." Kadd arched his back to work out a kink. "Remember that week we spent at that conference?"

They both burst out laughing, Kadd's deep draconic voice resonated louder than Tamtoc's human laugh but their sincerity was the same. Tamtoc smiled at Kalara. "Did Sire tell you about that?"

"I don't think he has." Kalara acted the part and winked at Kadd. "Do I need to know what you two did?"

"Probably not." Kadd interjected and then asked Tamtoc "This is your first time to Viptryx right?"

"Yes. It's nice."

"Wait till you go diving through the waves. There is nothing like it."

Tamtoc excused himself from the table. "If you don't mind I'm going to go check that out."

"Have fun." Kadd said, "And get familiar with the lair and area because trust me, after the rite you won't feel like it.

"Hey, one more thing." Kadd said.

Tamtoc paused.

"You'll have to be in your base form for the rite. The human body is too frail for it."

Tamtoc nodded and left.

Kadd looked down at his new mate. "How are you holding up?" He asked.

Kalara shrugged "I'd really like to go to sleep now."

"Why don't you release your form and rest with me?"

"How about I curl up next to you instead?"

"What? Why?" Kadd asked.

"It's just.... look, can't I just rest right now?"

"Sure." Kadd scooped her up and placed her in the warm curl of his neck. "And don't worry, I'll shield your thoughts for you from the others so you can truly rest – wouldn't want any more thoughts escaping."

Kalara woke up the next morning feeling a lot better. Tamtoc had released his human form to sleep. After he and Vritra awakened they left the lair to go fishing. Kadd also stirred awake in time to see them off.

"Looks like it's just you and me." Kadd said after they left.

Kalara stretched, then tamed her hair and straightened her clothes. She didn't want to sleep like that again. "Uh-huh" she mumbled. All Kalara could think about was the mistake of leaving her mummies and going down that hole. Her poor mummies were still there, hiding at the top. She hoped she could find the place again. All she had to do was hang on a bit longer and she would be free again.

"So when do you think they'll get here?" Kalara asked.

"It'll be tonight probably. They have to work with the airports' schedule you know."

Kalara walked over to the table and sat down. She just wanted this whole Acama business to be over with. Knowing she was going to have to wait all day depressed her. 'Why must they take an airplane?' she wondered but didn't want to ask. Of course her former self would know why. She also still wondered exactly how much Kadd had got from her thoughts. What all did he know? It couldn't be too much or else he would have killed her already.

"Let's go fishing." Kadd said as he flexed his wings.

"No, this is fine for me." she replied and grabbed a piece of fruit.

"Are you sure?" Kadd curled his purple-scaled mouth into a smile. "We could fly, entwine in the air like you always wanted.... then eat."

She shook her head "No, really. I'm good."

"Kalara, it is so rare to be here in Viptryx. We should get out and enjoy it. The waves, the penguins..."

"You go, really. I'll be here."

"Alright then, will you be OK?"

"Yes. I'm not sick or anything."

After Kadd left Kalara went over to the water way and found a good place to sit. Now that she was alone she was thinking of leaving. There was no wisdom in leaving though because surely they'd find her flying away and she'd have to explain herself.

So she made herself comfortable instead, her mind went to Kadd and how quickly she got to know him. He had asked her to release her human form – if only she could! But that meant he hadn't found out everything and apparently the part he did know didn't warrant killing her.

Kalara wondered if Ravanan lied about the Acamas killing her because he knew that Kadd loved her. She smiled. Kadd was in love with her – even knowing she had forgotten him totally. It sure didn't seem like Kadd could kill her, ever. Fear still remained in her heart though. What if Kadd did find out? What would he do? And did Ravanan know how Kadd felt? Once again she had too many questions rolling around in her head. Ravanan said he was her mate and it was him who searched for her. But she couldn't trust Ravanan, the way he had treated her, doubted her, and his brutal interrogation that had nearly squeezed the life from her. He'd been so cold with her, it was confusing.

But Kadd.... she decided not to ask the questions that came to her and keep her secrets to herself. Was she mated to him now? Did yesterday nullify all 2,000 years of her and Ravanan? Perhaps mostly on her mind was what would Kadd do when he learned she couldn't release her human form? She feared it would be today, the day of Tamtoc's rite. The wizard Kadd was nice on the eyes though, she hadn't minded yesterday, in fact it was fun. And she got the feeling from Kadd's aura that she could trust him. It was only her fear holding her back. After all, didn't she at one point feel like she could trust Ravanan? And what did that trust get her?

She ran her hand along the rock; knowing she could trust it and it wasn't confusing or malicious, it was just there, helping her. In her heart she planned to somehow get Kadd to take her back to the Acama Lair after the rite, it was the last place she'd been before traveling by all the anchors to where she was now. From there she'd part ways, collect her mummies, and use them to find her way back to Black Blade. She really needed to work on trusting herself to make (and use) anchors – not using them was becoming a detriment.

Kalara hoped Kadd wouldn't notice her mummies when they returned. She did tell them to hide and they were good at it. What would Kadd think of her mummies? That worried her. Of course they looked repulsive and very dead, but you had to look beyond that. There was no decay or rot in them and they had become her best companions. She trusted them, more than that she held their very existence with her will, it was complete obedience like a well-trained dog. But he may not understand all that.

Kadd returned before Tamtoc and Vritra. "Those waves are fun" he said as he came to lay near Kalara. "Before you leave you've got to go for a swim."

"Maybe I will."

Kadd looked over at the feasting table, now it had fruit and refreshing drinks laid out. "That was quite the dinner Vritra prepared for us last night."

"It was." Kalara agreed. "I hadn't eaten like that in a while."

"Well, you know she never has to cook here. She did that for Tamtoc and me."

"Oh?"

"Yeah, I eat what humans eat, like most of us do."

"But Ravanan...."

"I know. Ravanan likes to keep with tradition." Kadd interrupted. Then he nuzzled her. "But we're done with him finally, right?"

"Right." She leaned into Kadd's cheek.

"I don't want this day to end." Kadd said as they watched the little waterfalls.

"Yeah, I guess we're all pretty busy."

"So where have you been staying since you left Ravanan? At the Acama Lair?"

"Yeah, there and amongst the humans."

"And now? We need to set up a portal from my home in Nikhadelos to yours. I don't want to be away from you, not every night."

They were interrupted when Tamtoc returned. Vritra passed through too. She was clearly giving them space and spent the greatest part of the day calling on other dragonesses and polishing the diamonds in her horns. There was a whole society in Viptryx, it was a foreign world with different social protocols and graces. Kalara got the feeling that formality and etiquette meant everything here.

Kadd and Tamtoc talked a lot and left again for more wave diving. Kadd invited her again with no success. It seemed to her that he was purposely keeping Tamtoc busy to give her space. He was protecting her and she was thankful. The day passed slowly. Kalara was tempted to go outside but didn't want to make any mistakes, it wasn't worth it and besides she understood the outside to be quite cold. She might have attempted it had she been alone and could practice with mistakes but she wasn't alone and was so very far from all she knew.

The three of them were in the hot chamber when Tristan and Morada arrived late that night. They were in human form, Tristan carried a travel bag and Morada held a velvet-covered box.

"Tamtoc, come close." She said. "I've brought you something, I call it The Fifth. I even put one of your baby scales that I saved in it."

Tamtoc brought his head low to his Aunt Morada.

Morada unveiled her gift. It was a meticulously crafted scene set on a large piece of azurite and bound in platinum. The blue mineral represented the Southern Ocean, on one side was a pure white crystal of satin spar for an ice cap and on top of that was an amethyst carved into a statue of Tamtoc. "It's to commemorate this day when you become an Acama."

"Wow! Thank you Aunt Morada. It's a fine piece, perfect for my new home here on top of the world."

"You're quite welcome Tamtoc. I love you. You're going to have so much fun here, I know it. Do you see your baby scale there?" she pointed to the little dragon.

"I do!" Tamtoc could see it there inside the amethyst statue. "Is this what took you so long to get here?"

She laughed, "No. I made that statue years ago, knowing this day would come, I grew the amethyst around it to protect it and then carved it. Tristan helped me with the rest while we waited for the plane to depart."

"So you traveled by plane?"

"We had to" Tristan said. "For this." He pulled a tissue-wrapped pebble from his pocket with extreme care. "It's part of the comet – way too precious to travel by anchors with it. It must be scattered inside your heart so that 100% of its magic goes to you when released."

Tamtoc was surprised "Is the magic still in there?"

"Yes it is." Tristan said. He held it up, looking at it. "This is only a small piece of the comet that Acama himself found, and the fragment he found wasn't much bigger," he gestured the size of a small melon. "We keep it safe deep inside the lair."

The four Acamas and Tamtoc went back to the main chamber. Vritra was nowhere around. Morada let her human form go and found a good place to make herself comfortable.

"I assume Kadd and Kalara told you what to expect?" Tristan asked.

"They did." Tamtoc said as he laid down beside his Aunt Morada who cuddled him with love.

Kadd suggested that Tamtoc evoke his healing aloe. Tamtoc's version was cuffs.

"Are you ready?" Kadd asked.

"I am."

Kalara ended up standing near Tristan, feeling out of place she sought to be near anything remotely similar to herself.

Morada rubbed Tamtoc's chest while casting *"NUMB"*.

Kadd evoked a saber and sliced him open between his scales while Tristan dipped the pebble first in salt water then in powdered gypsum. Then Tristan cast *"AIR SEAL"* on the coated pebble so that it appeared to be floating off his hand.

Tristan held it out to Kalara. "Here you go, be careful."

Kalara was surprised. She hesitated to take it.

Kadd was instantly sending her a telepathic thought to take the coated pebble as he was holding Tamtoc's flesh open with his talons.

Their eyes met. Kalara caved and took the precious rock with a fake smile.

Inside her head Kadd told her "Walk over and shove it in Tamtoc's heart. You can't miss it, it's the big red thing I just cut a slit in. Don't slip on his blood."

Kalara had never walked so carefully before that moment. All eyes were on her. Tamtoc's dark red blood was pooled under him. At times she had been close to Ravanan and Kadd in their base form but this was different. She was now standing in Tamtoc's most vulnerable spot. There was so much trust in the chamber. The moment wasn't about her.

She walked under Kadd's arm and around Tamtoc's. She was there now, with her other hand she reached out for a stable hand hold on her son's massive purple scaled body. It was incredible. She could feel his body heat seeping from the incision.

"Anytime Kalara." Kadd said. Morada snickered.

Kalara made sure her feet were set firmly then thrust her hand into the cut and onward deep inside the heart to place the pebble. Blood was everywhere – not just on her arm but her armpit, face, and side too. Blood was even in her hair.

Kalara started to back off when Kadd said. "OK, ready? Do you want to breathe fire or pulverize it?"

Kalara answered "I think Tristan ought to get to do something, or Morada?"

Tristan came up "I've got the fire."

Kadd nodded "I'm ready."

Tristan breathed a narrow flame that only hit the edge of the heart but most went in as he targeted the pebble. "OK, close him up Kalara."

Kalara wanted to say 'ugh, not again' but thought wiser of it. She reached in and did her best to hold the heart together.

Morada cast *"BIND"* on the cut heart and it latched itself back together.

Tristan and Kalara backed away out of the blood puddle.

Then Kadd cast *"PULVERIZE"* on the coated rock, releasing the extraterrestrial amino acids that were some of the oldest in the universe. Kalara felt Tamtoc's new resonance in her head.

Tamtoc roared in agony, Morada and Kadd held him down. The cavern walls shook. Instinctively Kalara grabbed Tristan's hand. She thought she felt a trickle of hot blood escape her ears. She stole a glance at Tristan's ear, it was bleeding.

Tamtoc roared again, violently.

"CALM!" Kadd cast at his son. So had Tristan and Morada. Kalara looked to each one of them. They all had blood escaping from their eyes, nostrils, and ears. She reached up to wipe her nose and found her face was bloody too.

Tamtoc was quiet then. His Aunt Morada cast *"SLEEP"* on him.

"What a bloody mess!" Tristan exclaimed as he wiped his nose and neck. He shook his head. "It wasn't that bloody last time was it?"

"No." Answered Morada gravely. She stood up and walked off.

"BIND", Kadd cast on Tamtoc's scaly skin, it was an afterthought. "No, it wasn't. I remember there being a little pain and maybe a few drops but this was much worse." He said to the group. "Let's go wash off. Come on."

Tristan looked at his bloodied floor with a soured face. He released his clothes and walked off to let the human form go. Kalara noticed his older body, it didn't look so bad. She wondered if dragons could choose the apparent age of their human form. Maybe she should work with that as a way to change form.

Soon Kalara was alone with her sleeping son. She didn't know how long she had before everyone showed up so she made a beeline for the little river and washed off. By the time they got back she was seated at the dinner table having a snack.

"Is he doing OK?" Kadd asked.

"I think so, he's still asleep." She answered. She couldn't help but feel different, being the only Acama there in human form.

"Well what is everyone's thoughts on this?" Tristan asked.

Kadd spoke first, like his troubled words were glad to be spoken. "I think Tamtoc already had the extra magic in him and that it passed from us to him."

"I do too." Tristan answered.

Kalara gave an agreeing nod.

"But we've never felt the resonance from him." Morada countered. How were we supposed to know he had it already?"

"Do you feel it now? I do." Kadd asked. The others nodded. "How come we never tried to have him enter the lair?"

Morada rolled her eyes, frustrated with herself. "I don't know. We assumed he couldn't. Here again, he didn't have a resonance so why would he be able to? Maybe he couldn't have entered, we won't know until our next hatchling."

"We should have tried it." Kadd fired back. "That would have been a simple test. And I think you're right, we'll do it on the next amethyst hatchling."

Everyone agreed.

Tristan played with his feathered whiskers in thought. "Do all of our hatchlings have the explosive power? Not counting Tamtoc how many others have we made in the past 500 years?"

"14 for me. Kalara?"

Kalara was at a loss. Again Kadd was right there to help. In her head she heard 6. "6"

"Tristan, no," Kadd implored. "We can't worry with them. They are out there but we're not going to hunt down our hatchlings."

Morada chimed in too "If they have extra magic good for them. They are alive out there and using it, not harming anybody. Chances are they don't know they're different."

"I think it's a mistake to let them live. Any more we make, we should immediately kill if they're not amethyst."

"Tristan, I'm not hunting them down. None of us are. That would raise questions that we don't want to answer." Kadd was solid on it.

"Fine. I won't actively go after them but might find a new hobby when I'm not busy. Don't you all see why we can't allow our non-amethyst hatchlings to live?"

"It's hard to admit." Morada began, "and I want to think more on it – but not now. Back to Tamtoc.... I've heard him roar before and it didn't hurt. Does it hurt you all when I roar?"

"No, but I've never been inside your aura when you roared. We were right there." Kadd said.

Morada looked around at the Acamas "Definitely the aura makes a difference. But is this something he could do at range too?"

"I don't know. I wouldn't think so." Kadd responded.

Morada shot back "Have any of you gone head to head against him in magic? I haven't."

Tristan and Kadd said no. Kalara went along with them and shook her head no.

"What's your thoughts on this Kalara?" Morada asked.

"Well clearly," Kalara started "he's got a powerful roar." She said lightly and looked around to see if that was good enough. They were all still listening. "I wonder if he'll be OK." she added.

"He did lose a lot of blood which was odd." Tristan answered. "But his magic ought to preserve him. He isn't going to die under my care."

"He'd better not. I know you'll keep us updated." Kadd said.

"Maybe we should stick around for a few days." Morada offered.

"You can if you want but I can handle him. It's not like he is dangerous. We didn't change his personality."

"Well there is that at least. We raised him to be good. But with that kind of power...." Kadd's voice trailed off, unwilling to say such a thing.

"What have we done?" Morada asked.

"Well we can't undo it now." Tristan said. "I don't think we should tell him."

Everyone agreed. Already each of them was envious but scared.

Morada looked at Kadd "You've spent the most time with him, has he ever said anything Naga-like?"

"Not to my knowledge."

She went on, her purple eyes opened wide "It would be a bad thing."

"Well that won't happen. He knows the Naga are wrong. He won't lord over the herd." Kadd turned to Tristan. "Are you going to test him or not? How powerful is he?"

"I see no reason for that. We know what just happened. No need for senseless demonstrations. That would only shine a spotlight on his power."

"Agreed." Kadd said.

Again Morada looked at Kalara "Why aren't you saying more?" she asked suspiciously.

Kalara leaned forward "I agree with everything that has been said, except for killing hatchlings. And I don't think we should test Tamtoc. We don't need a roaring contest or one of magic." she paused to glance at her son "we don't need to wake him up right now either."

"Kalara, did you know his blood already carried the explosion?" Morada asked.

"No. Of course not. As you said, I felt no hum from Tamtoc."

Kadd intervened, "None of us did. This is all our fault."

"We couldn't have known." Tristan said quietly. "If nothing else let's be glad he is one of us. I think Kalara's right though, we should let him rest in quiet."

Kadd stood up "We should. And I should be off anyway. There is another deep sea launch next week, I need to make sure my dragons have their preparations made." He looked at Kalara. "Oh! One more thing guys. Kalara and I are mated now. Finally."

"It's about time. Good for you." Morada commented and Tristan agreed.

"We'll be in touch. Give Tamtoc our love. *ANCHOR*" Kadd cast. "Come on Kalara, let's go make another one!"

Chapter 26

All that night Ravanan dreamed of purple fire; it was more vibrant than the indigo ring of fire he was familiar with, and so beautiful just like Kalara's glistening scales. The fire haunted him. First he would see Kalara's amethyst eyes boring into his, loving him. Then he would feel the chill of her icy touch on him. He loved it when she used her aura like that, it was always the perfect bite of cold. And then she'd warm him up with that purple fire of hers, she only ever used it on him. It was such a cool heat.

He woke in the night thinking to keep his new young mate and use her, in a bizarre way it would be a memorial to Kalara, a chance to get to see her purple fire and scales in the flames every time he made fire with the red Ishida. He ran his hands through his hair. What was wrong with him? He wasn't crazy and shouldn't think like that. If he wanted Kalara bad enough to imagine her while bedding another then he should just go and get her.

By morning he had made his decision. He watched Ishida as she slept on his gold, thinking about her choice of form to make fire. He was surprised at first, thinking she, being Naga, would prefer the ancient way, but the way she moved on him revealed why she morphed, she liked it.... a lot. The human body was built for emotion and sensation, from the supple skin to flowing, always moving hair. Then add the many hormones, large brain, and nerve endings, and the human body became an amplifier of emotion. But it was so tiny.

He knew for sure Ishida was not a true Naga. Neither was he, although he now realized there were two things he agreed with them on – dragons should rule and should stay true to their form. Yes the human form felt great but it was soft and vulnerable during a fight, it was a bad trade off in his opinion. Even now it would be so easy to raise a foot and step on her head or crunch her skull with his teeth. She would be dead instantly. Ishida was too trusting.

Though he disapproved on principle, if he was going to make fire like a human from now on it would be with Kalara, his mate. He would do that for her out of love, he would stay in the puny human form with her always, until death took them both. If the Naga ever caught Ishida in human form they'd kill her. It was better to not get any more involved with the Naga than he already had.

The red enchantress stirred awake, smiled up at his towering blue body, then returned to her base form "Shall we go hunt?"

Ravanan followed her outside.

Ishida was in a good mood, with a light happy voice she said "We should make crowns for each other – to display this moment – the first pieces of our treasure together."

He paused in the morning light. "About that.... This won't work."

"What won't work?"

"Us. We're over."

"WHAT?!?"

"Bye Ishida. Don't make me fight you. Just leave."

"But wait!" she pleaded with him but found no give in his eyes.

Ravanan was done. He sat there unmoving and not talking, guarding his lair.

Ishida at least knew the blue dragon well enough to know when to quit. She flew away without another word.

With a renewed sense of purpose Ravanan made three new traps for Ishida and her invisibility robe should she try to come back. When they were finished he left to go get Kalara. He figured it would be good to make a fresh start with his purple mate in a new lair, Black Blade belonged in the forgotten past.

Ravanan entered Black Blade Lair through the seer pool. He couldn't feel her aura and saw all the food he'd sent piled up, some of it had been drained of blood but none of it eaten. He checked the wardrobe chamber and saw that Naught was in its case. She was not home. New worry filled his mind.

Back at the seer pool he began a location spell by thinking of Kalara. Since the target of the spell was one of love he had to drop his fluid onto the still surface of the water. Then he held a perfect crystal of Iceland Spar to his eye and cast *"LOCATE KALARA"*. He saw only a glow at the top edge.

"I shouldn't have left her." He said to himself. His concern grew. That was in the direction where he'd found her before. He turned back to the main lair, stood at a certain place and cast *"ANCHOR"*. The entire cavern floor began to weep dark red ink. Everywhere small circles bled into existence, each one with a small sketch of a place in his territory, there were too many to count. The whole chamber had become a map and was pretty much accurate to the four corners of the earth. He was within two steps of the one he wanted, he had done this so many times the ceiling was just as memorable to him as the floor was.

Ravanan traveled as far as he could then looked for a suitable body of water, it had to be unmoving, peaceful, and with life in it since the heart beats of the aquatic life gave the image its animation. If he could move fast enough he could save her in time. Why was she in that direction again? His fear was that like last time a protective veil would be placed over her so that it made finding her by seer pool difficult.

He continued at breakneck speeds until at last he saw her with two others he didn't know. Ravanan landed crying, happy to know she was no longer afflicted with that curse. How had it happened though?

He watched the trio moving through the night toward Tamtoc. He rolled his eyes. "Why here? What is she up to?" he whispered to himself. He wanted to go to her but needed to learn as much as he could before acting. "Who are those two with her?"

Then he heard the voices:

"..... Don't blame me if it breaks."
"It won't. - Man! This place is awesome. I had no idea it was so old!"
"Don't you guys feel the sacredness of this place?.."

When Ravanan heard Kalara say "Jeremy, feel like hunting?" he dove in, to test her and the other two. He needed to see what he was dealing with and this was a great opportunity to do so, not to mention it would be a great dinner and old-fashioned kill, a rare opportunity. He grabbed the target she named first, his talons ran fully through the flesh as his powerful jaws tore him in half. His soft flesh was delicate and hot. A few wing-beats later his aura stopped the girl's heart then he grabbed her up as well.

Ravanan kept himself far away to patiently watch, casting spells to heighten his senses. He didn't know who Jeremy was, only that he could run very fast. He felt no auras from Kalara's two companions. They also lacked body heat, a pulse, and breathing sounds. They didn't even have a smell! In every way they matched the forest. He dared not take his eyes off the odd pair for fear of losing them to the woods.

Kalara went almost directly to the Acama lair – Ravanan couldn't believe it. He watched her disappear at the rim of her second home while the other two stayed behind.

He'd been to the Acama lair every time with her, never allowed inside but he knew these woods well while he had waited for her. 'Why would she drape Naught before entering the Acama lair? Unless, that had to be it, she was trying to find her past. But how did she know to come here since he hadn't told her about it?'

Ravanan slowly closed in on the two companions, in his human form and wearing his own version of Naught called Cover. They had a tree-like quality to them, they were so still. He listened intently as he approached.

"Do you think she'll be OK?" the one called Jeremy asked.

"Oh for crying out loud! She is fine! Our Enchantress can hold her own. I ain't worried for her and you shouldn't be either. She ought to be out any time."

"I know. I know. It's just.... I'm her provider you know. I like worrying about her."

"Well, I'm sure if she needs us she'll call."

Though it sounded strained and aged, Ravanan had heard that female voice before from Kalara's memories, it was Annette's!

His blood boiled with anger at what he was seeing. It was her! The very dragoness herself! He had to find out more. He made his way to draw closer then stopped when he saw a purple dragon appear on the rim. It was Tristan, followed by Kadd and Morada. He knew they'd come.

'Great.' he thought. 'What could he do?' He hoped against hope Kalara could fake it. He absolutely could not get in there to help and so he backed off to wait the meeting out.

Everything concerning Kalara made him feel inadequate. A tear left his eye. And now to hear this Jeremy name himself as Kalara's provider - he never should have left.

He heard Annette ask Jeremy about the other three purple dragons "Do you think we should be worried about that?"

Jeremy didn't answer.

"Alright." She said. "We continue to hide."

While Ravanan waited for the Acama meeting to end his mind was anxious with worry for his mate and why Annette was with her. What was going on down there? Had Kalara got her memories back? The thought took over him. A worry that Kalara had regained her past and no longer wanted him. Why else would she have gone to the Acamas instead of summoning him back to her? Ravanan couldn't stop his mind from going there.

He knew things were delicate between them before Kalara was taken by Annette. That whole blasted nation in Anarchelos was a real source of headache for Kalara and him. They couldn't agree on anything up there. Once again he rehashed their worst contention, he simply had a different opinion on how to handle the Lincoln matter than she did; killing him wasn't the big deal Kalara made it out to be. But he really thought they were working it out. The tension between them didn't seem to be that serious as of late. But maybe he was wrong and he knew for sure it had been wrong to make fire with her when she couldn't even remember him. With her memories back now she'd know he had taken advantage of her state of mind.

It wasn't long until Ravanan saw two lightning balls in little clouds shoot out of the cave, but which two was it?

Time answered him when Ravanan saw Tristan and Morada rise out of their lair in their human forms, notably flying rather than traveling by anchor. Now his mind toyed with him. So it had been Kadd and Kalara.... where did they go together? Did Kadd know about Kalara? He couldn't know or else she'd be dead. Ravanan considered intercepting the Acamas to ask about Kalara but that would mean leaving Annette to her own business and he couldn't allow that to happen.

Where was Kadd taking her? What were they doing? KADD! Ravanan hated that dragon. He was always taking her side about Anarchelos. What did he know of it? He was working with much older nations and people. Half of everything he said only made sense when taking into account he wanted Kalara. If any dragon was taking advantage of Kalara it was Kadd.

Where did they go together? With all three Acamas together there was no way Kalara could have fooled them and they'd have killed her right then and there. No, she had to have got Annette to put her memories back and then went off to tell the Acamas. Now her and Kadd were alone. He probably jumped at the chance to make fire with Kalara. She had to have went with him for a reason.

Well he was going to find out - about the whole mess, and the one who could help him was sitting just over there. Annette of Anarchelos Vya!

Like a cat he moved silently into a good position to see them.

They didn't look right, sitting there. What was wrong with them? He moved closer and it was like their lines became more subtle. Ravanan squinted his eyes, somehow they got harder to see amidst the trees.

Now just steps away and still invisible he could see them clearly. They were looking straight at him! There was no way they could see him. But he froze in his tracks and just looked. What he saw disgusted him.

He studied their black eyes, there was no life in them and the windows were clouded over with milky void. All the signs – or lack thereof – pointed to dead bodies. But he had seen them move. The guy could run extremely fast and was strong enough to twist heads off.

And Annette the powerful enchantress....well, she was sitting before him when she should be at the bottom of the ocean waiting to be crushed.

They were dead. More than dead, they looked dried out. It was hard to gaze upon them without retching. Whatever fate had befallen them was nothing to be wished for. And in all his long years upon the Earth, some two thousand years, Ravanan had never seen this before.

As he stood there watching them they kept looking his way while eating choice handfuls of forest floor dirt. They looked like they were watching a movie and eating popcorn. They were unblinking and he was blinking as little as possible because every time he did he had to find them again.

Ravanan tried to control Annette but couldn't. He couldn't control Jeremy either. It was like their minds were not attached to their brains anymore. Somehow their spirits were controlling their bodies without needing the brains that were now so dead and dried that he couldn't get inside them. Mind control was one of his specialties and it unnerved him that it wasn't in his arsenal with these guys.

He was certain that he was looking at mummies and was in utter shock over it. In Kalara's memories Annette was alive. And now, months later, she was dead. Did Kalara do this or did Annette? If it was Kalara, how was she so powerful in such a short time? He had to talk to her, help her. How could she have done such a gruesome act?

But what troubled him more was that Annette wasn't a dragoness in human form; if she was then there wouldn't have been a body left to mummify. Annette was human.

And there was no way she could have captured and taken Kalara's memories unless she had magic. Annette had to have gotten magic from some dragon. Who then? And whoever it was was sure to have his treasure.

He so desperately wanted to kill Annette. But he had to be careful, Annette was dangerous – a human with magic. He hadn't seen a spellsword in many years, long before the Age of Acama. It was a special thing for a dragon to share its magical blood with a human; he had only done it twice, both times were in his youth. But now under Dragon Law to give a human magic was completely forbidden. How many other spellswords had been made besides Annette?

Spellswords were extremely volatile and crazy with power. He remembered both of his fondly and the pact he had made with them. One of them, the first one, Arekuna, he had actually brought to Black Blade Lair for a time of training. They became friends against Kalara's wishes. But his experiments quickly got out of hand and he had to kill them to clean up his mess. Not only kill them but also kill their apprentices, which took him over 40 years to do. A total of nine spellswords had to be erased.

Annette was not only a spellsword she was a living dead as well. It was more than wrong! Of course the humans have conjured up all kinds of stories through the centuries but no one ever actually achieved reanimating the dead. Every dragon knows you just simply don't take a dead piece of flesh and tell it to live, it goes against nature and life and wasn't supposed to be possible. Even the Chinese spellswords couldn't bring life to the dead.

These two were an abomination and had to be destroyed. He thought about all the humans' books and movies about the subject of ending a living dead – he had serious doubts that bullets, wood stakes, beheading, or silver would actually do any harm to them......

"Enough! You no-good *dragon*." Annette sneered at Ravanan.

Ravanan was jostled from his thoughts. Did she just speak to him? And she knew he was a dragon – how could she know that? How could she see him? She couldn't. No way. He retreated in his footpath to watch from further away.

"Yep, keep going. Don't stop." She urged him.

Ravanan stopped – yes, she was talking to him and he refused to obey a damn spellsword. His eyes darted from mummy to mummy. They were still sitting but that didn't detract from their ability to battle.

Jeremy remained silent, watching and deferring to his medicine woman. Although he did sneak a peek upward past Ravanan, in awe of Ravanan's glowing dragon spirit.

Ravanan glanced up to see what the mummy was looking at, he saw nothing.

"LEAVE." Annette commanded.

'Like hell I will!' Ravanan thought. He dismissed his clothes and morph and revealed himself. Towering over the two mummies he lowered his head to meet them. "I don't believe I will Annette."

Unimpressed and seeing that he wasn't so easily scared off, she replied "And you are Ravanan I presume?" She rolled her eyes, "I might have guessed. So you can see us....." her voice trailed off like she was making a note to work harder on hiding next time.

"You weren't hard to find."

"Well, fine. And I suppose you're looking for Kalara." She didn't wait for Ravanan's acknowledgment. "Know this. Kalara does not want you."

Ravanan didn't flinch. "She is not a topic I'll discuss with you." He reared back and let his wings snap wide before folding them back down. "I intend to kill the dragon that made you. Tell me where he is".

The mummies shared a glance as Jeremy updated Annette on Ravanan's latest thoughts, neither of them wore a smile.

"Don't lie to me. You intend to kill us!" Annette barked at the giant blue head.

The mummies felt the jungle air rush around their backs as Ravanan drew his breath. That was their only warning before the great blue dragon shot flames upon them both.

Jeremy fled fast away into the trees, his clothes were now part of his leathery skin.

Annette fell back from the blast but was able to deaden her flames into smoke. She was prone on the ground as Ravanan watched her agonize with blackened skin. She began to chuckle.

Ravanan's eyes narrowed. "Don't make this any harder Annette."

She didn't even try to get up but laid there sprawled out and laughing.

"Tell me where the dragon is."

Annette's laughter continued to fill his ears. If Ravanan could have seen her underside he would have seen her leathery skin healing from the moist soil. But he didn't.

Ravanan wanted his answer, not her crazy slow laugh. The air stilled and stiffened. Annette's smoldering hair started to separate and lift. Then his lightning jolt came up from the ground and sizzled all of her that was in contact with the Earth.

That pissed her off. The mummy sprang up in torture. It was the most feeling Annette had had since she'd died. Her laughter was gone and in its place was the dead of her eyes as she looked at her foe.

Again and with more force Ravanan shocked her feet and said "Tell me where the dragon is."

Annette danced in agony but then started chanting in beat with her step, calming herself, healing her leathery skin.

"TELL ME!" He roared at her.

"NEVER!"

Ravanan lost all his restraint. An unleashed bolt of lightning fed from him to Annette's chest, finding what little sap she had. All of his might fed into the bolt's power. The bolt shattered Annette just like a tree trunk, splitting her open. Pieces of her flew into the air as the lightning raced through her body just like a river of light. The bolt of lightning continued, feeding off Ravanan's aura. Annette's body couldn't contain the power as it was connecting Ravanan to the ground that was under her feet. The undead medicine woman looked like she was skewered on a glowing white bolt.

Finally Ravanan was empty of his rage. Finally Annette had stopped laughing.

She laid there unmoving in two large pieces. 'Was she dead?' he thought to himself. The other spellsword had ran off, he'd deal with him another time. But Annette? He had to be sure. Ravanan lit her body up with fire.

He watched the flames engulf her and added more as needed. If there was a hint of regret for killing Annette before finding the dragon that made her he didn't show it. The fire lit up the deep night. His breathing calmed. He thought once more of his beloved Kalara and making fire with her, he wished he knew where she was. The roar of the flame slowly quieted to a crackling heap. With watching Annette burn up and having no distractions he suddenly winced in pain. He looked down at his scales and saw them, several shards of Annette had splintered and shot into his skin, all over his chest and arms. He hadn't felt the spray during the explosion.

Ravanan began to pluck the splinters out and toss them into the fire. He also looked around for chunks of her that had flown into the trees and added them to her burning corpse.

After the flames consumed all the carbon Ravanan sifted through the hot ash with his long black talons. By dawn Annette was no more.

He needed rest. Yet Ravanan didn't want to leave the Acama lair entrance until Kalara returned. Surely she would come back, she'd left her mummies here. But by that nightfall Ravanan felt very tired from waiting around all day and the lure of his lair caused him to fly off. He returned to Black Blade Lair, thinking to maybe find her there.

The lair empty. Deflated, he went straight to sleep. The following morning he felt ill enough to just stay asleep. The day was filled with restless sleep. He couldn't get comfortable and when he did slumber odd black dreams filled his head. Just blackness, emptiness, it was black like Annette's stare. He was dreaming of that spellsword's stare! Finally he rose up and flew outside to watch the sunset.

The sun turned the sky red. The volatile colors deepened, and so did Ravanan's mood. What was wrong with him? Nothing had happened in that fight. Annette had done nothing to him. He re-played the encounter in his head. She didn't fight back. All she did was laugh, that laugh was maddening, still he could hear it in his ears – it was enough to make his skin crawl. Itching, tickling, teasing, reddening.... that was it, the memory of Annette was bothering him.

No wait, it was more than that. Could he really hear her laughing? Surely not. And his skin, was it itching? It was. Ravanan shook his head as if a fly was buzzing about. Then he carried the shake throughout his whole body, he would shake this off. He was fine. He was tired but he was fine, nothing another night's rest couldn't fix. He knew that now he was simply exhausted from the poor rest he'd been getting.

The following morning the great blue dragon woke to dawn light beaming into Black Blade, so soft and warming, he knew something was seriously wrong. He was weak and the dreams were much worse. Ravanan went to his wizard's alcove and cast Reveal on himself. Horror washed over him, he dropped his tools to the ground and stumbled backward in shock. He'd missed some shards of Annette and now, *somehow*, she was inside his blood, festering in there, inside him. She was alive! And she had one agenda, to kill him. He was dirty with her! Feeling grossed out he rushed to the seer pool to bathe. Deep down he knew no amount of bathing would clean him but going through the motions at least felt right. She was all through him. Ravanan couldn't sit still, moving constantly, imagining her wiggling inside of him, wishing he could get away but there was nowhere to run.

Ravanan walked all over the lair, trying to not think about it.

He wasn't giving up. And yet he stopped pacing at the middle of the lair and laid there panting, taking a rest. He felt so filthy, contaminated. He could taste her! She was growing stronger, he *knew* it. He had to fight her off. How had she fooled him and his aura? How could she be alive and growing like a weed inside him? She was thickening his blood, clotting it. Ravanan made himself think hard; concentrating his aura to fight her off. There couldn't have been more than five or ten pieces of her that got in, shards so small that they crawled into his veins. But how? His aura would have caused his magical blood to destroy all her copies. But then those pieces would have lived and grown to crawl further towards his heart and brain. Then once again his aura would destroy them, only to have twice as many or more come back to life! He was so worn out. Every time he killed Annette she just came back in smaller pieces but greater numbers. Why wouldn't she just die already?!?!?! He breathed out a loud mournful sigh. His shoulders quivered in a silent cry. How could this have happened? He banged his horns against the floor to clear his head.

The sound his horns made against the rock was a dead sound. All he could do now was think and let his blood fight. A glimmer of hope surfaced as his horns hit the rock surface again – what if he could read Annette's thoughts now that she was inside of him? There were so many copies of her now, what if he could hear more than just her singular command of KILL KILL KILL? He had to try.

Mustering his mental strength he listened. He was very good at reading thoughts and mind control. This was just a little different since she was dead. That thought grossed him out again, dead things were moving inside him, trying to kill him, but they were dead and rotten, what kind of germs come from that? He banged his horns again 'STOP THINKING LIKE THAT!' he ordered himself. He just needed to learn how to read the thoughts of the dead. It was a slow process, listening to your blood. It gave "introspection" a whole new meaning. He had to learn Annette, feel her. Ravanan had to re-acquaint himself with his own aura to do so. For centuries his aura fought alongside him silently and now more than ever he was depending on his aura to save him.

Each time Ravanan tore the Annette shards apart the more focused her thoughts became – he learned about the kinds of mushrooms she knew about, he knew all the tribal elders' names, and so many types of trees and flowers. He wouldn't give up, he picked her thoughts up one by one, examining them. Then he found the dragon: The Great Spirit, Mother Earth.

'Really?' Ravanan thought flatly. That is it? That wasn't anything! All this time spent wondering, hoping to get to probe Annette and THAT WAS IT? No name, no color or gender?

In aggravation he listened more, looked deeper, he became even quieter, he could hear his heart struggling with heavy beats. There had to be something. The hours ticked by. He learned all Annette's prayers and chants, he learned the recipe for her healing salve. This spellsword had really learned a lot and learned even more on how to fool people.

Annette continued her infectious pursuit, her shards were smaller and becoming more singular driven in thought, making it easier for Ravanan to find her hidden thoughts. Another nugget emerged as he found her knowledge of voodoo dolls and curses, finally he knew what evil curse had ripped open Kalara's belly. And then he saw the honey locust tree where Kalara's Pelt used to be hooked on its thorns. Then there it was before him, the frightened memory of seeing Mother Earth in her true form, a silver dragoness. It was a powerful memory, Annette feeling the shock of the revelation that Mother Earth was a dragoness. The whole meaning of her human existence had changed in that moment in those woods.

Ravanan got the location of Annette's hill easily enough and afterward all that remained was to end Annette's existence totally. Ravanan rested then, letting his aura finish the job.

Chapter 27

"Where do you go every day?" Todd asked Melissa over breakfast. "And I know it's not the bar because your boss called me looking for you the other day."

"Out. Shopping..... jogging.... the gym. A girl's gotta work for her body to look this good. I didn't know you'd be so nosy." Melissa left the table.

"Baby, Honey, look, I'm just saying it'd be nice to have you around more."

"I am around. And you know I'll always come home to that fine dick of yours." She gave him a kiss before leaving to go get dressed.

Todd put his own plate in the sink and started his own day.

Bill stopped by Todd's for a visit after work. The two friends grabbed their cooler and headed to the lake with the boat. Sometimes fishing and drinking beer was all that needed doing.

Bill cast out his line and settled back. The lap of the water on the hull was the best sound. Thinking a deep thought for a bit he took in a breath and laid it out there. "Ya know, sometimes I think Jenn is cheating on me."

Todd wiped the bait slime from his hands and looked crossly over at his friend. "You're still seeing her?"

"Hell yes! And things are the best they've ever been between us. Except that she ain't with me all the time."

The medicine man rolled his eyes and then cast out his line. "And so you think she is cheating on you?"

"It's just a feeling I get. She came home the other day and I smelled some cologne on her. It was weird. Not to mention she always has somewhere to go."

"Yea, Melissa does that too. She tells me she's working out and not to worry with her."

Bill grabbed another beer "You trust her?"

"Yes."

"Yea well, I think I'm gonna follow her tomorrow, see where she goes."

Todd recalled following his sister that one night. He had no explanation for her whoring around. "Nah man, I don't think I would."

"Why?"

"She's done a one-night stand before. Maybe she still does."

"You serious? Are you fucking kidding me?!?"

"No."

"Why THE HELL didn't you tell me before now?"

"I thought you two had broken up. The last time I saw Jenn I threatened her, told her to stay away from you."

"Oh thanks man!" Bill groaned sarcastically.

"Anytime."

Bill shrugged, "I don't know, she is a really hot piece of ass – maybe I can deal with it."

"Stop already! GROSS MAN!" Todd didn't know if he wanted to vomit or hit Bill.

"Sorry! Sorry!" Bill held his hand up like he was at gunpoint.

Todd took another drink "Look, I'd forget about it. Just bite her on the ass and pray for lockjaw."

It was after sunset when the friends got back from the lake. Before bed, Todd went to cleaning his catch. Melissa helped him so he could be finished sooner and get to their bed sooner. They really didn't talk much and that was curious because from what he remembered of Melissa before, she was a talker. And this new quieter Melissa was just fine with him.

As he scaled the fish he started comparing the frequency of when they fucked to when she wasn't around. Every time he would get to feeling like it had been too long since they'd made love she would be all over him, demanding it. The timing of their sexual desire seem to really match and he liked that very much because he was always wanting it to the point of madness.

There was something else different now also, she was a licker. Her mouth was always on his body somewhere, which again he didn't mind at all. But lately he started paying attention to the hickeys she gave him, there were always some tiny scabs with them but they didn't look like teeth marks. Even just thinking about the hickey he was going to get that night made him erect. Melissa was so very sexy. And she always gave him hickeys, sometimes he thought he even heard her purring once which he knew couldn't be. He had hickeys all over him at various stages of healing, there were even a couple on his junk – he still remembered the heated passion that came with them, those ones seem to happen when it had been a while since they'd been together. But he felt fine, great even, it was just her way.

The following morning Todd was taking visitors, it was a slow day and Melissa was gone again. At lunch time a couple came by, the husband, Jerry, was not able to perform for his wife and she was mad about it. She had to tell Todd all about it, how often they used to have sex, and in what positions, it was too much information, even for the care-giver who was tending to the problem. Apparently it had been four days since he had an erection and sex with her, it had been too long. Finally the woman was quiet and looking to Todd to fix it.

"Please come with me Jerry, let me examine you while your wife stays here." Todd stood up and turned on the TV for the wife, increasing the volume for a nice sound cover.

Todd did a basic quick look, it looked fine. He backed off and sat down, not seeing the healing bite mark on the guy's inner thigh.

"Jerry, do you have anything to add to what your wife said?"

"No."

"OK. How do you feel?"

"I'm okay. I just feel bad for her. I can't give her what she wants." It was obvious in his tone that his self-esteem was a wreck.

"Did anything happen to you recently?"

The man looked out the bedroom window through the dream catcher. "No."

"Come on, let me get you something that may help." Todd got up and went to the kitchen and crafted a special tea blend from his vast herb cabinet. "Make a cup of this tea every day for a month and see how it does."

A month later there was no improvement and the wife was really distraught. Todd prayed about it knowing he would hear nothing, it was all about faith now. Finally he made up his mind and went out back to the chicken pen to collect his meanest rooster.

Chapter 28

K add and Kalara arrived in Stanley on the Falkland Islands. After convincing the Bed & Breakfast owner they had reservations and to have dinner brought up in 30 minutes they went to their room.

Kalara sat down on the couch. "Kadd, this is nice and all but I need to get back."

"I know you do. And I have to get back to Nikhadelos – which makes this place the perfect place to part." He came to sit beside her. "After we talk."

She smiled and looked out the window. 'Trapped again' she thought.

"Kalara, are you alright?"

"Sure."

"I don't believe you. Let me ask it another way – if I'm a stranger to you that you're completely scared of then why make fire with me yesterday? – why pretend with me?"

"I pretended because I was scared. Besides," she grinned "you look good."

"Only when I'm next to you!" he joked "but you're not going to evade this with me". He reached out and played with her hair. "How can I help you?"

"You can't."

"That seems to be the only thing you are sure about. I am worried about you. For over 200 years I have longed for you – I'm not about to leave you. And if Ravanan thinks he can take all your memories of me away, that is still not enough to keep us apart. I know we can get through this."

"Ravanan isn't responsible for this."

"How can you know that? You know how good he is at mind control, it wouldn't be hard to plant a thought.... and it's to be expected – wipe and replace."

"Trust me, he's not."

"I'll trust you if you trust me, I could never kill you."

They held each other's gaze for a long time.

Finally Kalara's eyes welled up with tears. She easily felt his loving aura holding her warmly, he melted the wall around her heart. "Kadd, not only do I not know you I don't remember anything before a year ago."

"What happened a year ago?" Kadd asked tenderly.

"A medicine woman named Annette took my mind and stole me away. The first thing I can remember was being lost in a jungle in Brazil in this human form. I didn't know a single thing."

Dinner came and went. By the time she told Kadd about Ravanan leaving her alone at the seer pool they were on their balcony with an empty bottle of wine.

Kadd surprised her with his attitude about her amnesia. It was nothing like what Kalara had feared, instead of killing her he was sitting near her. His warm aura comforted her, if anything his company felt like what a friendship should be.

"And you've tried to let go of your human form?" Kadd asked.

"Well," Kalara thought back – what an obvious thing to try, to let the morph go.

"I've wanted to." She was puzzled by her own recent past. "But no, now that I think about it, I haven't." The realization came as a surprise to her. "I thought I needed my memories to be able to return to my base form." She thought some more "This whole time, that's what I've thought. That's what Ravanan told me. That I needed to know my dragon qualities to change back."

Kadd smiled, watching her work through it.

"He said I needed to stay as I am so we could get the clues from my head to find Annette. He said I must be who I am right now."

"Well maybe you should try it some time. Maybe you're not trapped in human form. Just because you have no memory doesn't mean you can't change forms, it only takes magic. But in any case you shouldn't worry about the Acamas killing you. Why would we when we are desperately trying to make more Acamas?"

"I only had what Ravanan said about you and also of me – that I could get myself killed and all of dragonkind with me. I learned to trust him. And then he....." She dropped the thought.

Kadd shook his head in amazement. "I can't believe Ravanan left you there."

"It hurt. But I'm better for it. So what if he thinks I'm a half-breed? I am the only one of my kind and I am an Enchantress. I like what I am."

"No matter what Kalara, your blood is Acama blood. It always will be. You are still you, no matter what shape, with or without memories, and the Acamas are stronger with you alive."

"He told me not to do *anything* that would make you all suspicious. Why would he say that? He was my mate and had to know some things about the Acamas, surely he knew you all wouldn't kill me."

"Ravanan went to great lengths to keep us apart."

"About that, what about Tamtoc? Ravanan never mentioned him. How could we have a son without making fire?"

Kadd smiled at the idea. "We didn't make fire. Ravanan didn't want us to touch. When I hugged you yesterday that was the first time I've ever touched you."

"But then how..."

"Let me explain. You know by now we are trying to bring more amethysts into the world. Our mates are fine with the normal way but Ravanan wasn't, even though you asked him to be. So every time you tried to get an egg it became a tedious job of transference without contact. It's unnatural, its bizarre. More like how a human would manage auto-fertility. Whether it was me or Tristan getting the attempt, all three of us had to be there with you and Ravanan to watch and help. We couldn't be in anybody's lair. We all hated it."

"So where would we do this then?"

"You suggested the temples in Acama's homeland. They're convenient because they are right next to the Acama Lair, and it honored Acama himself. I guess all the times we ate with him affected us. I agreed with you and Ravanan, we should use those cities that honored mates and mating, Oxte'tun and Tamtoc among others."

"I wondered if there was a connection for his name and that place I saw." Kalara said. "I was just there at Tamtoc."

"That is where all our hard work finally paid off. The Acamas have been trying for 500 years, we amethysts are rare even amongst ourselves."

"So you knew Acama before he died? Ravanan said he did and that I did too."

"Yes I did. His elaborate games were where I first met you."

"OK. Then will you please tell me our history? Ravanan wouldn't – saying it wouldn't help."

"He's probably right that it won't. Ravanan is extremely intelligent. But I see no reason why you can't know.

"I met you and him at Acama's games and feasts. I was just a little younger than you guys. When you and he took your mating flight I was still learning about the world and my magic.

"I like to think that you and I instantly connected, being the only amethysts in our little world. But you already had a mate that you loved and he loved you. He protected you and always placed himself between us. Then when Acama died and we met Tristan and Morada our lives changed as we took the Acama vow. We weren't happy about being forced to take on the responsibility but what could we do? All the dragons left except for Ravanan, Ahmat, Morada's mate, and Vritra, Tristan's mate. There the seven of us were, on the beach with Acama's dried up carcass. We made our initial plans and I moved to Nikhadelos."

"Could you and I be from the same dragoness?"

He turned towards her. "I know you don't remember but we have discussed that very thing before. We did both hatch from Kynasteryx, but from opposite sides, you from Ravyx and me from Diamid. We've looked into it more than once as the science has grown. Morada has done much in that area, looking for ways to increase the chances of making a purple. But no, we're not related."

"I'm glad." she took his hand.

"Me too. Kalara, the only reason I volunteered to move to Nikhadelos was that I didn't have you. Just making an egg with you is not enough. I can't stop thinking of you, even when making fire with others I'm envisioning it is you I'm with. I can't get you out of my mind."

"But do you still feel that way now? I'm not the same....."

"I want to." Kadd said as he pulled her to her feet. "Will you give me a chance to find out how I feel?"

"Why not? If nothing else I appreciate the conversation."

"Let's go inside, this wind is too much."

Back on the couch Kadd asked her "So how is that you escaped from Ravanan's entrapment and ended up at the Acama lair, which is exactly the best place you could have gone to?"

"Ravanan's entrapment...." she repeated. "I guess it was kind of like that wasn't it? Odd to put it that way. But I did escape. It was extremely painful.

"I started regaining my verbal skills with simple spells, Drape, Reveal, Starlight. The reveal spell helped me to learn all my clothes and armament. Then when I had that figured out I draped everything I could for healing and flew out of the lair. I don't remember much but the pain. I'd crawl when I had to, enchant the dirt to heal and calm me. When I found that pelt I destroyed it with fire.

"On my way home I found Tamtoc. I was feeling better by then and wanted to explore. I followed the river upstream. Eventually I heard the soft resonance of our lair. I didn't know what it was but I was drawn to it. And then you all found me."

"It's surprising you made that long journey all by yourself."

"Yeah, there were many times I didn't think I was going to make it."

Kadd pulled Kalara to rest against him."I get it that you and Ravanan haven't found Annette. Do you think she knows you destroyed the pelt?"

"I don't know and I don't care."

"Kalara, I don't think this battle is over by any means. You should care. If she is a dragoness we can find her easy enough, especially two of us together. We've got to at least try right? You do still want to find your old self?"

Kalara turned to face him "Of course I do! But after Ravanan's failure, and like you said, he is pretty smart, I don't know. I sometimes think I want to leave well-enough alone. I mean, I *did* get rid of that cursed pelt didn't I?"

"Right. But you should be looking over your shoulder always. Like this" then Kadd leaned and looked over her shoulder in such a goofy way it made her laugh. "And like this" then he kissed her shoulder. His kisses eventually turned into him picking her up and carrying her to the bed where he surprisingly left her alone under the covers. He kissed her once more and returned to the couch.

Kalara raised her head and gave him a questioning look "Why are you over there?"

"Because I shouldn't be there" he nodded towards the other side of the bed.

"OK, why the sudden nice guy act?"

"We can't do anything here, we'd burn the place down. Remember? Ring of purple fire?"

"Oh yeah." - 'Why didn't I think of that?' she asked herself.

"And besides," he continued "You just met me yesterday, what kind of guy do you think I am?"

After breakfast Kadd wanted to take Kalara back to the Acama lair, as he put it "We have Acama business to work out." He looked as though he'd been up all night.

The lair was just as it was before however this time the two of them entered by anchor which didn't summon the others. The map in the middle was the same except that a fifth purple marker was added to the southern continent. As they sat near the map Kadd asked "I'm pretty sure you haven't been doing any Acama business then for over a year right?"

"I haven't been. And I was wondering why you said I'm so busy in that meeting we had."

"Well, you are handling two continents, both crowded with humans and not all of them are uneducated. There is a lot of research going on and governments trying to rule the world."

"Right. But you were saying that you are really busy too."

"I did say that. It's just that the old you always made it a point to brag about your dragons and all the glorious things you all have done in Anarchelos – the past 150 years especially. Not that Kynasteryx isn't doing research but you think that nation – *America* – is above all the rest. We've all seen mighty nations grow and die though, time will tell.

"But anyhow, we've got to make rounds to your dragons, I'm sure they're starting to wonder where you are. In all this time have you ever felt the urge to just go in one particular direction?"

"Well yeah, I've sometimes felt like leaving Black Blade and before that my home in Oklahoma but it was simply out of the question. I couldn't leave. I can't say for sure it was in one main direction I wanted to go though."

"When you felt that urge it was one of your dragons calling you. We've got some catching up to do. I'll help you. Just so I make that call to mine about that upcoming deep sea plunge next week."

"So we're gonna be together like glue?"

"Well that is an odd way to put it but pretty much, like glue."

"I don't know Kadd, that didn't work out so well for me and Ravanan, he ended up hating me and all my questions. What if you decide I'm too much work to bother with? Then you'll leave me too, or worse."

"I told you," he took her hands in his "I could never harm you. Right now I'm thoroughly enjoying myself. This is where I'm supposed to be, I know it is. Do you not want me around?"

"Well, it's just that I tend to feel trapped."

"Oh! You did mention that last night. And I can see why you'd feel that way. I'll tell you what. How about I go now to deal with my work and then I'll be back in two mornings from this one? Surely that will let you know that I'm not trapping you. You can leave. Go, do whatever. Don't be here when I return if you want. I'll stay until the sun starts its fall. I only want to help you get back into your Acama work."

"What if we don't meet up but then later I want to summon you? I don't know how to summon – unless going through that door is the only way."

"Really? So when you said you don't remember anything you meant A.N.Y.T.H.I.N.G. I thought it was more selective, since you remember how to walk and talk. Let me teach you, first I'll show you, go to the far wall."

When Kalara got there Kadd cast *"COME HERE KALARA OF KYNASTERYX RAVYX!"* Icy pain seized her heart and Kalara

381

suddenly felt the urge to move. She started walking, as she did the coldness subsided but the pain didn't. Then she heard Kadd call out after a few steps "Good! Now try to walk in another direction, see how that feels."

Kalara turned and her pain grew. When she corrected her path the pain let up a little but it didn't go away until she was standing in front of Kadd.

"Wow. That hurt." she said.

"But now it doesn't, right?" he caressed her arm.

"Right."

"Now you're going to try it."

"OK. But I know Ravanan tried this when he was controlling me and it didn't work."

Kadd shook his head. "It's horrible that he did that to you, treating you like a human. I'm not surprised it didn't work. He's not an Acama, but you are. I'm sure your blood and aura fought him the whole time."

"You think so?"

"I know so."

"But I was willing and agreed to it."

"That makes no difference. You're not a puppet." he smiled "Now, shall we try it?"

"I'm ready. What do I do?"

"It shouldn't be hard for you to do. When you cast the spell you first need to know the full name of who you are summoning, mine is Kadd of Kynasteryx Diamid.

"Now you can also summon a group of dragons by the region you want but we don't summon them here. You have your usual summoning areas all over the land, really the place doesn't matter so long as it's open enough and not so overrun with the herd. When you send out a mass summons your aura makes a connection with that region, a painful tether coming from you to each dragon. As each dragon arrives your pain lessens by a degree and they are freed from the pain but not the tether. For those that lag their pain increases, taking on the pain of those "early birds" and your lost degrees of pain. This continues until the pain of all others is piled onto the last dragon out there. Your pain at that moment is minimal, just enough to let you know your summons is being ignored."

"Why did we make a spell of pain for this job?!?"

"What better way to assure compliance?"

"Well no wonder some dragons question us!"

"What do you mean, has something happened?"

"No. It's just something Ravanan said when he was telling me about the Acamas."

"Well it's true. Not every dragon likes the way we crafted our spell but they did leave it up to us. And we don't summon masses often; that is saved only for drastic times. We do our best to only call one dragon at a time, or maybe two or three depending on the job. So, are you ready to try to summon me?"

"It's going to hurt isn't it?"

"Yes" Kadd said softly as he leaned forward and kissed her, holding the back of her neck. "But your blood is strong and I'll come quick." he whispered.

Kalara wrapped her hand over his wrist, mustering her willingness to cause herself pain. Kadd held her gaze and neck, enjoying feeling her skin on his as she found her strength. After a moment longer she let him go. "OK, Go. I'm ready."

Seeing he was in position at the far wall Kalara cast *"COME HERE KADD OF KYNASTERYX DIAMID!"* That same icy pain grabbed her heart. Kadd leapt into flight. Just as before the coldness around her heart quickly went away leaving only the pain. Kadd veered for a second to show her that pain wouldn't change for the one doing the summoning. Then he flew quick to end their pain together.

"Did I get here quick enough?"

"You did."

"See? I knew you could handle it." He flashed her a gorgeous grin. "It's a lot less than what Acama had to endure."

"Why is the pain cold at first?"

"Cold is the signature of amethysts, right? For other dragons the cold doesn't go away. What you felt is the antifreeze in our blood rushing to help us."

"Now Kadd, you said all those times I felt like leaving it was my dragons summoning me. So why didn't their summoning hurt me like it did when you summoned me?"

"Because they aren't Acamas. Their summoning spells are weak. The comet's rocky power has enabled us to do mass summonings as well as increasing the effectiveness of our spells. But we don't talk about it, not even with mates, it wouldn't be good if word got out."

"Talking about mates, I've been wondering" she sat down "have you had a mate before now?"

Kadd followed her back to the dais. "I've had plenty but none I've really cared for. I haven't found any dragoness that matches what I want," he paused to gaze into her eyes "other than you. You have a way of sticking in my mind and they could always sense I wasn't theirs."

Kalara shifted her feet "So that's it then? We're mated. Just like that after one time?"

"If you want us to be. I needed to get you out of Tristan's lair. Morada was starting to ask questions. It was obvious you were acting differently and very quiet. I only knew a little about it but it was enough to make me want to protect you. Was I wrong? Did you want to stay?" His face hinted with mirth.

"No. I was glad to get out of there. Thank you! But I haven't agreed to be your mate."

"I know. The other night shouldn't have happened. If there is a next time it'll be because you desired it, not because you feel forced to." Kadd stood up. "Which is why I'm leaving. Is there anything else you want to know before I take off?"

"Maybe you could walk me through making and using anchors. The idea scares me."

"I bet it does." he laughed. "It's one thing to do verbal spells but quite another to basically destroy yourself."

"That doesn't make me feel better about it."

"But that is the basic idea, to tear yourself apart into molecules and travel lightning fast."

"I suppose you're right. It just sounds so scary. What if I make the runes wrong? I watched Ravanan make one and I've seen yours. You both write in runes that I'm just not getting. I've tried."

"The runes aren't so important to be in that language, that's an old language. You can use any language. What is important is what you write. When you write down your spell it's much more powerful than verbal spells and your aura knows it. They're high level and permanent so long as the rock exists. The aura takes the words you write and the thoughts you intend to do then tells the iron in the rock to carry out your will."

Kalara asked "Then I draw the place I want to go in the middle? I can't draw very well, Jenniffer tried to teach me but gave up. What if my cloud is forever lost trying to go to my crazy drawing?"

"That can't happen. As long you know where it is, so does your aura. You can trust your aura. Let's go outside and try it."

Chapter 29

K add left without a kiss after he watched Kalara make a few successful anchors. Kalara's last one took her back to the dais and map in the Acama Lair. And by anchoring to the lair she didn't automatically summon the other Acamas as she had the first time she entered through the door. She walked around the lair with new eyes, appreciating the space and glad it had no connection to Ravanan.

She was free! A smile grew on her lips and stayed there. Free to come here, free to live here, and free to leave whenever she wanted. She could definitely live here and already the place felt welcoming to her. The enchantress draped Heed and strolled to the food alcove for that pizza she had seen earlier.

The warmed pizza was sitting on the map somewhere in the Pacific Ocean, Kalara was hovering at the pinnacle of the room to learn what she could about herself and other Acamas. She stuffed the last bite in her mouth and then turned her gaze down towards the pizza far below her. *"ANOTHER SLICE!"* she cast and smoothly a slice pulled up and away from its neighbors with the cheese stringing into threads.

It wasn't difficult to tell which embossed gold tiles were of Tristan and Morada due to their distinctive crystals on their bodies. But Kalara had a harder time telling the difference between hers and Kadd's walls. That didn't bother her though. She wasn't the same sad dragoness that Ravanan had found so long ago. Kalara started planning how she would further her story on her wall, whichever one it was.

With a full belly Kalara went out to the rim to retrieve her mummies. "Annette! Jeremy!" Her eyes scanned the trees. Jeremy emerged and ran to her. "Where is Annette?" she asked.

"She's dead! He burned her!"

"Dead? No. She can't die. What do you mean he burned her? Who?"

"That blue dragon. He came here looking for you and when he didn't find you he blew fire on us!"

"But dragon fire wouldn't end her! Look at...."

Suddenly Kalara was whisked away.

Kalara reappeared in water and darkness. Super cold salt water forced her lips apart and gushed into her mouth and nose, filling her lungs instantly. She had no air! What was happening?!?!? Then just as suddenly her aura pushed the heavy water away to form an air bubble around her, the power drain of it caused Kalara to crumble weakly to the muddy ocean floor. She turned over and got on her knees to expel the salt water from her lungs. Her hands and knees sank deep into the cold soft mud but she could feel them start to warm from her body's natural antifreeze.

Her chest ached from the strong expulsion of the water. There was nothing but darkness all around and it was equally quiet except for her sniffling.

Coughing still, she managed to cast *"SUNLIGHT"* into the nothingness of the bottom of the ocean. Beside her was something big. She stood up and turned to look. A dragon. RAVANAN! He was dead and he had taken her with him just as he said he would!

How could he be dead?!?!? What killed him? She was done with Ravanan but wasn't ready for him to be dead! Without another thought Kalara targeted Ravanan and cast *"MUMMIFY"*. Ravanan roared, his voice dampened by the still water around him. And there in the deep of the ocean Ravanan the Dragon Lich rose up to kneel in front of his sunlit Enchantress.

About the Author

Rachal M. Roberts was born in 1972 and grew up in the forested hills of NE Oklahoma and still resides there with her husband and 2 children. Her heritage is ¼ Native American from the Upper Cayuga Band in Canada. She has always loved rocks and earned her B.S. and M.S. degrees in geology from Oklahoma State University in Stillwater, Oklahoma. While in college she was in the university choir and sang opera. Rachal is a licensed UST Remediation Consultant and has written many risk assessments since 1996. She began her own successful private consulting business in 2008 for leaking petroleum storage tanks and started writing The Cursed Dragon that same year. She is also an avid gamer of epic fantasy RPGs and MMORPGs but will also pull up a chair for tabletop RPGs and board games. Rachal never considered being an author until the stress of starting her own company unveiled her imagination, causing her to write her first novel, The Cursed Dragon.

CPSIA information can be obtained at www.ICGtesting.com
Printed in the USA
LVOW04s2319061114

412191LV00003B/3/P